IN THE
TUDOR COURT

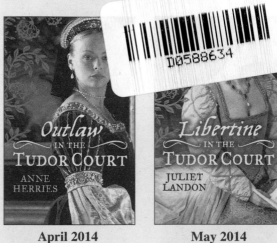

Outlaw
IN THE
TUDOR COURT
ANNE
HERRIES

April 2014

Libertine
IN THE
TUDOR COURT
JULIET
LANDON

May 2014

Notorious
IN THE
TUDOR COURT
AMANDA
McCABE

June 2014

Maiden
IN THE
TUDOR COURT
JUNE
FRANCIS

July 2014

Libertine
IN THE
Tudor Court

JULIET LANDON

MILLS
BOON
&

Published in Great Britain 2014
by Mills & Boon, an imprint of Harlequin (UK) Limited,
Eton House, 18-24 Paradise Road, Richmond, Surrey, TW9 1SR

LIBERTINE IN THE TUDOR COURT © 2014 Harlequin Books S.A.

One Night in Paradise © 2003 Juliet Landon
A Most Unseemly Summer © 2001 Juliet Landon

ISBN: 978 0 263 24619 3

052-0514

Harlequin (UK) Limited's policy is to use papers that are natural, renewable and recyclable products and made from wood grown in sustainable forests. The logging and manufacturing processes conform to the legal environmental regulations of the country of origin.

Printed and bound by
CPI Group (UK) Ltd, Croydon, CR0 4YY

Juliet Landon lives in an ancient country village in the north of England with her retired scientist husband. Her keen interest in embroidery, art and history, together with a fertile imagination, make writing historical novels a favourite occupation. She finds the research particularly exciting, especially the early medieval period and the fascinating laws concerning women in particular and their struggle for survival in a man's world.

One Night in Paradise

JULIET LANDON

Chapter One

23 June 1575, Richmond, Surrey

Adorna Pickering's ability to stay calm in the face of adversity was put severely to the test the day that Queen Elizabeth went hawking. They were in the park at Richmond and Adorna was noticed not so much for her superb horsemanship but for her graceful fall backwards into the River Thames and for her pretence that it was nothing, really. Though Adorna managed to impress the Queen, there was one who refused to be impressed in quite the same sympathetic manner.

It had all begun so well, the midsummer sun promising a windless day perfect for hawking, one of Her Majesty's favourite sports in which she always indulged when staying at her palace in Richmond. The park was extensive, well stocked with deer and waterbirds, and a select gathering of the Queen's favourite courtiers made a brilliant splash of colour behind her, quietly vying with each other to show off their finery, their horses, and their popularity.

As the daughter of the Queen's Master of the Revels Office, Adorna's presence in such company was not only accepted but encouraged. Living at Richmond so close to the royal palace had many compensations, as her newly appointed father had only recently pointed out.

Adorna had already attracted smiles and admiring glances, her striking beauty and pale gold hair reflecting the similar pale gold of her new mare in the blue-patterned harness given to her last week for her twentieth birthday. By her side rode Master Peter Fowler, another member of the royal household, a young man on the upward current who privately believed that his future would be enhanced by his association with someone slightly above his station. Not that he was oblivious to Adorna's physical attributes, but Peter was more ambitious than moonstruck, and his appearance by her side this morning was no coincidence.

In a sea of jewel colours, tossing plumes and a speckle of spaniels weaving between hooves, the company waited while the Queen and her Master Falconer cast their falcons up into the sky while down below the beaters flushed ducks from the river, putting them to flight. But, being on the edge of the gathering and not far from the river bank, Adorna's flighty young mare took exception to wings whizzing overhead, squawking loudly. The mare bunched and staggered backwards, quivering with fright, and it was with some difficulty that Adorna controlled her and stopped her barging into nearby horses whose riders were looking skywards. Then, thinking that she was over that semi-crisis, she gave her attention to the falcons, which, in bringing down the ducks, dropped two of them into the river in a flurry of white feathers.

Everyone's attention was now engaged in seeing who would be first to retrieve the flapping quarry for Her Majesty, none of them noticing how Adorna's mare, still restive, had decided to join the retrieving party of her own free will against all her rider's attempts to stop her. Moving backwards instead of forwards despite all that Adorna could do, the mare was beating a determined staccato with her hind hooves into the water around her. Men called, others laughed, including the Queen, some used their swords as fishing hooks, one lad plunged in bodily to earn the Queen's favour, but no one—not even Peter—noticed how Adorna and her pale golden mare were now wallowing, hock deep, into the current.

She yelled to him, 'Peter! Help me!' but his attention was on the ducks like everyone else's, and Adorna was obliged to use her whip to impel the horse forward as the water covered her feet, the hem of her long gown swirling wetly around one knee. But she had left it too late; the whip hit the water instead of the horse, which still refused to respond to her commands. Help came unexpectedly in the form of a large man and horse who plunged into the water ahead of her, grabbing unceremoniously at the mare's bridle only seconds before the current swept over the saddle.

Concerned only with getting on to the bank as a team, she paid no attention to the man's appearance except to note that his horse was very large and that he himself was powerful enough to drag the reins out of her hands and over the mare's head and to haul the creature almost bodily through the muddy water on to dry firm ground.

Well away from the applauding crowd, Adorna found her voice. 'Thank you, oh, thank you,' she said, clutching at the pommel of the saddle as the mare lurched forward. 'Thank heaven somebody noticed at last.'

Her thanks were misinterpreted. 'If you think that's the most effective way to be noticed, mistress, think again,' the man snapped, devoid of any sympathy. 'The applause you hear is for Her Majesty, not for your antics. Leave the retrieving to the hounds in future.'

It was not Adorna's way to be speechless for long, but that piece of calculated rudeness was breathtaking. What was more, the man's dismounting was far quicker than hers and, well before she could reply, she was being hoisted out of the saddle by two strong arms and set down upon the ground with the hem of her wet skirts and underclothes sticking nastily to her legs. His hands were painfully efficient.

'I was referring, sir, to my predicament,' she snapped back, shaking off his supporting hand. 'If I'd planned on being noticed, as you appear to think, I'd not have chosen to back into the river before the Queen's entire court, believe me. Nor was I in the race to retrieve a duck. Now, can I rid you of any more delusions before you go?' Still not looking at him, she shook the full skirt of her pale blue gown, catching a glimpse of Peter out of the corner of her eye. He was dismounting. Kneeling. 'Peter,' she said, 'get up off…oh!' Her rescuer was doing the same.

The crowd had parted and, as Adorna sank into a deep wet curtsy, the Queen rode forward on a beautiful dapple grey. 'Geldings make better mounts on these occasions, mistress, so I'm told,' the Queen said. 'Your mount is a beauty, but a little unmannerly per-haps?' The embodiment of graciousness, the Queen exuded a sympathy for Adorna's plight that came as a welcome change from the rescuer's brusqueness.

Yet Adorna could not allow the chance to pass. She stayed in her curtsy, sending a haughty glance towards the man before making her reply. 'Your Majesty is most kind. My mare is still young, though one would have to struggle to find a similarly good excuse for others' unmannerliness.' There was no mistaking the butt of her remark, the man in question glowering at her as if she were a troublesome sparrowhawk on his wrist, while the Queen and her Court's laughter tinkled around them like splinters of breaking ice.

But Adorna's glance had given her the information that she had already suspected, by his imperious man-ner and cultured voice—he was a self-opinionated wit-monger, albeit an extremely good-looking one, whose imposing stature was exactly the kind the Queen liked to have around her. Ill-featured people were anathema to her, especially men. He was dark-eyed and bold-faced with a square clean-shaven jaw, his head now bared to show thick dark waves brushed back off his forehead, a dent showing where his blue velvet bonnet had recently sat. His shoulders were broad enough to take her insult and, as the Queen signalled them to rise, Adorna saw that his legs were long and muscular, outlined in tight canions up to the top of his thighs to where his paned trunk-hose fitted. His deep blue velvet complemented her paler version perfectly, but that appeared to be their only point of compatibility.

The Queen was still amused. 'There now, Sir Nicholas,' she said. 'Apparently it is not so much what one does as the manner in which one does it. I shall expect more from you when I have the misfortune to fall into the river.'

Sir Nicholas had the grace to laugh as he bowed to her. 'Divine Majesty,' he said, 'I believe the Lady Moon will fall into the river before you do.'

'I hope you're right.' She accepted the compliment and turned again to Adorna. 'Mistress Pickering, there are few women who could look as well as you after such a fright. I hope you'll not leave us.'

Adorna knew a command when she heard one. 'I thank Your Majesty. I ask nothing more than to stay.'

'Then stay close, mistress, and let my lord of Leicester's man teach your pretty mare a thing or two about obedience. Sir Nicholas, tend the lady.'

Sir Nicholas bowed again as the Queen moved away to yet another scattering of applause at her graciousness, but Adorna had no intention of being tended by this uncivil creature, whatever the Queen's wishes. She turned to Peter Fowler, but the voice at her back held her attention.

'Mistress Pickering. Sir Thomas's daughter. Well, well.'

Adorna spoke over her shoulder. 'And you are one of the Master of Horse's men, I take it, which would explain why you are more polite to horses than to their riders. What a good thing the same cannot be said of your master.' It was well known that the handsome earl, Her Majesty's Master of Horse, was desperately in love with the Queen.

'My master, lady, has not yet had to drag Her Majesty out of the river in front of her courtiers. It's not your pretty mare that needs a lesson in manners so much as its rider needing lessons in control.' By this time the golden mare was eating something sweet from Sir Nicholas's hand, as docile as a lamb. 'Believe it or not, that is what Her Grace was telling you.'

Furiously, she rounded on him as Peter and two of her friends came to her aid, wringing the water from the hem of her gown. 'Rubbish! There is no one in the world who speaks more candidly than the Queen. If that's what she'd meant she'd have said so. Her Grace commands me to stay close and that is what I must do. I have thanked you for your assistance, Sir Nicholas, but now you are relieved of all further responsibility towards me, despite what Her Grace desires. Go and practise your courtesies on your horses.'

'Mistress!' Peter Fowler's alarm warned her that her own courtesy was fraying around the edges. 'This gentleman is Sir Nicholas Rayne, Deputy to Her Majesty's Master of Horse.'

Before she could find another cutting retort, Sir

Nicholas made a bow to Peter, smiling. 'And you, Master Fowler, are the gentleman with the longest title in Her Majesty's service. Gentleman Controller of All and Every Her Highness's Works. Did I get it right?' He was already laughing.

'To the letter,' said Peter. 'In other words, Head of Security.'

But Adorna was not prepared for any signs of amity. She thanked her two friends and turned to Peter for assistance in remounting, though by now he was diverted by laughter and forestalled by Sir Nicholas who, in one stride, caught her round the waist and hoisted her into the saddle as if she were no more than a child.

For a brief moment, her view of the world turned sideways as her head came into contact with his neck and shoulder, her cheek feeling the softly curling pleats of the tiny white ruff that sat high above the blue doublet. She caught a whiff of musk from his skin and felt the firmness of his hands under her shoulders, and then the world was righted and she was looking down into his face, into two dark unsmiling eyes that held hers, boldly, for a fraction longer than was necessary. Confused by what she saw, she blinked, took the reins from him and waited as he and Peter unstuck the clinging fabric from her legs and arranged it in damp folds around her.

The Queen's party had begun to move away.

'Thank you, Sir Nicholas,' she said, coldly, to the top of his blue velvet bonnet, watching the white and gold plumes lift and settle again. 'I think you should go now.'

He made no reply to that. Instead, he took his own horse from a groom and vaulted into the saddle in one leap, reining the horse over expertly to walk on her other side, his nod to Peter cutting across her stony face.

By the time they reached the wide open fields well away from the river, Adorna's composure was settling into an act which convinced those about her that she was comfortable. This was far from the truth, but showed the level of pretence of which she was capable. The wetness from her beautiful pale blue gown had now seeped up to her saddle, warm, sticky, and chafing her thighs: her golden mare's hindquarters were caked with mud and the shining bells on her harness were clattering instead of tinkling. Far worse than any of that was the disturbing presence of the one who had saved her from a complete soaking, whose inscrutable expression gave her no inkling of his real reason for staying nearby, whether because he wanted to or because he had been commanded to. The pressure of his hands could still be felt, but she would not let him know, even by a sneaking exploration, that he had had the slightest effect.

As the Queen had commanded, Sir Nicholas drew her nearer to the centre of things than she had been before, which did even less for Adorna's comfort. Having changed her peregrine falcon for a rare white gerfalcon, the Queen held it, hooded, on her wrist as a distant heron flew away upwards, ringing into the sky. The gerfalcon was released to pursue it, to climb even higher and then to stoop and dive, bringing the lovely thing down to the retrieving greyhounds whose speed prevented any injury to the precious raptor. Again, there was applause, then the announcement that they would have the picnic.

At this point, Adorna sidled invisibly back to her friends on the edge of the party, accepting whatever morsels of food were brought and passed around by the young pages. She made an effort to dismiss the incident of the river and to make herself affable to Peter, but her eyes had a will of their own, straying disobediently towards the tall well-built figure in deep blue braided with gold whose laughter was bold and teasingly directed towards a group of the Queen's ladies.

Dressed entirely in white, the young Maids of Honour made a perfect foil for the Queen's russet-and-gold that suited her so well. Like Adorna herself, she wore a high-crowned hat with a curl of feathers on the brim, a man's-type doublet that buttoned up to the neck, and a full skirt. But whereas Adorna's outfit was relatively modest in its decoration, the Queen had spared no effort to load herself with braids, chains and rings, frogging across her breast overlaid by pendants, and jewels winking from every surface, even from her neck-ruff of finest white lace.

Adorna's gown had begun to dry by now and they would soon be away again on a search for herons and cranes, perhaps larks for those with smaller raptors. She went to where the mare was tied to a tree, her muzzle dripping with water from a bucket. 'Your legs all right, my beauty?' she whispered, taking a look at the mud-covered rear end. 'We nearly came to grief, you and I, didn't we, eh? Are you going to calm down this afternoon, then?'

'That will depend,' a voice said behind her, 'on her rider more than anything else.'

Refusing to be drawn into another confrontation, Adorna clenched her teeth and slid one hand over the mare's muddy rump, preparing to examine her legs. Sir Nicholas managed the gesture with far more confidence than she, overtaking her hand with his own as he came to stand before her, continuing the examination with all the assurance of a horseman. His hands were strong and brown with flecks of fine dark hair on the backs, his nails clean and workmanlike, and Adorna watched in reluctant admiration how his fingertips pressed and probed almost tenderly. She drew her eyes upwards to his face as he stood, and found that he was already regarding her in some amusement, knowing that the progress of his hands had been marked with an interest of a not altogether objective nature. Against her will, she found that her eyes were locked with his.

'Well?' he said, softly. 'She's still sound after her dunk in the river, and there's nothing wrong with her temperament that a little gentle schooling won't cure. Show her who's master, though.' As he spoke, his hands caressed the mare's satin flanks, which twitched against the sensation, and Adorna knew that his words had as much to do with herself as they did with the mare. 'She's a classy creature,' he said, 'but not for amateurs.' On his last phrase, his eyes left hers and rested directly on Peter Fowler who was just out of earshot, returning to her in time to see a flush of angry pink suffuse her cheeks.

If he wanted to believe that Peter was her lover, even though he was not, she was content for him to do so, for it would afford her some protection, his innuendo being impossible to misunderstand. She was as angry at her own uncontrollable shiver of excitement as at his blatant attempt to flirt with her after his earlier hostility, and the stinging rebuke came out like a rapier.

'Don't concern yourself with my mare's requirements, sir,' she said sharply. 'Nor with mine. We have both managed well enough without your advice so far, so don't think that your one act of bravado makes you indispensable to us. I think you should go back to your master and make yourself *really* useful. I bid you good day.'

She would have walked away on the last word, but his arm came across her, resting on the mare's saddle, and she found herself imprisoned between him and the horse. 'Ah, no, mistress,' he said, without raising his voice. 'That's the third time you've ordered me to go, I believe. There are only a limited number of those who may give me orders, and you will never be one of them. What's more, when the Queen commands me to tend a lady, I will tend her until she gives me leave to stop. If you dislike the idea so, then I suggest you make your objections known to her. Now, mistress, make ready to mount.' And without the slightest warning other than that, he swooped and lifted her into his arms.

She should, of course, have been prepared for this, for he had already shown himself to be a man of immediate action. But strangely enough, she found that she was temporarily immobilised by his overpowering closeness, his refusal to be commanded, his boldness. Now his face was alarmingly close to hers and, instead of tossing her into the saddle as he had before, he was holding her deliberately tightly in his arms, preventing her from struggling.

'You are a stranger, sir,' she whispered, 'and you are insulting me. My father will hear of this.' Yet, as she spoke the words, she knew full well that her father would not hear of it from her lips and that, if this stranger was indeed insulting her, it was making her heart race in the most extraordinary manner that mixed fear with anticipation and a helplessness that made her feel guilty with pleasure. Or was it anger? Any other man, she thought, might have been expected to react with some concern at that threat, her father being Sir Thomas Pickering, Master of the Revels and therefore this man's superior.

His expression showed no such disquiet. 'No, mistress,' he said. 'I think not.'

She could feel his breath upon her face as he spoke, and she knew that he was allowing her to feel his nearness in the same way that an unbroken horse must be given time to get used to a man's closeness, his restraint. His unsmiling mouth was firm and well proportioned and his nose, straight and smooth, led her examining eyes to his own that sparkled beneath high-angled brows, unflinching eyes of brown jasper, dark-lashed and suggesting to her an age of about thirty, by the experience written within them.

'Let me go, I say. Please!'

As he moved to tip her upwards into the saddle, she saw a brief smile cross his face, which had disappeared by the time she looked again. He tapped her riding whip with one finger. 'That's for show, not for use,' he said, severely. 'Stallions need it, mares don't.'

Adorna felt safe enough from that height to pretend unconcern. 'Fillies?' she said. 'And geldings?'

The brief smile reappeared and vanished again as he recognised the return of her courage. 'Remind me to tell you of the first some time. Of geldings I know little that would be of any use to you.' And once again, she knew that neither of them was talking of horses.

The afternoon passed in a daze, though the only one to remark on her unusual quietness was Master Peter Fowler, who said, quite on the wrong tack, 'Did that wetting upset you, mistress? It's a pity you were not allowed to go home and change. You could have been back before Her Majesty noticed.'

That much was true, her home being a mere half-mile away over on the other side of the palace, a convenient place for Sir Thomas and Lady Marion to live when the Queen was at Richmond, and only one of several dotted about the home counties near the other royal residences. Life at court was a great temptation and Lady Marion, Adorna's lovely mother, had no intention of leaving her handsome husband to the attentions of other women with whom he was obliged to come into contact. As Master of Revels, he probably saw more of them than the average household official, being responsible for the special costumes and theatrical effects needed for Her Majesty's entertainment, an element of court life of great importance to balance the weightier matters of state.

Sir Thomas had expected to have Adorna's assistance that day, but then had come Master Fowler's request to take her to the Queen's falconry picnic in the park, and he had not the heart to refuse. All the same, Master Fowler had better not harbour any fancy ideas involving Adorna: she could do far better for herself with her looks and connections.

Adorna's looks were indeed something of which her parents were proud: pale blonde hair and startlingly beautiful features, large grey-blue eyes with sweeping lashes and a full mouth that, as far as her parents knew, had never been tasted by a man. Boys, perhaps, at Christmas, but never a man. Needless to say, there had been plenty of interest, so much so that Sir Thomas and Lady Marion had been criticised by family for being too lenient with her fastidiousness. At twenty years old, the elders said, it was time she was a wife and mother; let her put her high-faluting ideas aside and marry the richest of them, as other women did.

Fortunately for Adorna, her parents had so far ignored this advice, for they knew better than most how the Queen's Court was a notorious hotbed of intrigue, liaisons, broken hearts and broken marriages, deceptions and dismissals. Adorna herself was not one of the Queen's inner circle of courtiers nor had the Queen ever insisted on her regular appearance there, being sympathetic to the Pickerings' views that lovely young women were often targets of men's attractions for all the wrong reasons. Her Majesty had had enough problems in the past with her six young Maids of Honour, some of them losing their honour so quickly that it reflected badly on her, as their moral guardian.

Even so, Her Majesty was well aware of Adorna Pickering's existence and, because she liked Sir Thomas and his wife, she encouraged their talented family to attend her functions. It worked both ways; while the Queen surrounded herself with beautiful and talented people, Adorna's presence went some way towards advertising her father's success as a new office-holder. Even though still part of the Great Wardrobe under Sir John Fortescue, his position carried with it a certain responsibility, one of which was to be seen in the best company.

To have access to Court without actually being sucked into the vortex of it was, Adorna believed, a very pleasant place to be, especially as her home was so conveniently near, with her father always at hand for protection if danger came a mite too close. On more than one occasion, he had been a very efficient tool to use against a too-persistent trespass, and running for cover became Adorna's foolproof defence against over-attentive men, young or old, who would

like to have taken more than was on offer. Though
guests came and went constantly to her home at Sheen
House next door to the palace, there were at least a
dozen places in the fashionably meandering building
where Adorna could remain out of touch until danger
had passed.

True to form, she sought refuge with her father in
the Revels Office for, despite Sir Nicholas's refusal to
be put off by the mention of him, she could think of
no reason why the younger man would venture there
to find her. There was still time left in the day to see
how her father had proceeded without her, nor was it
far for her and her maid to pass from Sheen House
down what had lately become known as Paradise Road
and through the gate in the wall of the palace garden.

To Sir Thomas's annoyance, the Revels Office had
no separate buildings of its own and was therefore
obliged to share limited space with the Great Wardrobe where some of the Queen's clothes were stored,
others being in London itself. Consequently, tailors
and furriers, embroiderers, carpenters and painters,
shoemakers and artificers all worked side by side with
never enough room to manoeuvre. Adorna's creative
talents were often put to good use in the Revels Office
where men with flair and drawing ability were always
in demand to design sets, special effects and costumes
for the many Court entertainments.

Today, she had found a relatively private corner in
which to examine some of the sumptuous and fantastic
creations being prepared for a masque at the palace at
the end of the week. She had helped to design the

costumes and choose the materials and jewels, also to construct the elaborate head-dresses and wigs, for all the Court ladies taking part must have abundant blonde hair. She lifted one of the masks and held it above a flimsy gown of pale sea-green fringed with golden tassels, holding her head to one side to judge its effect.

'Try it on,' her father said. 'That's the best way to see.'

'That won't help me much, will it, Father?'

'Perhaps not, but it'll help me.' He grinned and, to please him, she took up the mask and the robe stuck all over with silver and gold stars and went into a corner screened off from the rest of the busy room. Maybelle, her maid, went with her to help, though Adorna was wearing no farthingale or whalebone bodice to complicate matters. In a few moments she emerged to confront her father, but found to her surprise that he was not now alone but in the company of Sir John Fortescue and another officer of the revels who assisted her father.

This was not what Adorna had intended, for she was not wearing the correct undergarments, nor was the pale green robe with stars even finished, and it was only the papier mâché mask of a Water Maiden covering her face that hid her sudden blush of embarrassment as she held the edges of the fabric together across her bosom. And there was only one sleeve; her other arm was bare.

Before she could retreat, they had seen the half-dressed sea nymph and immediately began an assessment of its cost multiplied by eight, the amount of white-gold sarcenet with Venice gold fringe and the indented kirtles with plaits of silver lawn trailing from the waist. Not to mention the masks, head-dresses, shoes, stockings, tridents and other accessories, multiplied by eight.

'Put the head-dress on, my dear,' Sir Thomas said. 'Which one is it? This one?' He picked up a conchshell creation covered in silver and draped with dagged green tissue to resemble seaweed and passed it to Maybelle.

'Er…no, Father, if you please,' Adorna protested.

But she was overruled by the three of them, and the thing was placed on her head, pushing down the mask in the process and making it difficult for her to see through the eyeholes. She must alter that before they were used. She heard murmurs of approval. 'I must go,' she mumbled into the claustrophobic space around her mouth. 'Excuse me, if you please.'

Blindly, she turned and was caught by a hand on her arm before bumping into the person who had been standing silently at her back, someone whose familiar voice made her tear quickly at the mask, lifting it and tangling it with her loose hair and the head-dress in an effort to see where she was. The fabric across her front gaped as she let go of it and was snatched together again by Maybelle's quick hand, but not before Adorna had seen the direction of the man's eyes and the unconcealed interest in them.

'Not a good day for water nymphs,' Sir Nicholas

whispered, letting go of her arm and stepping back to allow her to pass.

Summoning all her dignity, Adorna quickly snatched at a length of red tissue from the nearest tabletop and held it up to hide herself from the man's gaze. 'This is the Revels Office,' she snapped, 'not a sideshow.'

Amused, Sir Nicholas merely looked across at her father and Sir John.

Sir Thomas explained. 'It's all right, my dear. Sir Nicholas comes from the Master of Horse. He needs to know about our luggage for the progress to Kenilworth. Don't send the poor man away before he's fulfilled his mission, will you? Or I'll have his lordship to answer to.'

Fuming, Adorna swept past him and returned to the screen, her face burning with annoyance that the man had once again seen her at a disadvantage. That he had seen her at all, damn him!

'It's all right, mistress,' Maybelle whispered. 'He didn't see anything.'

'Damn him!' Adorna repeated, pushing her hair away. 'Here, Belle. Tie my hair up into that net. There, that's better.' Her second emergence from the corner screen was, in a way, as theatrical as the first had been, for now she was not only reclothed in her simple day gown of russet linen but, covering the entire top of her body in an extravagant swathe of glittering red was the tissue she had snatched from the table. It trailed over one shoulder and on to the floor behind her, blending with the russet of her gown and contrasting brilliantly with the gold net caul into which her hair had hurriedly been bundled.

Astounded by the transformation as much as by the sheer impact of her beauty, the four men's conversation dwindled to a stop as she approached, her head held high, and it was her father who spoke, at last. 'Quick change, nymph!' he laughed.

Sir Nicholas was more specific. 'Water into fire,' he murmured.

Sir John cleared his throat. 'Ahem! Yes…well, your designs for the masque appear to be well in hand, Sir Thomas. I trust you'll not leak any of this, Sir Nicholas. The masque theme must be kept secret until its performance.' The Master of the Great Wardrobe looked at the younger man sternly from beneath handsome greying eyebrows.

'I quite understand, sir. No word of the masque will be got from me, I assure you. My lord the Earl of Leicester is planning several for Her Majesty's progress to Kenilworth, and he's just as concerned about secrecy.'

'Ah, yes,' said Sir Thomas, 'you need to know how many waggons and carts we need for the Wardrobe, don't you? Well, why not come and join us for a late dinner on Wednesday? Lady Marion and I are celebrating my appointment with some friends. These two gentlemen will be there, too. Do you have a lady, Sir Nicholas?'

'No, sir. Not yet.' He smiled at their grins, and Adorna was aware that, had she not been there, more might have been said on that subject. But her father had blundered by inviting him to their home, which meant that both her places of refuge were now no longer safe from his intrusion.

Sir Thomas was clearly expecting his daughter's approval of the invitation. He looked at her, eyebrows raised. 'Adorna?' he said.

The expression in her eyes, though fleeting, said it all. 'No lady yet, Sir Nicholas? Perfect. Cousin Hester will be with us by tomorrow and Mother was wondering what to do about a partner for her. Now the problem is solved.'

Sir Nicholas bowed gracefully. 'Thank you, mistress. I look forward to meeting Cousin Hester. Is she…?'

'Yes, the late Sir William Pickering's daughter. The heiress.' That should turn your neat little head, she thought. 'Now, if you will excuse me, gentlemen?'

Moving away from the group at the same time, Sir Nicholas was not inclined to let her go so easily, but strode alongside her, weaving his way in and out of the workers at the tables. By some miracle, he reached the door before her.

She glared at him. 'I do not need lifting on to my horse, sir, I thank you. I left it at home.'

'You're walking? In this?' He indicated the trail of billowing red stuff.

'As long as you are gawping at me, yes. In this.'

'And if I stop…er…gawping?' He gave an impish smile.

She sighed, gustily, and glanced across at her father's group. 'Go back to your business, sir, if you please, and leave me to mine. You are in the wrong department.'

'I'll get used to it,' he said softly, 'and so will you, mistress.'

'No, sir, I think not. See how you fare with Cousin Hester.'

'And will Cousin Hester be in Water or in Fire?'

'In mourning,' she said, sweetly. 'Good day to you, sir.'

Chapter Two

To her father's question of why she had been so ill-disposed towards Sir Nicholas Rayne that afternoon, Adorna had no convincing reply except that she didn't much care for the man.

Sir Thomas agreed that the excuse was a poor one. 'I hope I'm not as short with those I don't much care for, my lass, or I'd not hold on to my office for too long. Is there more to it than that?' He was a shrewd man, tall and elegant with white hair and beard and a reputation for fairness that made him keep friends with all factions.

'No, Father. No more than that.'

'He's a well set-up fellow. The earl speaks highly of him.'

'Yes, Father. I expect Cousin Hester will like him well enough, too.'

'Then perhaps by that time you could pretend to, for everyone's sake.'

'Yes, Father. I'm sorry.'

'He has more about him than Master Fowler, for all his long title.'

'Oh, *Father*!'

'Well, you're twenty now, Adorna, and you can't be chasing them off for ever, you know. There are several who—'

'No…no, Father, I beg you will do no such thing. I shall know the man I want when I see him, and Peter will serve quite well until then.'

'Really? Well then, you'd better start looking a bit harder because it's time your mother and I were grand-parents. Perhaps you're being a bit too pernickety, my dear, eh?' He touched her chin gently with one fin-gertip.

'Yes, Father. I expect I probably am.'

Pernickety was perhaps not the word Adorna would have applied to her thoughts on men and marriage, though she might have agreed that they were some-what idealised. Having never been in love, she had relied so far on the descriptions given her by friends and those gleaned from romantic tales of King Arthur and Greek mythology. Not the most reliable of sources, but all there were available. Consequently, she believed she would recognise it when it happened, that she would know the man when he appeared. Ob-noxious, arrogant and presumptuous men were not on her list of requirements. For all that, she could not have said why, if he were so very unsuitable, Sir Nich-olas Rayne was continually on her mind, or why his face and form were before her in the minutest detail.

To her amusement, she had heard in the usual

roundabout manner that she was regarded by some men as being hard to get, not only because of her efficient safety nets, but mainly because she had never yet been prepared to bind herself to any man's exclusive friendship for more than a few weeks. There were men and women among her friends whom she had known as a child, some of whom were parents by now, but she and a few others enjoyed their state of relative freedom too much to let go of it. In the same way, she supposed, that the Queen enjoyed hers. While others involved themselves deeply in the serious business of mate-finding and binding, she was happy to indulge in men's admiration from a distance, sometimes playing one off against the other, but committing herself to none. It was a harmless and delicious game to play in which she took control, rather like the plays her brother wrote where actors acted out a story and then removed the disguise and went home to sleep soundly.

She found her father's sudden concern irritating. It suggested to her that he might cease to be as helpful to her as he had been in the past. It also suggested that he had recognised in Sir Nicholas Rayne a man he might be prepared to consider as son-in-law if she didn't make it absolutely clear that he was not the man she was looking for. Exactly who she *was* looking for would be harder to explain, for while she and her female friends accepted their own conquettish ways as being perfectly normal, none of them felt that fickleness in a man was desirable. A man must be constant, adoring and lover-like, and none of those commendable traits could be ascribed to Sir Nicholas Rayne, Deputy Master of Horse. Let him stick to his horses and she would stick to her ideals.

Sheen House was the most convenient of the Pickerings' houses, the nearest to Sir Thomas's place of work when the Queen was in residence. It was also Adorna's favourite, situated to one side of the old friary built by the Queen's grandfather when he rebuilt the old palace of Sheen, which had been destroyed by fire. Sheen Palace in its new form was then renamed Richmond after the earldom in North Yorkshire that had been Henry VII's favourite home. The palace was massively built on the edge of the River Thames, its gardens enclosing the friary which had its own private garden, known as the paradise, at the eastern end. Since the dissolution of the monasteries almost forty years previously, the friary had been left to disintegrate, its stone reused, its beautiful paradise overgrown, now used by the palace guests for walking in private. The road that led past Sheen House, past the old friary and down the southern wall of the palace garden to the river, had now become Paradise Road. Most of the friary land was visible from the garden of Sir Thomas Pickering's house, providing what appeared to be an extension of their own, the friary orchard and vineyard being used by the palace gardeners. The rest of Richmond's houses spread along the riverbank to the south, most of them timber-framed set amidst spacious gardens and orchards, free from the noise and foul air of London Town.

* * *

Sheen House, however, was built of soft pink brick like the palace itself, originally in the shape of an E for Elizabeth. Sir Thomas's latest addition to the buildings was a banqueting house in the garden, built especially for Lady Marion's entertaining, and it was here on the next day that the call reached Adorna and Maybelle that Cousin Hester had arrived. The small octagonal room was situated in one corner approached by a paved walkway above the fountain-garden, far enough from the house for them to remove their aprons and fling them on to the steps before greeting their guest.

They had fully expected to see some change in Cousin Hester, having last seen her as a mere child of ten on one of her father's rare visits to Sheen House. Hester's father had never been married, not even to Hester's mother, an unknown lady of the Court who had allowed her daughter to be brought up by one of Sir William's married sisters. Consequently, the astonishment felt by both women at the sight of each other was in Adorna's case cleverly concealed, and in Hester's case not so.

'Oh!' she whispered. 'Oh...I...er...Mistress Adorna?' Hester looked from Adorna to Maybelle and back again. Although a year older than her cousin, she was still painfully shy, twisting her black kid gloves together like a dish-clout, her eyes wide and fearful.

Bemused, Lady Marion laid a motherly arm across her guest's shoulders. 'Call her Adorna,' she whispered, kindly. 'And for all you're Sir Thomas's cousin rather than our children's, you must call us all by our

Christian names, you know. Sir Thomas and Seton and Adrian will be in later.'

That announcement did not provoke the delighted anticipation it was intended to, for the young lady looked as if she might have preferred to make a bolt for it rather than meet men and boys.

Adorna took pity on her, smiling with hands out-stretched. The wringing hands did not respond. 'Welcome, Cousin Hester. You must be tired after your journey from St Andrews-Underhill.' There was no real reason why she should have been, for her new home was only a stone's throw from St Paul's in the centre of London.

'Yes,' Hester whispered. She looked around her at the white plasterwork and the warm tapestried walls. 'It's cool and quiet here. I remember how I liked it before, long ago.'

'Well,' Lady Marion said, leading her towards the carved oak staircase, 'a lot's happened since then, and now you're a woman of independent means, free to do whatever you wish. You're our guest for as long as you choose to stay.'

There was no corresponding flash of delight at hearing her new status described. On the contrary, the very idea of having to make her own decisions was apparently not something she looked forward to with any relish. Sir William Pickering, Sir Thomas's cousin, had died at the beginning of the year, leaving his fortune and his house in London to Hester.

'Did you bring your maid with you?' said Adorna. 'If not, you shall share Maybelle with me. She knows how to dress hair in the latest fashions. Come, shall we find your room? The men will bring your baggage up.'

Cousin Hester's mourning-garb was only to be expected, in the circumstances, though neither the hostess nor her daughter would have allowed themselves to look quite so dowdy as their guest had the same thing happened to them. While they were not particularly in the forefront of fashion as those at Court were, neither were they ten years behind it as Hester was. Her figure could only be guessed at, concealed beneath a loose-bodied gown closed from neck to hem with fur-edged ties, puffed shoulder-sleeves and tight bead-covered under-sleeves. The hair to which Maybelle may or may not have access was almost completely hidden beneath a black french hood that hung well down at the back, though the bit of hair that showed at the front was brownish and looked, Maybelle thought, as if it needed a washing before it would reveal its true colour.

After her father's reproach the day before, Adorna now exercised all her charity towards her half-cousin, knowing little of the background of experience which had kept Hester inside her protective shell. For a woman of her age, she was impossibly tongue-tied and, for an heiress, she was going to find it difficult to protect herself from fortune-seeking men of whom there were countless hereabouts. Adorna managed it by virtue of her closeness to her parents; Hester would not manage it at all without some help. Yet on their guest list for Saturday, Adorna and her mother had already paired off this pathetic young lady with Sir Nicholas Rayne who might, for all they knew, be one of those sharks from whom she would need protection. On the other hand, they might suit each other perfectly. Strangely, the idea had lost its appeal for Adorna.

Having helped to unpack Hester's rather inadequate belongings and a very limited range of clothes, Adorna conducted her on a tour of the house, which she believed would make her feel more at home. Inside, there was much of it that Hester remembered, but outside, the large formal garden had been restructured into a series of smaller ones bounded by tall hedges, walls, trellises and stone balustrades, walkways, steps and spreading trees. The banqueting house was also new to her.

Adorna opened the double doors to reveal a marble-floored garden-room with windows on all eight of its sides. The ceiling was prettily plastered with clouds and cherubs bearing fruit, and the panels between the windows were painted to represent views of the garden beyond. In the centre of the floor was a round marble table supported by grimacing cherubs.

'For the banquets,' Adorna said, 'the suckets and marchpanes. I'm making them ready in the stillroom. We'll come out here after the last course and nibble while the servants clear the hall ready for the entertainment.'

'Tonight?'

'No, tomorrow. About thirty guests are coming to dinner. Didn't Mother tell you?'

The colour drained from Hester's face. 'Guests? Oh, dear.' Her hand flew to her mouth. 'Perhaps I should stay in my room. I'm in mourning, you must remember.'

'Hester, dear...' Adorna drew her down to a stone bench fixed to the wall '...being in mourning doesn't mean you have to avoid people. It's nearly seven months since Sir William died, and how often did you see him in your twenty-one years?'

'Two...three times. I don't recall.'

'So, you can still wear black for a full year, if you wish, but Sir William would not have wanted you to hide away for so long, would he? After all, he was a man who lived life to the full, I believe.'

She supposed Hester to know at least as much as she did about Sir William Pickering, who had once believed himself to be in the running for the Queen's hand in the days before the Earl of Leicester. She had shown him every favour and he had exploited that favour to the full, making himself extremely unpopular while he was about it. But the Queen did not marry him and he had retired from Court, permanently unmarried but not chaste.

'Did your aunt never tell you about her brother?' Adorna said. 'By all accounts your father was a remarkable man. In the Queen's Secret Service, a scholar, a fine handsome man. Women adored him, and he must have loved your mother and you very much to have wanted you to inherit his entire wealth. He doesn't sound to me like the kind of man who would want his daughter to hide herself away when she has the chance to meet people. My mother and father will be here, remember. We'll take care of you.'

Hester, who had been gazing at her hands until now, sighed and stared out of the window. 'Yes...but...'

'But what?'

'Well, you're so used to it. You know what to say, and you're so beautiful, and fashionable...and...'

'Nonsense! Some of the most fashionable ladies are not beauties, and some beauties are dowdy. Everyone has at least one good feature, and you have several, Hester.'

'I do?'

'Of course you do. The secret is to make the most of them. Would you like me to help? I can, if you'll allow it. Maybelle and I can do your hair, and we can find something a little prettier to wear?'

'In black?'

'In black, but more flattering. Yes?'

At last a smile hovered and broke through. 'All right. And will you tell me what to say, too?'

'Ah, now that,' Adorna said, 'may take a little longer, but I can certainly try. The first thing to do is to smile.'

By the time Sir Thomas returned to Sheen House in mid-afternoon, the transformation had begun and the outmoded mousy young lady who had been greeted by Lady Pickering was not quite the same one who curtsied gracefully to the master of the house, though the effort of it robbed her of words. Between them, Adorna and Maybelle had worked wonders. The hair had now been washed, burnished and arranged into a small jewelled cap that sat on the back of her head like a ripe hazelnut. Hester's straggly eyebrows had been plucked to form two slim arches, and her faint eyelashes had been darkened with a mixture of soot and saliva, which seemed to work very well. Even those few measures had been enough to convert an ordinary face into a most comely one, but Hester's greatest assets were her teeth. Once she began to show their dazzling whiteness, there was no reason why she should not smile more often, Adorna told her.

Under the loose gown, she was found to be as shapely as most other young women, if somewhat gauche, not knowing what to do with her hands. Or her head, for that matter. But when she tried on Adorna's black taffeta half-gown with the slashed sleeves and the blackwork partlet, then the new Hester began to emerge.

Teaching her how to move with confidence did not produce such instant results, for there were years of awkwardness and tensions to remove, nervous habits and self-conscious fumblings to eradicate which could not even be mentioned for fear of making them worse. So Adorna advised her to listen rather than to talk. 'It's easy enough,' she said. 'Men will talk about themselves until the moon turns blue and then some more. You'll only have to nod and they'll never notice you haven't said a word. You can't fail. They're all the same. Just smile at them, and they'll do the rest.'

Hester did not recognise the cynicism, never having found a pressing need to express herself on any particular subject, so the advice was well within her capabilities. She had noticed the palace wall beyond the Pickerings' garden and wanted to know if that was where Sir Thomas worked.

'No,' Adorna told her, 'my father's offices and workrooms are round the back, not far from the tennis court and bowling alley. That wall is the Queen's Gardens. Would you like to see?' She had noted Hester's interest in their own.

Predictably, the response was muted. 'Well...er, might we not be intruding?'

Adorna laughed. 'Meet somebody? Well, probably the odd courtier or two, or the gardener. Come, let's show off the new Hester.' The new Hester followed, dutifully.

The palace itself dominated a large area of the riverside, spreading backwards and upwards in a profusion of towers and turrets that pierced the sky with golden weather-vanes, shining domes, flags and chimneys. The colours of brick and stone mingled joyfully with flashing panes of glass that caught the sun, and the patterns that adorned every surface of the façade never failed to enchant Adorna. But Hester's eyes were too busy searching for any sign of life to enjoy them. On a rainy day, Adorna told her, one could still walk round the magnificent garden beneath the covered walkway that enclosed all four sides, but Hester was still unsettled. 'What's that shouting?' she whispered, nervously.

'The tennis court, over there at the back. Shall we go and see?'

'Er...there'll be people.'

'They'll be far too busy watching the players to see us.' Adorna took her arm and drew her gently onwards towards the sound of people and the curious pinging noise that became a hard clattering the nearer they walked.

The tennis court was a roofed building like the one at Hampton Court Palace that the Queen's father had had built. They entered through an arched doorway into a dim passage where suddenly the clatter and men's cries became sharper, and Adorna felt the resistance of Hester's arm as she drew back, already fearing what she might see. Although Adorna could sympathise with her cousin's dilemma, she saw no point in balking at the first hurdle. She placed Hester in front of her and steered her forwards, smiling to herself at each reluctant step.

The light came from windows high up on the two longest sides; the walls built up high had galleries running along them under sloping roofs upon which the hard balls bounced noisily before hitting the paved floor in the centre. A net stretched across the court, visibly sagging in the middle while four men, stripped down to doublets and hose, whacked at the ball with short-handled racquets. The two women sidled into the gallery where men and women leaned over the barrier to watch the play with shouts of, 'Well done, sir!' echoing eerily, laughing at the men's protests, their shouts of jubilation.

They found a space behind the barrier, Adorna nodding silent greetings to a few familiar faces, feeling

Hester flinch occasionally as the ball hit the wooden roof overhead and rolled down again. It was only when she gave her full attention to the players that Adorna realized she was within an arm's length of Sir Nicholas Rayne whose aggressive strokes at the leather ball were causing the marker to call out scores in his favour, though she could not begin to fathom out why.

Almost imperceptibly, she drew back, wishing she had not come, yet fascinated by his strength and agility, his amazing reach that scooped the ball up from the most impossible places, his quickness and accuracy. At one point, as the players changed ends, Sir Nicholas was one of those who pulled off their doublets, undoing the points of their white linen shirts. Rolling up their sleeves, they showed muscular forearms, at which Hester was obviously disturbed. 'Should we go, Adorna?' she whispered.

The name was caught inside a moment of silence, and Sir Nicholas turned, stared, and deliberately came to the barrier where they stood. He rested his hands just beyond Adorna's. 'The Mistresses Pickering. Welcome to Richmond, mistress,' he said to Hester. His appraisal, Adorna thought, must have been practised on many a likely-looking horse, though thankfully Hester would not realise it.

But his narrow-eyed survey of Adorna was of a more challenging variety, and his personal greeting to her was no more than, 'Enjoy the game, mistress,' which she was quite sure did not mean what Hester thought it meant.

She was given no time to find a reply, for he walked quickly away, swinging his racquet, while she was torn between making a quick and dignified exit or staying, hoping to put him off.

It was Hester's astonishing response to the greeting, predictably delayed by nervousness, that decided the course of action. 'Thank you, Sir Nicholas,' she said to his retreating back.

'What?' Adorna whispered, staring at her guest. 'You *know* him?'

Hester nodded. 'Uncle Samuel and Aunt Sarah often invited him to Bishops Standing before he left to join the Earl of Leicester's household. I've not seen him for a year or more. He's always so polite, but I never know what to say to him.'

For someone who didn't know what to say, that was the most Hester had said since her arrival. Which, Adorna thought, meant either that Sir Nicholas was the cause of some interest within the timid little heart or that her own efforts were already bearing fruit. Unlikely, after such a short time. 'Did he visit often?' she probed, watching him.

'Quite often. He and Uncle Samuel used to play chess together, and hunted, and talked about horses.'

Adorna was silenced, overtaken by the combined thudding in her chest and the crash of the ball against the wall. Had he pretended not to know Cousin Hester? Or had he simply not pretended anything? *I look forward to meeting Cousin Hester. Is she…?* Of course, it had not occurred to her to discover any previous acquaintance. So what had been the true purpose of his visit to Sir William Pickering's sister's home? Chess? Horses? 'Is his home near them?' she whispered.

Hester's reply came with an expression that suggested Adorna ought to have known the answer to that. 'His father is Lord Elyot,' she said. 'He *owns* Bishops Standing.'

The astonishment showing so clearly in Adorna's lovely eyes was caught at that moment by the player at the far end of the court whose mind was not entirely on the game. His keen eyes levelled at hers like a hunter stalking a doe, while his partner yelled at him to attend.

'Chase two!' the marker called.

'No. Chase one!' Sir Nicholas said to himself as he sent the ball crashing across the court. The next time he had chance to look, the two Pickering ladies had disappeared.

The full impact of what was happening to her began to take effect at the end of that day, by which time Adorna was too confused to sleep. She and Hester had strolled back to Sheen House, diverting their steps through the friary paradise especially to examine the overgrown roses, the heavily budding lilies, the rue and lady's bedstraw that symbolised the Virgin Mary to whom the garden had probably been dedicated. It was a magical place where, even now, the outlines of the beds could still be seen, providing Hester with a topic for suppertime when Lady Marion asked them where they'd been. It saved Adorna herself from having to reply, her mind being far away on another journey.

As the summer evening drew to a close, she made an excuse to be alone, to walk along the raised pathways to the banqueting house to see that the doors and windows were closed. There was a moon, silvering the pathways and the orchard below, outlining the derelict friary and staring through the glassless east window, lighting the high palace wall. She stared out across the paradise where she had walked earlier, frowning as she caught a movement beyond the shadows. A man passed through the garden door from the palace, leaving it slightly ajar, picking his way carefully across the space to stand under a gnarled pear tree, his broad shoulders well inside the low branches. There was no mistaking the shape of him, the long legs, the easy movement, the carriage of his head. Sir Nicholas Rayne. She was quite sure of it.

He had waited no more than two minutes when another figure came through the door, a woman, looking about her hesitantly. Sir Nicholas made no move to show himself, no rush to greet her or sudden urge to embrace. The woman searched awhile and then saw him, but still there was no laughter stifled by kisses but only a slow advance and the joining of hands indicating, Adorna thought, either a first meeting or a last one. The two stood together talking, his head bent to hers, her hand occasionally touching his chest, her finger once upon his mouth, briefly. The watcher in the banqueting house placed a hand upon her own breast to still the thumping inside, to quell the first

awful, sour, bitter, agonising pangs of jealousy so foreign to her that she did not recognise them as such.
She thought it might be guilt, or something akin to it,
telling herself that the man and his woman mattered
nothing to her. Less than nothing.

Do you have a lady, Sir Nicholas?

No, sir. Not yet.

What was this, then? An attempt to acquire one, or
to get rid of one? He was a flirt. He was already welcomed by Hester's foster-parents, no doubt as a potential suitor for their niece. There was surely no other
good reason for them to encourage his visits, for they
had no other family. What did it matter to her, anyway?

The couple was moving apart. The lady was preparing to leave, stretching the last touch of their hands
to breaking point. She was weeping. Quickly, he took
a stride towards her, reaching out for her shoulders
and pulling her with some force towards his bending
head. His kiss was short and not gentle, ending with
a quick release and a faint cry from her that reached
Adorna, wrenching at her heart. She clung to the wall,
watching as the woman picked up her skirts and ran
to the door, leaving it open behind her.

Sick and dizzy from the impact of a kiss that had
not been for her, Adorna stood rooted to the spot, staring at the back of the man she had tried to keep away
with her coldness, willing him to turn and come to her
here, in the soft shadowy night. He did not move.

A call came to her from the house, her father's call,

loud and unmistakably for her. 'Adorna! Come in now! It's getting late, Adorna!'

She must answer, or he'd come looking for her. 'Yes, Father.'

As she knew he would, Sir Nicholas turned towards the high wall behind him where the banqueting house was built into one corner. She could not leave without him seeing, and her loose blonde hair would show him her exact location. Reluctantly, she closed the double doors with a snap and locked them noisily behind her, tossing her bright hair into the moonlight. If she must reveal herself, then she would do it with aplomb. She did not look below her as she went to meet her father. 'Coming!' she called, merrily.

The reflection in the polished brass mirror kept up a steady and silent conversation with the blue-grey eyes, and the candle flame bent in the light breeze from the window, barely shedding any light on the messages of confusion and soul-searching that refused to untangle. What had now become clear to Adorna, after her reaction to the secret tryst in the garden, was that she had blundered in the wrong direction by her attempts to make Hester more attractive. Even to herself, she could hardly pretend that she had done it for Hester's own sake alone, for at the back of her mind had been the possibility that a young and personable lady with a fortune would surely be of more interest to the man who had behaved with such familiarity towards herself. Then, it had seemed imperative that a way be found to get rid of him or to keep him at a more manageable distance, at least.

But now there had developed within her deepest self a reluctance to exclude this man quite as forcibly as she had been doing, especially now that there seemed to be a real chance of him seeing Hester in a new light. Her foster-parents apparently approved of him, and doubtless Hester herself was impressed by his connections. Another more relaxed and enticing meeting between the two might just be enough to do the trick, and she herself would have helped to bring it about.

Yet she could not like the man. He was too aggressively male, too experienced for her, probably promiscuous, too presumptuous. And rude. And what was he doing speaking so pertly to her when there *was* another woman, in spite of his denials? No doubt he had a long line of mistresses somewhere, all of whom he would deny whenever it suited him. Yes, let him make an offer for Hester, since she had come into her fortune. A man like him would appreciate more wealth, rather than the Master of Revels' daughter.

She lifted the sleeve of her chemise to look once more for the imprint of his fingers on her upper arms. There they were, like a row of shadowy blackberry stains. She caressed them, wondering which part of her he had seen yesterday that the other three men had not. Slowly, she slipped her chemise down to her waist and stood, holding herself sideways to the mirror and raising her arms to enclose him, feeling his imaginary grip upon her shoulders, the hard dizzying kiss upon her mouth. How would it feel? Something deep inside her belly began to quiver and melt.

Guiltily, she folded her arms across herself and tip-toed over the creaky floorboards to her bed where she stretched, aching, seeing him again in the moonlit paradise as he turned to look. No, this could not be what they called falling in love; this was confusing and painful; there was nothing in it to make her happy. In the darkness behind her wide-open eyes she watched him at tennis, saw his appraisal of Hester's new image, saw his hands on her mare's flanks, his control of his own great mount. His bold words and stare had stirred her to anger and excitement as no other man had done. But no, of course, this was not love. How could it be? She was right; this was not the man for her. Let Hester take the field.

Chapter Three

This resolution, nursed by Adorna until she fell asleep, had vanished completely by the time she woke, which meant that the whole argument had to be reconstructed from the beginning in order to establish any reason why Sir Nicholas should have been on her mind in the first place. Which was difficult, in the light of day.

Another disturbing development was that, overnight, Hester had apparently discovered how to smile. Adorna suspected that she must have been practising in front of the mirror, but this newest enchantment showed itself first at breakfast and was then rehearsed at intervals throughout the day so that, by the time the two of them had put the finishing touches to an array of subtleties for the banquet, Adorna was forced to the conclusion that Hester was happy. There was surely no other explanation for it.

Not that Adorna had any objections, as such, to Hester being happy, only a reservation that the reason behind it must mean only one thing. Sir Nicholas. After a year or more, Hester was happy to make contact again.

Even Lady Marion noticed it. 'She'll dazzle the men with that smile,' she said to Adorna. 'They'll be writing sonnets to it before the week's out.'

Adorna stood back to look at the effects of the trailing ivy interlaced with roses hanging in swags across the oak panelling of the great hall. 'She's learning more quickly than I thought,' she said with her head on one side. 'Is that level with the others?'

'More or less. I think she ought to have her own maid though, dearest. Perhaps I'll suggest finding one for her. If she's going to improve as fast as that, we can't let her choose one who doesn't know a farthingale from a martingale, can we?'

Visions of Hester wearing a strap from her chin to her waist to keep her head down caused an undignified halt to the proceedings that lightened Adorna's heart, if only temporarily. Her mother's relief at having an extra male guest to partner Hester had grown to far greater heights once she discovered that the two were already acquainted and from then on, no instruction was too detailed to make sure that Hester and Sir Nicholas were to be regarded as a pair. From which it was obvious to Adorna that her father had made very little of the man's visit to the workshop two days ago. Knowing her parents' tendency to see potential suitors even before they appeared, Adorna was very relieved by this.

Although they had never regarded Master Peter Fowler as a serious contender for Adorna's hand, Peter himself did, being one of the first to arrive for the dinner party, bringing a gift for his hostess in the shape of a tiny silver padlock and key. A symbol, he told her, of his protection for her most precious jewel.

Smiling courteously, Adorna said nothing to contradict this, for it was precisely this aspect of Peter's company that had singled him out from other young men. He was tall and well made, personable, correct, agreeable and utterly dependable, as his job demanded. Protection was not only his profession but also the reason for his attraction, for if Adorna could not be safe with Peter, then who could she be safe with? Naturally, his lapse at the Queen's hawking party in Richmond Park had been unusual, but Adorna did not blame him for that. Brown-eyed and curly-haired, he offered her a brown satin-clad arm while expertly assessing the security of the pale pink bodice that skimmed the swell of her breasts with a hint of white lace to half-conceal the deepest cleft. A lace pie-frill ruff clung enticingly to her throat.

She laid the tips of her fingers on his arm. 'Peter,' she said, 'I want you to meet our house guest. She's appallingly shy. Will you talk to her?'

Hester curtsied with lowered eyes while Peter, bowing to the shy black-clad figure, thought the contrast to Adorna could hardly have been greater. Even in black, the dowdiness had been replaced by a beguiling vulnerability to which Peter instantly responded, for Hester's nut-brown hair under a jewelled velvet band had suffered hours of Maybelle's ministrations and now, framing her face in a heart-shaped roll, suited her perfectly.

Peter's response to Adorna's introduction was even more immediate. 'Sir William Pickering's daughter?' He beamed. 'Why, mistress, I have admired your late father's exploits since I was so high—' he held a hand level with his waist '—and I even met him, once. Come, will you speak of him to me?' His large fingers closed warmly over the trembling ones and Hester was obliged to abandon Adorna's advice concerning smiles and nods in order to talk of a father she had hardly known. It was good practice, but not exactly what Lady Marion had had in mind.

Sir Thomas's musicians were by now in full swing high up in the gallery at the far end of the hall. Below them, the guests entered from a porch at one side, adding another layer of sound that rose in waves of laughter and drifted away into the great oaken rafters. Even while she chatted, Adorna could identify the booming stage-voice of Master Burbage, their actor friend, followed by the reed-pipe squeak of Master Thomas Tallis whose wife Joan held him up by one elbow as a stool was placed beneath him. Yet, though she was soon surrounded by friends and acquaintances, Adorna felt the effect of someone's eyes on the back of her head that pulled her slowly round and drew her away like a netted fish.

Although Sir Nicholas was part of a newly arrived group, he took no part in their conversation but aimed his narrowed eyes towards Adorna, meeting hers as she turned, throwing out a challenge for her to come and welcome him. To refuse would have been too discourteous.

She lifted the golden pomander that swung on a chain at her waist and went forward, unable to withdraw her eyes from his though, even as they met, there was not the smile of welcome she had given to others.

'Your lady mother bade me welcome,' he said, softly.

'Of course,' said Adorna. 'She would see no reason to do otherwise.' Her heart beat loudly under her straight pink bodice, making her breathless.

'And you, mistress? Do you see a reason to do otherwise?'

'I see several reasons, sir, but don't concern yourself with them. It cannot be the first time a woman has taken an aversion to you. But then, perhaps it is.'

He glanced around him as if to find an example, but saw Hester instead. 'Ah, Cousin Hester. Was it your doing that transformed the lady, or had it already begun? Quite remarkable. She's learning to speak, too, I see. Well, well.'

Coming from another, she might have smiled at this sarcasm, but a mixture of pride and protection quelled it. 'I was not aware,' she said, 'that you and she knew each other. She tells me that you found the hunting good at Bishops Standing.'

'Is that all she told you?'

His blunt question made her pause, not knowing how to learn more without betraying her interest. Mercifully, she was prevented from saying anything by the Yeoman of the Ewery's arrival, whose invitation to dip their fingers into the silver bowl of scented water signalled an end to most conversations. She dried hers on the linen towel and handed it to Sir Nicholas. 'I am expected to take you to her,' she said. 'Will you come, sir?'

'Gladly,' he said, smiling. 'I can hardly wait.'

For some reason, she would have preferred a token show of reluctance, but now there was just time, before the procession to the table, to present Sir Nicholas to Mistress Hester Pickering and to watch like a hawk as his eyes smiled into hers and quickly roamed, approving or amused, over the new image. By this time, the effect of conversation and the warmth of the hall had brought a most becoming flush to Hester's cheeks and a sparkle to her eyes and, though she kept the latter modestly lowered, the newly darkened lashes made alluring crescents upon her skin. This show of mutual pleasure left no doubt in Adorna's mind that Lady Marion would be delighted to see how her plan was falling into place so neatly.

Peter took Adorna's arm to steer her to one side, noting the direction of her interest. 'I thought you said she was shy,' he said.

Adorna looked puzzled. 'Did she tell you of her father, then?'

'Only a little. She talked of Sir Nicholas, mostly.'

Once again, the conversation was curtailed by the ceremonial observed by every noble household at meal-times, the waiting, the seating, the ritual carving and presenting, by which time there were obligatory gasps of delight at the array of dishes, their colours, variety and decoration. Lady Marion had, for this event, brought out the best silver dishes, bowls and ewers, the great salts, the best spoons and knives, the finest monogrammed linen. On the two-tiered court-cupboard stood the best Venetian glasses, while an army of liveried servers attended diligently to every guest's needs.

Adorna tried to avoid looking at Hester and Sir Nicholas, but her curiosity got the better of her, her sneaking looks between mouthfuls and words feeding her snippets of information as to Hester's responsiveness to Sir Nicholas's attentions. His attention was required from other quarters, too, for the table of over thirty guests was merry and light-hearted, and Sir Nicholas was an excellent conversationalist. Adorna would have been blind not to see how the women, young and old, glowed when he spoke to them, prompting her to recall his uncivil manner as he had hauled her out of the river, his familiarity afterwards, even when he had discovered whose daughter she was.

With renewed assiduity she turned all her attention towards the other end of the table and to her partner, taking what pleasure she could from the safe predictability of Peter's good manners and to the chatter of her friends, all the while straining to single out the deep cultured voice of Sir Nicholas Rayne. At the end of two courses, they were led into the garden where the double doors of the banqueting house had been thrown open to receive the slow trickle of guests. Here was laid out an astonishing selection of tiny sweet-meats on silver trays, candied fruits, chunks of orange

marmalade, sweet wafers and gingerbreads, marchpane and sugar-paste dainties covered with gold leaf.
Jellies and syllabubs were served in tiny glasses, and
biscuits were placed on wooden roundels, each guest
nibbling, exclaiming, and moving outside to admire
the formal flower-beds, the view over the friary orchard and the river in the distance.

Purposely, Adorna kept some distance between herself and Sir Nicholas while she spoke to many of the
guests, laughing at their jokes and listening to their
opinions, never straying far from Peter's side. From
there, she could signal to Sir Nicholas that she had no
wish for his company. Her mother, however, had already begun to waver on this point.

She whispered in Adorna's ear, 'You didn't *tell*
me!'

'Tell you what, Mother?' Acting total innocence
came quite easily to her.

'That he was so handsome. And distinguished. If
I'd understood that he was my lord of Leicester's deputy, I'd have had him instead of Master Fowler partner
you. Is Sir Nicholas the one who helped you out of
the river?'

Adorna's eyes strayed once more to the midnight-
blue taffeta doublet, velvet breeches and black silk
hose, to his elegant bearing, to the gold buckles and
jewels on his swordbelt and scabbard. His hand rested
on one hip while with the other he held up his wooden
roundel, reversed, from which he read the poem
painted on the rim.

'Lord Elyot's eldest son,' her mother continued, 'I

think, dearest, that you ought to be making yourself a little more agreeable to Sir Nicholas. He's going to be wasted on Cousin Hester.'

'I'd much rather he played the part you invited him for,' Adorna replied. 'Though I think Hester's wasted on *him*.'

But Lady Marion was only half-listening. 'Don't be difficult, dear. Come along!' she called to Sir Nicholas's group. 'You must sing your roundelays, you know. I think you should be the one to start them off, Sir Nicholas, if you please. Show them how it should be done.'

The idea of having guests to sing for their suppers was not a new one, each one expecting to contribute to the others' entertainment in some way either by singing or by playing an instrument. At thirteen, Adorna's youngest brother Adrian usually had to be held back forcibly from being the first to perform, but this time he added his voice to his mother's. Although Sir Nicholas's roundelay was short, he made it last longer by singing it several times over to a simple tune of his own devising.

And so my love protesting came, but yet I made her mine.

His voice was true and vibrant, but Adorna refused to watch him perform, not wishing to see who he looked at while he sang. Yet as soon as the applause died down and another guest followed, a whispered comment at her back closed her ears to everything except the exchange of riveting gossip.

'Pity he doesn't make them his for longer than three

months,' a man's voice said, half-laughing. 'He goes through 'em faster than his master.'

'Hah! Is that how long the last one was?'

'Lady Celia. Traverson's lass. Handsome woman, too, but ditched after three months. Penelope Mountjoy afore that and heaven knows how many afore her. He has 'em queueing up for him.'

'But he's only been in his post for a year or so.'

The voice chuckled. 'Trying out the new mares.'

'They're happy to assist, eh?'

'Aye, but not so happy to be left, apparently. Still, if he's after old Pickering's heiress, he'll probably not find any protesting there.'

The two men joined in the applause though they had not listened to the song, but Adorna's blood ran cold as she sidled away to the back of the crowd to avoid an invitation to sing, shivering with unease at the sickening words. Even among men it seemed that Sir Nicholas's reputation as a rake was chuckled over, envied, plotted and predicted, his victims pitied. From the corner of her eye, she identified one of the gossips as her father's colleague, the Master of the Queen's Jewels, the other as a superior linen-draper who held a royal warrant.

Ditched after three months? Trying out the new mares? It was as she had suspected; the man had been amusing himself, teasing her to make her respond to him, despite her obvious antagonism. Then he would blithely go on to the next before choosing how, when and where to include Cousin Hester in his schemes, sure that she would defer to his convenience more than any other. For the hundredth time, she heard the woman's sob echo through the evening, saw again her last slow touch, her hurried departure into oblivion. Her heart ached for the woman's pain and for Hester, too, who would have no experience of how to deal with a man's inconstancy, being unused to dalliance and light-hearted love affairs. Hester would not recognise insincerity if it was branded on a man's forehead.

That much was true, though at that precise moment Hester was having no problems with her own brand of innocence or with other people's kindness, whether the latter was sincerely meant or not. Dear Adorna and Lady Marion had identified her deficiencies, which were many, and had offered her every assistance to overcome them, and it would be both churlish and unnecessary to deprive them of the pleasure of success. Moreover, the pleasure was not all theirs. She practised her smile once more on a young gentleman who offered her a heart-shaped biscuit and saw how his eyes lit up with pleasure, as Sir Nicholas's had done.

What a pity Aunt Sarah had not made her aware of such delights, but then, her foster parents were much older than Adorna's and had had neither the time, experience nor patience to be plunged into parenthood with a ready-made child. They had provided her with an elderly nurse and tutor, shelter and food, a good education and firm discipline and, if she wanted company, there were always the horses. Uncle Samuel was a passionate horse-breeder: Aunt Sarah was not passionate about anything. Passion, she had once told Hester, was a shocking waste of energy.

Hester was satisfied, almost pleased, that Sir Nicholas had noticed the changes enough to compliment her. He had always been most kind, and it was quite obvious that Lady Marion had asked him here especially to put her at her ease. The least she could do in return was to remember what they had told her about smiling, listening and keeping her hands still.

She glanced across the long shadows that now striped the lawn, seeing Adorna talking animatedly to a group of men, her expressions so graceful, her hands and head articulate, her back curving and set firmly against Sir Nicholas from whom she had made no attempt to conceal her indifference. They had scarcely spoken to each other at the tennis court, nor had Adorna joined the ladies who surrounded him, but Hester supposed that the gentlemanly Master Fowler was Adorna's special friend and that she preferred his company to anyone's. Which Hester could well understand, though for their sakes she would make herself most agreeable to Sir Nicholas since that was clearly what they wished.

Her aunt and uncle had, naturally, warned her that once she was on her own, there would be fortune-hunters, but her mind was at rest as far as Sir Nicholas was concerned, he having a fortune of his own. Apart from that, if he had ever entertained thoughts along those lines, he had had plenty of chances during the six years or more he had been visiting Uncle Samuel.

The guests were beginning to move back into the house again, Adorna firmly linked to Master Fowler. To Hester a dear gentleman offered his arm, which she daintily laid her hand upon, smiling at him, picking up her skirts over the grass and thinking how much easier this was than she had once believed.

In the great hall, the tables and benches had been cleared to leave a space for the entertainments, and here Hester was happy to watch as sheets of music were handed to those guests who were prepared to perform on viol, flute and lute. Nothing could have been lovelier than when Adorna played a beautiful melody by William Byrd on the virginals, for she was able to sing at the same time in a voice so sweet that the guests were spellbound, making Hester appreciate even more how much she herself had to learn.

There was dancing, too, which had never been Hester's strongest point, so she remained at one side in the company of yet another gentleman who talked non-stop about his fishing visits to Scotland when she would rather have listened to the music. She did, however, notice how Adorna kept her eyes lowered whenever she went forward to take Sir Nicholas's hand, and how he looked at her without the smile that he had bestowed upon herself, which seemed to indicate that he was as little interested in Adorna as she appeared to be in him.

Then there was the play, written by seventeen-year-old Seton, Adorna's brother. He had persuaded some of his friends from the theatre company known as Leicester's Men to join him in this short and extremely funny performance, made all the funnier because it was entirely unrehearsed. Master Burbage, their leading actor, kept it all together somehow, but even he could not keep his face straight when Adrian, who had begged on his knees for a part, began to *ad lib* most dangerously, throwing the other characters off track. It brought the house down, the evening to a close, and Hester to the conclusion that, if it got no worse than this, she might begin to get used to dinner parties.

As duty demanded, Adorna stood with the rest of her family to bid each of the guests farewell, promising Master Burbage that she would rectify one glaring omission by attending one of the Leicester's Men's performances at their London venue before long. With a quick squeeze of her mother's hand, she slipped away from the family group, along the passageway leading to the back of the house and out into the walled herb-garden. Here she waited until the calls of farewell had begun to fade. This was another of her refuges, used on this occasion as an escape from Peter who had earlier left her in no doubt that tonight a formal kiss on the knuckles would not be enough. Without seeking to argue about it, Adorna was convinced that anything more than that would be too much. It was better, she had whispered to her mother, if she disappeared and explained tomorrow, if need be. Lady Marion had had experience at making excuses.

It was almost dark, but still she could just see the brick pathway leading through the garden door on to the lawn where the guests had strolled earlier. There was the walkway that led to the banqueting house in the corner, the fountain still tinkling. Distant bursts of laughter and chatter still floated through the open win dows, shapes moving in and out of soft candlelight.

Keeping to the shadows, she entered the small room with a feeling of relief that the evening was over, that she had escaped Peter's personal leave-taking and that the act she had kept up all evening could now be dropped. The banqueting-house floor was still littered with crumbs in the light of a single candle that the servants had left burning, and a heap of wooden roundels, painted side uppermost, lay discarded on the table, their rhymes sung and forgotten. Holding them towards the candle flame, she went through the stack one by one until she found the one she wanted, peering to make out the words and touching them with the tips of her fingers.

'And so my love protesting came,' she whispered, reading as she turned it.

'But yet I made her mine,' came the reply from the doorway.

She half-leapt in fright, clutching the plate to her bodice and whirling to face him, angered by the intrusion. 'I came here...' she began, ready to resume the act. But the lines had already faded from memory, and she could only glare, defensively.

'I know why you came here.' Sir Nicholas closed the door quietly behind him. 'You came here to escape Master Fowler's attentions, in the first place. Isn't that so? Poor Adorna. Saddling yourself all evening with him to keep yourself out of my way. Was it worth it, then?'

'It worked well enough until now, sir!' she snapped.

'Tch, tch!' He shook his handsome head, smiling with his eyes. His hair and the deep blue of his clothes blended into the shadowy room, but could not conceal the width of his shoulders or the deep swell of his chest. Though he made no move towards her, Adorna found his presence disconcerting after a whole evening of trying to avoid him. He held out a hand for the plate. 'May I?' he said.

Evading his eyes, she placed it back on the pile. 'A silly jingle,' she said. 'Quite meaningless. I must not be seen with you here alone, Sir Nicholas. We have nothing to say to each other, and my father will—'

Before she could say what her father would do, he had stepped forward a pace and nipped the candle flame with his fingers, plunging the room into darkness except for the lambent glow from a rising moon. At the same time, Adorna's neat sidesteps towards the door was anticipated by the intimidating bulk of his body. 'Then we must make sure,' he said, 'that we are not seen here alone, mistress. But I cannot agree that we have nothing to say to each other when you said so little to me earlier in the evening. Do you not recall the moments when you could have spoken but chose not to? Shall we reconstruct the dance to ease the flow of conversation?' In the darkness, he held out his hand.

She had noticed his graceful dancing, but this was a game she did not intend to play, nor was she by any means ready to fall into his flirtatious trap, as she was sure many others had done. Far from queueing up for his attentions, she wanted nothing to do with him, especially after what she had heard that evening. It was time someone taught him a lesson.

Taking up the act where she had left off, she let out an exaggerated sigh and turned away from him to stare out of the same window where, two nights ago, she had watched him kiss a woman in the friary paradise. 'Sir Nicholas, I have had a busy day and I have little inclination to wake all Richmond with my screams. But I am prepared to do so if it's the only way to get out of here. Now, please will you go and make your courtesies to my parents and leave me in peace? Others may find your ways diverting, but I don't.'

In one step, he came to stand close behind her with his knees enveloped in her wide bell-shaped skirts. 'For one so unmoved by my diverting ways, mistress, you send out some strangely contradicting signals,' he said, his voice suddenly devoid of his former playfulness. 'You came in here to seek my—'

'I did not come in here to *seek* anything!' she snarled at him over her shoulder. 'The poem was one that caught my eye.'

'I see.' He allowed the explanation to go unchallenged. 'So perhaps you came here to remind yourself of something you saw out there. Eh?'

'I saw noth—' She bit her words off, remembering that he had seen her. She started again. 'What I caught the merest glimpse of, Sir Nicholas, in no way concerned me. If you choose to tell my father that you have no lady, that's entirely your own affair. I care not if you have a different lady for each day of the week. All I ask is that you don't *ever* consider me to be one of them.'

'You may be a marginally better actor than your brothers, Adorna, but I still say that your signals are in a tangle. Shall I tell you why?'

Again, she made a move towards the door, but her skirts hampered her and this time his arm came across her to form a solid barrier. She willed herself to maintain an indifference that had nothing to do with the facts, to make her voice obey her head instead of her heart. It was not easy.

'No,' she said. 'Don't. If you find my signals conflicting, then you are obviously not reading them correctly, sir. Master Fowler finds them easy enough to understand, and so do other men. When I keep out of their way it means that I do not want their company. Now, what part of that message do *you* not understand? Shall I put it in French for you? Or Latin?'

Even in the darkness, she could feel the changes that crossed his face, his silence verifying that she had scored at last, checked his cocksureness. For once, he was nonplussed. But it did not last long. 'You mean it, don't you?' he whispered. 'Do you flee from all men on sight, just for the fun of the ride?'

His temporary unsureness gave her courage. 'What I do with all men is none of your business, Sir Nicholas. But one thing I *will* tell you is that any man who compares me to a horse, however delicately, may as well take himself off to the other side of the Christendom. And if you've finally understood that I mean what I say, then I shall sleep better at nights. Now, return to your long line of *amours*, sir. They'll be awaiting you.'

'When I'm ready. I find it interesting that you feel able to indulge in equine double-talk when you are looking down at the top of my bonnet, but it's a different matter when your feet are level with mine, isn't it? Now, that can mean only one thing.'

His arm still held her back against the wall, but his closeness spelt a dangerous determination, and her act of indifference began to falter as his warmth reached her face and the bare skin below her ruff. She gulped, moistening her mouth.

'You are obviously about to tell me,' she whispered, 'though you must have performed this jaded ritual so many times before.' She turned her head to one side. 'Tell me, if you must, and then allow me to go in. I'm getting chilled here.'

It was a blunder she could hardly have bettered, but in one way it prepared her as nothing else would for what he might do. Although there was a part of her that wanted him with a desperate longing, she had never anticipated yielding to a man in the middle of an argument about the exact meaning of her signals. If she herself didn't know what they meant for certain, how could he, for all his experience? No, this was not the way she wanted to be wooed, not like his other easy conquests; small talk, gropings in the dark, a kiss and a fall like ripened fruit into his lap. She was *not* like the others.

Before he could take hold of her, she had knocked

his hands sideways and rammed one elbow into his doublet, swinging herself away into the darkened room to find the table as a barrier. Caught by the side of her hand, the pile of wooden roundels clattered onto the floor, halting her long enough for Sir Nicholas to reach her again with a soft laugh and an infuriating gentling tone that she was sure he used on restive horses. 'Steady…steady, my beauty. You're new to this, aren't you, eh? I knew it. Scared as a new fill—'

Her hand found its target with a terrifying crack on the side of his head that shocked Adorna far more than him. Never in her life had she done such a thing before, nor had she ever needed to. The success of her assault, however, gave her no real advantage except to reinforce her anger and fear, which Sir Nicholas was already aware of. Even in the dark, he was able to catch both her wrists and pull them to his chest, holding her firmly to him, panicking her by his closeness and by her own unusual helplessness. This was not how she wanted to be wooed, either. She had never thought that fighting might be a part of it.

To fight and twist away was one thing, but a whale-bone corset beneath the pink fabric of her bodice was quite another and, though she might have screamed, the breath was not in place before he spoke without a trace of the facetiousness she had dreaded.

'Adorna…hush now. You've got it wrong. Listen to me.'

'I don't want to…be here… Let me go!'

'I cannot let you go.'

'Words…words!' she hissed. 'I'll *not* be your latest conquest!'

'Adorna, what is all this about my conquests, my long line of *amours*? What is it that you've heard? Give me a chance to refute it. I'll not deny that I enjoy women's company, but it's not the way you think.'

'I don't think anything!' She pushed at him, angrily.

'Yes, you do, or you'd not be so fierce. I'm not trying to force you into a relationship. Did you think I was?'

'Then what are you doing with my wrists in your hands, sir?'

'Persuading you to listen to me, for you'll not listen any other way. There, I've released you, see. Now, you can do whatever you wish with your hands while I tell you how lovely you are.'

'Oh, for pity's sake!' she yelped. 'Tell me that my hair is like the moon's rays, my mouth is like a rose-bud, my eyes are like—'

'Adorna!'

'Like two faded periwinkles, my nose…oh… whatever the best noses are like nowadays, but spare me the rest, I beg you. I've had all that and more, and you can have nothing to add that I've not already—'

Apparently there *was* something that he could add that, so far, no one else had ever succeeded in doing, something that stopped the flow of scorn as effectively as a gag. She tried to talk through it, but he was no amateur like the one he had identified at the Queen's picnic, and his was not the kind of kiss that pushed and hoped for the best. Knowing that she would try to avoid him, he caught her head and turned it sideways on to his chest, wedging her there while he cut off the scolding words with a sweet tenderness that dried up her thoughts, too. This, he was telling her, was more potent than words, beyond argument, and totally beyond her experience.

Her hands, now freed, could have torn at him but lay unhelpfully upon his doublet instead, feeling nothing. She had sometimes wondered how a woman was supposed to return a man's kiss when he was doing all that needed to be done, and now she stopped thinking altogether for, after the first startling invasion of his mouth on hers, her mind closed as effectively as her eyes, and she was swept away into the deepest, darkest, most overpowering sensation she could ever have imagined. And she *had* imagined, often.

Drunk with the new experience, her mind was slow to adjust and, when he paused, just touching her lips with his, her pretences had deserted her. Without any prompting, her hands knew what to do, reaching up through the darkness to touch his face and to find their own way over his ears and hair that parted under her fingers. Shadows of shattered conscience warned her of some former conflict, some contradiction, but it was too dark to identify them before they fled, and his lips returned to take what, this time, she was yielding up without protest. He was tender, carefully disturbing the surface of her desire until a moan began to rise in her throat.

Then he released her, easing her upright and supporting her in his arms while her head drooped, almost touching his chin. 'You were saying?' he whispered, eventually.

She shook her head, saying nothing, thinking nothing.

'Then will you listen to me awhile?'

'Another time,' she whispered. 'Please? Another time? My father…the servants will be here soon to…' she peered about her and disengaged herself from his arms '…to clear up, to lock the doors.' Unsteadily, she stepped aside, hearing a loud crack from beneath her skirts. 'Oh, no!'

Sir Nicholas bent to lift her foot and to retrieve two halves of a roundel, placing them on the table. 'Can't be helped,' he said. 'Adorna, just one thing before I take you back.' He took her hand and held it against his chest. 'Whatever you've been hearing of me, and you know how people gossip at Court, don't allow it to prejudice you against me. If there is no scandal, people will invent it. It's gossip, Adorna.'

There was nothing she could reply to that except to remove her hand and hope that her cheeks and lips would be cooled by the night air before she entered the house. The last remaining guests were departing as they appeared together, though one who lingered was, to Adorna's consternation, Master Peter Fowler. He came to greet them with some eagerness, his expression as he looked from one to the other showing that he recognised what Adorna had hoped to conceal.

'Peter,' she said, reading his face.

'There you are!' Peter said, breezily. 'Sir Nicholas, I was hoping to catch you, sir.'

'Me? Whatever for?'

'I've been across to the palace just now. The keys, you know. Bedtime.' He smiled apologetically. The handing over of the keys of Her Majesty's chamber at bedtime was a ritual he could not evade. 'And I've been given two messages for you. You're a popular man, sir.' His expression, Adorna thought, held a glint of sheer mischief as he came to her side, ready to lead her away. 'One from his lordship's man to say that he'd be glad if you'd take a look at the bay stallion again before you retire.'

'Certainly. And the other?'

'Oh, from Lady Celia Traverson's maid. It appears her mistress was expecting you to visit her this evening in the east tower room, sir. Seemed a bit upset. I said I'd see you got the message.' He glanced again at Adorna with a suggestion of triumph in his merry eyes. 'Wonderful evening,' he said.

'Yes,' she agreed, taking the arm he offered. 'Wonderful.'

As if to verify the effect of Peter's ill-timed messages, she met the eyes of her former companion as he made her a formal bow and saw the anger that washed briefly across them, drooping the lids with a stifled frown. Their glances agreed that there was no explanation that he could offer to which she would want to listen, and that Adorna's former hostility, far from being lessened, had now increased. Her coldness turned to a relentless freeze. She did not need to ask who Lady Celia Traverson was, having heard the same name that evening in connection with his last love affair. Nor was there any doubt in her mind that Lady Celia was the woman he had met in the friary paradise while she had watched, yearning for such a kiss. And now, her first kiss had turned bitter upon her lips.

Chapter Four

Sir Nicholas straightened, dropping the stallion's hoof gently into the deep straw. He patted the sleek brown rump and looked across at his noble employer over the top of it. 'Perfect,' he said. 'It was the same last night. He's sound enough, sir.' He leaned back against the stall.

The Earl of Leicester, the Queen's favourite and the handsomest man at Court, some said, leaned against the other side of the stall and folded his arms across his wide chest. 'Samuel Manning certainly taught you a thing or two, Nicholas,' he said. 'You believe it was the mare, then?'

Sir Nicholas smiled. 'Almost certainly, sir. They can do a fair amount of damage when they're new to it, as you know.'

'Then we shall have to make sure he's well padded next time, eh?'

The laughter was mutually rueful. The earl looked pointedly at the reddened skin along the left side of Sir Nicholas's eyebrow, unable to conceal his interest.

'Don't tell me,' he said, 'that you need some padding, too. I'll not believe it. Was that the problem?'

A hand went up to comfort the tender place. 'Nothing to speak of, sir,' Sir Nicholas smiled. 'A misunderstanding.'

'Not Lady Celia, surely?' the earl said gently. He was as tall as Sir Nicholas and, even with his sleeves rolled up to his elbows, his graceful bearing and proud head showed him to be a man of considerable importance. He crossed his long elegant legs, well muscled and encased in brown leather thigh-boots.

'Lord, no, sir.' He sighed, taking hold of the stallion's tail and slipping his hand down its silky length. 'No, Lady Celia departs from Portsmouth today. She and her mother and sister will embark as soon as they get a fair wind, and she's distraught, naturally.'

'At leaving England, or you?'

'Both, sir. Nor does she like the idea of marrying her Spanish duke.'

'Mmm...I heard about that. Her Majesty's not keen on the connection, but Lord Traverson is adamant about it. Says it's too good an opportunity to miss.'

'He would, being of a Roman Catholic family. We ended our relationship weeks ago, but she asked me to meet her, for a last goodbye. Except that it wasn't the last, of course.'

'Hah! Never is, man. They say a last goodbye at least three times; I could have told you that. Recriminations, then?'

'Oh, no, sir. No bad feeling. Just a sadness. Our

parting was mutual, but I'd not have wanted her to go all that way, just the same. We were friends.'

'Sad,' the earl said. 'So who's the unwilling one?'

'Sir Thomas Pickering's daughter, sir.'

'Ah! The Palomino!' A slow grin spread across his face. 'The one you hauled out of the river the other day? Well, you'll not get that one eating out of your hand so easily. Nor will you be the first to try.'

Nicholas was, however, reasonably sure that he had been the first to succeed in areas where others had failed. 'No, sir. That's what I heard, but I think now's the time for some schooling.' He grinned back at the earl. 'I also think I'm in for a rough ride.'

Studying the stallion's beautiful hindquarters, the earl leaned forward and rested his arms across the broad satin back. 'Then you may be glad of a word of advice, my friend.'

'Sir?'

'Keep her guessing. You'll get nowhere with a woman if you're too predictable. They can second-guess you every time. And don't be too kind too soon. Fillies like *that* one need to know who's master from the start.' To his surprise, he saw that his deputy's chest was heaving with laughter. 'You don't believe me?' he said.

'Certainly I believe you, sir, but maybe I should tell you what this was for.' He placed a palm upon his temple.

'I was hoping you would.'

'For talking to her as if she were a horse.'

Their laughter made the stallion look round, his

muzzle caught by the earl's hand. 'So then you began to praise her beauty, I suppose?'

'Yes, as a matter of fact...'

'Lost your wits of a sudden, man? Tch! You know better than that.'

'I do now, sir. But I shall have to move fast if I'm to make any headway. There's Her Majesty's progress to your castle at Kenilworth in a few days, and young Fowler has got a foothold already.'

'Argh! She'll not be serious about him, man. He's only for show. Nor would her father consider him. Anyway...' his voice brightened '...she can come up to Kenilworth with Sir Thomas, if you wish. Would that help?'

'Indeed it would, sir, I thank you.'

The earl smacked the stallion's back and ran a hand down its tail, fanning it like tissue. 'I'll see she gets a royal command, then. You need to keep your hands on the reins and stay firmly in control at this stage. As for young Fowler, if he'd been attending to his business, he'd not have let her slip into the river in the first place, would he? Think on it, man. Now, let's go and take a look at those new Irish geldings. They're supposed to be fast-goers, too.'

There was probably no other man of Nicholas's acquaintance from whom he would have accepted advice on such a delicate issue, never having been the kind of man to discuss his love life with others, as many did. But Lord Leicester was as experienced with women as he was with horses, though his stormy relationship with the Queen had been one of the most talked-about since her accession seventeen years ago. At forty-two, they were both as enamoured as ever, though hardly a month passed without some complication arising to set her snarling at him like a wildcat. The earl's invitation to the Queen to make a royal progress to his magnificent castle at Kenilworth was, as Sir Nicholas knew, a last major attempt to remain permanently high in her favour after so many serious indiscretions, though if the Queen had known what Nicholas knew about his master's extra-marital activities, she would probably have decided on a progress in the opposite direction instead. His lordship had a huge capacity for intrigue and a magnetism that few women could resist, a combination which seemed to Nicholas like a recipe for disaster.

Had he been faint-hearted, Nicholas might have viewed his own predicament in the same light, last night's ending being as close as one comes to disaster, thanks to the help of a certain Master Fowler who knew exactly what he was doing. Although he had never before encountered the same relentless resistance in a woman as in Mistress Adorna Pickering, his experience told him that she was certainly not as immune to him as she pretended to be and that her act last evening had been impossible for her to maintain until the end. Then, she had lost it in his kiss, after which he discovered what she had been trying to conceal, even from herself. She wanted him.

With that satisfying knowledge firmly in place, he mused over his master's advice about the tight rein and decided that a little variation on that theme would not come amiss. She had eaten out of his hand once; she would do it again. Eventually.

Adorna would not at that moment have agreed with this theory if she had known of it. Having wept with anger and other unidentifiable emotions, she had slept badly, waking up to the same reflection of how little regard men paid to the truth in order to win a woman. The truth, she told herself, would have been easier to deal with. At least it would not have left the same sour taste in her mouth as his pathetic lies had done, especially after...no...she would not think about that. But she did. What did it matter, anyway, except that she had given her first kiss to a man to whom it would mean very little except yet another trophy?

Lady Marion could not help but notice her daughter's swollen eyelids and pink nose. 'A cold?' she said, looking doubtfully sideways. 'Come here, child. I know a tearful daughter when I see one. What is it?' She took Adorna's hand and led her back to the cushioned stool she had just vacated. 'You've had no breakfast, and it's no good saying it's nothing. It's men, isn't it?'

Adorna nodded.

'Ah! Well, if it's any comfort, love, there's probably not a woman in the whole world who hasn't wept over a man, one way or another. Which one, Sir Nicholas?' She didn't wait for a reply, having guessed it already. 'Yes, well, I admit I got it wrong about having him partner Hester when it's obvious he's more interested in you. We can't tell her so now, of course; that would do her confidence no good at all. But we can soon put it right. I'll get your father to invite him—'

'No, Mother!' Adorna objected. 'Please, I don't want him to. I don't like the man. I prefer Peter.'

'Don't like him, love? What is there not to like? I thought he was perfectly charming.' She scrutinised her daughter's face for signs, and found them. 'Ah, I see. So he kissed you.' Her eyes strayed through the sunlit window where the wobble of green glass distorted the banqueting house grotesquely. 'So that's how my best wooden roundels found their way on to the floor. We thought a fox must have got in.'

Adorna laid a hand over her mother's puffed pink sleeve. 'I'm sorry about that, Mother. It was my fault, I shall have to find a better hiding place next time.'

Lady Marion's hand enclosed hers in sympathy, but not too much. 'Well, you know, love, I'm not so sure that hiding is the answer any more. It served well enough while you were a lass, but your father and I think it's about time—'

'Oh, Mother! Not *you*, too!'

'Listen to me, love. A determined man is not going to be put off because he can't find you. And what are you going to do when he *does* find you alone, as he did last night? You cannot blame him for getting the wrong idea.'

'Yes, I can, Mother. He should learn to take no for an answer.'

'Did you mean no?'

Coming from her mother, the question was a surprise, and Adorna didn't know how to answer it.

Since the calamity was not quite as serious as she had expected, Lady Marion saw no need to hide her smile. 'One day,' she chuckled, 'you will see how unreasonable that is. Since when did a man ever take no for an answer? I'm glad your father didn't.'

'Didn't he?'

'Lord, no, child. Four times he asked me to marry him. I only said no just to see how long he'd keep on, but it was me who cracked, not him. Did Sir Nicholas ask you to…?'

'To marry him?' Dramatically, Adorna's voice was loaded with scorn. 'No, of course not. Men like him are not looking for marriage. He has a reputation to uphold.'

Slowly, her mother stood up as Hester entered the sunny parlour. 'If that's so,' she said, 'then I think, my child, that you could easily put an end to it. And what's more…' she lowered her voice for Adorna alone '…he might have it in mind to put an end to yours.' She smiled at Hester.

'My…?' Adorna's eyebrows squirmed, but Hester was close, having no thoughts about an intrusion on a private moment, and the intriguing subject of Adorna's reputation had to be shelved until Maybelle was obliged to continue it in the privacy of the bedchamber.

'Your reputation, mistress?' Maybelle said, giving the full pink skirt a shake. 'Well, everyone has some kind of—'

'Oh, don't hedge, Belle. Just tell me what you've heard.'

Maybelle sat on the carved pine linen-chest, deflating the pink silk like a balloon upon her knees. 'Well, you know what the Court ladies' maids are like.'

'And?' She waited for Maybelle to verify what she herself had already heard.

'And, yes, they say that you're hard to catch. But,' she added hastily, 'it could be much worse. Better than being easy to catch, isn't it?'

Adorna had no ready answer to that as she pondered yet again on the apparent ease of her capture by a known master of the art and then, to crown it all, on her capture by default by the one she had been trying to avoid. There was no comparison, Peter's amateurish goodnight peck being nothing like the earlier sensuous experience from which she had not, at the time, recovered. In that moment, as Maybelle watched for her seemingly artless observation to filter through, the question itself seemed to crystallise Adorna's dilemma more quickly than all her nightly cogitations. She *did* want to be caught. She wanted, more than anything in the world, to be crushed against him and to feel his hard arm across her back, his lips touching hers, making her taste his and forget how to protest. *And so my love protesting came...*

'Yes,' she said, finally. 'I suppose so.' With one finger, she traced the sinuously entwined frond embroidered on her coverlet.

Maybelle, aged eighteen, prettily dark-eyed and as sharp as a knife, placed the pink bundle to one side and came to sit next to her mistress on the bed. 'You suppose so?' she whispered with her neatly coiffed head on one side. 'Look, if you've discovered he has something you want, you can still have it and give him a run for his money at the same time. Why not slow down a bit and let him think he's caught up with you? Then, when you've had enough of him, you sprint off again. You're good at putting on a show when you need to, mistress. You can act your way through that, easy. You take what you want and then you can go back to Master Fowler. He'll always be there to help you out.'

'But that would be, well, asking for a different kind of reputation, wouldn't it?'

'Who'd notice? He'd hardly be likely to brag about the fact that you'd dropped him before he could do the same to you, would he? Bad for his image.'

The conversation had rested there, with just enough of an idea to keep Adorna's thoughts occupied all that day while employing herself in her father's Revels Office with Hester who, they discovered, was more than content to assist with the embroidery. Before supper, they rode together across Richmond Park with friends, Hester surprising them once again by her excellent horsemanship.

Like words that turn up on a daily basis after an absence of years, Sir Nicholas and some of the men from the Royal Mews were seen in the distance studying the paces of some large greys. Although her party watched them awhile, Adorna trotted off smartly in the opposite direction as soon as Sir Nicholas ap-

proached. It was, she told herself, too soon for unrehearsed pleasantries.

She was still unrehearsed when she was presented
with another chance on the following day while keeping her promise to Master Burbage, principal actor
with Leicester's Men, the ones who had caused such
merriment at the dinner party.

For almost a year, Adorna's brother Seton had been
one of their members, chiefly as a writer of plays, at
which he excelled, and more recently as an actor, at
which he did not. It was one thing to cavort about at
home when all of them were equally inept, but it was
quite another to perform professionally when all of
them except him were very good.

At seventeen, Seton Pickering was so remarkably
like his elder sister that some said, in private, that he
ought to have been born a girl. They had the same
colouring, the same classic features, the same willowy
grace, but Seton's ability to write plays had brought
him, through family friendships, to the attention of
James Burbage, who instantly recruited young Seton
to write for his company under the patronage of the
great Earl of Leicester, no less.

Unfortunately for Seton, the unknown side-effects
of his acceptance concerned the company's constant
shortage of suitable young men to play the female
roles, a tradition that for reasons of modesty were
never allowed to women themselves. So, as one who
knew the whole cast's lines by heart and who had a
head start when it came to disguising as a woman,

poor Seton was exploited in a direction he would have preferred not to go, having no wish to perform the way his younger brother did. At thirteen and-a-half, Adrian was rarely *not* performing.

Adorna's decision to visit the specially built play-house at the sign of the Red Lion at Whitechapel did not meet with Seton's immediate approval, in spite of her promise to Master Burbage. 'You won't like it,' he told her, pettishly. 'It's noisy. Hester won't like it, either.'

'But it's you we want to see,' Adorna said. 'And Master Fowler will be there to see to our safety. I know you'll be good.'

'I won't,' he grumbled. 'I never am.' All the same, he gave her a hug and a watery smile.

They made the journey on horseback from Richmond to the city, and it was two hours after noon when they were eventually allowed into the building with the eager crowds paying their shillings for seats in an upper gallery supported by scaffolding. Hester, already uncomfortable, was unsure about the wisdom of the whole venture, but Peter's protective instincts were already alert, for this kind of place was well known to swarm with pickpockets. He shepherded them into a shady corner and did his best to divert Hester's attention from the press of bodies.

'Look down there,' he shouted, pointing to the stage. 'If we'd paid more we'd have been allowed to sit on the stage itself, as those gallants are doing. I hope they don't stop the performance.' The clamour made any attempt at conversation quite impossible, and it was Hester's nudge that made Adorna turn to where she was looking, not at the stage but to the gallery at one side of it.

A group of fashionably dressed people had just entered and were arranging themselves along the benches, laughing and chattering with excitement, one of whom Hester had already recognised. The sunlight fell on him as he waited to be seated, dressed elegantly in dark green and red, his small white ruff open at the neck to accentuate the strong angle of his jaw. Sir Nicholas Rayne.

Holding her breath, Adorna pulled herself back from the edge of the gallery wondering why, of all times and places, they would be obliged to sit within sight of each other to remind her of a moment she was trying to forget. The trumpets sounded for the start of the play, the audience turned to face the stage, but Adorna was sure that, if she could hear the beating of her heart, then surely everyone else could. She would not, *could* not look at him.

'He waved,' Hester said as the din settled.

'Did he?' said Adorna. Indirectly, she had scrutinised every one of his companions, two other men and three young, pretty and vivacious women whose chatter was unaffected by the arrival of the first actor. But then, nor were others until at least five minutes had passed by which time the words could be heard. All the way through, there was a continuous upstaging from the rowdy group of young gallants who had paid well to sit on stools within reach of the actors, and when Seton made his entrance as a lovely young woman, their loud comments would have made a sailor blush.

Adorna's glance across at Sir Nicholas's group showed that some of them thought it was hilarious while she squirmed for her brother's predicament, having to suffer that kind of thing each day in a different role. Though his acting was not quite as bad as he had told her it was, it became clear to her, knowing him as she did, that this sensitive young man was enjoying the performance even less than she was. She applauded loudly and enthusiastically at each of his speeches, ceasing to care whether Sir Nicholas was watching her or not, determined to make Seton aware of her support.

As the actors took their bows, Adorna shouted to Peter that she was going backstage to find her brother. 'I know where the horses are,' she called to him in the pandemonium. 'You take Hester and wait for me. I'll be all right. I can look after myself.'

'No, don't go!' Peter yelled back. 'You'll be trampled to death.'

'Don't be dramatic.' She smiled, squeezing Hester's arm. 'I must have a word with Seton. See you outside.' Slipping past them, she climbed over the bench and found her way at last into the dark shaky stairway that led her in the direction of the stage, elbowing her way against the crowds. To her consternation, she came face to face with those in Sir Nicholas's group who, although not known to her personally, had been aware of her presence in the gallery. She smiled and squeezed past, seeing Sir Nicholas's concerned expression over their heads, fortunately too far away to make contact.

His eyes followed her, disapproving. 'Mistress Pickering,' he called.

But Adorna pressed forward, ignoring him, finding herself in a shabby wooden passageway where actors, their faces grotesque with thick sweating paint, squeezed past her on their way to curtained cubicles. She peeped into two before she found Seton.

Beneath the pale pink face-paint, the ridiculously red cheeks and painted lips, Seton was beaded with sweat. His eyes were wide and sad, his fair lashes blackened, his head still covered by a massive blonde wig that fell in luxurious curls over his lace ruff. From a distance he had looked convincing; now, he looked absurd. His sweat had made dark stains under each arm and the two bulges on his chest had been trussed until they almost met his chin. The jug of ale in his hand shook uncontrollably.

Miserably, he placed it on the small littered table. 'Dorna!' he said, croaking. 'I saw you.'

They fell into each other's arms, swaying in mutual comfort, Adorna as pained to see her brother in this state as he was to be seen. He had not wanted it. His malformed shape reeked of sheep's wool, and she could not tell whether his shaking was for relief, distress, or laughter. 'Shh!' she crooned. 'You were very good.' Then, hearing the inadequate words, she added, 'Well done, love. Even Master Burbage didn't know his lines as well as you.'

'I should do,' he said. 'I wrote them.'

'By far the best play I've ever seen. Wonderful story.'

'Thank you...thank you, love.' He turned them both to the sheet of polished brass on the wall that served as a mirror. 'Look, Dorna. Look at us both.'

Still clinging, they saw two sisters, identical in so many respects that they might have been twins.

'Well!' Adorna smiled at his reflection. 'Shall I call you sister now?'

Seton broke away, eager to be rid of the stifling disguise. 'Not for the world,' he said. 'As soon as my voice breaks, I'll do this no more. I'm counting the days.'

'It won't be long, love. It's going already.'

'You heard the squeaks?' He gave a rasp of laughter. 'Yes, I know. I shan't be able to keep it up in that register much longer, thank heaven. It hurts with the strain.' Seton's voice had been late to change, though there had been those, Master Burbage, for instance, who hoped it never would. Such things were by no means unusual. 'Here, help me off with this thing.' He put a hand to his forehead to peel away the wig.

But before Adorna could comply, the curtain rattled to one side to reveal an unknown figure who stood swaying on the threshold, his face bloated and purple with drink, his eyes swivelling from one female figure to the other. 'Eh?' he said, thickly. 'Two...*two* of you?' He swept a hand over his face. 'Can't be. I'm seeing things again.' He kept hold of the curtain for

support while he fell into the cubicle with an out-
stretched hand ready to grab at Adorna's bodice.

She lashed out, yanking at the man's hair as he
came within range while Seton, in the confined space,
picked up the jug of ale to hit him over the head. The
curtain and its flimsy pole came down with a splin-
tering crash as the intruder was yanked firmly backwards by a dark green arm across his throat and, above
the mesh of curtain and limbs, Adorna identified the
green-and-red-paned breeches of Sir Nicholas. Standing astride the prostrate drunkard, his eyes switched
from brother to sister and back again, his expression
less than sympathetic.

'Congratulations on your performance, Master Pickering. Are you hurt, mistress?' he said to Adorna.

There had not been time for any injury except to
her composure, which had suffered even before her
meeting with Seton. 'No, I'm not hurt, I thank you,'
she said. Curious faces had appeared behind Sir Nicholas, and a pair of stage-hands came to drag the man
away by his feet, still parcelled. The curtain rail lay
smashed across the passageway. 'Who was he, Seton?'
she asked.

'The usual kind of backstage caller with his congratulations. It's quite a common occurrence, love.'

'You mean they come here to…?'

Seton smiled and pulled off his wig, making himself
look, in one swift movement, utterly bizarre. 'Yes, all
part of the business. You have to get the wig off first.
That usually stops 'em.' He took Adorna's hand. 'Now
you must go. Let Sir Nicholas take you home. He

appears to be more security-conscious than your Master Fowler. Sir...' he turned to Sir Nicholas '...we were glad to have your assistance. I thank you. Could you see my sister safely home, please? She should never have been allowed to come backstage on her own.' His voice wavered over an octave.

'Your sister didn't come here alone, Master Pickering. I was waiting at the other end of the passage for her. And you may rest assured, I intend to see that she gets home safely.'

On that issue, there seemed no more for Adorna to say except to hug Seton once again and assure him that she would give good reports of the play to their parents. Outside, however, in the emptying space of the shadowy theatre, she began her objections, suddenly realising how impossible it would be to follow Maybelle's advice at a time like this. 'Sir Nicholas,' she said, slowing down, 'I came with Master Fowler and Cousin Hester and our servants. We shall be quite safe enough, I assure you. I thank you, but—'

'No need to thank me, mistress,' he said, coldly formal with his use of her title. 'You will be going home with Master Fowler, as you came. But I told your brother I would give you my personal protection, and that is what you'll get, whether you want it or not.'

She stopped in her tracks. 'You came here, sir, with your own friends and I came with mine. I prefer not to join you.'

Unmoved, he stopped ahead of her with a loud sigh, only half-turning to explain as if to a difficult child.

'You are not joining me,' he said, wearily. 'I'm joining you. My friends have gone home. They are Londoners. Now, can we proceed? The horses will be getting restive and your cousin Hester will be worrying, I expect.' Whether about Adorna or the horses he did not specify.

She could not explain why she preferred Peter's company to his, nor why she felt embarrassed that he had seen her brother at less than his best and unable to shield her from harm, the way *he* had done. The afternoon had not lived up to her expectations, and her heart bled for Seton, whose discomforts had been far more acute than any of theirs.

Rather like the play itself, the journey home was long, uncomfortably hot, and tense with an act which, as far as some of the characters were concerned, made them relieved to reach the end. Whether she would admit it to herself or not, she had been further nettled by this latest display of Sir Nicholas in the company of women, though the thought no more than skirted the labyrinth of her mind that there was no good reason why he should not be at a playhouse with friends of either sex. New to jealousy, she still did not recognise its insidious tentacles.

Just as bad was the small howling voice of reason that reminded her, at every glance, of the prejudice he had pleaded with her not to hold. A dozen times on that journey from London to Richmond, she watched him and listened to his deep voice as he talked easily with both Peter and Hester, and she wondered whether this unpredictable return to his original abruptness signalled an end to his efforts to win her interest and, if it did, then why had he followed her when she went to see Seton? She recalled her father's persistence, his four times of asking, and wondered how her mother's nerves had stood up to the uncertainty.

On reflection, it could only have been by design that, as they entered the courtyard of Sheen House in the early evening, Sir Nicholas manoeuvred his horse near enough to hers for him to be the one to lift her down from the saddle, leaving Peter to assist Hester. As her feet touched the ground, she would have removed her hands from his shoulders as quickly as she could, but he caught them tightly and held her back, unsmiling.

After miles of contemplation, Adorna would have pulled away, angrily, her hurts being multiple and confused and not to be easily soothed. Certainly not in the temporary shelter of her horse in a crowded courtyard. But she was surprised enough to wait as he touched both her knuckles with his lips, sending her at the same time the quickest whispered message she had ever heard. 'At bedtime. In the banqueting house.' Then he released her, turning away so fast that she might even have imagined it.

Her first reaction was of an overwhelming relief that, like her father, he had not given up too soon. Hard on its heels came the heady thrill of fear and promise; already she could feel his arms, his mouth on hers. Then, what if she refused to meet him, to show him once and for all that she had no intention of being added to his list, whether at the bottom or the top? How that would teach him a lesson more swiftly than Maybelle's version, though it would leave her longing for something she had tasted and would never taste again? Was she experienced enough to deal with that?

As she had half-expected, Peter and Sir Nicholas were both invited to supper and, since it was already an hour later than supper-time, they readily accepted. Hester, exhausted by the three-day effort of being sociable, left the conversation to the others and retired to her bed soon after the meal. Adorna, however, was compelled by the circumstances and by her own confusion to maintain a pretence of indifference towards Sir Nicholas, which, she believed, would give him no hope that she would accept his invitation. At times she came close to being sure that she would never do so, for that would be to walk into his trap like a drugged hare. Her resolution veered by the hour.

Peter and Sir Nicholas took their leave of the Pickerings together, the duties of Her Majesty's Chamber coming before pleasure and, whether for friendship or to make sure of the competition, Sir Nicholas rode with him back to the palace, presumably to return later, unseen.

'I do wish you would try to unbend to Sir Nicholas a little, Adorna,' Sir Thomas said as they watched the guests depart. 'He's a most pleasing and competent chap. Knows his job, too, by all accounts.'

'You've been making enquiries, Father?'

'Yes,' he said, taking her arm. 'Of course I have.

He's Lord Elyot's son and he's gleaned most of his horse skills from Samuel Manning, Hester's uncle. Good connections.'

'And what about his connections with Lord Traverson, Father? Do you know anything of those?'

'Traverson? No, nothing at all. All I know about Traverson, the old fool, is that he's sent his eldest daughter off to Spain to marry some duke or other. That's as near to being a royal as he'll ever get, for all his efforts. What do you know about him, then?'

'Nothing at all, except that he's one of the Roman Catholics that Her Majesty objects to.'

'So that's why he's sent his wife and daughters off to Spain, I expect, to get them to safety. No Protestant would risk the Queen's anger by taking the daughters on, her views being what they are, and nor would Traverson allow it, either. So much for religious tolerance. Come on in, love. Time for bed. You've had a busy day.'

'Yes, Father. I'll go and lock up the banqueting house.'

'Eh?' he frowned. 'Lock up the—?'

His arm was caught, quite firmly, by his wife's hand; she pulled him back and closed his mouth at the same time.

Chapter Five

Reciting her opening lines, Adorna opened the door and went inside, sure in the pit of her stomach that this was not a sensible thing to do, and certainly not the way to show a man how consistently unaffected she could be. It was not so much that a well-bred young woman would not have done this kind of thing; she would, there being few enough places where one could be private, let alone with a lover. Every nook and cranny had to be made use of. But having acted the hard-to-get with such force, this would seem to him like a remarkably sudden capitulation after so little effort on his part. Even her mother had put up more resistance than this, apparently.

On the other hand, the invitation may have been no more than a cruel jest. The thought sent shivers of fear across her like an icy draught.

The place had been swept and tidied with the sun's warmth still locked inside, the first deep shadows of night clothing the painted walls and blackening the windows. She waited, straining her ears towards every sound, picking up the distant hoot of an owl and wondering vaguely how she could be at such odds with herself that she could do the exact opposite of what she had planned to do. Could she be in love against her will? Was that what love did?

From the palace courtyard a clock chimed the hour, then the half-hour. She sat, stood, and sat again, starting at every sound, watching the lights go down in the house, one by one. Another hour chimed. Numb with anger and cold, she closed the doors behind her, quietly, this time. One last look towards the wall where the door led from the paradise into the palace garden, then she picked up her skirts and went into the house with a painful knot burning in her throat, knowing that this must be the snub she had predicted, though not quite so soon. That, and the coolness since his appearance at the theatre, would be his way of teaching her that it was he who had the upper hand.

There was one thing, however, that this fiasco had taught her; that she would never be caught like this again, that it had mercifully prevented her from continuing from where they left off and that, in effect, she had had a narrow escape. She should be thankful. This time, she would not weep or admit that her pride had taken a fall. She could act, as Maybelle had reminded her. Let them see how well she could perform.

Yet in her dark bed, the act was abandoned and the mask of nonchalance removed, and she gave way to the surge of uncontrollable longing that his kisses had awakened in her. After that, she fumed with anger at the man's arrogance, his sureness that she would come willingly to his hand. Never again. Never! She would die rather than become one of his discarded lovers.

The timing of it could not have been better even if Dr John Dee, the Queen's astrologer, had looked into his scrying-glass and forecast the best day for forgetting, this being the day of the masque in the royal palace for which she and her father's men had put in weeks of preparation. To have every prop ready on time, they would have to work nonstop.

Hester went with Adorna to the Revels Office, insisting that, although neither of them would be taking part in the masque, she could assist with the embroidery. 'Is this the *bodice*?' she whispered to Adorna, her eyes widening at a mere handful of tissue. 'This bit here?'

'Yes, that's it.' Adorna smiled. 'Many of the Court ladies show their breasts nowadays at this kind of event. This is modest compared to some.'

'You designed it?'

'Yes, four like this and four with a silk lining. This one's for Lady Mary Allsop. She likes to be seen.'

'But you can *see* through it!' Hester didn't know whether to laugh or to appear shocked. 'What does Her Majesty say to this?'

'Her Majesty is very careful not to let anyone outshine her,' Adorna whispered, laughing. 'She bares almost as much herself, occasionally.'

Only a few days ago, the idea of Cousin Hester sewing spangles on semi-transparent masque-costumes for ladies of the Court would have been unthinkable.

But there she was, beavering away with her shining brown head bent over a heap of sparkling sea-green sarcenet at five shillings the yard, actually enjoying the experience. Even the apparent contradiction of women taking part in a masque while not being allowed to act on stage had been accepted by Hester without question. Adorna had also noticed how the men made any small excuse to attract Hester's attention and how she was now able to speak to an occasional stranger without blushing. Cousin Hester was taking them all by surprise.

Sir Thomas smiled at his daughter, lifting an eyebrow knowingly.

By evening his smiles had become strained as he supervised the magnificent costumes being packed into crates for their short journey across several courtyards to the Royal Apartments at the front of the palace, along corridors, up stairs, through antechambers and into a far-too-small tiring-chamber. As the one who knew how the costumes were to be fitted, Adorna went with them to assist the tiring-women amidst a jostle of bodies, clothes, maids, yapping pets, crates and wig-stands.

'Here's the wig-box, Belle,' Adorna called above the din. 'Keep that safe, for heaven's sake.' The wigs were precious golden affairs of long silken tresses weighing over two pounds each, obligatory for female masquers.

She checked her lists, ticking off each item as it was passed to the wearer's maid, waiting with suppressed impatience for the inevitable late arrival. 'Where's Lady Mary?' she asked one of the ladies.

The woman wriggled out of her whalebone bodice with some regret. 'Don't know how I'll stay together now,' she giggled, happy with her pun. 'Lady Mary? She wasn't feeling well earlier, mistress. Anne!' she called to the back of the room. 'Anne! Where's Mary?'

'Which Mary?' came the muffled reply.

'Mary Allsop!'

'Not coming. Indisposed.'

Adorna's heart sank. 'What?' she said. 'She can't—'

'Indisposed my foot,' the courtier simpered. 'I expect she's chickened out at the last minute.' She glanced at the costume Adorna held.

'As usual,' someone else chimed in.

'But we can't have seven,' Adorna said. 'There have to be eight Water Maidens in four pairs. There are eight men expecting to partner you.'

The courtier held her breasts while her maid pulled a silky kirtle upwards to cover her nakedness, fastening it at the waist. 'This is like wearing a cobweb,' she grinned. 'Well then, Mistress Pickering, you'll have to take her part. You'll fit that thing better than anyone, I imagine.'

Adorna was not going to imagine any such thing. 'Er…no. Look, one of your maids can do it. Now, who is the nearest in height to…?'

There was a sudden surge of protest as Adorna's

suggestion was rejected out of hand. 'Oh, no! Not a maid. No, mistress.'

'The masquers must be from noble families.'

'Or Her Majesty would be insulted, in her own Court.'

'Adorna, come on, you can do it.'

'Yes, you're the obvious stand-in, and you won't need to wear the wig, either. Come on, mistress.'

'I cannot. I've never worn...well...no, I can't!' Even as she refused she knew the battle to be lost, that there had to be eight and that she would have to take the place of the inconsiderate absconder. At the same time, she could still remember what pleasure she had derived from designing each costume which, although slightly different in colour, style and decoration, had made up the eight Water Maidens. She had imagined herself wearing each costume, floating in a semi-transparent froth that swirled like water a few daring inches above the ankle. She had tried some of them on when only herself and Maybelle had seen, sure that no one would ever see as much of her as they would of the Queen's ladies.

The masks had been adjusted to hide the wearers' identities from all but the most astute observer. No one would know it was her except, perhaps, by her hair.

'Wear the wig,' said Maybelle, 'then they'll not know till later that you're not Lady Mary.'

But Adorna knew how unbearably hot the wigs were. 'Not if I can avoid it,' she said. 'I'll risk my own hair. I'm only one of eight, after all.'

'Then you'll do it?'

'I think I'll have to, Belle. But…oh, no!'

'What?'

'This is the one with the…oh, lord! What would Cousin Hester say?'

'She's not going to know unless someone tells her. It's what Sir Nicholas will say that's more interesting,' she said, cheekily. 'Think of that, mistress. This'll show him what he's missed better than anything could.'

'I had thought of that, Belle.'

'Well then, step out of this lot. Stand still and let me undo you.' She spoke with a mouthful of pins as she detached the sleeves, bodice and skirts while Adorna still ticked off her list and handed out silver kid slippers, silk stockings, tridents and masks to the ladies' maids.

There was only the smallest mirror available for her to see the effect of her disguise as it was assembled, piece by piece, upon her slender figure. But both maid and mistress noticed the women's admiration as the silver-blue tissue was girdled beneath her breasts, neither fully exposing nor hiding the perfect roundness that strained against the fabric at each movement. Others were more daringly exposed, but not one was more beautiful than Adorna, so Maybelle told her as she placed the silver mask over her face and teased the pale hair over her shoulders.

'There now,' Maybelle said, placing the papier-mâché conch-shell on Adorna's head. 'It'll take 'em a while to recognise you in that.' Not for a moment did she believe her words, for there was dancing to be got through before the masquers could be revealed, and Adorna's shimmering pale gold waves were far lovelier than the wigs.

'So this,' Adorna muttered, 'is what Seton means by stage fright.'

With the last checks in place and the head-dresses imposing an unnatural silence upon the eight Water Maidens, they waited for the trumpet-call to herald the entry of the masquers. Then the door was opened, assailing them at once with a blaze of light and jewels, colourful and glittering clothes, eager faces and the dying hum of laughter. Blinkered by the small openings in the masks, they saw little except the immediate foreground, but now Adorna realised how this hid their blushes as well as so many leering eyes that strained to examine every detail.

Surrounded by her favourite courtiers, tall and handsome men, the Queen was seated on a large cushioned chair at the far end of the imposingly decorated chamber that glowed warmly with tapestries from ceiling to floor. The latter, clear of rushes, had been polished for dancing and now reflected the colours like a lake through which the eight glamorous masquers glided in pairs, each pair led by a semi-naked child torch-bearer with wings.

One child, mounted on a wheeled seahorse, asked the Queen to approve of the masque, but Adorna's eyes had rarely been so busy in trying to seek out, without moving her head, someone she recognised. Her father would be otherwise engaged with the props behind the scenes, the organisation and mechanics of

the clouds, the little Water Droplets, the noise of the
thunder and the giant sun's face that smiled and
winked. While she paraded and danced a graceful pavane she could not help wondering what he would say
when he knew.

The doubt about his approval nagged at her, blunt-
ing the pleasure of seeing Sir Nicholas's reaction to
what she intended to deny him. The pleasure waned
even further as she became quite certain that Sir Nicholas was not present. Some of the other masquers were
having no such qualms, for they had already made
some minor adjustments to reveal more than had originally been intended, but it was after the pavane that
a shriek and a sudden parting of the crowd indicated
that there had been an invasion of sorts. A group of
tall silver-clad men, glittering in satin-beaded doublets
and silver-paned breeches, strode fiercely through the
open door, yelling and whirling white fishing-nets
about their half-masked heads.

'Ho-ho!' they called. 'What treasures do these fair
Water Maidens bring? Yield them up, Maidens! Yield
up, we say!'

This was the part of the masque about which
Adorna had been kept in the dark, being concerned
only with the women's department, but now she recognised at a glance both the Earl of Leicester and Sir
Christopher Hatton by the shape and colour of their
beards. They threw their nets about with gusto, making
the women guests yelp with excitement, but it was the
Water Maidens who had to be netted, and it was they
who fled furthest.

There were some, naturally, who did not make it too difficult for the fabulously dressed Fishermen with the white ostrich-plumed caps, but Adorna was not one of them, suspecting that Sir Nicholas was probably a Fisherman with his sights on one of the others. This was her perfect chance to be netted by someone else, to let him see, as Maybelle had said, what he was missing.

'Here, my lady,' she laughed, removing her conch-shell head-piece and handing it to a courtier old enough to be her mother. 'You could be netted, if you wish it.'

Willingly, the lady held it above her head, drawing the Fishermen's attention while Adorna skipped aside to find one of the eight who looked least like Sir Nicholas, a ploy that misfired when, as she dodged Sir Christopher's net, she whirled round to find that the man she had hoped to evade had spotted her. His wide shoulders, proud bearing and dark hair could not be concealed by the silver half-mask any more than she was by her complete one.

Across the long room they surveyed each other, one with legs apart, menacing and determined, the other equally adamant that any man would be preferable to this one, at this moment. She slipped away to where guests shoaled like fish, but it was too late to mingle with them before his net flew through the air towards her.

She threw up a hand to ward it off, catching it and hurling it aside scornfully, feeling a surge of triumph as she planted both feet firmly on it, glaring at the

Fisherman. The guests, unused to anything but a token show of resistance, roared their approval of her clever ruse and turned to watch what would happen next while, at the far end of the room, the Queen's head appeared above all the others to see what was going on.

Ready to sprint off again at the first hint of approach, Adorna was not prepared for the sudden shift under her feet as Sir Nicholas yanked hard at the net, pulling it on the slippery floor to unbalance her and bring her down on to her side with a sharp slap. Then, laughing softly, he hauled his net back and shook it out unhurriedly, his voice challenging and strong. 'Come on, Water Maiden!' he called. 'You should be as used to this performance as I am by now. Come, let's have a look at your bounty, eh?'

The men yelled and clapped, but Adorna's expression was well hidden behind her mask, though her voice betrayed enough to suggest that this was not all an act. 'I'm a cloud, Sir Fisherman! A mist. A waterfall. I have no fish, no bounty. You'll get nothing from me. Go and seek your bounty elsewhere.' Quickly, she scrambled to her feet, vexed that her flimsy bodice had not been designed for this kind of activity and that her legs, usually concealed, were now perfectly outlined for all to see. Hoping once more to hide in the arms of the guests, she turned towards them. But they were far too occupied in cheering her bravado and in ogling her charms to move aside and, before she could think of an alternative, the net came swinging towards her once more to fall neatly over her head and shoulders.

A roar of approval went up in the crowded room, the men calling for Sir Nicholas, the women calling for Adorna to do something. But it was obvious who would win with the net tightening about her, pinning her arms helplessly to her sides and, unlike the others who had been carefully drawn towards their captors, she was hauled unceremoniously across the floor to the slow clap of the guests, totally unable to resist the strength of his arms.

'Now, my beauty,' Sir Nicholas said loudly as she drew nearer, 'are you going to reward my efforts? What's it to be this time?'

In the Queen's presence, her answer would have been totally inappropriate. His taunts infuriated her, as did the guests' enjoyment, nor did the concealing comfort of her mask last long when he pulled her close and lifted it to reveal her flushed and angry face.

'Mistress Adorna Pickering,' he laughed. 'I would have recognised your...er...face anywhere.' His eyes were not on her face. Then, as if she had indeed been a netted mermaid, he picked her up in his arms and brought her head slowly up to his and, before his lips met hers in this public and humiliating display of mastery, she saw the gleam of exultation in his eyes, the white flash of his teeth.

'No!' she whispered, angrily struggling against his wicked grip. 'You are making it look as if I am...we are...'

'Yes,' he said. 'I am, aren't I?'

Even here, in the worst of circumstances, when his kiss was the very last thing she wanted, there was a moment when she became deaf to the yells of approval and heard only the way her heart danced to a rhythm of its own. He kissed her through the net as if no one else had been there, as if the reward he took was no paltry thing but worth all the discernment he could give to it, and it was only when the kiss ended that her other senses returned, with her anger. By then, it mattered nothing to anyone except herself, for the crowd were dispersing and making ready for the dance, still laughing at the rough diversion, both men and women envying the two masquers.

The Earl of Leicester slapped Sir Nicholas on the back as Adorna was carried to one side, his lazy and open examination of her dishevelled attire adding to her chagrin by his unconcealed approval of the contest. 'I see what you mean, man,' he murmured into his ear. 'Time for some lungeing then, eh?'

'Put me down!' Adorna snarled, hating them. 'How dare you manhandle me in this way before Her Majesty, sir?'

He placed her upright within the shadowy window-recess that opened immediately on to the River Thames, admitting the night air that helped to cool her flushed face and neck.

'Her Majesty is as much amused as everyone else.'

'Except me!'

'And you cannot go before she does. That would be a breach of etiquette. Besides,' he said, easing the net away from the tangle of fringes and stars, 'the masquers have to dance together first.'

She tried to step away, but he pulled her back and

held her against the wall while he untangled her hair. 'Stand still,' he said, 'or I'll have to hobble you.'

'Don't *dare* to speak to me as if—'

His kiss was meant to be a gag and, in that, it was more effective than even he had expected, given Adorna's fury. He did not allow her to recover herself, but seemed intent on keeping a firm hold on the authority he had won. 'As if you were a filly?' he said, holding her eyes and beating them down with the unflinching brown jasper of his own. 'You believed that a box on my ears would bring me up short, did you, lass? Well then, just recall that day you sat up there so safely in your saddle and asked me about fillies, and I said I'd tell you someday. Ah, I see you remember that. Well, I'm telling you now, Mistress Adorna Pickering, and we'll take it in easy stages, shall we?' He removed his mask at last. 'The introductions are over. Your education begins here. Now, the musicians are starting up again, the galliard, and you must dance with your captor.' He stood back to release her, holding out his hand.

She shook with outrage, more than ever aware that, for all her plans, this was going disastrously wrong. She would not give him the satisfaction of her immediate obedience; instead, a myriad of schemes fought for the right to make her as difficult, rebellious, intransigent and downright impossible as any woman had ever been or could ever be, just to show the arrogant savage what he was up against. Seething with vexation at her own lack of opportunity, she ignored his hand just long enough to see a slight movement of his body, a warning that she had better give in.

Haughtily, she placed her hand in his and felt his warm fingers close over hers. She had never seen him look so handsome. Or so dangerous. 'My captor only for this dance, Sir Fisherman,' she said, darkly. 'A net is not the best means of catching water, you know. You'll have to do better than that before you start your self-imposed role as tutor.'

'Oh, I will, Maiden. I will,' he whispered. 'I'll do much better than that, believe me. I won't even need half a chance.'

'Not a ghost of a chance.' She allowed herself to be led into the formation for a galliard, though her mind was churning over the fact that so far he had offered no explanation or apology for last night, not even a reference to it. Which showed him to be both heartless and mannerless, a man to whom Hester was more than welcome, if she wanted him. From now on, she vowed to herself, she would not only place Hester in his path, she would hurl her bodily into it, whether she wanted him or not.

He was, as she had seen before, an excellent dancer, and more than once during the lively galliard, she felt the Queen's scrutiny as she received whispered information into one diamond-weighted ear. As a partner, he could not have been bettered; graceful, sure of his movements, strong and athletic, and during those brief moments of physical contact, she could almost believe that their animosity was a thing of fiction. He would not let her go, but kept hold of her for the next dance, and she was too close to Her Majesty to make a fuss.

The coranto, with its leaps and little running steps, was one in which the Queen herself was an expert, an even more intricate measure than the gay galliard. Here the man could vary the steps at will, taking his partner with him as long as she concentrated. Adorna came close to containing her anger in the heat of the exercise, particularly when he held her above him with his hands around her waist, both of them in complete unison, at one with the rhythm, the steps, the lifts, as if they had rehearsed together. None of which should have been possible between two people so incompatible on every other level.

For the sake of good manners, not to mention the Queen's presence, she was obliged to swallow further biting comments with the dainty tid-bits he offered her from the banquet prepared in the chamber next door, though it was she who drank liberally of the wine being offered. More than once he reminded her that it was undiluted, that the Queen herself always took water with it, but the impulse to gainsay him at every opportunity had now taken on the dimensions of a crusade against his tyranny, and she took far more of the wine than she needed to quench her thirst, just to thwart him. He need not treat her like a schoolboy. Education, indeed!

It was at the informal banquet that she saw Master Peter Fowler from the opposite side of the chamber. She could have sworn he had not been there earlier, but then his duties could have been the reason for that.

All the same, she was relieved that he had not seen the undignified duel between herself and Sir Nicholas, though it appeared to be the presence of the latter at her side that prevented Peter from coming to speak to her. She smiled at him, but her smile was acknowledged only by a bleak expression of discontent that slid from her to Sir Nicholas and back again. She made a move to go to him, but found that the firm hand on her waist was manoeuvring her round to speak to other guests, as if on purpose to deflect her interest, and she knew then that the rivalry between the two had begun in earnest with neither her consent nor approval. It looked as if Peter had been warned off and that he had accepted the instruction, being in no position to do otherwise. She made a note to herself to reverse the situation as quickly as possible, but when she next looked, Peter was nowhere to be seen.

More than once, in the hours that followed, the idea of seeking her father's protection came and went. It had always been a useful gambit, always successful. But for once, and for a medley of strange and disturbing reasons, she was glad that her father had not been present, the same reasons telling her that, this time, it would be best for her to handle the problem alone.

'You've had enough,' Sir Nicholas said, in a low voice, returning the full glass to the server.

Adorna tossed her pale hair over her head and reached out to retrieve the wine from the man's hand, downing it at one go before he could move away. She handed him the empty glass with a smile. 'I think I'm the best judge of that, Sir Shiffer...shiff...Fisherman,' she said. 'Or had you intended to instruct me on what to eat and drink, too?'

His reply was lost as the room fell silent, the ladies sinking into billowing clouds of lace, feathers, silk and jewels, the men to their knees like dwarves in a rainbowed forest. The Queen was leaving. She halted in front of Adorna.

'But for you, Mistress Pickering,' she said, 'one of our Fishermen would have had an empty net. We have you to thank for stepping into Lady Mary's shoes. That was courageous, as it turned out. You are not hurt, I hope?'

Adorna looked at the forty-two-year-old face, still remarkably handsome and shining with intelligence through piercing topaz eyes. 'Your Majesty is most gracious,' she said. 'I'm not in the least hurt, I thank you, though I do seem to be perpetually wet these days.'

The Queen's laugh was merry and tinkling. 'But I notice that you made it a little more difficult for Sir Nicholas to haul you up, this time. Was that because you do not care for the mode of capture or because you do not care to be netted by Sir Nicholas?'

'I am not yet ready, Your Grace, for any man to capture me.'

'I'm glad to hear that.' The Queen nodded. 'Then we are of the same mind on that score, mistress. I agree that we should not make it too easy for them.' She walked on, smiling until the doors closed quietly behind her.

Sir Nicholas placed a hand on the small of her back, continuing from where he had left off. 'No,' he replied to her facetious question. 'Anyone who can converse so clearly with the Sovereign after as much neat wine as you've had needs no instructions from me. Even if it *was* nonsense.'

'It was *not* nonsense, sir, it was...'

'Yes, it was. You *are* ready for a man.'

'Now who's talking nonsense? You know as much about that, sir, as you know about fishing. Nothing at all. I bid you goodnight.' She kissed several friends on the way to the door, as was usual, but Sir Nicholas was not one of them. Indeed, she was relieved to find herself at last in the peace of the tiring-room where only Maybelle and a handsome young man were having a quiet conversation in a dimly lit corner. The clothes were all in order, and her own garments had been laid out ready for her. The young man bowed courteously and left. 'Is he waiting for you, Belle?' Adorna asked.

'Yes, mistress.'

'Then just help me out of this thing and into my kirtle and chemise. If I throw that cloak around me I'll not look any different in the dark. Get your young man to go home with you and take my other things at the same time. I'll slip through the palace garden as soon as I've gathered my wits together.'

'Didn't you enjoy it, then, after all? Lift your arms.'

'Slip it downwards, Belle. No, I didn't. And my head's reeling. I need to sit still a moment.'

'Too much wine?'

'Too much everything.' Her tongue's usual agility had begun to fail her, suddenly. 'Hurry up. No, leave my loos and shippers.'

'Stockings and slippers?'

'Tha's what I said. Now, get me into my…there, that'll do.'

'But you can't go home only half-dressed.'

''Course I can. Who's to see me? There, you go and take these with you.' She bundled the heavy skirt, bodice and stays, sleeves and ruff into the maid's arms. 'Don't be late back, Belle. Who is he?'

'His name is David, only he says it Daveed. He's French.'

'One of the French mission to the Queen?'

'Yes, mistress. You be all right alone? You sure?'

'Better than I've been all evening, Belle. Go.'

Alone, she pulled her cloak closer around her shoulders, sitting down suddenly on a clothes-chest as the room swayed dangerously. Fresh air was what she needed, and sleep.

The door opened, disturbing the beginning of a dream. Her heart sent drumming beats into her throat, but she was immediately defensive. 'What?' she said. 'Advice on how to dress?'

'Come,' said Sir Nicholas, holding the door. 'I'll see you home.'

'Why? You think I may have an assignation with Faster Mowler? Fowler. If so, you may well be correct.'

'There is no assignation and you should be in bed.'

'Whose?'

'Can you walk, or shall I carry you?'

She stood up, hearing her words take on a boister-ous life of their own. 'Neither, I thank you. I can carry myself home.'

'Yes, I'm sure you can. Sooner or later.' He lifted her heavy hand and pulled gently, and Adorna saw a flicker of surprise as her cloak fell open to show that her full overgown was missing.

Wearily, she pulled the cloak back into place, snapping at his helping hand. 'No more than you've seen already, and no different from all the others.' Walking without legs was something new to her, although she placed the experience together with all the others of that unforgettable evening. The shock of the cool night air reeled like gunpowder through her head, making her clutch at the door-frame as they passed from the Queen's Apartments into the covered walkway surrounding the royal garden.

She felt his arm go around her, supporting, and the events of the evening fell about like skittles in her mind while her body responded in the only way it knew how, instinctively and uncontrolled. Blindly, she turned to him, reaching up with her hands to search him in the darkness, understanding the reason for his hesitation but knowing that here she could taunt him and take his response in private without the act she had been forced to adopt before the Court. Here, she could fight him with knives unsheathed and be damned to the consequences.

Holding his head only a whisper away from hers, she whipped him with her scorn, oblivious to the danger. 'So what was all that about the lungeing-rein, Sir Nicholas? You think you can school every filly, do you? Well, sir, I believe you might have bitten off more than you can chew this time, because I don't stand around waiting for—'

His hesitation was shorter than she had predicted before his mouth closed over hers, the scathing words she had just delivered wiped from her memory in a ravenous avalanche of kisses that buried them for ever. She was never able to recall what she had said to provoke him, only that it might have seemed that he was waiting for just such a provocation.

The loss of her words was nothing to her gains in other respects for, despite her taunts that she was equal to his experience, she had no idea what she was talking about except kisses and mild caresses of the kind she and her gossip-friends had giggled over. Going to bed with a man, according to their information, was what some unmarried women did, but exactly what this entailed was still something of a mystery, and the sex acts they had witnessed between animals could surely bear little relation to humans.

But now her body burst into flame at his touch, urging her to press herself against him while revelling in the hard restraint of his arm across her back, the width of his shoulders, all those details she had unwillingly watched this evening while hating his strength, his mastery, his arrogance.

In the enclosing darkness, she was only dimly aware of being lifted into his arms and laid upon the pine bench that lined the walls, their cloaks beneath them.

His weight lay half over her, his legs heavy upon her own sending new shockwaves upwards through her body as the imprint of every contour made its way through the soft linen of her kirtle. His mouth came again to hold hers captive while his hand moved carefully over her embroidered chemise, coming to rest, at last, over her breast.

'No!' She pulled her head aside, breaking his kiss and expecting the amazing sensation to stop. 'No,' she gasped, when it did not.

His lips stayed in contact with hers, just short of a kiss, just close enough for her to expect it at any moment. 'Steady...steady,' he whispered. 'It's all right...steady!' Moving his hand over the full roundness, he kept her lips waiting and her awareness flitting between hand and mouth. Then, as she stilled, he slipped his hand beneath the fabric while claiming her mouth just as a gasp filled her lungs, ready to protest again. The shock turned to a moan of ecstasy and the hand that had grabbed at his wrist slackened its hold, allowing him to explore, softly, slowly, tenderly raking her nipple as his lips nibbled hers. She gave a cry, unaware of its precise meaning. 'That's good,' he whispered. 'Very good. Now, what else are you going to teach me, eh? About this...?'

Her breathing quailed under his hand that plotted the next unfamiliar warm voyage across the skin of her ribs and stomach, sliding over her hips and making her cry out again with the unbearable suspense of it. 'No,' she whispered, meaning yes. Reaching up with her free arm, she slipped her fingers into his hair and pulled his head down to meet hers, her words and needs no longer in unison. His dizzying kiss made her moan with desire, but she heard it only from a distance, like the denials she had voiced since their first meeting, fading at his command.

'More?' he said. 'This is but the beginning.' His lips moved downwards on a different course over her neck and breast, straying across to her other side to torment her nipple with his tongue and teeth, taking her hand and holding it firmly away as she writhed and arched, pinning her down. 'Now, my beauty,' he said, kissing the taut skin, 'is there something else you wanted to show me? What was it you had in mind, back there, that I haven't a ghost of a chance of getting? Eh?' His deep voice vibrated across her lips.

But a slow and exquisite ache that began somewhere in her thighs had now centred in a mysterious place, telling her that things were happening that she could never have dreamed of, that she had started something of which she had never been in control from the start, that he had the power to mould her with his touch. As to what she had meant by her riposte, her mind was a blank as she shook with the impact of her own body's responses. She was silent and trembling as his teasing hand made a slow and inexorable progress over her breast and stomach, reaching down until it came to rest on the soft mound between her legs. By which time he had claimed her lips once more with a kiss that was intended to make protests difficult, but not impossible.

However, he was more aware than Adorna that

some kind of protest was necessary, for although he intended that she should remember this first chastening lesson, there would be far better times and places to continue it when her senses would be clear instead of dulled by wine. Her contrariness had served his purpose well, but she would blame herself as much as him for this memorable episode before she would be tempted to return for more.

'Well?' he said, caressing. 'Have you remembered?' When she made no answer, he understood that she was already on the verge of surrender and so, to provoke her, he tightened his grip on her wrist and shifted his weight.

'No...no! Please...don't!' Her voice shook itself into a whisper, full of the premonition that, whatever his next move was to be, it was up to her to make him understand that no matter whether this was what he did with other women, he could not do it with her. She could not have said why, having no experience to go on, but the certainty was there.

Instantly, he withdrew his hand, gently pulling her clothes back into their proper place. 'Shh...shh...all right. I've stopped. That's enough for now, I think.' Carefully, he swung himself away, easing her upright to rest in his arms until her trembling was under control.

Even in her fuddled and confused state, she could not have denied that the capitulation already begun in the banqueting house was now well under way in the Queen's garden. But though her fear of being added to his conquests remained as great as ever, he had shown her with appalling ease how close she had come to ignoring every one of her objections. The thought was terrifying.

'Let me go home,' she whispered, shakily. 'You have taken advantage of me, sir.' She stood, clinging to one of the wooden pillars for support.

He came to stand behind her, his hands beneath her cloak covering her breasts and pulling her back to him, possessively. 'Oh, no,' he said into her ear. 'Oh, no, sweet maid. That I did not, and you know it. If I had truly taken advantage of you, I could have plied you with more wine instead of telling you to stop. I could have taken you into any one of a dozen dark rooms. I could still have you stark naked and on your back right now, if that's what—'

'No!' she panted. 'That you will *never* do! Now release me.' For all its apparent fervour, her plea lacked momentum under his persuasive hands that cleverly drew her mind from resentment towards the breathtaking response of her body. Still tingling from his attentions, she had no will to protest as his wandering hands reinforced his first lesson.

'You started this, my beauty, and now you're in it up to your pretty little hocks again, aren't you. And no guardians to run to.'

'Master Fowler will…be my…' Her mouth was taken over by his kiss.

'Yes,' he said at last, 'run to your Gentleman Controller as often as you wish, but he'll never have control of you as I shall. You can stop playing your game of run-and-hide now, Adorna. It's time to face reality.'

He caught her wrist and swung her round to face him, taking a fistful of her golden hair to tilt her face under his. 'I want you and I shall have you. Fume and fight as much as you like; your opposition will make my winning and your losing all the sweeter.'

'Fine words,' she snarled, 'from one who makes a secret assignation with no intention of keeping it. If that's the reality you intend me to face, sir, I'll stick with my so-called games a while longer, I thank you.'

'So that's niggling at you, is it? Well, if I'd thought you'd have accepted my explanation any earlier, I'd have given it to you, though there's hardly been a good moment for apologies, has there? I was foaling a mare. A first foal. Premature.'

'And you could not have sent a message?'

His voice softened with an invisible smile. 'Oh, yes. Yes, I could have. I could have sent your Master Fowler. He was with me in the courtyard when the stable-lad came to tell me that the mare had started. I could have asked him to go to the banqueting house where you'd be waiting for me and tell you not to. Should I have done that, do you think?'

The idea was absurd, she realised that now. He could not have sent anyone with such a message. 'I was *not* waiting for you,' she said, angrily pulling at his grip on her wrist. 'I went in.'

'Ah, I see.' He smiled, releasing her. 'Then there is no real harm done after all, is there? And no apology needed. Now, anything else before I take you home?'

'Yes, there is. Have you warned him to stay away from me?'

'Who? Master Fowler?' His smile grew into a soft laugh. 'No, mistress. I do not warn men off. I don't need to. Our Gentleman Controller will get the message soon enough without any extra help from me. I think you've already seen that tonight.'

'And I think, sir, that the less I remember of this night the happier I shall be. I choose my own friends and I shall choose my own lovers when I'm ready. And you will not be among them. Master Fowler would never have behaved as you have.'

'In which case, Mistress Adorna Pickering,' he said, pulling her to him once more, 'you would not have behaved the way *you* just have, would you? And that would have been a pity.' Like his first kiss, he gentled her lips with his own, reminding her of how she had responded to him and luring her into another betrayal of her slumbering protests. It also made her aware that this theory, though probably sound, was way beyond her understanding at that moment and had better be analysed on the morrow.

Chapter Six

Fortunately, Lady Marion was entertaining some friends when Adorna arrived home like a sleeping child in Sir Nicholas's arms, and Sir Thomas had not yet returned from the palace. Consequently, no one except Maybelle and the Pickerings' chamberlain were there to see how carefully she was deposited on the bed from which she did not wake until well past dawn. And then she wished she had not.

It was not so much her head that pained her, though that was worse than anything she could remember, but the shattering burden of self-reproach that grew with each of her searching questions to Maybelle about her behaviour, her clothes—or lack of them—and about Sir Nicholas's part in getting her home. The pain worsened as her mother kindly lectured her on the dangers of allowing a man too much familiarity. How did she know about the journey home? 'Because I pay my chamberlain to tell me what's going on in my own house,' she replied. Unfortunately, it was not possible for Adorna to discover exactly what the chamberlain had implied, or how much her mother suspected, or indeed how far Sir Nicholas had gone. And having no one but herself to blame for her determination to drink too much undiluted wine, she realised that she must get herself out of this situation with the same defiance she had used to get into it.

Neither the pain nor her temper was improved by Hester's somewhat ill-timed opinion that Sir Nicholas would make a good husband. 'For you?' Adorna said, wincing at the sunlit garden.

'Well, yes. My inherited wealth and his inherited title would go together rather well, I think. And Sir Nicholas has noticed how much I've changed. Isn't that nice?'

'Very nice,' Adorna murmured, watching a butterfly head off towards a gaudy marigold. 'That makes all our efforts worthwhile.' Secretly, it rankled that the plan she had been so eager to put into action only a short time ago had now begun to look as if it had Hester's approval and, what was worse, that it might actually work. The only comforting thought she could find was that, one day quite soon, Sir Nicholas and Peter would both be gone up to Kenilworth with the Earl of Leicester to prepare to welcome the Queen.

Adorna had missed the Sunday-morning service in the Queen's royal chapel, but felt obliged to attend the evening one at which she hoped Sir Nicholas would not be present. Her hopes were soon sent packing. He came in with the earl's household only moments before the Queen herself, fitting into a space on the bench immediately behind her. It was Hester and Lady

Pickering who turned to smile at him, but the unkind lurch of Adorna's heart had already responded to some strange telepathy, and from then on it was all she could do to keep her mind on course instead of on his presence at her back, his hands so close, his eyes taking in every detail.

She devised a series of strategies for evading him afterwards, but her father and Hester demolished them by keeping her between them as they turned to speak to Sir Nicholas, compelling her to respond to his query about her health. His 'You are well, I hope?' was accompanied by a lack of gravity in his eyes that suggested he might already know the answer.

She had no intention of telling him the truth. 'Well enough, I thank you, sir.' Against her will, her eyes evaluated the impeccable green silk doublet and matching trunk-hose, its surfaces slashed to show long puffs of pale gold silk beneath. A small white ruff sat neatly beneath his chin, but her examination stopped at his mouth, lacking the courage to meet the laughter in his eyes.

Hester, apparently, felt that Adorna's response was sadly wanting in detail. 'She is *now*,' she said, in the awkward silence that followed. 'She's been unwell all morning with a terrible headache. Poor Adorna.' She looked pityingly at her cousin, trying to imagine what a headache felt like.

'Hester!' Adorna said through her teeth. But the damage was done.

'Really?' Sir Nicholas replied, adopting an expression of extreme concern. 'Is that so, mistress? Now what could possibly have caused that, I wonder?'

Sir Thomas came to the rescue, dismissing the problem with his usual bluffness. 'Well,' he said, 'anyone who has to dress eight noblewomen as Water Maidens all at the same time is entitled to a headache, I'd say. It gave me one just to think about it. Hah! Now, Sir Nicholas, I believe I owe you our thanks for escorting Mistress Adorna home last night. Very thoughtful. Mighty good of you. I was tied up till the early hours, you know.'

Sir Nicholas's response was a slight bow, though his eyes and voice still denied a proper seriousness. 'No thanks are necessary, Sir Thomas, I assure you. It was a great pleasure to escort your daughter to her bed...er...room. In fact, it was the highlight of the evening for me.'

But any deeper meaning of Sir Nicholas's words was quite lost upon Sir Thomas as his attention was caught by another friend, and he began to move away. Not so with Hester, who appeared to be getting the hang of social chit-chat with a remarkable degree of clumsiness. 'Oh, you didn't tell me that,' she said to Adorna, ignoring the bright pink flush that had risen in her cousin's cheeks. 'Did Sir Nicholas...er...did you really...?'

'Sir Nicholas is *jesting*, Hester dear,' Adorna almost snarled, looking daggers at the man to warn him not to say another word. 'Remind me to tell you how some men enjoy making ladies blush, will you?' She took Hester's arm in a firm grip to steer her away.

Hester, however, had taken the bit firmly between her teeth. 'But Sir Nicholas would not do that, would you, Sir Nicholas?' she said, resisting the pressure.

'Yes, he would,' Adorna said, under her breath. Her glance across at her parents gave her even more cause for concern, for now there were eyes flickering in her direction as snippets of gossip were passed back and forth by their friends, heads nodding, smiles of surprise, grimaces of shock. She could not doubt that she and Sir Nicholas were the topic of their conversation.

Sir Nicholas himself offered her little consolation. 'Yes, I would,' he said to Hester. 'But you should also ask Mistress Adorna to explain that a blush of embarrassment doesn't necessarily imply guilt. Ask her about it, Mistress Hester.'

This was getting too deep for her. 'Yes, sir,' she said, looking as if she had already lost the thread. 'Yes, I will.' She bobbed a curtsy, glanced once more at the rosy signs of Adorna's extreme vexation, and moved away to join Lady Pickering, presumably to hear the details with which Adorna had not supplied her.

Adorna herself would have left Sir Nicholas at that point had he not kept hold of her arm. 'No, sir,' she hissed. 'Let me go now. How could you have begun such a conversation before my father and Hester? Now they'll think—'

'What will they think?' he said, close to her ear. 'Are you pretending that your parents will never hear that we were together at the masque? That they'll never know how you stood in for Lady Mary? Of course they will. Look at that crowd. They can hardly wait to talk about it. What d'ye think they're saying, then?'

The temptation to look was strong, but she could not do it while the embarrassment was so plainly written upon her face. She could not even meet Sir Nicholas's eyes as she replied, 'How could I possibly know what they're saying?'

'Well, I'll tell you.'

'Don't.'

'They're talking about the Water Maiden who refused to be caught. About how she—'

'Stop!'

'How she wore a gauzy bodice everyone could see through and—'

'Please!'

'And how the Deputy Master of Horse kissed her there before them all, while she struggled in his arms. Then they danced with each other and no one else. Can you hear that roar of laughter? Your father. Your mother and Hester are looking shocked. Well? Would you prefer to go and join them and be invited to explain, or would you rather leave with me and not have to explain anything?'

There appeared to be no choice left to her. The blush, now intensified, was certainly not what she wanted to exhibit to anyone, nor did she wish to see their expressions of shock and amusement. She could guess what they would be saying. 'Adorna Pickering caught at last? Do explain…she *what*?'

Without bothering to answer, she followed him

quickly out through the small north door into a court-yard and from there through a maze of passageways, smaller courtyards and doors that led on to Paradise Road. 'I can find my own way from here, sir,' she said, looking to see if anyone else was about. The track was deserted.

He began to walk with her. 'You couldn't find it last night though, could you?'

'Sir Nicholas, it really is most discourteous of you to insist on reminding me of an incident I would rather forget. Now that there is no one to see, there is no point in continuing to embarrass me. Whatever happened last night is past and gone. It will never happen again. Never. I regret the whole incident and, most of all, I regret the part you played in it. It's a mercy to me that I cannot recall much of what happened, which you will no doubt see as a chance to make up whatever you like and tell all your gossipy friends. Now, please will you go and leave me to walk home alone.'

'You have little choice in the matter, my girl,' he said with his arm across her back. 'You can either walk sedately by my side to Sheen House or you can be carried there as you were last night. Make up your mind. Which is it to be?'

'You are insufferable, sir!'

He smiled at her fury, urging her forward. 'Pity you remember so little, you in your flimsy kirtle in the garden afterwards, and me wrapping you in my—'

She drew back a hand to hit him, to put a stop to the shameful picture she had no wish to see. But this time he was prepared, and she was slowed by the dull

thudding in her head. He caught her hand well before
it made contact, pulling her uncomfortably close to
him in a restricting embrace. 'That's enough!' he said,
sternly. 'So I shall not give you any more details except for one reminder that you must have missed.'

'And that, sir?'

'That the game of chase has ended and that you had
better start to regard yourself as mine. Which is exactly how those people in there...' he tipped his head
towards the palace wall '...are seeing you, whether
you like it or not. Far better to go along with it. Less
confusing for everybody.'

Only a week or so ago, she would have argued herself in circles at his arrogant assertion that she belonged to anybody. To be held in his arms was something kept only for the night's secrets, but to be added
to his list of conquests was quite a different thing. Yet
the appalling headache of the morning had left her
feeling distinctly unsteady, and now she was unable
to summon up enough strength to continue the contest.
'Let me go, sir, please, just let me go. We can finish
this conversation another time. Tomorrow, perhaps.'
The fields and trees swirled dizzily into a black void
as a tingling sensation froze her arms and legs. She
had had nothing to eat all day. 'Please,' she whispered,
'I need to sit...down...'

And so it was that Adorna Pickering, against every
resolution to keep this man at a distance, was carried
once more up Paradise Road, this time in broad daylight, to Sheen House where Maybelle and the Pick-

erings' loyal chamberlain were there to take receipt of her yet again.

It was not the most dignified way to end the day, but at least it gave her an excuse to avoid the interrogation that her parents had intended for her after church.

By Monday morning, when they had had time to put the events into some perspective, they had agreed that, all in all, Sir Nicholas's appropriation of their beloved daughter at the masque was probably no bad thing, even if she had suffered some embarrassment by it. After all, they reasoned, she could have been even more embarrassed *without* his protection, and he had, apart from the horseplay, behaved in a careful fashion. A storm in a wineglass, one might say.

Sir Thomas returned to Sheen House from the palace, mid-morning, waving a letter he had just received from the Queen thanking him for his efforts last evening. He found Adorna in the still-room preparing some rosewater, her hands deep in a bowl of petals. 'Well, my lass,' he said. 'Her Majesty must have approved of your performance at the masque enough to invite you to go up to Kenilworth with me on Wednesday. I shall have to go with the Wardrobe, even though his lordship is doing his own entertainments, but I shall need all the help I can get with the robes. Are you interested?'

No, she thought, Sir Nicholas will be there. Travelling with us, too. I must stay well away from him now. Far better if I remain here, beyond his reach. But the Queen's invitation was not something one could decline. It was a royal command. 'Yes,' she said. 'Of course I am, Father.'

'Good,' he said, picking up a handful of the petals and smelling at them. 'You must take Maybelle and Hester, too. Seton will be there with the players to put on a couple of performances at his lordship's request, so now we only have to remind your mother that you're twenty years old instead of fourteen. Eh?' He laughed, replacing the petals in the wrong bowl. 'Perhaps if I tell her that Sir Nicholas will be sure to keep an eye on you, she'll feel easier about it.'

Adorna scooped up the petals and replaced them with the rest. 'Father,' she said, 'I don't want her to get any ideas about a connection simply because he's escorted me home a few times. It was not looked for, I assure you. It's no more than a coincidence.'

'Ideas about Sir Nicholas, love? Too late, she's already got them. Look,' he said, removing her hands from the bowl and taking them in his own, 'stop worrying about it. I shall be there, too, with hundreds of others. Safety in numbers. So why not go in and start packing? If you and Hester need some extra gowns, I'll borrow some from the Wardrobe for you. Now, go in and tell your mother and Hester.'

'Is the earl's household to go up to Kenilworth with us at the same time?' She tried to sound only mildly interested.

'Ah no, lass. They've gone. Early this morning.'

'What—*all* of them?'

Sir Thomas looked intently at her expression of surprise. 'Well, the earl is the host at Kenilworth, you know, and he'll be escorting the Queen. But his men have had to take the horses up ahead of them. Didn't Sir Nicholas tell you?'

For all she knew, he might have done while she, once again, had been in no position to remember much of what he'd said, though she found it strange that the memory of his hands upon her was sharp enough to send waves of weakness into her legs. 'No, he didn't,' she said. 'But it doesn't matter.' By the time I arrive, she thought, he'll have found others to keep his mind off me. Yet the picture she painted did not give her the satisfaction she had expected it to, nor did Hester's controlled enthusiasm for the venture convince her that this was the right course to follow.

One who did come to make a more specific farewell was Master Peter Fowler, who felt it to be his duty whilst barely concealing his dismay at the part she had played at the masque. He had little time, for his party was ready to move off, and there were many venues where the locks on the doors must be changed, *en route*, for Her Majesty's security.

As kindly as she could, Adorna reminded him that she was free to choose her own companions and that to meet them however she wished was of no concern to anyone but herself.

'And presumably Sir Nicholas Rayne's?' he said, coldly, before immediately relenting. He took her arm. 'Can we talk reasonably for a moment? I have to join the party before we cross the river. Will you walk with me?'

Adorna lifted her golden-yellow skirts, placing her fingers briefly over his. 'Peter,' she said, 'we must not quarrel over this. I'm not responsible for what Sir Nicholas says to me. He probably says exactly the same things to many other women. But nor am I answerable to anyone except my parents for what I do or don't do. If you cannot accept that, then I shall be sorry for it, after being your friend since Easter.'

He trapped her hand over his sober grey sleeve. 'I had hoped to be allowed more of a place in your life than merely a friend of three months, Adorna, but I suppose I shall have to either accept your terms or lose you altogether. I'm prepared to wait. It's too soon, I see that now.'

'Yes, Peter. Much too soon. Despite what you believe, I am no nearer committing myself to a man than I was when we first met.'

'Yet you appeared to be approaching some kind of relationship with Sir Nicholas after Lady Marion's dinner party,' he said softly. 'Or was that my imagination, too? And again at the masque. Does he know of your attitude towards non-commitment?'

She removed her hand. 'You have no right to ask me that, Peter. Sir Nicholas knows of my friendship with you and yes, if you must know, he has been told that I am not available. But I'm having as hard a time convincing him of it as I am you.'

'From what I've heard, Adorna, his purpose in pursuing a woman is not the same as mine. He is not best known for his fidelity with women, you know. Perhaps it's as well that he'll be away from you for a few weeks, too.'

'Neither of you will, Peter. I go up to Kenilworth with my father on Wednesday.'

He stopped abruptly, leaning one hand on the gateway to the courtyard. 'You...you're going?' he blinked. 'Oh, I had no idea.'

'I've only just found out myself. Will you look out for me? I shall be glad of an escort.'

'Of course I will. So Sir Nicholas doesn't expect you?'

'No,' she said, airily, already seeing the handsome figure leading the Queen's horses, glancing in her direction, keeping company with her father, no doubt.

When Peter had departed, however, she felt a pang of regret that she would not have the pleasure of his company on the journey, for it would have been a comfort to her. Not only that, but the effect of arriving at Kenilworth with Peter would have gone some way towards getting her own back on the one who had, apparently, taken some kind of liberty with her and then left her to think about it while he went off to enjoy the company of other women for several weeks. And if that was what she had secretly predicted, dreaded, and warned herself of, she had only herself to blame for allowing it.

Alternative plans immediately began to form before it was too late. She could change her mind, refuse the Queen's invitation, stay well out of the way here in Richmond. That would be discourteous but by far the safest course. She could follow Maybelle's advice and her own inclination, go to Kenilworth and ignore the man, stick to Peter, flirt, and enjoy herself; all the things she would normally have done when pursued too hard by any pushy young man. But perhaps what she dreaded most of all was the look on his face when she arrived, unexpected, at Kenilworth. That was something she did not know how she would be able to bear.

8 July 1575. Kenilworth Castle, Warwickshire

Shading his eyes against the glare of the afternoon sun, Sir Nicholas Rayne watched the distant progress of yet another advance party towards the Earl of Leicester's castle at Kenilworth, probably the last to arrive before the Queen herself on the morrow. The bluish heat haze shimmered over the mere where a line of ducks fled in alarm at the splash of wading men hammering stakes of fluttering pennants into the water, the clack-clack of their mallets sounding like castanets between the blaring of trumpets.

To his left, along the Warwick road, the cavalcade wound like a gaudy ribbon accompanied by the barking of dogs and the excited yelling of children who could not be convinced that this was merely the Royal Removing Wardrobe with her Majesty's articles of daily living. Chests of robes, fan-cases, hatboxes, crates of shoes, leather coffers, linen cloak-bags, her feathers and jewel-cases, cases for her parrot and her monkey, curtained to keep them quiet by the order of Sir John Fortescue. With them rode her tailor and shoemaker, her silk-woman and their assistants, ushers, maids, grooms and pages, musicians and messengers.

Behind Sir Nicholas in the castle's outer courtyard, known as the bailey, men tangled with carts, waggons, packhorses and suppliers that would seem to leave little space for yet another incursion. Every summer the Queen went on progress to see and be seen by her countrymen and, even though the cost of accommodating and entertaining hundreds of people for a few days often crippled them, the townspeople believed that the honour was worth it.

Those who were forced to bear the burden alone, the grand houses, the castles, the favoured courtiers, were not so sure. She had been to Kenilworth Castle once before to please her favourite, the Earl of Leicester, but never had the preparations been so extensive. This time, the earl had almost beggared himself to impress her, and Sir Nicholas had no doubt that she would take it as no more than her due when she arrived to an extravaganza of adoration.

His eyes, however, were not presently focussed on the preparations or on the state of the castle, but on anything in the cavalcade that might reveal the presence of a pale golden horse with a fair-haired beauty in the saddle. She would be there somewhere, he was sure of it. No, correction. He was not sure of it. He smiled, briefly.

'A fine sight, sir,' said the liveried man at his side, picking up the expression of approval.

'Yes, Watt. A fine sight, indeed. Keep the stable

area clear, though. We don't want them round there, only those on the list. Send for me if there are any arguments.'

'Yes, sir.' The man turned his horse and trotted away.

No, he could not be sure, only reasonably confident. Her curiosity had come alive from the start, with her resentment of him, but now it was more than curiosity she had revealed. Now it was an untapped well of desire that had probably surprised her more than it had surprised him. He smiled again, remembering. Not that she would recall much of it except the headache and the anger, but not even an excess of wine could have released something which had not been there in the first place.

He could imagine her reaction to the Queen's invitation, how she would first have refused, accepted, refused again and then thought of all the ways to pay him back for revealing something she had wanted to keep to herself. Her own passionate womanhood. She would not pass up a chance like this. She would put on an act of coolness, as before. Ignore him. Flirt outrageously. She would cling for safety to young Fowler who wanted high connections, and to her father. She would use all her old tricks to avoid any suggestion of a serious involvement although by now she must have realised that she *was* involved, like it or not. And that was why she would come. The Palomino, the earl had called her, teasing him.

A moment later, the bright toss of a pale cream mane showed through the mass of riders, the young woman behind it sitting like a lance poised for her first sighting of him, her first attempt to put him in his place. His smile turned into a huff of laughter. He would bring her back to him when he was ready. There was Mistress Hester, too; a useful ally to him in more ways than one.

He moved his bay gelding forward to meet the leaders at the gatehouse beyond which a raised artificial causeway banked up on one side of the great lake that seemed to float the moated castle upon shimmering water. 'Welcome, Sir John,' he called. 'Welcome, Sir Thomas. On behalf of my lord the earl, welcome to Kenilworth.' As the earl's deputy, it fell upon Sir Nicholas to take the place of his master who was at this moment escorting the Queen to his home. He turned his most complaisant smile in Adorna's direction, intentionally showing no trace of surprise. 'And to the Mistresses Pickering, welcome to you both. Your rooms will be here at the castle. They are ready for you. Master Swifferton will show you the way.'

A young man stepped forward as Sir Nicholas dismounted to take the bridle of Adorna's mare while Hester's mount was led behind. By now, the outer bailey was rapidly filling with the huge body of guests, household servants, horses and waggons, only those in the earl's company knowing exactly where to go. The rivalry for accommodation at the castle itself was intense, everyone preferring to be lodged near to the Queen, though many were billeted at houses in the town, at inns, in tents, or even miles away in the large houses of the gentry. No one was allowed to refuse the Queen's guests.

Both Hester and Adorna had expected to be amongst the latter category, at a safe distance from the action, but it was Adorna whose curiosity surfaced first. 'Here?' she said to the top of Sir Nicholas's black velvet cap. 'Are you sure? I don't think we were expected.'

'I think you will find, mistress, that you are both on Master Swifferton's list. Is that not so, John?' he called over his shoulder. 'In the Swan Tower, is it?'

'That's correct, Sir Nicholas. The top two chambers. Bit of a squash but better than most. Overlooks the water. Lovely views.'

Sir Nicholas released the mare's bridle at the corner of the great keep and pointed to the round tower on the furthest corner of the bailey set into the battlemented walls. 'Swan Tower,' he said, smiling at her with the same complaisancy he had shown earlier. 'Nest up there, Palomino.' He ran his hand over the mare's golden rump and stood back, laughing inwardly at her stubborn refusal to ask what he meant, though a dozen questions showed so clearly on her lovely face.

Turning back to the other guests, he prepared himself to explain why they had been given accommodation in town. 'Sir John, Sir Thomas and Master Seton, you're at the sign of the Laurels in Kenilworth,' he told them, heartily. 'The whole inn has been taken over for you and your men. It's as near to the castle as any building in town. Plenty of room there. I shall

take you over myself, if you will kindly follow me?'
He extended an arm, asking so sincerely after their
welfare that their temporary annoyance was forgotten.

The removal of Adorna from his side was, however,
something of a set-back for Sir Thomas Pickering,
who had assured his wife that he would be with their
daughter and cousin at Kenilworth. It had not occurred
to him that he might not be, yet he was aware that to
be given one of the castle towers was a mark of es-
pecial favour, set as it was at the corner of the earl's
newly-built magnificent garden. With the moat and the
lake on the other two sides, it would have been fit for
a princess, but for its smallness.

Lady Marion's exhortation came to him sharply as
he followed the handsome horsemaster through the
gatehouse and over the moat bridge. 'Find out exactly
what he has in mind,' she had said the night before
he left. 'If his intentions are serious, we ought to be
knowing about it. If they're not, then Adorna must be
warned. I fear he may already have taken her too far.'

'You mean…?'

'No…no, not *that*. Just…well, too far. She's confused, Thomas.'

Sir Thomas had snorted. 'Confused, is she? She's
had 'em all confused for years, love. Us, too, for that
matter. Time someone confused her for a change.'

'Don't be unsympathetic, dear. You know what I
mean.'

'Stop worrying. I'll find out what he's up to. She'll
be all right with me.' He had given some thought to
the timing of such an interview, to the tone of it, for-

mal or informal, and then, as usual, had decided that the manner of it would be dictated by the circumstances.

The time came after supper that same evening when not even he could have helped noticing the distinct coolness of his daughter towards Sir Nicholas, or the man's apparent indifference to Adorna's icy demeanour. To other eyes there seemed to be nothing amiss, not even Master Fowler's unusual buoyancy, but Sir Thomas tended to see things from a typical father's viewpoint where matters were either positive or negative, even affairs of the heart. He tapped Sir Nicholas on the arm as the tables were cleared in the great hall. 'A word, sir, if I may?' he said.

As if knowing the subject in advance, Sir Nicholas obligingly led the Master of Revels towards the large oriel window at one end of the hall that looked westwards over the castle wall and to the water beyond. It was more like a small private chamber where the Queen herself would be sitting at this time tomorrow. The two men stood, their amiable regard lit by the pink evening sky.

'Sir Nicholas, there is a matter, a private matter, that concerns me and my wife regarding your relationship with our daughter.' Sir Thomas watched carefully for a sign, but found none. 'There *is* some kind of relationship, I take it?'

It would, after all, have been difficult to pretend otherwise after the days of gossip from courtiers who had little else to say. Sir Nicholas made no attempt to deny it. 'There is, as you say, sir, some kind of relationship between myself and Mistress Adorna, though it is not easy to define, at present, exactly what it consists of, except admiration on one hand and deep distrust on the other.'

'Admiration, Sir Nicholas? No more than that?'

'*Much* more than that, sir.'

'I see. And the deep distrust? Is there a particular reason for that, do you think?'

'No reason other than gossip, sir, and a couple of misunderstandings. You know how things are at Court. An unattached male comes on the scene and before you know it he's saddled with a reputation whether it's deserved or not, simply because he spends some time playing the field. Which I believe is what Mistress Adorna has been doing these last few years.'

The older man pulled in his chin and rubbed his nose as the truth of it could hardly be contradicted. That was exactly what she had been doing, of course. 'Well, I suppose you have a point there, Sir Nicholas, although my daughter has been most careful not to encourage one man's attentions more than another's.'

'Except Master Fowler's?'

Sir Thomas made a gesture of dismissal. 'Oh, that young man can hardly be counted, Sir Nicholas. He must know that he'll never be in the running. He's her companion for safety's sake, that's all. I'm talking about men like yourself. Aristocrats. She's never allowed a serious relationship. Won't entertain the idea of marriage.' There was a note of resignation in his voice that Sir Nicholas was quick to detect.

'And you and Lady Marion believe it's about time she did, sir?'

The sigh was released slowly. 'Her mother says she's being careful,' Sir Thomas said, looking far out across the pink satin water, 'which I suppose it not a particularly bad thing in this day and age when so many young women rush into relationships as if it were their last chance. They seem to have forgotten how to say no,' he added, thoughtfully.

'I can assure you, sir, that Mistress Adorna has made good use of the word recently.'

'Hah! Lady Marion gave me a no five times until she tired of the game.' His mouth twitched inside the white beard as he added an extra no for effect. 'However,' he said, pulling himself back into the discussion with a jolt, 'there's a difference between being careful and making oneself unattainable, and we're neither of us unaware that Adorna has been steering towards the latter position this last year or more.'

'Which, I feel sure, Sir Thomas, must have its basis in some very sound reasoning, even if we don't quite understand it. For a lovely young woman at the centre of men's attention, it would be quite unrealistic and a waste if she were prevented from enjoying it while it lasted. And yet...'

'Well? And yet what?' Sir Thomas swung his head attentively.

Sir Nicholas came to stand beside the tall stone mullion that supported the window as far as the ceiling, his arms folded across his embroidered doublet. The sun caught the top of his dark shining head and

washed it with pink. 'I've been doing the same, sir, as
I'm sure you did. Yet there comes a time when a man
sees a woman he *knows* is the one he wants. For life,
not simply for the chase.'

'I see. And have you told my daughter of this?'

There were dimples of tension around Sir Nicholas's mouth as he replied, recalling the poor timing
and Adorna's disbelief. 'Yes, sir. But I fear the lady
is more preoccupied with my so-called reputation than
with what I said to her on one occasion. The other,
she will probably not remember.'

'Ah, the masque, you mean. Yes, she's headstrong,
and wine is not her usual tipple. I suppose, as a father,
I should ask you exactly what happened afterwards.'
He looked uncomfortable, this being a new role to
him. 'Did anything happen…you know…er…that…?'
The rest of his breath blew itself away between pursed
lips.

'Nothing that Mistress Adorna did not initiate herself, sir. And nothing that happened against her will.'

'That's not quite what I asked, Sir Nicholas.'

Sir Thomas had not asked anything specific, but Sir
Nicholas let it go. 'No, Sir Thomas. Mistress Adorna
is quite unharmed, you have my word on it. She may
have been compelled at the time to face a few facts
about herself and her feelings towards me, but that
won't do her any harm. Naturally, she's angry with
me and with herself, and I expect some heavy opposition from her while she's here, but I believe my patience will last longer than hers.'

'You'll have to have more than bloody patience,

man!' Sir Thomas growled, leaning one hand against the carved stone tracery. 'I've had patience, and I can tell you it's wearing a bit thin. I want the very best for my daughter, Sir Nicholas, but if Adorna can't see it when it's staring her in the face, then perhaps I ought to—'

'I beg you to leave it to me, sir.' Sir Nicholas had not missed the reference to his being among the best. 'If I have your approval, I'd like to go about winning her in my own way. Any sign of pressure from… elsewhere…might be a hindrance rather than a help. As you say, she's headstrong.'

Sir Thomas studied his foot. 'So your attentions are honourable, then?'

'Entirely, sir.'

'And you have marriage in mind, do you?'

'I do, sir. I intend to win her, however long it takes.'

The flash of grey eyes from beneath dark eyebrows held a glint of both approval and relief. 'Hmm! You'll have your work cut out, you know. She's always been free, never one to hanker after bairns. Might lead you a merry dance, eh?'

Sir Nicholas smiled at the picture. 'Yes, sir. I have your permission?'

'Well, you've already started, by the look o' things, so you might as well carry on. If you want any help, tell me. It's just as well I brought her with me, then, isn't it? What would you have done if the Queen had not invited her? Hoped for the best for six or seven weeks?' He looked over his shoulder to see that Sir Nicholas was almost laughing. 'Ah, I see,' he said, stopping. 'So *you* had something to do with this, did you? Hence the Swan Tower and its closeness to the Royal Stables. Well, well. Friends in high places.' He laughed, slapping Sir Nicholas on the back. 'Well then, perhaps you'll be good enough to show me the new stable-block before I see where you've put my daughter?'

'Certainly, sir. There's a good hour of light left yet. Come.'

Chapter Seven

Ever vigilant for anything which might affect her mistress's chance of happiness, Maybelle moved sharply away from the double-lancet window of the high chamber in the Swan Tower to confront Adorna, ostensibly to begin removing her lace ruff. 'Look out there,' she murmured, flicking her eyes towards the fading light. 'Your father and someone else.'

The someone else hardly needed a name, especially not here before Hester and her new maid Ellie, a young woman who was as irritatingly eager to please as a month-old pup. Adorna had no intention of appearing too interested. She moved without haste to the window-seat and glanced to the right where, outside the large stable-block built against the castle wall, her father and brother stood in deep conversation with Sir Nicholas Rayne. Still talking, they began a leisured approach towards the Swan Tower.

'Leave it on, Belle,' she said in an undertone. 'They're coming up.'

'Who's coming?' said Hester, pricking her ears, her

hands already clenched upon her skirts, ready to scuttle away down the spiral staircase.

'Only Sir Thomas and Seton,' Adorna said, turning away from the window. 'No need for you to go, Hester. I expect they want to see how we fare up here.' There was a tightness in her seemingly nonchalant reply that she knew sounded strange. 'Move these gowns, Ellie. Are they Mistress Hester's or mine?'

'We haven't yet decided, mistress,' Ellie said, gathering the colourful silks up off the canopied bed. 'These are the ones from the Wardrobe department for both of you.'

Four heads swung in unison as a knock sounded on the heavy bolt-studded door, the click of the latch and the appearance of a snowy head happening almost simultaneously. 'May we come in?' Sir Thomas said, stooping to avoid the low pointed arch. Seton squeezed in behind him, suddenly crowding the small chamber and immediately dashing Adorna's expectations that Sir Nicholas would be with them.

Reproving herself for caring one way or the other, she reacted with self-possession. 'Of course, Father. Maybelle, you and Ellie take those below to Mistress Hester's room and hang them in the garderobe to air. There,' she said, watching them go, 'that gives us a bit more space. Come over to the window and take a look at this garden. You can see the knot-pattern from up here, and there's a raised walk across on the far side with an aviary in the centre of it. You can hear the birds if you listen.' It was an impressively large garden surrounded by high walls, one of which housed the Swan Tower in a corner. Adorna's gaze, however, had already shifted sideways to the ground between the garden and the castle walls to search for a figure she had hoped—expected—to see at closer quarters.

Her father peered down, pointing to the end of the stable-block. 'Your palomino's at this end,' he told her. 'Sir Nicholas asked if you'd like to go down and see her before you retire. And Mistress Hester, too, of course.'

Once so hesitant and indecisive, Hester now needed no persuasion. 'Yes, we'd love…er…well, I'd love to go and see.'

'You go down by all means,' Adorna said. 'I'm sure the mare's seen enough of me for one day.' But she could hardly keep her surprise from showing when Hester slipped out of the room, apparently happy enough to see more of Sir Nicholas and the horses. 'You'll send a message to Mother, won't you, to say we've arrived safely?' she said to her father.

Sir Thomas placed an arm about her shoulders as he closed the little door. 'I shall write it tonight and tell her everything, love. Tomorrow will be far too busy.'

'The Queen will be here,' Seton said, 'and then the fun will begin. Why didn't you want to go down and meet Sir Nicholas, Dorna? You're not too tired, are you?'

Unwilling to answer directly, Adorna asked one of her own. 'What's a palomino, Father? Is it a new breed?'

Her father's arm dropped as he went to test the

bed's resilience, patting the soft yellow brocade cover and lifting up the hem to study the deep twisted fringe. 'Hmm! Very nice. Not so much a breed as a colour,' he said, dropping it. 'Called after a certain Juan de Palomino who was given one by Cortés when he became governor of Mexico. Still highly prized because they don't breed true, so Sir Nicholas tells me. You never quite know when you're going to get one, even with two golden parents. He'd like to breed from your mare, he tells me.'

A warmth stole up Adorna's neck to her cheeks, forcing her to seek the deepest shadow in the room. 'I'm sure he would,' she whispered. 'I hope you've not agreed to it, Father.'

'Of course not,' he said, standing up and pulling out the crumpled panels of his breeches. 'I would never interfere in a young lady's love-life. The mare is yours to mate as you please. Or not.'

'Not,' Adorna said, with finality. 'Definitely not.'

Reverting to a less controversial topic, Sir Thomas pointed out to her the layout of the town from the northern side of the tower, and the inn where he and the Wardrobe were quartered, the moat already reflecting the earliest lights. She followed her father and brother down the staircase as darkness fell, meeting a breathless Hester and her maid on the way up, the heiress glowing with the familiar talk of horses. Apparently, the company of Sir Nicholas had brought a healthy pink flush to her cheeks and a twinkle to her eyes. 'He asked after my aunt and uncle,' she said.

At the outer door, Seton laid a hand on his sister's

arm to hold her back while her father spoke to Hester. 'Dorna,' he said, 'have you read it yet?'

'Yes, love. Well, most of it. It's very good.'

'You wouldn't like to go through it with me, would you?'

She blinked. 'That's not like you. You know everybody's lines.'

'I know. I just wish…'

'Wish that you didn't have to perform?'

The misery clouded his face like a sudden rainstorm. 'Yes,' he said, looking beyond her shoulder. 'It's in four days' time and I don't know how I'll perform in front of…oh, never mind. In front of Father, too.' Loaded with gloom, he dropped his hand into hers as he had often done when they were children. 'I'm a man, Dorna. I wish they'd understand that.' His voice squeaked in protest.

Adorna's hand squeezed. 'First thing in the morning, love. We'll find a quiet spot in the garden and go through it together. The Queen won't arrive until midday. She's already reached Warwick, so Peter says.'

Seton's face cleared. 'Right. Bring your copy. I'll be through the gates as soon as they're open.' He lifted her knuckles to his lips. 'Thanks, love.'

'Sleep well, and stop worrying. Father wouldn't be Master of Revels if he minded men dressing up as women.'

His eyebrows bounced, wickedly. 'Or women dressing up as fighting Water Maidens?'

'You've heard about *that*?' she whispered.

'I'd have to be deaf not to. The whole Court must

know by now.' His voice chortled up and down an octave. 'In fact, they seem to be waiting for Act Two.'

'Well, there isn't an Act Two,' she snapped.

'You mean, that was *it*? So what d'ye think *he*'s after, then?'

Frowning, Adorna turned to look where her brother's eyes rested and saw, to her confusion, that Sir Nicholas was strolling towards them down the path from the royal stables. There was no way round him.

'Goodnight, Seton,' she said. 'See you tomorrow.' Three yards behind her, she took her father by surprise with a quick peck on his cheek. 'G'night, Father,' she said. Her vanishing act would have been the envy of William Shenton, the Queen's Fool.

Still sure that Sir Nicholas could not have anticipated her arrival that day, Adorna was as puzzled as Hester at their luxurious accommodation, though it had crossed her mind more than once that it might have been more to do with Hester herself than with Sir Thomas's high office that had gained them this distinction. By now the whole Court would know that the heiress was not only available but amongst them. One had only to see how, on this first evening, the men had sought Hester's attention as well as Adorna's, though the former's colour had not been so high then as on her later return from the stables. Adorna nevertheless congratulated herself on avoiding Sir Nicholas, though the manner of it had perhaps been a little more obvious than she had intended. She would do better tomorrow.

The stillness of the night and the sweetly scented

air from the garden below did less than she had hoped to quell the excitement that had mounted over each day of their journey, each stop-over hardening her resolution to take matters into her own hands after her shameful submission on the evening of the masque. If the man belicved that she would now succumb at the next snap of his fingers, he would soon discover his mistake. Nor would there be any more problems with Peter after their talk. As for Hester, she would be easy enough to steer into Sir Nicholas's path, for Adorna believed that her readiness to talk of him and his superb horsemanship had teetered on the brink of hero-worship at times.

By the light of a candle, she lay next to Maybelle and read to her the last scene of Seton's play, one of two he had written for this visit to Kenilworth. 'Wake me at daybreak,' she whispered, closing the pages. But Maybelle was already asleep and Adorna was left to wonder how safe this ivory tower would be in comparison to her Richmond refuge, and whether her father would be as willing to assume his usual protectiveness from an office so inconveniently situated. The contradictions within these hopes failed to register with her when, only an hour ago, she had actually hoped Sir Nicholas *would* invade her privacy. But then, she had been consistent in wanting to have her cake and to eat it, too.

The early sun cast deep shadows across the garden and set light to canopies of diamond-dusted spiders' webs from leaf to leaf that trembled as Adorna walked carefully past, lifting her skirts so as not to disturb them. Silently over the grassy pathway, she stalked the darting wrens and shy thrushes, always the first to begin feasting. Situated on the north side of the castle, the symmetrical beds of fragrant herbs were divided by walks that led towards a circular fountain in the centre, while the exotic birds chirping in the aviary added yet another element to the garden's magic.

Seton hardly noticed her arrival, his head almost hidden behind a sheaf of papers that flailed the air in time to his whispered narrative. He lowered the script with a sigh as she approached, looking down at her from the high-terraced walk. 'It's no good,' he said in a loud whisper. 'It sounds worse every time I read it.'

'How do I get up there?' Adorna said, looking for a flight of steps.

He pointed to the far end. 'That way. Steps. Be careful, they're slippery.'

Joining him, she was able to see his troubled face. 'You've not slept, have you?' she said. 'What on earth is it? You're not usually so worried.'

'I don't usually perform before the Queen and her Court, do I?' he said, wearily. 'And these performances are so important to the earl. He's our patron, and all this palaver is meant to impress the love of his life, you know. Nobody believes he'll get another chance. Nor does he, either.'

'To get her to accept him? After all these years?' Adorna looked out across the formal, static, ordered enclosure and saw in her mind's eye how it hid a seething mass of life, just like the Court, full of complications, competition and dependency. 'And you want the plays to be the best ever. Yes, I can see how you think it will reflect on the earl if they're not, but Father obviously thinks they're acceptable.' It was the wrong thing to say; as Master of the Revels, their father was obliged to censure everything performed before the Queen, but he was no critic of good writing.

'I don't want acceptable, love,' Seton said. 'I want brilliant.'

The silence was broken by a distant clamour of ducks out on the mere. A line of swans honked softly across the castle and disappeared.

'Show me what's bothering you,' said Adorna, turning her pages.

Seton turned to the last scene. 'I'm supposed to be the beautiful Beatrice who finally admits her love for Benedict. The trouble is, I can say it in my head as if I'm her, but I'll never be able to say it out loud to a hundred people or more. It's so private.'

'It's the loveliest part of the whole play,' Adorna said. 'Here, you be Benedict for a change, and I'll be her. Let's see if that helps.' She pointed to the beginning of their dialogue. 'Shall you start there?'

Seton began, unconvincingly.

And is your heart of the same mind, sweet Beatrice,
Or are the twins conjoined as close as ever in dislike
of me?
Or perhaps it is your fear that freezes them in perpetual winter
And makes you less than bold to look at summer in the face.

Adorna replied:

Nay, my lord, I pray you let me speak
Of how once my heart refused to thaw or bend to
thine,
Of how since then my yearning's like a flower grown,
Opening its petals to the sun, the dew, the day's long
hours
And every nourishing thing that Nature owns.
Now I am persuaded to accept, to love, to be no more
aloof,
To say that what was mine shall now be yours, for-
sooth.

There was disbelief and scorn in Seton's Benedict:
Thou'lt not find me so easy to persuade, though all—

He stopped abruptly as a quiet voice interrupted to remonstrate, as if he had been the director.

'Oh, no, Master Seton. No, that would be too discourteous by far.'

'What?' Seton's papers hit his knees with a slap. 'Sir Nicholas, my sister and I were hoping for—'

'For some privacy. Yes, I know. Don't go, Mistress Adorna, please.' From the shadow of the gilded aviary the tall figure of the knight emerged to lean against one side of the trellis and look down upon the two fair-haired players. 'Forgive me, do, but I was unable to ignore the poetry. It's very moving,' he said, obviously sincere, 'but Benedict's reply to that wonderful confession is unworthy. No gentle man could disbelieve such a genuine submission. Your Benedict would have to have a heart of stone, surely?'

'And you would know about such things, would you, sir?' Adorna said, coolly.

'Of a man's reaction to a longed-for declaration of love? Certainly I would. None better. May I suggest a change there, Master Seton? It may help you to feel more comfortable as Beatrice.'

'Well…er…yes, if you think so, Sir Nicholas.' Seton placed a hand over Adorna's arm as she stood and laid her script on the bench. 'Stay, Dorna. You said that far more convincingly than I could do. Stay and see what Sir Nicholas has to suggest.'

She resumed her seat, placing Seton between them yet unable to tear her eyes away from the countless differences between the two males that could not be explained by age alone: Seton's delicate white fingers against the strong brown hands with a dusting of dark hair on their backs, the knight's solid wide frame and muscular neck against Seton's slightness, the size of their heads, the length of thigh, the sheer bulk of Sir Nicholas against the young man who looked and sounded so much like herself.

Her eyes were drawn to the powerful hunch of his shoulders under a sleeveless blue velvet doublet, to the thick dark hair that touched against the high collar of his white shirt, hair that she believed she may have fingered, somewhere, some time. She watched, under the pretext of following their discussion, how the skin stretched over his cheekbones, how the muscles in his jaw rippled, his eyes and eyelids moved beneath angled brows, the mobile mouth that had so expertly taken hers, and more. What more?

Catching her examination, he held her eyes and read them. 'Do you not agree, mistress?' he said, watching the colour flood into her cheeks.

'Er…yes, if Seton agrees. He's the author.' Her eyes dropped to the script, now written upon in his large bold hand. Of all the people in the world, she would rather it had been anyone but he who had heard her speak Beatrice's lines, for now he was sure to be hearing them as if they were her own. 'May I see?' she said.

Seton sounded relieved. 'It's much better like this, Dorna. My Benedict was too ill-natured, whereas this one keeps his authority but is more kindly. Thank you, Sir Nicholas. Shall you read the new bit, sir? Please?'

Sir Nicholas took the page from him. 'If you wish. Mistress Adorna? You will be Beatrice again, for the moment?'

She felt trapped. 'Who is this Beatrice, Seton?' she said, suddenly irritated. 'And what has this Benedict done to deserve such a climb-down?'

'They're nobody, love. Just people. Read it.'

As soon as they began, sharing the amended script, the two characters became stand-ins for Adorna and Nicholas, who were saying to each other what they might have said in real life if things had been different, if she could have been convinced that his intentions were serious and that she was not simply the latest in a long line of potential conquests. This time, Benedict's scepticism was exchanged for loving acceptance with a hint of teasing, a far more credible ending than Seton's. Adorna's hands were trembling as the scene ended with a kiss which, in this rehearsal, was acted only in the two players' minds.

She could not look at him, nor did she reply when Seton jumped up, hurriedly brushed a tear away with a knuckle, and took the script from Sir Nicholas. 'Thanks,' he croaked. 'Amazing. I'll go and find Master Burbage. He's Benedict. He'll have to learn the new ending. Thanks.' His footsteps padded on the soft grass, his dark suit melted into the wall.

Like so many other things, this was not what Adorna had intended. She stood up. 'Excuse me, I must go, too. I'm sure you must be especially busy today.'

'Well read, Beatrice. Now we both know how it ends, even if the getting there may vary in detail.' Sir Nicholas stood with her, escorting her along the terrace to where the steps led downwards. A gardener and two ladies with a dog had entered the lower pathways to walk waist-high in lavender and St. John's wort, their voices hardly audible, only the gardener's hoe clinking on the soil. 'You are unusually subdued, mistress. Were you convinced by it, or are you musing on the bit we missed out?'

She accepted his hand down the slippery steps and then removed it quickly. 'Missed out? I don't recall missing anything. Does Seton know of it?'

'Oh, most certainly. Bear with me. I'll tell you by the gate. I'd not want to be overheard and have the plot spoiled.'

She had lived with the sensation of being close to him, yet nothing she remembered could compare with the reality of his presence, of vibrating to the warmth of his hand as it deliberately claimed hers again. For the benefit of the curious women, she thought, cynically. She left it there, feeling his grip tighten as they reached the gate in the high wall. The touch of her arm on his sent a thud of excitement into her chest and, struggling to keep her voice level, she glanced down at the script in her hand. 'Which bit did Seton miss out?' she said.

'Not Seton. Us.' He pulled her to one side where the eastern sun caught the pink brickwork full on, facing her into its rays so that he became, for that moment, a dark silhouette. By which time it was too late to evade his arms, and she was bent into him with her head pressed into his shoulder, his lips already taking hers with a fierce urgency that belonged as much to her as it did to him.

She had nursed her fears and resentment for well over a week since their last eventful meeting, during which time she had schooled herself to adopt a façade of unconcern. But at this first physical contact the façade was flattened; it was as if he had reached behind it to drag forward the response he wanted. Helpless to keep up the pretence, she was angry that he had not been fooled by it, and shamed to have her needs exposed as if they were as accessible as he chose to make them. A storm of hunger shook her like an earth tremor, and she responded, blind and unthinking, ravenous for the hard pressure of his body, warm and overpowering. A memory stirred and then faded.

His mouth opened and she felt him shudder, sending

a soft gust of air like a sigh through her lips. 'That,' he said hoarsely, 'is what we missed. Both of us. And that's what you'll have to imagine when you watch the play. As I shall.' His voice was harsh and angry. 'And I've told you before, woman, that if you try to evade me, I shall find you. Run as fast as you like; it will make no difference.'

Her breath was exhaled in a sob before she could stop it. 'Then ride your fleetest horse, Sir Nicholas,' she panted, 'for I shall never wait for a man. Not for you, not for anyone. I waited once, but never again. Never.'

'You will, woman,' he said roughly. 'You'll come to me within days.'

'Never!'

'We'll see, shall we?' His release of her was so sudden that she fell back against the wall while he clicked open the gate and disappeared, leaving it ajar for her to follow at her own pace. The two women stood by the fountain, staring at her instead of at the water and ignoring the dog's constant yapping.

Her eyes welled with sudden tears as she turned her back on them to avoid their pitying eyes, silently cursing herself for allowing him to see, yet again, how she melted at his touch. Just like all the others. Fool. *Fool.* Now she would have to begin again, to work even harder to rebuild the façade, to stem the inevitable gossip already being generated behind her.

Straightening the crumpled sheaf of papers, she waited and then slipped through the gate. But what had he meant by 'I've told you before'? What had he said? When?

Hester's chamber door opened as she passed. 'Come in,' Hester called. 'Come and tell me how this looks.' She twirled, half-dressed and pinned into the skirt of a mulberry silk over a pale grey petticoat. 'Ellie says this one will suit me best. Do you agree, Adorna?'

'Yes, as it happens, I do,' Adorna said.

The twirling stopped suddenly, but Adorna had already moved upwards to her own chamber where Maybelle was clearly indignant. 'Someone's going to have to tell that Ellie,' the maid hissed, pointing to the floor. 'She's chosen that—'

'Yes, I know,' Adorna said. 'I never wanted it anyway. She's welcome.'

'But you're angry. I can see.'

'It's nothing. Come, find that lovely cream silk with the embroidered flowers. And jewels. And feathers. And a saucy hat. The Queen will be here by mid-day and I have some serious flirting to do by then.'

Maybelle smiled her broadest smile. 'Cream silk it is, then. With feathers.'

For all her determination to prove how wrong his prediction was, Adorna was not only shaken by his kiss but by his noticeable anger, too. That had been something unexpected; exasperation, perhaps, or a gentle reprimand such as that given by thwarted young men like Peter, but not anger, not the rough handling Sir Nicholas had meted out. And why the talk of avoiding him, which he had patently noticed, when he had not known she would be here in the first place?

Or had he? As for coming to him in days, he for one would be far too occupied to notice her coming or going, once the Queen's party arrived.

In fact, it was almost evening when the Earl of Leicester escorted Elizabeth and her train across the high causeway with water on each side that reflected the columns decorated with fruit, birds in cages, fish, armour and musical instruments. A cannon salute boomed from the castle, the clock on the tower was stopped at the time of her arrival, and the glittering cavalcade entered the castle bailey like a tidal surge of jewels and lace, silver and gold, faces almost lost in a sea of priceless fabrics, tinkling harnesses, hands lifting and voices laughing in extravagant greeting.

Surrounded by admirers and friends, Adorna stayed well within Peter's range, but was unable to stop herself searching at regular intervals for the Queen's Deputy Master of Horse, lavishly attired in cloth of silver with gold embellishments, and an ostrich-plumed and tasselled cap. His grey stallion was hardly less magnificent.

That evening, wearing the exquisite cream silk gown with an open ruff that enhanced her long neck and lovely bosom, she danced and laughed and flirted as heartily as she had always done, though few could have guessed where her thoughts lay, or how irksome it was for her to see Sir Nicholas apparently so popular with the ladies of the Court, many of whose bosoms were shockingly exposed to view. After the fiasco at the masque, that was something against which she had no intention of competing, the men's leers being with her still.

The earl had invited about thirty other guests, including his sister and her husband and son, and the countess of Essex, whose husband was away on service in Ireland. With all their servants and attendants, it still surprised Adorna that she and Hester had been made so comfortable when many others were being squashed together like rabbits in a burrow. Diplomatically, she did not broadcast her good fortune, though she was unable to prevent Hester from doing so.

'Does Mistress Hester need rescuing, d'ye think?' Peter said to Adorna after the supper had been served. 'She's hardly used to this kind of thing, is she?'

Hester was by now quite out of her depth, her attempts at indiscriminate flirting having given false hopes to a clique of confused and bickering young men, none of whom interested Hester in the slightest. The situation was about to become heated as she was being invited to dance by two equally determined admirers.

'Yes, Peter. Go and calm things down, or there'll be a riot.'

Hester looked relieved as Peter approached, holding out his hand to her. But Sir Nicholas had also noticed and, despite Peter's approach, he too had gone to her rescue, both men now adding to Hester's choices, though with more success. She accepted both their hands, smiled wistfully, and allowed herself to be led away from the disgruntled group without knowing what she had done to cause their discontent.

The musicians, playing the introduction to an alle-mande, prompted Peter to go one step further and ask Hester to partner him before Sir Nicholas did. Sir Nicholas bowed and stepped back while Adorna, sure that he would continue to leave her to her own devices as he had done all day, prepared to turn back to her friends. Instead, she found her hand being lifted into his and firmly held, not so much requesting as ex-pecting her to join him. The surprise must have shown in her face, though he said not a word to persuade her while waiting for any one of a variety of responses, disdain, scorn or refusal.

She might have taken this chance to snub him in retaliation for his overbearing behaviour that morning, but he had partnered no one else that evening until now, and the thought of allowing the chance to slip past her was more than she could bear, for he was the most exciting partner she had ever danced with. So, with only two reasons to accept and at least a dozen not to, she moved slowly forward with him into the stately beat of the allemande, their eyes having not once unlocked in this duel of wills.

Changing couples moved gracefully forward and backward, meeting and parting, sweeping past, eyes reuniting with hands, bodies swaying and responding, while onlookers stilled to watch the couple who might as well have been alone for all the notice they took of anyone else. The rhythm altered and the pace quick-ened. As at the masque, they excelled all others in their grace, she in her cream-flowered silk with a shadow of pale violet, he in tones of violet and silver that made it appear as though they had consulted each other beforehand. Once again, they danced for themselves and for each other, their harmony of mind and body temporarily negating previous conflicts as if, for those rare and precious moments, the music was holding them in another world. Neither of them spoke, for there was no need, yet their bodies, hands and eyes said far more than words until, at some time in the distant future, one of them would be prepared to concede.

'Lavolta!' someone called as the music changed again to a determined beat in the Italian style. 'Remove cloaks and rapiers, gentlemen!'

Partnered by an earl stripped down to his doublet, the Queen took the centre of the floor while those about her watched entranced as the two, perfectly matched, executed the complicated movements and astonishingly intimate lifts of this most daring of dances. Then came the signal for others to take over, though there were relatively few who knew it well enough or who had the energy for it. Except Sir Nicholas, who had kept hold of his partner's hand till now, who unbuckled his sword-belt and threw aside his short cloak and drew Adorna straight into the movements without hesitation, appearing to appreciate her ability with a wholeheartedness that quickened every one of her responses.

His lifts threw her high into the air as if she were a child while women yelped with excitement and men stood silent with admiration. And when he lowered her with infinitely slow control down the length of his body, there was nowhere for her to place her hands except round his neck. She had seen it performed before at Richmond, but this was the first time she had danced it, her dancing-master having drawn the line at the capriole. She was breathless with exhilaration, yet not unaware of the fact that it was her partner's expert direction that reminded her of each move; she had only to watch his eyes, feel the pressure of his fingers, the swing of his shoulders.

Sir Nicholas was not the only one to recognise that here was another common ground on which they could be, at least for a time, at peace and in unison. While he held her mind and body in the rhythm of the dance, she was obedient, willing and sweet-tempered, giving in to his control without those recurring doubts and defiances with which she was otherwise besieged. But if this was the key to his success, then it was a fragile one, for who could dance their way through a courtship?

The others to see the connection were her father and the Earl of Leicester, who stood together as the last beats faded to the dancers' flamboyant courtesies.

'Well, Sir Thomas,' said the earl, watching his deputy lead Adorna towards them. 'As long as you can keep your musicians playing dances you have a chance of keeping your daughter within reach of her partner, it seems. Ah, here they come. Isn't it time we were formally introduced? The last time I saw the lady, she was less than happy with her lot.'

Hearing the earl's last comment, Adorna easily recalled their last meeting when introductions would
have been difficult, if not impossible. She sank into a
graceful curtsy before him as her father smilingly went
through the ritual words, still chuckling from something the earl had said.

'My Lord,' she murmured.

No one could have been surprised by the Queen's
long-lasting infatuation with this man whose exceptional good looks and manly figure were paired with
an equally exceptional intelligence and good nature,
though they were not by any means his only attributes.
His heavy-lidded scrutiny missed nothing as Adorna
took his offered hand. 'Mistress Pickering,' he said in
a melodious voice that women swooned over, 'welcome to my humble home. We look forward to enjoying your brother's performance as much as we have
enjoyed yours just now with my deputy here. He and
I will be offering a performance of our own to Her
Majesty tomorrow morning. I shall see that you and
Sir Thomas, your brother and cousin are given a good
view. I think you'll be impressed.'

'You are most kind, my lord, I thank you.'

'And your quarters? They are comfortable?'

'Indeed they are, my lord,' she smiled. 'We are hon-
oured.'

'A small thing to do for one I value so highly, mistress.' He glanced at Sir Nicholas and back to her so
quickly that, if she had not been watching carefully,
she might have missed it. In that moment, her earlier
suspicion grew apace. 'I'm relieved to see that it ap-

pears to be working, eh, Sir Thomas? You, too?' Bowing to them both, he released her hand and moved away, bending towards Sir Nicholas as he passed. 'Got the Palomino in your stable at last then, man? Well done.'

It was too late for Sir Nicholas to make any reply, the earl already having begun a greeting to others.

Frostily, Adorna took Sir Thomas's arm, pretending not to have overheard. 'Come, Father, it looks as if Hester may need your help.'

'Again?'

They turned together, but Sir Nicholas was already on his way, and Adorna had the dubious pleasure of seeing her cousin's face light up at his approach, her ready acceptance of his hand towards the banquet table. She watched just long enough to see Hester accept a glass of red wine, but not even at the amazing show of fireworks later on did Adorna look again to see where he and her cousin were, though she knew that Peter did, more than once.

Next morning, she discovered from Maybelle that Hester had returned some time later than herself, though it was too dark to see who her escort had been.

Trying hard to play down the impression that Sir Nicholas's attitude towards her appeared to be alternating between the courteous and the severe, Adorna began to waver in her plan to ignore him completely, especially after his warning that any evasion of him would fail. Formerly, this would have made her even more adamant, but his firmness with her had begun to add a new dimension to the affair that filled her with unease, shaking her certainty that she would be able to handle it in her usual way. Clearly, there was nothing usual about it, for never before had any man treated her with such arrogance or left her so unsure about what to expect from him next.

Another awful thought that recurred with sickening force was that her original plan to avert his attentions by throwing Cousin Hester in his path was now also going askew, for Hester seemed to be quite capable of throwing herself in his path without any assistance from Adorna, if her face last night was anything to go by. And that was not supposed to happen except in controlled circumstances. The dancing was all very well, but it had been Cousin Hester he had stayed with after that.

The Earl of Leicester's display of horsemanship before the Queen and her Court was yet another example of Cousin Hester's admiration for Sir Nicholas, for she had been there when he and her uncle had practised together at Bishops Standing. Like the earl, Uncle Samuel had brought over an Italian horseman to teach him the higher arts of equestrianism, the complicated manoeuvres which were now all the rage both here and in France and, like the earl, they had used Grisone's manual of 1550 to teach them how to school their best horses.

Not surprisingly, it was Hester who whispered to Adorna what to watch for as the horses and riders performed on the sand-covered tournament ground, though it was Adorna who was best able to compare his skills on dancing horses with those she had encountered last night. She also understood the significance of the earl's remark when he assured her that she would be impressed, for he was obviously thinking of the similarity between the two forms of exercise, the mutual harmony of two creatures, one of them controlling, one obedient, responsive and supple. The horses and riders, in perfect accord, turned, pirouetted and circled, changing direction, every movement named for them by Hester.

'The levade,' she whispered, as Sir Nicholas's horse squatted on to its haunches and lifted its front legs clear of the ground, staying powerfully motionless until he let it down. 'Takes years to teach that,' she said. 'This one's called the piaff, like a trot on one spot.'

'Why doesn't the horse go forward?'

'Because they train it facing a wall so it can't. Sir Nicholas is so good at this.' The horses were galloped and pulled up on the spot, wheeling round on their hocks. Sir Nicholas, according to Hester, was brilliant at that, too. They changed legs, leapt and cavorted. 'Uncle Samuel would be so proud of him,' she said, applauding, flushed with pleasure and more animated than Adorna had ever seen her.

In the privacy of the tower chamber, Maybelle regarded a white lawn chemise with blackwork round the neckline. 'Plans not working?' she said.

Adorna sighed and glanced at Seton's script that lay on the window-seat. She had been learning his lines to keep her mind off other matters. 'Not yet,' she admitted. 'He doesn't accept the cold-shoulder like others do. He seems to think he's in control.'

The maid searched amongst a pile of clothes on the bed, flinging aside smocks and stockings in annoyance. 'Don't tell me that girl has helped herself to your—' she hauled out a bodice in two parts, stiffened with whalebone '—your pair of bodies,' she said. 'Do you know, I saw her give Mistress Hester a note yesterday that she read and tucked down the front of her bodies. Looked mighty pleased with it, too, she did.'

'Who from?' Adorna said, squirming inside the contraption.

'Now that, mistress, I cannot say. She's not lacking in admirers though, is she?'

'With all that wealth, no one would.' That was uncharitable, and she regretted it, instantly. 'No, well, she's begun to look pretty, too. Prettier clothes, no problem with listening. Men admire that. But I wonder who's sending her notes, Belle.'

'Could be anyone.'

Adorna did not agree, but for want of a better strategy, accepted Maybelle's opinion that her own avoidance tactics had not had much effect so far because she had been too half-hearted about them. With all these daily activities, Belle said, it ought to be possible for any woman to make herself inaccessible. 'If she really wants to, that is.'

'Oh, Belle. I don't know what I want.'

'I think you probably do,' Belle said, pulling at the laces. 'But unfortunately you can't have your freedom,' she grunted, 'and his controlling arms…ugh…

at the same time…ugh…can you? There now. Are you still breathing?'

'Well, that's what *he* seems to want!' Adorna said, testily. 'Having me in his sights doesn't seem to stop him having a good time with whoever he pleases. I wonder how many women he's bedded since he's been here. Too many to count, I expect.'

'Or perhaps none at all. What have you been hearing?'

'Nothing, but I've seen how they swarm around him.'

'Bees swarm,' said Belle, dropping a cloud of underskirt over Adorna's head.

'Flock, then. Silly sheep flock.'

Regardless of her misgivings about the effectiveness of trying to stay out of his way, the programme of events at Kenilworth was so full, as Maybelle had pointed out, that she seemed at last to be managing it. At night, she was reminded of his kisses as well as of his warnings, and tried to recall how far things had gone on the night of the masque, partly to bathe in the bliss of his lovemaking and partly to haunt herself with the folly of it. His dancing whirled her into sleep. His performance with the horses pervaded her dreams except that, here and there, things became confused and she woke to find that the restraint against which she fought was Maybelle's arm across her neck.

The sparkling days of the Queen's visit were indeed packed with a constant round of entertainments of the most extravagant sort where boating on the lake be-

came a sea-symphony of mermaids, dolphins and musicians, and where archery, tennis and jousting became
picnics and pageants rolled into one great festival. The
feasts sparkled with the earl's best gold and silverware, glass and jewels, ivory and damask, the foods
concocted into masterpieces of ingenuity that had
taken a fleet of cooks weeks to prepare. When the
Queen mentioned that she could not see the knot-
garden from her south-facing window, the earl hired
men to work in silence throughout the night to construct one on the flat ground below her apartments. By
morning, the Queen's new garden was complete.

They hunted, attended masques and a country wedding at which the poor bridegroom hobbled on a broken leg, injured at a game of football. There were
more fireworks, bear-baiting, acrobatics and wrestling,
water-games and music parties and plays put on by
local people who were allowed to attend wherever
there was enough space. Even at church, Adorna surrounded herself by a tight company of friends, thereby
keeping herself bodily apart from Sir Nicholas, though
her father remonstrated, gently. 'You didn't even allow him to help you dismount,' he said.

'Peter was there first.'

'And even at the picnic by the lake…'

'The mare doesn't care for water, Father. I stayed
well away from it. It's the ducks, I think.'

'He was waiting to take the mare back to the stables.'

'Well, I sent it with Hester's mount. I'd promised
to learn the tennis game.'

'That's not for ladies, Adorna.'

'No, I discovered that, soon enough. Good fun, though. The men beat me.'

'All the same, I believe he's serious about you, if only—'

'Father!' Adorna scoffed, laughing. 'Men like that are not serious for more than a week or so. You know that as well as I do.'

'Then you'd better start reckoning backwards, my lass!' he scolded, watching her swing away. 'If you have a spare moment!' His sarcasm was lost in her laugh.

From the Swan Tower, Adorna's view of the beautiful knot-garden was probably better than the Queen's new one, for this one had the octagonal fountain, the gilded aviary, and the colourful gowns of guests that floated knee-high through hummocks of flowering herbs. An arbour at one end made a tunnel of roses where ladies and gentlemen strolled in the perfumed shade, though by evening they were coupled with the shadows of their lovers, their chatter and laughter muted to whispers, like the fountain. Some of the courtiers called it the paradise like the one at Richmond, though for Adorna it did not have the same connotations until, that night, its scented magic drew her to the window to breathe in the warm air and to search the blue-grey patterns.

Her heart thudded as she recognised the shape of a tall man standing alone on the grassy pathway, his back to the moonlit fountain. He faced the window from which she leaned, his posture telling her that, this time, he was waiting for her and no one else. Across the dark plots of foliage, their eyes met as a silent entreaty was sent again and again, and was rejected. Too afraid of what might happen, or of relinquishing her hard-earned successes, she drew back and closed the shutters. And when she looked out again, much later, he had disappeared. Then she began to reckon backwards.

Chapter Eight

A light shower of rain held the company indoors for most of the morning, giving the Queen a chance to attend to state business and then to rest. It gave Adorna a chance to ride to the sign of the Laurels in Kenilworth to help her father sort out some of the robes; they were getting into a mess, he said.

In an adjoining room of the rambling inn, Seton was nervously biting his nails, already in a lather about his first performance that evening, his voice more unstable than ever.

'Hardly eaten a thing,' Sir Thomas said, busily sorting through piles of used liveries. 'Those are finished with.' He handed Adorna a pile of velvet hats. 'They go in that basket over there. They'll need cleaning up. Poor Seton. I've never known him so nervous. I thought he enjoyed it.'

'I'll go and have a word with him,' said Adorna.

She sat with her brother on his bed where he stared gloomily at the window, his eyes like grey saucers.

'Want me to go through it again, love?' she said. 'It might help.'

'I can't do it,' he croaked, miserably. 'I can't, Dorna. Honest.'

'Oh, come on, love. Of course you…'

'I can't! Not before Her Majesty when my voice is cracking up. I'm a writer, not an actor, and I'm not a woman, either. I have to kiss Master Burbage, Dorna,' he almost squealed in disgust. 'Can you imagine *kissing* Master Burbage at the end?' He stared at her, panic-stricken.

Adorna could not. 'Well, you don't actually…kiss, do you?'

'Yes,' he squawked. 'He insists on being convincing. I can't do it. I shall be sick.'

'Oh, dear,' she whispered. 'There has to be a way round this.' They both knew, at that same moment, where the answer lay, though neither of them wanted to be the one to suggest it. It was unthinkable. Women did not make exhibitions of themselves in public. A woman performer would get the earl and his company—Leicester's Men—into serious trouble with the Revels Office of which their father was the head. Seton would never be employed again, Sir Thomas would lose his office, and she would be talked about for the rest of her life as the woman who acted before a public audience. Personifying a Water Maiden for the Queen's private masque in music and dance was not the same at all. None of the family would live it down if it became known, but nor would the earl gain any favour with the Queen if the leading female role,

Seton, made a mess of the production. Even so, Adorna's involvement was quite out of the question.

'No one need know,' Seton said in a low voice. 'Just this once. You and I are so alike, not even Burbage would know if you wore my wig.'

Adorna stood up, shaking her head. 'It's a nonstarter, love,' she said. 'I'm supposed to be in the audience with Hester. Are *you* prepared to be *me* for the rest of the evening? Don't be absurd. You *have* to go through with it.'

'You know the lines,' he said, bleakly. 'You told me you'd learnt my part.'

'That's nothing to do with it. Now come on, buck up.' She left the room, closing the door with a sigh, knowing she had failed him when he needed her most. 'He'll be all right,' she said to her father. 'He'll have to be, won't he?'

The Queen hunted that afternoon in the forests around Kenilworth, followed by the whole Court who were used to its lengthy rituals, its standing about, its distant removal from the real thing. On occasions such as this, the ladies were not expected to chase after the deer as the men did, but to station themselves with the Queen inside a carefully constructed bower ready to shoot at them as they were driven past. It went without saying that the bolts from Her Majesty's crossbow never missed their mark.

There were some women, however, who chose to join in the chase, people like Adorna and Hester for whom the fun was missing if there was no riding. They were well surrounded, and there appeared to be no obvious reason why any of them should be in danger except, perhaps, from the effects of the recent rain. Yet they had not been galloping long when Adorna discovered that Hester was not amongst the group and that Peter had already pulled up and was heading back towards the woodland. She waited a while and then followed, eventually spotting Hester in her emerald green hunting-dress lying on the wet ground with Peter bending over her.

'She's hurt?' Adorna cried. 'Oh, Peter! What's happened?' She leapt down from the saddle, fearing the worst.

'Don't know. Her mare didn't fall. Must have refused that log. She's had a nasty tumble, poor lady. Looks to be in a bad way.' His face was a picture of concern.

'Careful, she may have broken something.'

Hester was not unconscious, nor did she have any visible signs of injury, only a badly muddied gown, much loosened hair, and a face contorted with pain. 'Oh, dear,' she moaned. 'Oh, dear. Is that you, Adorna?'

'Yes, dear. Me and Master Fowler. Lie still. Let him lift you.'

Peter was strong and Hester was not particularly heavy. Between them, they managed to lift her on to his saddle where he held her before him all the way back to the castle, Adorna following with the chestnut mare. This was a worrying development. Her father would say that they should have stayed with the Queen and her other guests. Poor Hester. It was unlike her to part company with the saddle, for her horsemanship was one of her stronger attributes.

They took her back to the Swan Tower where Ellie, full of sympathy for her poor mistress, helped to undress her and put her to bed, though neither Adorna nor Maybelle could find the slightest sign of bruising. 'It's my head,' Hester moaned. 'My head hurts so badly. I think I must have hit it when I fell. Oh, dear!'

'Rest,' Adorna said. 'Ellie will bring you a warm posset from the kitchens and we'll stay here. Thank goodness Peter found you. It's not like you to take a fall, is it? Was the ground slippery, or was it the mare?'

'Treacherous,' said Hester, holding her forehead.

'I think I may seek the advice of her Majesty's physician,' said Adorna. 'You may have done more damage than we can tell. You're obviously in great pain.'

'No...oh, no! Don't do that. I shall be well enough with some rest. Really. Just rest and quiet. That's all I need. I'm not used to all this activity, you know. Maybe it's all been a little too much for me after such a journey.'

'Poor Hester. You'll miss tonight's entertainment.'

'Yes, I shall not feel like attending yet another event. It's too much.' She turned her head on the pillow and closed her eyes, snuggling into the soft coolness with a sigh.

Leaving Ellie in command, they left Hester to sleep in peace, though Adorna's prime thoughts were for some professional attention for the patient. Her secondary ones were for the evening's activities, the play being scheduled for after supper. For Seton's sake, she must help him to prepare; that was the least she could do.

She told her father about Hester's accident later that afternoon as he came to escort her to supper, though she felt that his reaction to her cousin's distress was a little hard-hearted.

'She'll be all right,' he said, outside the door. 'I expect she's fallen off a horse plenty of times before, though I doubt she's received anything like the attention she's getting now. If you were to ask me, what she needs most is a bit of fuss. Let her stay there.'

'But what about her head, Father?'

'If it's anything like her father's it'll be a damn sight harder than yours. Nothing much wrong there or there'd be other symptoms. Take a look at her urine in the morning. Now then, come on, I'm starving.'

'Should I stay with her this evening?'

'What, and miss Seton? No!'

Seton did not appear at supper, and by that time Adorna's concern for him had done little for her own appetite. She made her excuses as soon as the Queen had left the hall and went to search the small chambers set aside for the actors' dressing-rooms. It took some time to find him amongst the orderly chaos of costumes and props, assistants and actors, every cramped space piled with baskets of weapons, wigs, wine-jars and shoes, but when she did, her worst fears were confirmed. In a small chamber lit by a pair of candles he sat alone with his head in his hands, shaking with fear and as white as a sheet.

'Heavens above!' Adorna said, closing the door quietly behind her. 'Where's your dresser? Don't you have one?'

'Dressing Master Burbage,' Seton whispered. Beads of sweat sprinkled his forehead like dew. 'I've told him I can manage. I thought you might come.'

'Well, we can make a start, can't we? Oh, dear, love, you *must* try.'

The effort of speaking made him double up over a basin, his stomach cramping with another spasm of pain. 'Dorna,' he gasped. 'Help me!'

The dead weight of fear grew at the bottom of her lungs. 'Don't you have an understudy?' she said, mopping the dark points of hair at the back of his neck. 'There must be somebody else, surely?'

'No,' he said, miserably. 'Nobody.'

She had always been stronger than Seton, and the thought of seeing him fail in front of so prestigious an audience tore at her heart. She could not let him do it. Moreover, the situation had changed since morning and now her absence from the audience would be taken as an indication that she was with Cousin Hester. 'I don't know the stage directions,' she said, flatly, eyeing the large wig of brown hair. 'I've no idea what to do.'

'It won't matter,' said Seton. 'You'll pick it up from the script, and the others will help you like they do with me.'

'This is ridiculous,' she snapped, gently.

'Please,' he whispered.

'Tch! Put a chair against the door. Where does Master Burbage dress?'

'Next door. I can hide in here while you're on. No one will come.'

'I hope you're right. Show me what I'm supposed to wear and tell me what I'm supposed to know, or my performance will be worse than yours.'

Even to Seton himself, the transformation was truly remarkable. Having no need of padding, Adorna used the extra time to fit the bulky wig over her own hair, a problem that Seton with his trimmed fair locks did not share. Their features were so alike that it required only the stage rouge, lip-carmine, soot-darkened eyelashes and brows to change her into Seton's Beatrice, and by the time they had found a large clothes basket for Seton to hide in, she was primed about what to do in the first act. The second and third would have to wait. The call came almost immediately. She took a deep breath.

Master Burbage peered at her in the dim passageway. 'You all right, lad?' he said. 'Let's have a look at you.' He moved her towards the nearest flickering torch on the wall and looked pointedly at her bosom. 'Hm! You seem to have got that lot in the right place for a change instead of stuck under your chin. Now don't let your voice squeak, lad, eh? And keep your head up. That's it. Right, let's get on with it, then.'

'Yes, sir,' Adorna said, following him.

Until that first public performance, she had suspected nothing of the inner excitement, the power, or the extra level of experience that acting could bring. She forgot Seton, Sir Nicholas, the Queen and the earl, her father, the audience, even Master Burbage, the principal and most experienced actor. He was Benedict and she was Beatrice and, while she was separated from everyone else in that large hall by a footlight of glowing torches, another life enveloped her.

The story took her into an experience similar in many ways to the one she shared with Sir Nicholas, disliking and being a little afraid of a man, yet being totally bewildered by an overpowering attraction that could not move beyond a battle of two minds, both of them so determined not to yield an inch that their fragile relationship seemed doomed to failure. Consequently, she brought to the part an authenticity that Seton could not, and an innate love of performing that not even she had realised until then. She knew the lines as if they were hers; the stage directions she either picked up through some extra sense or made them up as she went along, the other players following her rather than the other way round. James Burbage was a good actor, yet he too was surprised to see his Beatrice take on a new realism that he could never have foreseen. The audience were enthralled, greeting each scene with ecstatic applause, carrying her, lifting her confidence.

She hurried back to Seton at the end of each act but found him fast asleep in the basket. Placing a coat beneath his head, she left him there and went on with the deception, floating on her success into the next two acts. It was as if she knew not only the words but the feelings behind them, the pretences and heartaches, the self-deception and the love she dared not admit, adding a new layer of meaning to Beatrice's simplest lines by her expressions and gestures. When the two lovers came to Beatrice's last heart-stopping admission that she could no longer maintain her coldness, the one she had read to Sir Nicholas in the garden, James Burbage responded with the most moving speech of his life, which had been written by Sir Nicholas himself. The kiss that Seton had dreaded followed so naturally from their reconciliation that Adorna felt no sense of strangeness, for they were still in a private world of their own. Apparently Mr Burbage suspected nothing, nor did he have any reservations; he was, as Seton had said, all for a convincing act.

At the end, the audience went wild, laughing and crying, rising to their feet, utterly won over by the magic of it all. It was many minutes before the actors were allowed to leave, by which time Adorna's scrutiny of the audience had shown her that Sir Nicholas was not amongst them.

Behind the scenery, Master Burbage and the other actors poured out their congratulations. 'Well done, lad,' the great actor said. 'That was some performance you gave. I knew you had it in you. Well done. Now, go and get cleaned up before we go and see Her Majesty.'

'Yes, sir, thank you. Shall you go on? I'll see you there in a little while. I need a rest first.'

'A rest? Oh, yes, of course.' He studied her closely,

but his eyes showed nothing unusual. 'But you'll come, won't you? His lordship expects us.'

Trembling with relief and elation, she was swept along the passageway, just managing to open the chamber door and close it again before anyone could follow her. What she saw brought her down to earth with a crash. 'Oh...God...no!' she whispered.

'Beatrice?' said Sir Nicholas. He had been sitting on a stool opposite the open basket where Seton still slept like a child, but now he rose to meet her, taking her hand and drawing her away from the door. 'He doesn't look at all well,' he said, following her eyes.

'He's not,' Adorna snapped. 'But look...this is not his fault. And why do *you* have to be here? If you suspected something, couldn't you have kept it to yourself for a while? There's no harm done. No one else has noticed, not even Master Burbage.' She kept her voice low but there was no hiding her fury. Still tightly wound-up from her performance, she was still Beatrice being brought too suddenly back to reality. 'Couldn't you have let it go?'

She sat on the stool he had just vacated, shaking with exhaustion and a return of the earlier fear that the worst had actually happened, despite the success of the play. Seton's play. Her eyes skimmed over his elegant Court dress, pale grey velvet and white satin, cloth of silver spangled with gold and, instead of a ruff, the collar of his shirt was a falling-band of fine lace that framed his square jaw. He was not smiling, but there was an admiration in his dark eyes that made her blush beneath the rouge. She pulled her hand out of his, feeling suddenly ridiculous in the brown wig and Beatrice's strangely gaudy clothes. 'Well, I expect you can't wait to go and break the news to everyone. Don't let me detain you, sir.'

Sir Nicholas poured a beaker of ale and handed it to her. 'We can discuss the implications later, if you wish,' he said, calmly watching her drink. 'But now we have to get you out of those things quickly and get Master Seton back on his feet. He'll be expected to join Master Burbage before long. Come on, my lass, this next bit of acting will have to be every bit as good as the last. Now, where do we start? With that dreadful wig?'

'I need Maybelle,' she said, bleakly. 'It's Seton who needs your help, not me.'

'Then I'll get her. Leave it to me.'

Outside the door, he took hold of a passing lad by the scruff of his neck. 'Hey, lad! What's your name?'

The lad flattened himself against the panelling. He was young, stage-struck, and not supposed to be backstage at all. 'It's Will, sir. Please, sir, I'm not thieving, sir, honest. Let me go back, sir. Please.'

'You were in the audience just now?'

'Yes, sir. With my father. It was brilliant.'

'Then run as fast as your legs can carry you to the Swan Tower and ask for the young lady called Mistress Maybelle. Say Sir Nicholas has sent you. Escort her back here. Fast, boy!'

In less than ten minutes Maybelle was with Adorna, her fingers rebraiding the pale blonde hair and coiling pearls into the strands as it had been before. Then, with the stage-paint removed, the true beauty took shape once more, the oyster and cream silk petticoats and bodice, the tiny lace ruff, the ropes of pearls and the earrings, the stockings and slippers. Maybelle missed no detail. 'Is Master Seton going to be all right?' she whispered.

Adorna glanced across to the corner where Sir Nicholas was holding a wet cooling rag to her brother's forehead. 'He will be,' she said, 'but he needs some of that black stuff on his lashes. That's the worst part to remove.'

As Maybelle obliged in the deception, Adorna's fears grew, for now two people knew of the offence. 'That messenger you sent,' she said to Sir Nicholas. 'Does he know, too, d'ye think?'

'Not a chance.'

'Is he one of the company?'

'No, he's a little eleven-year-old lad from Stratford-upon-Avon, about three hours' walk away. He came to see the festivities with his father, a glove-maker. Will, his name is. Will Shakespeare. I gave him two pennies and he thinks Master Seton is the Archangel Gabriel. Stop worrying. It's time we were out of here. Are you ready to go?'

'I'm ready. But…Sir Nicholas…are you going to…?'

He took her by the shoulders and spoke so that only she could hear. 'You think I'm going to shout about this from the rooftops? Think again, woman.'

'I see. So there'll be a price to pay, will there? I should have known.'

'I think,' he replied, 'that this is neither the time nor the place to be discussing terms. Later on, perhaps. Come, you are now Mistress Adorna Pickering who has come with her maid to attend her brother after his performance. You, of course, didn't see it, but you heard from me that he was quite sensational. And you will, naturally, stay close by my side at all times.'

'Of course,' she said. 'How could I think otherwise?'

Seton, pale but steady, had been perspiring and shivering and, now that his lashes had been darkened, had the look of an exhausted actor more convincingly than his sister did. Although the stomach-cramps and sickness had abated, he was still far from recovered. 'It'll pass,' he whispered. Then, like a child, he threw his arms around Adorna and hugged her. 'Thank you, love. Sir Nicholas has told me you were amazing. The best ever, he said.'

'Must have been the rehearsal we had,' she said. 'But Seton, you'll have to pretend now, just the same. It was *you*, remember.'

'Yes, love. I know. I'll do it. You go and enjoy the rest of the evening.'

Over Seton's shoulder, her eyes met Sir Nicholas's and now, as well as admiration, there was something in them she found difficult to read but which might conceivably have been triumph.

The dramatic change from Beatrice's brunette to Adorna's startling fairness no doubt helped to make any comparison more difficult, especially when she rejoined the company with her brother at her side, whose boyish good looks were what everyone expected to see. While he was instantly surrounded by applauding people, Adorna and Sir Nicholas went without delay into a stately pavane that had begun to form to the musicians' first notes, the concentration needed for its measured steps being exactly what was required to draw her mind into some kind of order. Its four-four-time beat a way into her heart, pacing it, slowing it, moderating it to accept what had happened and what was about to happen, events no longer under her control.

She had read his face correctly. He was triumphant about the outcome of her grave offence, about his prediction and about reminding Master Seton of his sister's talents. As he had suspected, it was not only acute stage-fright from which the lad was suffering but also a stomach infection so common on visits to different parts of the country where food was handled by all and sundry. Somebody always caught it. But Seton's loss had been his gain, the lady's mind already seeking a bargain for his silence, a development he had no intention of refusing if it was offered. He would never have told a soul what had happened that evening. He loved the courage she had shown by saving her brother from humiliation. But although she obviously believed he, Nicholas, intended some kind of blackmail, he would not be surprised if she used the situation, unconsciously of course, to do what she could not otherwise do without appearing to change her mind. Like

Beatrice, she was a proud woman, not used to backing down without a very good reason. This, for her, would be the best of all possible reasons. It would salve her conscience.

The pavane finished and her second ordeal began with a volley of comments about Master Seton's amazing performance. She handled it well, as he had expected her to do, and when he thought she had had enough, he took her elbow and led her away, to her relief, he thought.

Her father could not be kept at arm's length. 'Adorna! Ah, there you are. What a pity you missed Seton, m'dear. You were right about him, you know. He *was* all right. You should have heard that last scene, though. Not quite as I remember reading it, but absolutely marvellous writing and acting.'

'He's not too well though, Father.'

'Rubbish! He's as fit as a fiddle when he has to be, our Seton. I saw him. How's Hester?' Maybelle had told Adorna how Hester was sleeping, but Sir Thomas's enquiry held no real interest, for he was already looking elsewhere. Again, she responded quickly to the gentle tug on her hand.

'Come,' Sir Nicholas murmured. 'You need something to eat.' Normally, she would have argued, but not this time. He found a quiet corner where they could speak in low tones while a troupe of acrobats performed spine-bending contortions. He brought her a platter heaped with tiny pastries, gilded marchpanes and biscuits, a goblet of watered wine.

She drank it without comment but could not wait

for her mouth to empty before launching into the subject uppermost on her mind. 'Well?' she said. 'What's the price to be, sir? Is this to be the start of it?'

Sir Nicholas took a gold star-shaped biscuit and scratched the foil off at one corner to reveal the brown underneath. He looked at it hard and then ate it. 'This?' he said. 'Meaning what?'

'You know what I mean. My company for your silence.'

'Is that what you are offering me? Your company?'

'Isn't that enough?'

He sat up and turned to her, helping himself to another biscuit. 'I think, mistress, that you had better let me ask the questions while you supply some answers. Yes?' He picked a crumb off her chin and ate it. 'Now, it makes more sense if you tell me what my silence is worth to you. Have you thought—?'

'Well, of *course* I've thought, Sir Nicholas!' she snapped, taking the pastry from him on its way to his mouth. 'I've done nothing *but* think. This is as serious for Master Burbage and the company as it is for our family, yet it would have been equally serious for his lordship if Seton had performed tonight.'

'Shh! Keep your voice down.'

'But if you are quite determined to make some capital out of it, I can't prevent you.'

'Yes, you can.'

'Well, that's arguable. You know how it is when people make demands. They keep on making greater ones.'

'So I believe. Just as well then that I haven't made any, isn't it?'

'You've been careful, I grant you that. Still, the implication is there.'

'It is?'

'And you know how opposed I am to what you have in mind.'

'What do I have in mind? Remind me.'

'I will. You said I would come to you within days. You planned this days ago, didn't you? You must have.'

'If you mean, my lovely Adorna, that I knew Seton would be unwell tonight of all nights, then you must think I've been blessed with second sight. If you mean that I had a hunch he'd try to persuade you into it then, yes, I did. But as for planning anything, well, that would hardly have been possible, even for me. However, you *have* come to me, and so far so good. Now it remains for you to decide, as I said before, exactly what my silence is worth to you.'

'You mean...how far...?'

'I mean,' he said, helping her out, 'that the time has come for us to be seen as a pair, for me to have prior claim to you at all times, and for you to make yourself more accessible to me.'

'In other words, to add me to your list.'

'Ah,' he sighed, 'the list again. No, I'll scrap the list and start a new one, if you like, with your name on it alone. Will that do?'

'For how long? Are we speaking of days? Weeks? Months?'

'I shall let you decide, but I had years in mind.'

'Now I *know* you can't be serious.' Her hands twisted the rope of pearls that hung down to her waist. 'You realise, don't you, that this kind of bargain goes against all my intentions? I would rather you had demanded money.'

'I have money, thank you. And I haven't demanded anything. I asked you to make me an offer and you have done.'

'Same thing.' She did not contradict his statement, though she could have done.

'If you say so. Nevertheless, it had better be understood that you have accepted me as a suitor and that, to all intents and purposes, you are mine. My lady, my woman, call her what you will. There will be no more evasions or refusals.'

If that pronouncement had come a mite faster than she expected, it must have showed on her face, for her eyes filled with deep concern. 'We're not talking about…you know…are we?' Her voice was breathless, almost lost beneath the peals of raucous laughter that filled the hall.

He put out a forefinger and tenderly smoothed away the folds between her eyes that had puckered with her words. 'Easy…easy,' he whispered. 'One step at a time, eh? I'll not go too fast for you.'

'You did before, I think.' Her voice found an accusing ring.

He had by now turned himself to her so closely that their faces lay openly exposed to every nuance of expression, and although Adorna had proved her ability to act, there was neither script nor make-up nor scenery to help her here. Her concerns were never more genuine than those he saw in her eyes at this moment, for she had backed herself into a corner and was already fighting at shadows. Metaphors, he thought, could be so apt at times like this.

'Yes,' he said. 'I did, didn't I? There was a challenge, I seem to remember. Irresistible, in the circumstances, but no harm done.' He saw her eyes flash, angrily. 'Maybe I should start at the beginning again, d'ye think?' But her thoughts on the matter were hidden as he watched her eyelids close over them, the softness of her lips being the only reply he needed. He felt the intake of her breath as his mouth claimed hers, and he knew a pang of pity for the conflict that raged within her, like Beatrice, wanting yet furiously denying, and angry with herself for this blatant self-deception. For her sake, he would pretend she had no choice, yet the one question she could, and should, have asked was the one she had studiously avoided. *Did he intend to expose the two actors?*

The kiss ended. Her eyes opened and shifted, nervously. 'In public?' she whispered.

'It's allowed, between lovers.'

'My father…!' She placed her hands against his chest.

'He approves of me.'

'How d'ye know?'

'He told me so.'

Her lips tightened. 'I thought as much. But what about Hester?'

'She does, too.'

The fine brows squirmed. 'That's not what I meant.'

'Then what did you mean?'

'You know...'

'No, I don't. Hester and I are friends of long standing, that's all.'

'That's not what Hester would like to believe.'

Their eyes, inches apart, searched for more information until Sir Nicholas asked with a frown. 'Exactly what would Hester like to believe?'

Adorna looked beyond his ear to the dark silhouettes of figures and the occasional face that turned in their direction. 'She's very fond of you. She speaks of you, often.'

The facetiousness returned. 'Hester speaking often. That's new. Then I shall keep her on the old list. There, how will that do?' When she made no reply, he moved away carefully and stood up, taking her hands and pulling her upright. 'Come on,' he said. 'As soon as Her Majesty leaves, I'll take you back. And listen...' he pulled her even closer until she was within his arms, ignoring the open stares and smiles '...I'm going to suggest to your father that your brother stays here in the castle with me. I have a man who'll tend him. He needs rest and time to prepare for the next play. Have you seen the script yet?'

'I have a copy, yes. I've read it.'

'Good. Let's hope he's well by then.'

The next play was to be in three days and Sir Nicholas did not believe that Seton's problems would be gone in that time. Rather the opposite. Sir Thomas

Pickering, however, would be hard to convince that the problem existed at all. He would insist that Seton pull himself together: Seton would be a disaster: questions would be asked about how he could be so bad after being so good: the truth would be sought and Seton would admit the deceit. It was essential that Adorna should prepare, and that Seton should be kept calm until then. The play could be cancelled, of course, but the earl needed all the credit he could accrue and disappointments would not help.

'Sir Nicholas,' Adorna said, pushing gently at his chest, 'people are looking, and I'm not used to being seen like this.'

He was unmoved. 'Gets easier with practice,' he said.

Half-an-hour later, Adorna was beginning to understand something of what it meant to be seen as Sir Nicholas's new lady, a kind of emotional captivity she had sworn to run from until she grew too old, docile or broody to run any more. Which she had hoped would be light years away, God willing. With the full force of her antagonism brought back by the chill of the dark summer night, she rebelled against the decision she herself had taken only an hour ago. 'I suppose the Swan Tower was your doing, too,' she panted, trying to free herself from his grasp as he held her back against the wall. 'Which is why you were...let me go!'

'Not surprised to see you? Of course, woman. Yes, I had you invited to Kenilworth; what use is it having

the earl as patron if one doesn't make use of the connection, once in a while? I knew you'd come.' He held
her hands together in a cruel grasp. 'At least you're
comfortable here.'

'I should never have come. It was a mistake.'

'You couldn't stay away, could you? You knew
what would happen.'

'No, that's not—'

His mouth closed over hers, stopping the last futile
protest, his body attuned to her every move, sensing
the exact moment of her surrender. To reinforce his
victory, he made it last.

There were to be no more words that night, she
having digested as many in one short time-span as she
had in a whole week, and he having achieved his aim
by different methods. He took her to the door of her
room and delivered her to Maybelle. 'She's had
enough for one day,' he told the maid. 'Straight to
bed.'

Maybelle recognised the new development immediately; no man except her father had ever told her
mistress to go to bed, that she had had enough. 'Yes,
sir,' she said, marvelling at Adorna's compliance.

The damage had been done and there was now little
or nothing she could do to undo it, however much she
vacillated over the solution that had all too readily
been accepted. She had wept before falling asleep and,
understanding her mistress as well as she did, Maybelle had rocked her to sleep in her arms without ven-
turing any opinion one way or the other. The confusion was great enough to be left alone.

* * *

In the morning, some of the old opposition surfaced alongside premonitions of disaster. 'What am I to tell Peter?' she said to Maybelle, holding her foot out for a soft blue kid slipper. 'He'll think I've gone mad after all he's been helping me to do to avoid Sir Nicholas.'

'If Master Fowler isn't used to your ways by now,' Maybelle said, straightening the blue silk skirts, 'then he never will be. I shouldn't waste too much pity there, if I were you. Besides, he'll have to move on to the next venue soon, won't he?'

'Mmm, Staffordshire. But what about Hester? She's going to be a bit put out, to say the least. She was entertaining some hopes, Belle.'

'Mistress Hester's not going to be entertaining anything for a day or two, and then she'll have to accept that she doesn't stand a chance. Well, not for a while, anyway,' she added with unfortunate candour.

'No, not until he returns to the original contenders.'

The cynicism was not lost upon the maid. It was time for some plain speaking. 'Look,' she said, sitting on the chest opposite Adorna, 'things have moved on. *You*'ve moved on. And if Sir Nicholas has got Sir Thomas's approval, as you say he has, then he'll have to be careful what he gets up to, won't he? If you stop to think about it, he was actually helpful last night after the performance, and he's going to look after Master Seton, which is more than most men would do. And anyway, you'll probably tire of him by the time he's tired of you, then you can both go your own ways again.' Her barb found its target.

'The whole point, Belle,' Adorna scolded, 'is that

he *will* find someone else who takes his fancy *long* before I do, and that is *precisely* why I didn't want anything to do with him in the *first* place. I'd rather not be one of his old flames if I can't be...' She put up her hands to cover her face.

'Can't be what? The last love of his life?'

'I thought you knew that,' she said, hoarsely.

I did know that, Maybelle said to herself. *How could I not know?*

Later that morning Adorna found that her father had already been approached about allowing Seton to stay in Sir Nicholas's quarters and had given his immediate consent. She suspected that he welcomed the move by Sir Nicholas to involve himself with the Pickering family, but she made no mention of it even when Sir Thomas teased her about Peter's reaction to her apparent change of heart. 'Spent the evening looking like a dog that's lost its best bone.' He laughed. 'Didn't you see him glowering?'

'No, Father. I didn't.'

'Not surprised. You were otherwise engaged, weren't you? Still, I'm pleased to see you and Sir Nicholas on better terms. He'll look after you.'

It was not long before Master Fowler found his way to Sir Thomas's side with a similar custodial request that had nothing to do with Adorna or Seton. His concern was for Mistress Hester. 'She's quite unwell, sir, so I'm led to believe,' he said as they walked together over the moat-bridge to the castle. 'She has quite a delicate constitution. I wondered if I should escort her back to Richmond.'

'No!' Sir Thomas said, with a usual lack of sympathy. 'The Pickerings are not as delicate as all that, lad. She'll be fine after a day's rest.'

'But the conditions in the Swan Tower are not spacious, and—'

'And she'll be as bored as hell at Richmond. She's created quite a stir here amongst the young men, our heiress. No, she'll be fine. Leave her where she is.'

Aware of the Pickering obstinacy, Peter knew better than to press the point, for it could be argued that a journey was not the best cure for a sore head.

There was a tournament in the Queen's honour that day. Sir Nicholas was splendidly equipped in a suite of shining jousting armour, his helm topped by a tall crest of dyed ostrich feathers that echoed those set between his horse's ears, while embroidered on his horse's caparison were his family coat of arms like those on his shield. Round his upper arm he wore a streamer of cream satin ribbons which Adorna had removed from her own girdle to tie there in full view of the spectators, which had seemed to both of them to be some kind of turning point in their new relationship. The spectators, seated on stands draped with costly silks, had applauded, and although Sir Nicholas was well known for his skills at jousting, she had whispered private prayers for his safety throughout the contests. The action was brutal and fierce, despite the blunted lances; a fall in full armour from a careering horse injured many a knight that afternoon.

Adorna hid her concern from the friends with whom she sat to watch, just as she secretly hoped he would do nothing more to demonstrate his new hold over her. But he did better than that, sending a message to request her presence in his arming-tent, an invitation she was strongly urged by some of the young men to ignore. The young women laughed enviously, chiding her on her fickleness, knowing her teasing games and wondering if, this time, she was about to get her come-uppance from the accomplished knight.

She was not inclined to risk the consequences of a refusal. She was led to his blue-and-white chequered pavilion by his squire, a young man of impeccable manners and lineage whose face gave no sign that he might have performed the same kind of errand dozens of times before. He held the tent-flap open for her, bowed, and left her to face Sir Nicholas alone inside the shady canvas.

He had not finished dressing, but was tucking his white linen shirt into his breeches as she entered, the fabric sticking to his body as if he had not had time to dry, and showing a wide V of chest thickly forested with dark hair. His hair, still wet from his bath, fell onto his forehead in a tumble of spiked curls, and on one cheek was a red bruise where his helm had buffeted him. Adorna had seen her two brothers and her father in similar stages of undress more than once, but no domestic scene at home could have prepared her for this encounter. Her first reaction was to make a quick exit.

He caught her in one long-legged bound that startled her with its speed, drawing her into the tent with the kind of soft sound he would use to a startled filly. 'Whoa…whoa…lass!' he laughed. 'Shh! I'm dressing, not undressing. Sit ye down here, see.' He led her firmly to his arming-chest, slammed the lid shut and eased her down on to it, standing between her and the exit to prevent a departure.

There were two angry spots of red on her cheeks. 'There is no need for this, Sir Nicholas,' she said, refusing to look at him. 'I know what a man looks like.'

He squatted on his haunches before her, his knees enclosing her full skirt. 'Then why did you think of bolting?' he whispered, touching her cheek with one finger. It meandered gently downwards over her bare neck while she held her breath and let it out slowly, finding it impossible to answer him, his touch drawing all her senses towards a delicious peak of delight. He held her eyes with his own as he traced a path over the swell of her breasts and lingered, caressing the softness above the hard edge of her bodice. She knew, at the back of her mind, that he had been further than that and that he remembered it better than she. His eyes were telling her so.

The caress continued. 'Well, lady?' he said. 'Did you pray for me to win? Do I deserve your approval?'

'Yes,' she whispered. 'I did. You do.'

'And you are going to reward me?'

'Isn't this…this your reward?' she gulped, trying to take hold of his wrist.

His hand twisted and caught hers instead. 'No, it's yours.'

'Then…?'

'This,' he said. He guided her hand to his own throat and left it there. 'Come on,' he whispered.

She hesitated, not knowing that the caress could be almost as exciting for her as it would be for him. Then she found, as she explored, that the hair on his chest was soft, not harsh, and that as she slipped her hand beneath his damp shirt, the warm vibrancy of his skin was like no other sensation she had ever encountered, the contours being quite different, the softness only skin-deep over iron-hard muscles.

Suddenly aware that she was enjoying it against her will, her hand changed course, slipping upwards to his cheek where her fingers came to rest against the raw bruise. She caught the approval in his eyes, his maddening controlled approval. This had, of course, been a lesson. She snatched her hand away. 'So controlled, Sir Nicholas,' she said, turning her head. 'Always so very controlled.'

He brought her back to face him with his fingers beneath her chin. 'And that's something else you're not used to, isn't it, my lass? But you will. You're learning to come to me.' He stood upright, pulling her to her feet. 'And that's a good start.' She would have loved to prove him wrong, but he seemed to read her mind. 'No, we'll go together,' he said. His kiss was sudden and hard like his grip upon her arms, and she was left with tears burning her eyelids and no words to wound him as she would have liked.

They did leave the tournament ground together, she riding pillion on a cushion behind him with one arm about his waist from where she could see the expressions on the faces of those who had witnessed her earlier attempts at avoidance. She saw nothing in them to offer her any comfort, only various renderings of 'I told you so.' Nor could she escape the foreboding that she must now be prepared for similar public displays of his victory in the days ahead. That was a development she had not anticipated, though it would have made little difference if she had. Nor did it seem that she would be allowed to balk, his hands on the reins having noticeably tightened, so to speak.

She was relieved to find that Peter's attitude to his loss was more philosophical than the sulk her father had described. 'I saw it coming,' Peter said. 'We can still be friends?'

'Of course we can,' Adorna said. 'I don't intend to lose friendships this way. It'll not last. Give it a few weeks. Months, at the most. You'll see.'

'Are you talking about you, or him?' said Peter, though he neither expected nor received a reply.

Slightly more disturbing was the nagging problem of Seton, whose continuing and acute nervousness threatened to call a halt to his association with Leicester's Men. After the brilliant performance before the Queen, Master Burbage said, he was not prepared to coach one of the other young men in the part if there was the slightest chance that Master Seton would by then have overcome his tiredness and stomach upset, which were the reasons given for Seton being unavailable to rehearse. He was therefore in complete agreement with Sir Nicholas that Seton should be given total peace in which to study. There was still, however, the problem of rehearsals.

'He was rather under-rehearsed on that last one,' James Burbage told Sir Nicholas, meaningfully. 'Superb, I grant you, but it would have helped if he'd let us know in advance what he was about to do. If you see what I mean, sir?' He stroked his neat beard and waited for the younger man to suggest a solution.

'Then I think the answer, Mr Burbage, is that you and Seton should rehearse in my room, in private. In that way you could discuss stage-directions without tiring him too much before the performance.'

'An excellent notion, sir. And Mistress Adorna? Perhaps she would like to attend the...er... discussions? Just to give her brother some support?'

'I shall see that she is there on each occasion, Master Burbage.'

'Good, good. That's understood, then. Quite a relief!'

Sir Nicholas told Adorna of this arrangement at the masque that evening, after which she became quite certain that Benedict's convincing stage-kiss had not been intended for Seton at all, neither by Sir Nicholas nor Master Burbage.

There was better news about Hester's condition,

though Adorna could not help wondering exactly what the connection could be between her rapid recovery and a letter that she hurriedly pushed under her pillow as Adorna walked into the tower chamber. Not being of a particularly suspicious turn of mind, Adorna put this act of secrecy down to the admirers who had constantly asked about Hester's health, though she wondered why, if it was so innocent, Hester could not have shown it to her. Still, she was relieved to know that Hester did not feel quite well enough to attend the masque, for Adorna wished to delay for as long as possible the news that she herself was now being widely regarded as Sir Nicholas's woman. That, she believed, would do Hester's head no good at all.

Chapter Nine

From the very first of these private rehearsals to which she had been invited ostensibly as an onlooker, Adorna realised that she was in fact the one for whom they had been arranged. Nothing was said to this effect by any of the three men, not a word, nor did Master Burbage consult her except via Seton, while she made her own tentative suggestions as if they were for Seton's consumption rather than for hers. It was all rather bizarre, and although they had to be careful, it appeared to give back to Seton some of the confidence he had lost as a playwright and to restore Master Burbage's stability as principal actor.

What it did for Adorna was less easy to define, except to highlight the way that things had slipped well beyond her control since coming to Kenilworth and how, by the same token, her love for Sir Nicholas verged on hate, so intensely painful was it for her to see him even speak to another woman.

She supposed, in her more rational moments, that her own semi-romantic experiences would have cushioned her from such fears and given her enough self-confidence to deal with love's waywardness. But it was not so. Her dealings had been with boys, youths seeking experience, and widowers looking for second wives, not men like Sir Nicholas who challenged rather than adored. She had heard of jealousy, but had never encountered its terrible madness until this.

'Why are you doing this?' she asked him as they walked through the stable after a meeting. 'One performance was bad enough, but another one makes it even worse. What if I'm found out? Has it crossed your mind that I'll be ruined? And Seton? And the rest of us? Except you, of course.'

They turned into the palomino's stall and stood in the warm space at the mare's side, Sir Nicholas with his arm across the silken coat. 'Well, of course it's crossed my mind,' he said, taking Adorna's hand. At such times he was tender and exceptionally patient. 'But what good would it do your brother to abandon him at this stage, to tell him he must perform as best he can? How would it look now if he had to become Queen Titania of the Fairies? Could you let him do it, sweetheart?'

Her knees quivered at his use of the endearment. 'No,' she whispered, crossly. 'But if he knew how unsuitable he would be for the part, then why did he write it? He dreads this part even more than the other.'

'Well, a playwright doesn't simply write parts that he wants, he writes whatever is appropriate for the occasion. Perhaps Master Burbage suggested the fairy queen theme to him. Who knows?' His hand slipped around her back, easing her into his arms. 'And I can see no other woman who more closely resembles the Queen of the Fairies than the one who'll be playing her. Beautiful, talented, tender-hearted, fierce and womanly, yet still an innocent in so many ways.'

'Then you haven't read Seton's play all through, sir. She's also a flirt and a tease who's not willing to be ruled by a man. She's more vindictive and strong-willed than Oberon thought when he married her.'

'Then if I were Oberon,' he said, touching her cheeks and mouth lightly with his lips, 'I would teach her how to accept him as master. She'd not find it too uncomfortable.'

Adorna eased herself away. 'Then I'm glad you are not, sir. Seton's Oberon is made to prove his constancy. I much prefer that version.'

In retrospect, that was one of the few occasions on which she was allowed to have the last word on a subject so close to both their interests. Maybe, Adorna thought later, it was because he was anxious not to disturb her any more than she was already before the play. Maybe that was why his lovemaking was suspended altogether for those few days, and why she was required only to be seen at his side during the *al fresco* meals in the grounds, the hunting, the water pageants and the dancing, which was, in a way, as close to lovemaking as one could come in public. It suited her well enough, though she did not suppose the situation would continue in that way, judging by his sometimes transparent expressions.

Convinced that Cousin Hester's affections were still

directed more towards Sir Nicholas than anyone else, despite the competition of others, Adorna made every effort to include her in their party so as not to hurt her feelings by any display of fondness. She had no wish to antagonise Hester, being equally sure that, once he got what he wanted, Sir Nicholas's attentions would probably be diverted once more. If Hester was, as he had implied, on his old list, her total innocence in such matters would hardly prepare her for the ebb and flow of inconstant dispositions. Such were the effects of jealousy that coloured Adorna's view of things and showed her the contortions of her own mind rather than what was actually there.

If it had been jealousy alone that caused her to remain adamantly opposed to being Sir Nicholas's woman, her brother Seton might have been able to make her more aware of it. But there was more to it than that. After one of the discussions in Sir Nicholas's quarters, Seton stood lethargically by the window watching the door close behind Master Burbage. 'You're in love, aren't you?' he said, quietly.

They had just been over one of the quarrelsome scenes and Adorna's eyes had begun to fill. It was too much for her. She pressed a hand over her bodice. 'Am I?' she said. 'Is that what it is? It hurts.'

'Haven't you told him?' Seton's voice sounded reassuringly low and manly.

She shook her head. 'He's so...so sure of himself. So confident that I'll give in, as if nobody could resist him. I'm not ready to give in, and when I do it will be to somebody who knows how to hold my heart for life, not just play around with it for a while and then drop it.'

'And what have *you* been doing since you were fourteen?'

'That's different. You know it is. That was just... oh, flirting. Nothing serious.'

'You mean *he* takes women further?'

'Much further.'

'Yet you've allowed yourself to be caught, Dorna.'

'*Allowed* myself?' It was all she could do to keep silent after that, for she could never tell him that it was by helping him out of his dilemma that she had put herself in this position. It had been for him. Or had it? 'Yes, love. I suppose I have, haven't I?' she said at last.

Seton was not the only one that day to remark on Adorna's capitulation, for while the Queen took a ride on the palomino mare that had attracted her attention on several occasions, Adorna was left on one side of the Queen's Irish grey where, unseen by two of the royal courtiers, she became the subject of their speculation.

'So, the Palomino is well and truly stabled then, is she?' one of them said.

'Looks like it, certainly. She took a bit of catching, mind you,' said the other.

'We'll see how long the schooling takes. What'll you wager—weeks or months?'

Then their horses were turned and she caught the word 'mare' and no more. Promptly, she walked the Queen's grey across to Sir Nicholas in full view of the two riders, determined to retaliate. 'Sir Nicholas!' she called. 'We're the subject of a wager, I believe.'

He came riding towards her, smiling, and took from her the grey's bridle. 'Are we really? Tell me, fair lady.'

'There are some here who need to know how long it will take me to school you. Will it be weeks, or months? Are you a difficult colt, sir?'

He understood immediately what had taken place, and his reply was suitably loud enough to reach the ears of the two embarrassed courtiers. 'No!' He laughed. 'Weeks? Never! I'll be eating out of your hand within the hour, sweetheart. Come up, my lass!' He leaned down and extended a hand to her, knowing exactly how to stem the gossip.

Placing one foot on top of his, she grasped his elbow and sprang up behind him, settling herself like a cloak across his back and hugging his waist, relieved by the speed of his response, by his protection, and by his contempt for their critics. For the rest of the ride she clung like a limpet behind him, partly to confound their calculations and partly because it seemed like a wonderful place to be.

For his part, Sir Nicholas wished she would encounter comment like that a bit oftener, if this was to be the result, and made sure that their kiss at the castle stables was seen by the gossips. Nevertheless, Adorna experienced some anger and bewilderment as a result of the men's jest, and wondered how much further things would go before she could find a way out of her plight.

* * *

By the time the performance day had arrived, it was scarcely necessary for Seton to plead his case a second time, so sound had been his sister's preparation and so subtle that not even by a gesture had Master Burbage acknowledged that his leading lady might not be Master Seton himself. The company prepared as usual, and Master Seton went to his dressing-room with his sister and her maid to help him dress, while Sir Nicholas kept a careful guard outside the door, having put it about that Mistress Adorna would be staying backstage, the costumes being excessively complicated.

Adorna had tried, that same day, to take some control of her immediate future by asking her father to take her with him the next day when he returned to Richmond with Seton. They were to set out from the inn at dawn. She could meet him there: she longed to be back home, she told him. He refused, as she had half-expected, saying that she was to go on up to Staffordshire with the Queen's entourage. Sir Nicholas would take good care of her and Cousin Hester. He was glad she and Sir Nicholas were getting on so well together. He would tell her mother the good news. If only he knew, Adorna thought.

After all the preparations, the performance itself was an outstanding success, not only because Adorna's disguise was totally believable once more but because her portrayal was consistent with her previous one. Backstage, the presence of Sir Nicholas ensured that no one disturbed her, that Seton remained well hidden, and that it was only Master Burbage who came to give a final check to her appearance. Then, Sir Nicholas escaped to the audience. At the end, it was Master Burbage who clapped her on the back with, 'Well done again, Master Seton! Another great success, my boy!' in the hearing of the company. 'Now, let this young man get back to his dressing-room, you lot, and leave him in peace till later. Eh, young master?'

A stage-hand grabbed him by the arm. 'Master Burbage, sir! Her Majesty wishes to meet the cast. You're to bring them back, sir!'

Adorna's arms prickled with fright. 'No, Master Burbage,' she said. 'I cannot do that. You must see…I cannot!'

He took her to one side, his face still strangely unfamiliar as the grotesque fairy king, his wings lending another element of unreality to the scene. 'You *can*, Master Seton,' he whispered. 'Everyone is deceived, even me. Keep it up. And keep your voice down now,' he added.

'Down, sir?'

'Yes, down. Master Seton's voice has gone this last week. Hadn't you noticed?'

Of course. The drop from soprano to baritone was now complete and it was true that she had hardly been aware of it. Now she must try to do the same. Her head reeled, dizzily.

Fanning herself with a massive cluster of coloured feathers, the Queen scrutinised the actors who dropped to their knees before her, not knowing how the fairy queen quaked before the dozens of eyes that examined her in minutest detail from head to toe. It was the Queen's questioning, however, that was almost

Adorna's undoing, and had it not been for Master Burbage's quick thinking, she might have given the game away.

As always, Her Majesty was gracious. 'I hear that your brother is a keen actor, too,' she said to Adorna. 'We must try to persuade him to perform with the company to see how he does. Is he presently at Richmond?'

Adorna's efforts to reproduce Seton's new voice were thrown off-track by talk of a brother. 'Er...no, Your Majesty, he's in the...' she squeaked and growled alternately, completely at a loss. Where was he?

Master Burbage stepped in quickly. 'Master Adrian stayed at Richmond, Your Majesty. He wishes to perform with us like Master Seton here, but he is still young. They make a talented pair, the two Pickering brothers.'

'Indeed. A talented family, Master Burbage,' said the Queen. 'I knew their uncle, Sir William, quite well. He and my lord were rivals for my hand once, eh, Robert?' She turned to the Earl of Leicester, and the discussion swung quite naturally to embrace her doings rather than the players, allowing them to retire at last.

But Adorna was visibly shaken and close to tears at the way, after all their efforts, her over-excited wits had refused to cope with both Seton's newest voice and with her triple-identity before an assembly of eagle eyes, all keen, she was sure, to find fault with her disguise. She sobbed as Maybelle removed the outlandish make-up and restored her looks through the tears, refusing to be comforted by Seton or by the appearance of Sir Nicholas.

But once Seton had left to join the Queen's company, Sir Nicholas took matters into his own hands and, waiting until fewer people were about, he escorted Adorna back to the Swan Tower, though the summer night was still streaked with light in the west.

She was still overwrought. 'No more,' she croaked. 'Never again. I'm done with this charade. My head doesn't work in three directions at once.'

'I'm relieved to hear it,' Sir Nicholas murmured, opening the door of her chamber, 'though I have my doubts on both points.'

'And you shouldn't be up here at this time of night, sir.'

The distant thudding of tabors reached them through the open window, the high whine of viols and pipes, a man's shout and a woman's excited laugh. 'Since you have now rejected all pretence, sweetheart, this seems to be the best place for me to be. There now, it's all over…shh!' He took her gently into his arms as a late sob sent tremors through her body. 'Shh! You were superb, my lovely woman. They'll never have another leading lady like that. Never. But now you can forget the whole thing. Seton and your father and the players leave in the morning, and I can replace Burbage's kisses, can't I? Yes?' He gathered her up and laid her on the bed, slipping her fine kid pumps off her feet and straightening her skirts. 'What you need now is some rest. I'll leave you to Maybelle when she arrives.'

'Oh,' she said.

He smiled and sat beside her, bridging her body with his arm. 'Was that an ''oh'' of relief, or disappointment?'

Unwilling to commit herself to either, she remained silent, but her eyes could not hide the needs of her body now that the last few hours of deception were over. They roamed over his face, lingering on his lips and watching as they came closer. Her eyes closed and her arms lifted to feel the warm bulk of his body pressing her into the coverlet, releasing her into the need that had plagued her for what seemed like years. Eagerly, she took her reward with hardly a pause for breath, surprising him, delighting him.

The door opened without warning, breaking them dreamily apart. Maybelle had returned. But no, it was not Maybelle, it was someone who stood on the threshold for long enough to see what was happening, then closed it again.

Adorna pushed him away. '*Hester!* Oh, no! I don't believe it!'

Sir Nicholas sat up and eyed the door. 'I can't see that it matters,' he said. 'She must know by now, surely?'

'She mustn't!' Adorna said, sitting up. 'Now she'll think...'

'What?' He eased her backwards again and held her there with one hand. 'That we're lovers? Well, if she hadn't guessed before, she'll discover soon enough, won't she? Let her deal with it in her own way, sweet-heart, there's nothing you can do about it, and she'll recover from the surprise, take my word for it.'

'It's not me she'll be bothered about, but *you!*'

'Why should she be? Because you think...? Oh, that's lunacy. I told you, we're friends, that's all. It's not my problem or yours if she wants to think other-wise. She'll soon get the idea. Now, you stay there and let Maybelle tend to you.' He turned as the maid entered carrying a bundle of clothes from the Ward-robe. 'Good timing, Belle. I have to go.'

'Where to?' Adorna said, already dreading what he would say.

He showed no sign of impatience at her wariness, but sat down again on the bed and took her hand. 'I am going,' he said deliberately, 'to prepare my lord's horses, coaches and furnishings for tomorrow's events. We'll all be going up to Staffordshire the next day and preparations must be in place by then. I doubt if I shall be in bed much before dawn.' His thumb brushed ten-derly across her lips. 'Sober, manly occupation.'

'You had no need to explain,' she said, ashamed.

'No, of course I didn't. Sleep well. It's all over now.' He kissed her fingers and laid the hand on her bodice. 'I bid you both a goodnight.'

Dumping the clothes on the chest, Maybelle closed the door behind him and came to sit on the end of the bed. 'Who'll soon get the idea?' she said. 'Was that Mistress Hester he was talking about?'

Adorna pulled herself upright, swinging her legs over the edge. 'Yes it was. Did you see her?'

'Did I *see* her! She nearly knocked me flying as I came in at the lower door. She went haring across towards the garden as if the hounds were after her. What's wrong?'

Adorna's sigh became a groan. 'Oh, Belle. She saw us, here on the bed. Tch! I'd better go and find her and explain that it's…oh, where are my pumps?'

They were, at that moment, being slowly kicked under the bed by Maybelle's toe. 'Never mind Mistress Hester,' Maybelle said, soothing with her voice. 'Come on, love. You're shattered. It'll do tomorrow. Time enough to explain then if you still think you must, though for the life of me I can't see that it matters. You've got enough on your plate without bothering about Mistress Hester's heart-strings. It's time you were out of this bodice, for a start. Turn round.'

Overpowered by exhaustion and the forces of common sense, Adorna gave in without protest. But the night was a different matter, for then her thoughts refused to leave her in peace.

By daybreak she felt as if she had not slept at all, for she could not agree that Hester's heart-strings were none of her concern, since it was she and Lady Marion who had intended to set them quivering in the first place. She did not believe that Hester had a lover. She believed that the expression on Hester's face had been one of horror and that she would probably not deal with the shock half as well as Sir Nicholas had suggested.

When she found Hester's tower room deserted except for some baskets and a clothes-chest, Adorna assumed at first that she must, after all, have gone with Sir Thomas to Richmond, although this had not been planned. She sent a young page to the inn at Kenilworth to find out, but the reply was negative and her father's party had already left. Nor had Hester's horses been taken from the stable. Adorna's concern grew as she sent two pages to scour the castle in case she had changed her accommodation, but there was still no sign of her or the maid Ellie. Meanwhile, Maybelle asked at the gatehouse that led towards the Warwick road. A lady with her maid and two packhorses had passed through at dawn, refusing to tell the gatekeeper where they were going, though it was obvious to Maybelle they were not intending to meet Sir Thomas, whose exit from Kenilworth was from a different direction.

'You see?' Adorna said. 'She must have packed up last night after seeing Sir Nicholas with me. She's gone, and it's my fault. All my fault. I shall have to get her back, Belle. She's never travelled alone before and she'll not know what to do. I doubt she'll even know which direction home is. She must be very distressed.'

'If she wanted to go home to Richmond she'd have gone with Sir Thomas and Master Seton, wouldn't she?' Maybelle said with disarming common sense.

Leaning on the wide stone window-ledge that overlooked the garden and the keep at the north side of the castle, Adorna gazed at the throng of men, horses and waggons that gathered outside the kitchens. They had already begun to move off round to the south side of the bailey to begin the day's events when Adorna shifted back sharply.

'There's Sir Nicholas,' she said, 'getting the Yeomen into position. Now look, Belle, if we're quick about it, we can pack as much as we can carry and go after her before they all return. She's only had a few hours start and we may be able to find her before suppertime.'

'Go without an escort?'

'Well, it doesn't look as if *she* has one, and there's always Peter. He'll go with us, I'm sure of it.'

'Unless he's gone up to Staffordshire to prepare for tomorrow.'

'Without saying goodbye?'

'Why would he?' Maybelle's cynicism was justified, for their search revealed that Master Fowler had indeed left the castle. Making use of the plain and comfortable linen clothes that Maybelle had 'collected for repair' from the Wardrobe last night, they dressed in the manner of ordinary country women who might normally have been travelling to market on horseback, with a packhorse behind them bearing, among other necessities, food from the kitchens.

It was still a risk, lone women being targets for rogues, vagabonds and thieves on the loose, and had Adorna not been hopeful of overtaking Hester before nightfall, she would have hesitated to set off without a proper escort. Sensibly, she left her own palomino in the stables in favour of a large gentlemanly bay gelding which, she hoped, would be less conspicuous to fellow-travellers. The stable-lad had not thought of asking why, or refusing them the use of a sturdy cob for Maybelle and a packhorse with panniers. He had even helped them to load it, believing it to be a part of the disguisings that took place every day, in one form or another.

Danger, however, seemed remote in the bright morning sunshine, the main concern being Cousin Hester's safety, her vulnerability and the wretchedness she must be suffering It was up to Adorna to put the matter right, to explain that Sir Nicholas's interest was only likely to be temporary. She said as much to Maybelle as they tried, with limited success, to pass through the eastern gatehouse without being recognised.

'And you think that'll reassure her, do you?' said Maybelle, clapping her heels into the cob's chestnut flanks. 'What makes you think Mistress Hester will last longer than you? What makes you think she even has a chance?'

Adorna was empathic. 'She does. She adores him. Talks about him. Everything. It's obvious.'

'No, it's not,' Maybelle argued. 'These things have to be two-sided, you know. And anyway, you and Lady Marion were keen for her to pair up with Sir Nicholas at first. She's very obliging and dutiful. Perhaps she's simply been trying to oblige you.'

'You didn't see her face, Belle. She was shocked.'

'Well, that's not so surprising. How many times will she have seen a man and a woman together on a bed, d'ye think? I doubt Uncle Samuel and Aunt What's-her-name were much of an education.'

'And what about those letters? Why would she hide them?'

'Because she's never had any before, I expect. You did the same with your first love-letters, didn't you? Now, you just laugh and burn them. Anyway, you can't seriously believe they were from Sir Nicholas. It's not his way to send women love-letters.'

They were silent except for a cheery 'good morning' as they passed a cow-herd with two cows and their calves. Eventually, Adorna responded to Maybelle's reproof. 'Is that how I appear, Belle? Hard-hearted? Insensitive?'

Maybelle tugged at the packhorse's leading rein. 'No, love. 'Course not. I didn't mean that. I suppose what I'm saying is that you've had so much more attention than Mistress Hester that you've learned to ignore it, and I suppose that...' She sighed, wondering how to continue.

'That what?'

'That you could go on ignoring without ever finding out that it was the real thing. Sometimes you have to stand back and look at it a bit longer. I know I suggested trying the dropping game, but I've never known a man quite as determined to win you as Sir Nicholas, and I think he deserves more respect than that. Look at the way he's helped you and Master Seton out in the last few days. And at the water. And at the playhouse in London. And the masque.'

'Helped us *out*? Belle, what on earth are you talking

about? Because of him poking his nose in, I'm now in an impossible position that I don't know how on earth I'm going to get out of.'

'Then let him get you out of it. Trust him a bit more.'

'Trust him? Huh!'

'You're not seeing things too clear, are you? People in love see things differently, you know. They see things that are not there and they miss other things that are staring them in the face.'

'What things?'

But Maybelle felt she had said enough. 'Just things,' she said.

With more silence between them than chatter, they reached the town of Warwick well before mid-day without mishap. After a month of riding her skittish mare, Adorna was impressed by the gelding's perfect manners, his ability to anticipate commands, and his obedience at water-crossings. She welcomed the change from the flashy mare whose inclinations were far from predictable. Perhaps, she thought, the mare could have been better trained.

Following the River Avon did not turn out to be as inspired a decision as she had thought at Warwick for, only a few miles further on was a small town which, she told Maybelle, had not been there when they came north ten days ago.

'On the other hand,' Maybelle remarked, 'neither were we.'

They stopped at the sign of the White Lion for refreshment and discovered that they were at Stratford-upon-Avon, which made sense but was not what they wanted to hear.

'We're supposed to be at Banbury.' Adorna sighed.

'Well, how are we supposed to know? Intuition?'

'We've been going south-west instead of south-east. That's the trouble with the sun being overhead. It's no help at all.'

'So remind me, why are we heading for Banbury when for all we know Mistress Hester might be going anywhere?'

'Because,' Adorna replied sharply while preparing to mount, 'I don't have any of that intuition, either. It's the only place I can think of that she might be going, since it's south and so is Richmond.'

'But she might be—'

'Look, get on your horse, Belle, and stop arguing. We've lost valuable time.'

It was, however, further to Banbury than they thought, travelling at the pace of the loaded packhorse. As exhaustion slowed it down, the light began to fade and, as if to protest even further, the creature cast a shoe and began to limp. To be out in the middle of the countryside, alone, was no place for ladies.

With the greatest good fortune, they came to the beautiful pink-brick house of Compton Wynyates set in a deep hollow of green hills and surrounded by a glassy moat that shone pink and purple with the last of the evening light. The glowing serenity of the picture lured them on across the moat bridge where they were welcomed by Lord Henry Compton and his lady who knew Sir Thomas and Lady Marion Pickering and whose connections with the Royal Court stretched back many years. They had often entertained the Queen here and given hospitality to her officers on their progresses. Like kindly relatives, they welcomed the travellers and accepted their modified explanation as praiseworthy, if a little risky. Two extra mouths to feed at the high table were nothing at all in a household of over seventy.

At dawn, they were away on the road to Banbury with a fresh packhorse and the warm sun in their eyes, though now the possibility of finding Hester had grown more remote than ever. It was a ride of less than eight miles, yet they could not have known, as they approached the first of the whitewashed cottages from the west, that Sir Thomas Pickering's slow and cumbersome cavalcade of waggons was leaving Banbury from the south towards Oxford, which they hoped to reach by nightfall. After enquiring at all the most likely-looking inns, the two women found no indication that Hester had been there, and Adorna was then forced to agree that her cousin must have taken a different direction for reasons best known to herself.

As they rested outside an inn where the sign of the Swan hung above the doorway, something else was responsible for delaying them, a feeling that had been growing ever since dawn when they had broached the new day with only hours of peaceful riding ahead of them. Rather than having their time directed, manipulated and planned to fit each minute around the

Queen's entertainment, they now had no plans except to find Hester, few clothes to change into or out of, no noisy formal meals, meetings or evasions, no worries about Seton. They were free.

'I like it, Belle,' Adorna said, watching the world go by. 'Why don't we stay for a while? The Queen will probably think we've gone back with my father, if she notices at all.'

'Make our own way home? Yes, but what about Sir Nicholas? Is he going to come after you, d'ye think?'

There was the agreement, of course, which she had broken by removing herself from his sphere. He would not be best pleased about that. But, with all the miscreants gone perhaps he would think twice about revealing the deception, especially since he himself had helped in it, at the end. 'He can't,' she said to Maybelle. 'They'll be going on up to Staffordshire today. He has responsibilities. Let's go and pick up the horses; we have a brand new day to spend as we please.'

She was mistaken on one point and only half-right on another. Sir Nicholas's responsibilities could, in an emergency, be delegated. He approached the Master of Horse as soon as they returned to the stables and made some infuriating discoveries about Mistress Adorna Pickering and some of the horses. He had cuffed the stable-boy's ears for the blunder.

'I don't know what's going on, sir,' he said, 'but I think I'd better go and find out. Neither she nor Mistress Hester have gone with Sir Thomas, and her leaving the palomino suggests that she doesn't want to be recognised.'

'Not as well-stabled as you thought then, man. Maybe you should have bolted the door tighter, eh?'

'I intend to, sir, with your leave. Can Paddy and Osbern fill in for me till I get back?'

'Of course they can. They know what's to be done. Take your squire and two men with you for the horses. I wish she'd not taken one of the best high-school bays though, Nicholas. She'd better be taking good care of him. Damn women!'

'Then I'll set off straight away, sir. I can be at Banbury by dusk.'

'Go to it, man. I told you to use a tighter rein.'

'So you did, my lord. I shall attend to it.' He smiled.

'And Nicholas!' the earl called. 'Take your time. Best not to rush it!'

'Thank you, sir.'

A young woman and her maid emerged from the doorway beneath the sign of the Swan just as Adorna and Maybelle turned the corner of the cobbled yard that led to the stables at the rear. They missed each other by a whisker. Two horses, already saddled, were being led up to the stone mounting-block, though it was clear from the weariness on the woman's face that she was tired of riding and was not looking forward to more. 'Do we have everything?' she said to her maid.

'Everything. Shall we...? Why, what is it, my lady?'

'Wait!' The woman shaded her eyes against the sun, frowning a little as a group of three riders pulled up on the cobbles and dismounted, the tallest of them passing his reins to his squire as he looked keenly at her, his handsome face a picture of astonishment.

'Celia!' he whispered. 'No, it cannot be. Can it?'

She held out her kid-gloved hands, shaking her head. 'No, it cannot be *Nicholas*, of all people.' She laughed. 'What in the world are you doing here? You're supposed to be up at Kenilworth, aren't you?'

He took her hands in his as he had done in the paradise garden weeks ago. 'And you're supposed to be in Spain. Aren't you? What happened?' He shook her hands gently, noting the fatigue in her eyes.

Mistress Adorna Pickering and her maid rode round the corner of the inn at that very moment, ready to take to the road and glancing casually at the space they had so recently vacated, now crowded with horses and travellers. Though of a different order, Adorna's shock at seeing these two together was every bit as great as theirs had been, causing her involuntarily to pull the bay gelding to a sudden standstill. Maybelle's cob swerved to one side with a clatter of hooves and a snort of protest.

'Sir!' a young man's voice called.

Sir Nicholas turned sharply to look. 'Damn!' he snapped, softly. By the time he was back in the saddle, Adorna had dug her heels into the responsive bay and was away in one huge bound, leaving Maybelle to hold the packhorse and to exchange bewildered glances with the elegant woman in fashionable but dusty black.

The bay was willing, but its progress was far from straightforward through a narrow street bustling with traders, their carts and baskets, and the firm hand on its bridle soon brought it to a complete standstill.

'Let go, Sir Nicholas! Leave me! Go and tend your lady!' Adorna's voice was not loud, but already an amused audience had gathered to watch. Sir Nicholas was not inclined to give them a show, but instead hauled both horse and rider unceremoniously back to the Swan at a smart trot without a word of explanation. Then, before the astonished group, he pulled Adorna down out of the saddle and marched her boldly into the inn with his hand under arm. The woman in black followed, brimming with curiosity to see at closer quarters the one she had seen only from a distance, interested also to see how Nicholas would handle the situation. She had never seen him react quite so aggressively towards a woman before, and Mistress Pickering was indeed of a direct turn of mind, by the look of things, and very beautiful.

Fuming at this rough and humiliating treatment, Adorna turned on her captor as soon as the door-latch clicked shut. 'You have no right to do this, sir. If you think I want to know what your business is with this lady then you are mistaken. It's no concern of mine and I am no concern of yours. Now, allow me to go on my way, as I was about to do.'

The room was low-beamed and plastered between wooden supports, furnished only with a table and some stools and a sweet aroma of clean rushes on the floor. But in the light from the small-paned window, Adorna was able to see at last the face of Lady Celia Traverson whose name and shadowy form had been the cause of so much heartache, the woman who clearly had bonds with her former lover so acute that she had turned away from marriage for love of him. Well, what other explanation could there be? Her looks were quite remarkable, for she had a strong nose and high cheekbones that gave an impression of being able to make her own decisions. Her dark eyes, straight brows and firm full mouth were handsome rather than lovely. Her figure, Adorna saw at a glance, was superb, her full skirt of finest black velvet and puffed silk sleeves showing her to be a lady of great quality. The white lace ruff was large and quite inappropriate for long-distance journeys, but her rich brown hair was dressed exquisitely in a jewelled bilament that sat around her head and winked in the beams of sunlight. By contrast, the hem of her skirt was stained with dust from the road.

Lady Celia stripped off her kid gloves and laid them on the table before Sir Nicholas could reply. 'Mistress Pickering,' she said, 'please don't leave us without giving at least one of us a chance to explain.'

Still furious, Adorna was not open to suggestion. 'Thank you, Lady Celia, but neither of you owes me an explanation about anything. I'm really not—'

'All the same,' Sir Nicholas said, folding his arms and leaning against the door, 'one of us *is* going to explain and you *are* going to listen.'

Lady Celia was more diplomatic in her approach, seeing Adorna appreciate the sight she was presenting in contrast to her own, not to mention the treatment she alone had had to endure at Sir Nicholas's hands. Not that Mistress Pickering could be anything but lovely, whatever she wore, but her simple country-woman's dress of blue linsey-wolsey and padded doublet, the casually coiled hair in its netted caul, were a far cry from her usual modish appearance. 'Please, Nicholas,' said Lady Celia, 'will you leave us alone for a while? Women's talk? In this, I think we shall do better without you.'

'I'll wait outside,' he said, leaving them to it.

Still defensive and extremely angry, Adorna was determined not to be seen as the loser who must take the bad news with courage. Even so, she felt the sickness inside begin to grow as Lady Celia settled herself upon a stool and invited her to take the other. Seeing them together like that, hand in hand, had enraged Adorna, but she would not allow either of them to see how it hurt. 'Lady Celia,' she said, 'whatever you think, I have no claim whatever on Sir Nicholas and he has none on me. My maid and I were—'

Lady Celia placed a sympathetic hand upon Adorna's arm. 'Your maid and you were doing exactly what my maid and I are doing,' she smiled sadly. 'We are all seeking freedom, I believe, though in a way our freedom is also a refuge, isn't it?' She squeezed on Adorna's arm as she felt an interruption coming on. 'But you are mistaken in thinking that my meeting with Sir Nicholas was planned. On the contrary, it was as accidental as yours and mine. He supposed me to be halfway to Spain by now, but I spent last night here on the way to Stafford where I shall seek refuge with Lord and Lady Gifford. I'm running away, you see, like you, but for vastly different reasons. As I came out of the inn ready to go, Nicholas arrived looking for you, if I'm not mistaken. Well...' she smiled '...I'm *not* mistaken. He's been in love with you since before I left, and there'd be absolutely no point in me trying to reopen our relationship along those lines. None at all. It's been over for some time. Now I have to remove myself as far away from my father as I can, once he gets to know that I didn't sail for Spain as he intended. So you see, Nicholas came to find you, not to meet me.'

The relief almost swamped Adorna, stinging her eyes. 'Lady Celia,' she said, 'I'm so sorry. I misunderstood. Have you really abandoned your marriage to the Spanish duke?'

'Yes, I prefer to make my own choice of husband. I managed to escape at Portsmouth before we boarded, which is why—' she looked down at her dusty skirt '—I'm most unsuitably dressed. Not an easy ride, I can tell you.'

'But how do you know of Sir Nicholas's feelings towards me? He's never spoken of love, though he must have loved dozens of women. How can one take a man with his reputation seriously? You must be as aware of it as I am.'

'Reputations!' Lady Celia scoffed, gently. 'Show me a good-looking man at Her Majesty's Court who does not have a reputation for his friendships with women. They all do. Some deserved, some not. Look at Sir Christopher Hatton, for instance; even he doesn't escape scandal-mongers, though he's one of the most loyal and gentlemanly knights alive. And anyway, what's wrong with a man who knows how to love? Nicholas has never betrayed a woman, nor did he betray me. Nor have I ever known him to chase after a woman as he has done today, especially in the middle of a Queen's progress.' She laughed.

'Probably to recover the horses.'

'No. To recover you. There's a very determined look in his eye.'

'He doesn't like to be defeated, does he?'

'I wouldn't know, Mistress Adorna. But he did tell me that you were singularly unwilling. I see you still are, so I suppose there must be a very good reason.'

'Not one that Sir Nicholas appears to take seriously.'

'Would I understand, do you think? As a woman?'

Adorna could not help admiring this unique young lady in black. What courage she had to defy her parents, disappoint her unseen and unloving future husband and his foreign family, to fly off to seek her freedom over half the length of the country. What spirit. And what compassion, too, to explain to Adorna that she had no cause to misunderstand. 'Yes,' she said, 'you would understand. I think you would understand most things, and I believe that Sir Nicholas will be the poorer for allowing you to go.'

'It was mutual,' Lady Celia whispered. 'Different

religions, too. But what is it that holds you back, mistress? Is it pride, perhaps? You *do* have the distinction of being a sprinter, I believe.' Again her smile softened her words.

'Is that what's said about me?' *Why had it suddenly begun to matter?*

'"Not a stayer" is how the men put it. Crude, but you know what the men are like. They talk about the whole business as if we were either horses or goddesses. Personally, I prefer the first. It's more realistic, isn't it?'

Adorna felt, in those few moments, as if she was at last changing from a girl into a woman. What common sense this woman spoke. How matter-of-fact and yet sensitive. If she didn't like something, she changed it: if she did, she accepted it. 'Well,' Adorna said, 'I suppose they're probably right, though my reason for not staying the course is that I've not found a man who interests me. When I did, I heard that he was not a stayer, either. To be fair, Sir Nicholas tried to persuade me that that was not a true picture of himself, just as he tried to show me what I've been missing. But unfortunately the circumstances worked against us, and every time I came remotely close to changing my mind, something turned it all sour again. Jealousy, I suppose. And fear. They're both new to me. I don't know how best to deal with them.'

'Trust him, my dear. The best part is to come: the finding-out is something you'll want to lose so that you can find it out all over again. There's nothing in it to fear, not with Nicholas. And jealousy *is* fear, by the way. The two are the same thing. Go with him. You'll be quite safe.'

They stood up together and embraced as spontaneously as if they had been sisters. Adorna took Lady Celia's warm hands to her own. 'I envy you your courage, my lady. I shall think of you and pray for your safety. It must have been fate that brought us both to the Swan at Banbury on the same morning.' The same fate that had brought them so close at Richmond one night.

'Of course it was. Now,' she warned, 'not *too* pliable. Let him think he's still got something to work at, eh?'

They laughed, and were still laughing as they came out on to the inn's forecourt where the sun and Sir Nicholas were waiting for them.

Chapter Ten

Better protected than they had been so far, Lady Celia Traverson and her maid were launched unexpectedly into the last stages of their journey with the added escort of one of Sir Nicholas's men who had orders to deliver her safely to the door of the Giffords' home in Stafford. There, with one of the few remaining Roman Catholic families to be free of serious persecution, she would be able at last to make her own choice of husband.

Still under the influence of Lady Celia's short acquaintance, Adorna already felt that she had just lost a friend, a loss made even more poignant by Sir Nicholas's uncompromising control that showed no sign of abating. Far from offering her a chance to discuss what had been said in the inn, which he must have known concerned him, he appeared to take it for granted that an explanation had been given and accepted. He would neither add anything to it, nor gloat, nor ask for her reaction.

His sternness unsettled her as much this time as it

had before and did nothing to convince her of Lady Celia's statement that he was in love with her. If this present attitude was a sign of it, then the lady was obviously in possession of some evidence that she was not. Twice in the last twenty-four hours, Adorna had been advised to trust him, yet in his present mood he appeared to be quite indifferent to the chance of any change in her opinion of him.

She watched him silently checking the gelding's stirrup-leathers, girth and bridle with sure strong hands, pulling at the forelock to tidy it. He was dressed in workmanlike clothes, but no less elegant for that, buff-coloured suede breeches that ended below the knee, a brown leather doublet under a padded buff jerkin, a white shirt, open-fronted. She tore her eyes away as he suddenly confronted her.

'Now,' he said, skimming her bare neck with a cool appraisal, 'we can catch Sir Thomas's party if we get a move on.'

Instantly, his tone rubbed her up the wrong way. She had a right to be consulted. 'I do not intend to catch my father up, sir,' she said. 'I am going my own way.' She gathered the reins up into her left hand.

'You are going my way, mistress, like it or not.'

'Sir Nicholas, I cannot imagine how I have managed these last twenty years without your interference, but I shall keep trying. Now, will you please help me to mount, if that is what you intend to do, and then leave me alone.'

'Very well, let's see how far you get before you come back.'

Taken aback by his sudden reversal, Adorna swallowed her sudden misgivings. She had intended to show some appeasement, but he was giving her little chance in this matter of where she should go. She allowed him to help her into the saddle and then, with a curt nod of thanks and farewell, signalled Maybelle to follow her away from the inn in the opposite direction from that taken by Lady Celia. She had not gone more than twenty paces along the busy street when a distant whistle made the gelding's ears swing wildly backwards and forwards. He stopped dead in his tracks and turned about to face the way they had come, despite all she could do to stop him and move him forward.

'No!' she shouted, kicking with her heels. 'What's the matter with you? Get on...this way...stupid horse!' But he snatched at the bit and trotted disobediently back to the inn, ignoring every one of her commands and oblivious to her humiliation. Sir Nicholas was mounted, waiting for them. 'You wretch!' she yelled. 'This is your doing!'

'Stop fighting him or he'll throw you off. Come on. I told you. We go my way.' Quickly, he leaned and pulled at one of the gelding's glossy ears. 'Well done, boy,' he said, laughing.

Adorna was close to tears. 'I don't *want* to travel with my father,' she snarled. 'We're looking for Cousin Hester, and we're just beginning to enjoy a taste of freedom. If Lady Celia can be allowed her freedom, why can't I?' She knew the answer before she asked it. Lady Celia was running because she had courage: she herself was running because she was afraid. She had yet to discover the exact reason for Hester's escape.

'Then I'll help you to taste it. How will Aylesbury do for a start?'

She had no idea where Aylesbury was except that there were ducks there, but the temptation to reject his suggestion was by now almost second nature. 'No,' she said, knowing that he would ask for an alternative.

'Then where?'

'The Thames,' she said, on impulse. It was the river that flowed through Richmond. 'I intended to follow the River Thames to home.'

'Then it's a good thing you didn't get far just now or you'd have been in Scotland before you realised it.'

'Don't exaggerate!'

'All right, so we'll pick up the Thames and follow it to Richmond. We should be home by about Christmas.'

Now that *was* an exaggeration, and well he knew it, but it made the two men and Maybelle smile. It did not, however, make Adorna smile. 'Sir Nicholas,' she said, low-voiced.

He noted the lingering uncertainty, the one glistening teardrop clinging to her lower lashes, the top lip pulled in and let go, and he guessed what had taken place with Celia in the inn room. They were both remarkable women; their conversation would have reflected that. He moved away to one side, leading her horse. 'What is it?' he said, knowing what it was.

'It was Cousin Hester I came looking for,' she said.

'Yes, and it was you I came looking for, as you know.'

'Do I?'

'You know you do. But there's no need to continue the search for Hester, because I happen to know that she is not alone, or lost, or in any danger.'

'What? You know where she is?'

'I didn't say that. I made some enquiries before I left and now I have a reasonably clear picture of what's happened. She's with somebody.'

'An admirer?'

'Yes.'

'She's been abducted? Merciful heavens!'

'On the contrary, she's been planning this for some time. And that's all I shall tell you except to say that by the time we reach home, Hester and her companion will probably be there, or in London. Now stop worrying about her moral welfare. She's not nearly as helpless as you appear to think.'

'But she *is*! She's—'

'No, she's not. I've known her longer than you. She's as tough as old boots. Naïve, I grant you, but she'll be a bit more worldly by the time we catch up with her.'

'You mean…? Oh, dear, I should never have allowed her to run off like that.'

'Look, clear your mind of this business once and for all, Adorna. What she saw had no bearing on what she decided to do, I tell you. I'm quite convinced she intended to make a run for it well before that.'

'How d'ye know?'

'I know. And now your search for her has developed into something else, hasn't it? A few days of freedom, eh? Without me to curb you?'

She stared hard at the glossy mane before her and felt the shift of the horse as he changed his resting-leg. 'I was enjoying myself,' she retorted. 'I need to be alone, to sort myself out without—'

'Interference?' He smiled wickedly at the thought. 'Well, that's something you're going to have to put up with, because we made an agreement, remember, which you have already broken.'

'Which I suppose puts me at a disadvantage again.'

'It puts you, Adorna, in the position of being my wife for the purposes of this journey, at least. Unless, of course, you prefer to be known as my mistress? I have no objection to that. You understand what I'm saying?'

Their eyes met at last, each reading the other, hers in bright sunshine and his in the shadow of his black velvet cap, but as compelling as that first day by the Thames when he had told her that there was nothing here that a little gentle schooling could not cure.

She knew what he was saying, and the hair prickled at the back of her neck. Her eyes lowered meekly as she nodded, an almost imperceptible movement that belied the defiant set of her mouth.

'Lady Adorna,' he said. 'Sounds good. Looks good, too.' He viewed with some appreciation the countrified dress which, although full-skirted, was clearly not supported by the rigid whalebone bodice she usually wore. Now, her beautiful contours filled the soft fabric with the natural lusciousness of young womanhood and her neck, without a lace ruff to hide it, had begun to soak up the sun and the breeze.

Flustered by her new status and by his scrutiny, she tucked stray wisps of hair back into her caul and wished she had paid more attention to her toilette.

'One more thing before we go,' said Sir Nicholas. He passed her a small velvet bag. 'Find a convenient moment to put that on some time today. It will avoid the need for explanations.'

She took it without question, for she recognised the bag as belonging to Leicester's Men, having worn its contents in her role as Beatrice when she had married Benedict. 'I hope Master Burbage won't mind,' she said, attempting to make light of it. But the situation had become almost too serious for quips and, as they moved off at last, it escaped neither of them that they presented a perfect picture of a genteel married couple travelling with a maid, a squire, a groom and a pack-horse, apparently at peace with each other and the world.

Although this was a development she had not anticipated, it took only a mile or so for her to admit that having men in the party made a vast difference to their comfort. Fellow-travellers instantly moved to one side of the track instead of forcing them off; no one made ribald remarks, asked them where they were going, or suggested that they might need company. One look at the men's array of scabbards hanging from belts made the deference due to a lord and his lady a foregone conclusion. She felt as safe and protected as she had when she had ridden pillion behind him only a few days ago.

On the other hand, their relationship had now entered a new and potentially conclusive stage, for he was clearly expecting from her a commitment she had never faced before, the giving up of something she held dear, claimed by a man used to winning. Understandably, she was worried and apprehensive, despite Lady Celia's second-hand revelation that he was in love with her, which came without any form of guarantee. One worry was out of the way, however; the problem of Lady Celia herself was now over, their friendship understandable, acceptable, and in no way threatening. In fact, Adorna mused, their meeting had been a godsend.

It was late in the day when they emerged from the woodland below Woodstock and came at last to the top curve of the River Thames where the water level was low enough for them to wade across to the opposite side.

'Not far now,' Sir Nicholas told them.

'How far is not far?' Adorna said, wearily.

'Another mile, that's all. There's an inn at Wytham.'

Nestling on the edge of the great wood at Wytham, the White Hart was small but welcoming, the landlord overjoyed to see prestigious travellers on his side of the river. 'They usually choose Oxford on the other side, m'lady,' he said to Adorna. 'Never enough bridges, that's the problem. Come inside if you will, sir. My goodwife will show your lady to the rooms. Clean sheets on all the beds. No need to share. This way, m'lady.' His shining bald head led them to the small but clean parlour where the goodwife curtsied, tying on a clean pinafore.

There was an aroma of new-baked bread in the creaking oak-lined passageway, the faintest whiff of woodsmoke along the staircase, and newly cut rushes in the small bedchamber. The goodwife opened a small window just above floor level, letting in the distant sound of a mill-wheel slowing, then stopping. 'Ye can have both rooms up here, if you wish,' she told Adorna, patting the blanketed tester-bed. 'This one is the biggest. The two men can sleep above the 'osses in the stable. Now, what'll you have for your supper, m'lady? We have roast pigeons, pickled beef, mutton pie, a cheese and egg pasty and new bread. Or perhaps you'd prefer a chimney-smoked gammon with garlic and turnips?'

'No garlic,' said Sir Nicholas, entering the room unexpectedly.

Adorna smiled at the goodwife's astonishment. 'The men will be hungry by the time they've seen to the horses,' she said. 'I dare say they'll make short work of whatever you have. We'll be down presently.'

She bobbed another curtsy, looked sideways at Sir Nicholas, and closed the door mumbling, 'No garlic! Tch!'

'Where's Maybelle?' Adorna said. 'I need her.'

The room was not as large as the goodwife had implied, the oak beams only just clearing Sir Nicholas's head and allowing the canopied top of the tester-bed to fit cosily between two of the great timbers. He ducked, cautiously. 'She's chatting up Perkin still,' he said. 'They're getting on rather well, hadn't you noticed?'

'Then there's going to be trouble; there's a young man called David at the palace.' She turned away, suddenly confused by his nearness.

'David has gone back to France with his master.' His voice dropped to a whisper. 'Speaking of which—' he came to stand behind her with his arms enclosing her shoulders '—don't get any ideas about Belle sleeping in here. This is where *your* master sleeps.'

She stopped his caressing hands with her own. 'Hasn't this gone far enough, sir?' she whispered, hearing him smile.

'Good try,' he said, kissing her sun-warmed neck. 'But no, it hasn't. Not nearly far enough.'

With determination that he clearly did not expect, she lifted his arms and shook herself free. 'No,' she said. 'No!' She turned to face him, looking everywhere except into his eyes. 'This is *not* how it should be.' Her voice wavered, searching uncertainly for the words.

He took her face tenderly in his hands as if it might break and held it until her gaze settled upon him at last. 'Tell me,' he said softly. 'Tell me how it should be.'

'I swore...' she began as if reluctantly parting with a secret.

'Yes?'

'I swore I'd make it hard for you.' She took his hands away and held them together before her. 'And now…look at this…' Her eyes skimmed the room. 'Look at me…cornered! Trapped!'

'You think it's been *easy* to get you this far, lass? Take my word for it, it hasn't.'

'I don't know. All I know is that I've ridden dutifully with you all day and now I'm expected to eat dutifully with you downstairs and make dutiful wifely conversation and then come dutifully back up here and let you…dutifully…' Tears brimmed, squeaking the words. 'And that's *not* how it should be. If I have to give myself to you, I'm damned if I'll give it to you here…' she glared at the bed '…where everyone knows what's happening. What choice do I have?' she croaked. 'Four walls. A locked door. How difficult will *that* be for you? Have you ever had it easier?'

He would not give her the answer to that. Not yet. 'Don't say any more,' he said, keeping her hands. 'I understand. What we need, I think, is some exercise. We'll take a walk after supper, shall we? There's still some hours of light left.'

Adorna nodded, breathing out at last. 'Yes.'

'And you can lead. And I'll follow.'

'Yes.'

'And you can be as bloody difficult as you like. Yes?'

A huff of laughter escaped as she brushed a tear away. 'You're not supposed to understand,' she said. 'You're a man.'

'I'm sorry. I'll try harder next time.'

So after the roast pigeons, the new bread, the cam-
embert cheese, baked apples, cream and ale, but no
garlic, Adorna excused herself and left the parlour.

'Should I go with her?' Maybelle asked Sir Nicholas.

He rose to his feet. 'No, go to bed, all of you.
There's a fair way to go tomorrow.'

But beyond the garden and the dovecote besieged
with plump white pigeons, Adorna crossed the wooden
bridge over the stream into the meadow where a path
ran along the riverside. The innkeeper had mentioned
an abbey; Godstow Abbey, ruined for many years;
they would have passed it and seen it but for the trees.
The grass here was already shin-high, waiting for hay-
time.

The trees soon enclosed her again, shading the river
with black shadows, and soon the stone walls of the
old nunnery appeared as if by magic in a sheltered
clearing, massive foundations rising up steeply to tow-
ering reminders of security and peace. How ironic,
then, that she should seek her last vestiges of freedom
in such a place where nuns had forfeited theirs. Each
for their own reason, as Lady Celia had said.

Slowly, she picked her way over wide rubble-filled
walls now level with the grass and smoothed with
time, moss and lichen, shading her eyes as the low sun
shafted orange light through branches and pointed
arches. She stood to listen to the last call of the birds,
comparing this new tranquillity to the last frenetic

weeks, to her most recent burst of anger and resentment, and to her apprehensions which seemed now to have lost their sting. *There's nothing to fear with Nicholas*, Lady Celia had told her.

Beyond the ruined eastern end of the scattered conventual buildings was an open space, part enclosed by a stone wall where ridges of once-cultivated ground showed that this had been a small garden. It was private, secluded, warmed by the sun, where wild roses flung themselves about in heaps and overpowered the leggy mallow, one of whose pink flowers she plucked and held to her breast. Then she stood by a large stone and waited. This would be the place and no other.

He must have been watching from close by for he appeared almost immediately, like a moving shadow, slowly, as if half-expecting her to leap away like a doe in a clearing. He stopped a few paces from her. 'Now, my beauty,' he whispered, 'is this to be the place?' He moved slowly towards her. 'Perfect for wild creatures, eh, lass? Stand still...softly...' He reached out a hand and pulled at the open-mesh caul that held her hair, shaking it loose in a white gold flood down one shoulder to her waist.

She knew he would have seen the mallow flower trembling in her hand, but there was no trace of frivolity in his manner nor even of the harshness he had brought to their meeting earlier that day. The quaking flower was removed from her fingers and its stem was woven amongst the strands of gold. 'There,' he said, taking her hands and kissing the knuckles, 'you'll need these, I think. What do you remember, I wonder? Anything?'

'Very little,' she said, speaking to his hands, 'except the headache afterwards.'

He smiled at that. 'Shall I tell you what I remember?'

'Best not to,' she said, looking away.

His knuckle brought her back to face him. 'I remember the most stunningly beautiful and headstrong woman I've ever met,' he said, softly, 'lying by my side after an evening of opposition and showing me a part of herself that she'd tried hard for a long time to convince me didn't exist. Yet I knew it did, and I wanted to prove it to her. And I find she doesn't remember much, which is just as well because now...' he lifted her into his arms '...I can prove it to her all over again.'

He placed her in a shadowy corner of the garden upon a soft mossy bed warmed by the sun, and it was here that their kisses, held off for so long, came together like a star-burst in which all their doubts, misunderstandings and schemes faded, replaced by sensations that had been left starved and wanting till now. He had intended gentleness; she had feared revenge for his waiting; yet what emerged in the blind heat of their union was an amalgam of all this and so much more that Adorna's fears became joys, his intentions merely preludes to the next fiery duet. As with their dancing, they partnered each other in a perfect accord that neither of them could have predicted.

Once, at the beginning, she took hold of the hand

that untied her laces, delaying its investigations. But his lips on hers diverted her while he proceeded, skin touching skin, fingertips, palms, lips, teeth and tongue, her breasts coming alive with an urge that touched chords in every part of her being. 'Nicholas!' she cried. Just that. But the birds in the trees above fell silent, listening.

The wide expanse beneath his shirt would alone have been enough for an afternoon's exploration but, combined with her own body's new experiences, the excitement drew her on faster, ever faster. When his hand slid down over her hips and groin to the warm cavern between her legs, a vague memory of fear dissipated in a groan of ecstasy. Her hands on his back curled into claws that dug into his firm flesh, and she arched against his searching hand, turning her face into the tumbled mass of her hair. Panting, she cried out to him, 'Nicholas! I want you…now, now!'

Her legs opened as he nudged them apart with his knee. 'Lift them, sweetheart. Wrap them round me, that's it…easy.'

She was moist and ready, but had not been prepared by anything her mother had told her for the almost frightening experience of having another body so close to that most isolated of all parts. She cried out, not with pain but with shock as she felt the gentle invasion, the insistence, the first surging thrust, the incredible locking, the hunch of his body over hers, the tender male weight of him, his restricting arms, his pulling her into him with a hand under her back. His control. Her breathing shuddered to a stop.

'Sweetheart, I hurt you?'

'No,' she said, getting her breath back.

'You cried out.'

'Did I? Is this it, Nicholas?'

He smiled and began to move, heady with victory. 'Yes, my beauty. This is it.'

Her mother, come to think of it, had missed out so much of the whole business of loving that Adorna, lying quietly in his arms afterwards, felt bound to mention the uselessness of similes as opposed to hard facts. 'Rather like a warm bath, she told me. Really!' she said, combing his chest with her fingertips.

'And was it? Like a warm bath?'

'Nothing at all like a warm bath unless you take one in the middle of a blizzard, just for the excitement.'

He raised himself onto his elbows to look down on her, 'Well, it can be, if you want it to. Every time is different, or it should be, if the man is doing his job properly. And that was quite exceptional.'

'Was it? For you, too?'

'Unbelievably good. As I knew it would be. So now we could go back to the inn and try that warm bath experience, if you like.'

'In bed?'

'Just for comparison.'

Later, as they strolled back through the darkening meadow, he teased her just a little. 'And *are* you going to be bloody difficult, or was that as bad as it gets?'

'I'm saving it,' she said, perversely, 'for tomorrow.'

'Forewarned is forearmed then, my lady.'

For the rest of that night, she was more than willing to be led and to be introduced to the slow and leisurely loving of Lady Marion's—probably recent—experience that verified Sir Nicholas's assurance that the variations on the theme were endless. In the warm and comfortable darkness without a shred of clothing to inhibit them, they used their heightened senses to discover what had previously only been hinted at. Hands caressed and fondled to the brink of rapture and beyond, the control that Adorna had balked at now so sweet that there was no part of her that she would not allow him to explore. That alone, she told him shyly, was sheer bliss, not having believed it could be so exquisite.

He raised his head from her breast. '"And so my love protesting came, but yet I made her mine,"' he quoted, 'but not without a fight. Perhaps that should have been written on the other side of the roundel.' He resumed his teasing of her other nipple.

'You are bragging,' she warned. 'And pride cometh before a fall, sir.'

Inch by inch his mouth moved upwards until it reached her mouth. 'I have your measure, my lady,' he growled. 'I can handle you.' His kiss was both commanding and possessive, meant to show that, even in teasing talk, she had capitulated and he was the winner. Her silence confirmed his claim. 'Good,' he whispered. 'Open your legs.'

Excited as much by his fierce command as by the hard bulge of his muscular shoulders, she received him willingly yet tried to remain passive and unresponsive in the face of his boast. It did not work, for his exceptional tenderness was the last thing she had expected from him, and soon she was drawn like a reluctant dancer into the rhythm of his body, sharing every moment, following his lead, crying out at the gathering speed that only he could control.

It burst upon her without warning, whirling her away into space and keeping her breath deep in her lungs as the beat slowed and swirled away into her thighs. Dizzy and exhilarated, she lay beneath him as the warm flood of exhaustion overtook her, and she rocked him in her arms as his exceptional vigour ebbed into deep languor. Seamlessly, sleep overtook them.

Waking at intervals during the night by the strangeness of the large male body at her side, Adorna asked herself over and over why she had wanted to evade him and how strong were her reasons. The main stumbling block had been dealt with in one chance meeting that very morning, and she had been urged to trust him. But did she dare? Had he threatened her with exposure if she didn't co-operate? She knew that he had not, though he had gone along with her pretence because it suited him to. And she had proposed it because, in her heart, she wanted an excuse to surrender. And now she had surrendered, what would be the outcome? Abandonment and disgrace? Or life with the only man she had ever wanted?

She turned to him and snuggled deep into him, marvelling at the unaccustomed hardness of his welcoming arms, plotting the rise and fall of his powerful chest under her hand. What if she bore his child? Would that be enough to keep him? Had other women had the same ambitions? Well, if this was what she wanted to hold for life, and it was, then she would have to make sure of keeping his interest. Not too pliable.

'You knew of the White Hart Inn beforehand, Sir Nicholas?' Adorna said as they rode away next morning. She tried, unsuccessfully, to keep the extra curiosity out of her voice.

His mouth twitched but his eyes looked straight ahead. 'This area belongs to the Earl of Leicester,' he said. 'Near here is another inn called the Bear and the Ragged Staff. His arms, you remember. And at nearby Cumnor is the house where he and his first wife lived until her death. I've visited all his lordship's properties, for one reason or another.'

'For one reason or another?'

He caught her eyes and held them, amused rather than critical. 'Yes, lady. On my lord's business. Anything else?'

'And now we head for...where is it? Abbey?'

'Abingdon.' His smile broke as he recognised her train of thought. 'We pass through Radley where Lord Thomas Seymour lived.'

Adorna remained silent. She had heard tales of Seymour, Lord High Admiral, the Queen's handsome and foolish late uncle. Everyone had. Poor young Elizabeth. Her love life in ruins, despite all Leicester's attempts.

Sir Nicholas's observation regarding Maybelle and his man Perkin had not been exaggerated, the young man's interest in the vivacious maid being every bit as keen as hers in him. The development suited Adorna well enough, for it kept Belle's curiosity about her mistress well in check. Young Perkin, a solid, bold and efficient man, was well able to make best use of his time with Maybelle and to keep her occupied while his master and Lady Adorna went off on their own with Lytton, the squire, to hold the horses.

Their journey to Abingdon took them along the riverside path through woodland and lush meadow, past thick hedgerows, wading knee-deep in fallen blossom, buttercups and meadowsweet. But his authority still caused Adorna some contradictory emotions, for while she loved his masculine assuredness, she did not care to be anticipated on every point, nor for him to know what she wanted better than she knew herself. Not even her father went so far. Last night, that had been close to the truth, but telling her that she would like Abingdon was stretching her new-found compliance too far. She would *not* like Abingdon. She had no intention of liking it. She told him so.

'I don't know why we're here at all,' she said, crossly, pulling the bay to one side as an ox-team and waggon lumbered past without any apparent form of steering.

'We're here,' Sir Nicholas said, 'because you wanted to follow the Isis all the way to Richmond.'

'I didn't want to follow the Isis,' she snapped. 'I wanted to follow the Thames. How could you—?'

'The Isis *is* the Thames, woman!' he snapped back. 'It's called the Isis on this stretch of Oxfordshire. And pull your horse out of the middle of the road.'

'But we've been heading west for the last half-hour. Look at the sun.'

He groaned. 'Well, that's because the river doesn't flow in a straight line like a Roman road,' he said, pulling at the bay's bridle. 'Come. If you don't want to stay here we'll move on down the river, though what's wrong with Abingdon I can't imagine. Sounds like a clear-cut case of that bloody-mindedness you promised me. Is it?'

Denying him an instant confirmation, Adorna had already taken a route away from the track and was following the river southwards which, she mumbled under her breath, since they couldn't go east, was better than going west. Suspecting that he knew at least one good reason for her rebelliousness, Sir Nicholas rode alongside her without comment for a mile or so until, quite out of the blue, she spoke to him in a low voice. 'I'm sorry. There's nothing wrong with Abingdon. It's just...' she shrugged her shoulders '...I don't know.'

'I think I do, though,' he said, smiling.

She glanced at him and saw the laughter in his jasper eyes, a look that sent waves of pink upwards into her cheeks.

'It's all right,' he said. 'You're allowed to take the reins occasionally.'

'As long as it doesn't interfere with your plans.'

'Easy, my lass. Easy,' he whispered.

Nevertheless, she could not help thinking that, on this matter, she had taken the reins into her own hands only to ride along his chosen route by default, for the small village of Kings Sutton, which lay less than two miles south from Abingdon, was owned by Sir Nicholas's father, Lord Elyot. The manor house there was kept in a habitable state for his periodic use and, as they arrived, only the steward, the bailiff and a handful of servants were there, as delighted to see Sir Nicholas and the lady as he was to find somewhere, at last, which she appeared to like.

In all conscience, she could not have objected to the delightful old place where buildings had once been erected to provide a retreat and convalescent home for monks from Abingdon Abbey. The old Abbots' House had been their country retreat set in a secluded garden bordered by limes, elms and yew. The ancient church stood beside what had now become the manor house.

'Will this do for the night?' he said, lifting her down from the saddle.

'Better,' she said. 'Much better, I thank you.'

But although the fine oak-panelled chambers lacked nothing in comfort, it was to the scented and well-tended garden that Adorna went alone after a private supper when Sir Nicholas believed she had gone upstairs. The sun touched the horizon in a ball of fire, and the tall trees awaited with open arms for the last crows to settle into their lacy spaces. In the mirrored pond the lilies had closed for the night, and a lone blackbird warned its mates from a rosemary bush that something was astir. Adorna felt it, too.

'You,' she said to the shadowy figure that approached, soundlessly.

'There was a time,' he said, reaching her, 'only a few nights ago, when I stood in the paradise at Kenilworth Castle to wait for a certain woman who declined to come to me.' He took her hands in his. 'And I have an inkling, just an inkling mind, that this certain woman...'

'Who shall be nameless.'

'...who shall be nameless, may be trying to put that right by coming to this private monks' paradise, and to the nuns' paradise at Godstow, to wait for *me*. I wonder if that's what could be happening.'

It was still light enough for him to see her smile at that. 'You may wonder, sir, if you wish, but the woman may have quite a different reason for drawing her lover into such a place.'

'Is that so? Will she tell me, d'ye think?'

'Eventually. If all goes according to her wishes.'

'Ah, so she has wishes, does she?' He pulled at her hands and held her close. 'So I must try not to divert her, is that it?'

'She would prefer to be humoured on this, I believe.'

'This is indeed gentler talk, lady. There was also a time when she would have insisted, stridently. She would have flayed me with her tongue, told me that she didn't care one way or the other.'

'She cares, sir,' she said, breathing the words on to his cheek like a kiss.

He seemed to hold his breath and let it out so carefully that she could not tell whether it was a sigh or a gasp. His arms tightened about her like the approaching darkness. 'Again,' he said. 'Tell me again.'

She lifted her arms to caress his wide shoulders, her hands skimming his hair, his ears. 'She cares, Nicholas. How could she not care?'

'Sweetheart.' His kisses rained on her face and throat, bathing her in his delight, while she marvelled that he should be so affected when her words were still so minimal and when he must have received the unqualified adoration of many another woman.

He carried her at last through the hall of the timber-framed house where an old servant ignored them, up into their chamber. With barely enough light from the pale glow in the sky, Nicholas unwrapped her as if she were the most precious and delicate parcel, slowly prolonging the discovery of her body as if for the first time, caressing each beautiful limb and mound.

Wrapped only in her hair, she stood naked before him, melting at his touch and vaguely recalling the time when, in her room at Richmond, she had imagined this occasion without knowing anything of its realities. Deftly, her fingers went to work on his fastenings, each revelation punctuated by her lengthy examination of his magnificent body, an examination that involved lips as well as hands. She had never known that a man's body could be so comely, so well proportioned or so impressively virile, nor had she understood that the mechanics worked so obviously fast until now. Overawed, she hesitated as the phenomenon was revealed, not sure how to continue.

'I could make love to you with my boots *on*,' he offered, pushing at his knee-length breeches, 'if you wish.' He pulled them off and threw them aside in a tangle, reaching out for her in one smooth movement.

But she held him off, laughing at his impatience. 'I thought one of us,' she said, holding his hands, 'had unlimited control. I thought…'

'Correction,' he whispered, lifting her off the floor, 'one of us has more than the other, but only at certain times. And this is—'

'Not one of—?'

'Those times.' He placed her on the bed, but already the waiting had stretched beyond breaking-point and, making up for every moment when they had each burned for the other, their consummation could be delayed no longer. She was as fierce as he, urging him on with a relentlessness that brought them both to a shattering release even before the linen sheet had been warmed by their bodies.

Groaning, he lay softly upon her, still throbbing and as amazed by her fervour as by his own sudden inability to prolong the act. 'What have you done to me, woman?' he said. 'That's not happened to me since I was sixteen.'

Adorna lay smiling into the smooth warm patch of skin behind his ear, and he took her silence for exhaustion. Which was not entirely the case.

* * *

By early morning they had left behind the idyllic manor and paradise at Kings Sutton to follow the winding river eastwards through Appleford. From here, they cut across a loop of the river and left the horses with young Master Lytton to climb to the top of a hill where a clump of beeches huddled together. 'Like a tuft of hair on a bald man's head,' Adorna said, merrily. Hand in hand, she and Maybelle were pulled along by the two men, preventing them from lifting their skirts, tripping them into the long grass from where they had to be hauled, speechless with laughter. Sheep stared, then walked away, munching. The top of the hill gave them panoramic views across a plain ridged with small hills, and the river like molten silver weaving through them.

'Over there, to the right. See,' Sir Nicholas said, 'in the distance, that's Wallingford.'

Adorna shaded her eyes. 'I wonder where Hester is,' she murmured. She had had her hair plaited into one long rope that hung to her waist, and she wore another simple gown of dusky rose pink, already tasting the freedom she had once been sure she would lose by accepting Sir Nicholas's escort. She could never have travelled like this in her father's company. Or Peter's. Maybelle had remarked on her mistress's new vivacity, but she herself was in love and had found a new sparkle for her laughing eyes. The separate rooms had allowed them little time together to explore the consequences, yet here on the hilltop they both saw an opportunity at last. 'I think it's time we had a dip in that water,' Adorna said. 'Can we escape them, d'ye think?'

An hour later they came to a secluded bend in the river, sheltered on one side by trees where the sun had warmed slow-moving pools. Rocks and sandy slopes provided little bays for undressing, and it was here that the two women left their clothes and entered the tepid brown water, gulping and puffing at the coolness that crept upwards and clung to their bodies. Further in, they pirouetted and splashed, rubbing themselves down with handfuls of moss, then floating down on the slow current to the bend, protesting mildly at the change in temperature. They turned to go back, but Maybelle touched Adorna's arm, signalling her to silence and patting the water. 'Keep down,' she whispered.

Looking in the direction of Maybelle's wide-eyed stare, Adorna saw that, further round the bend and hidden from their own entry into the river, the heads and shoulders of two people were clearly visible, closely entwined beneath the water and quite oblivious to their amazed audience. A man and a woman, shining and sleek as fish.

But for their overpowering curiosity, the two women would have quietly departed, but the intimate scene held them transfixed as the woman's arms wrapped and clung. She threw her head back in ecstasy as the man's dark head bent to her throat and then, with her straddling him like a child, he carried her to the shallows and lay upon her.

Adorna and Maybelle turned at once and waded back to their clothes, their hearts beating like tabors. 'It's Mistress Hester,' Maybelle said. 'I'd swear it.'

'With Master Peter Fowler,' said Adorna, grabbing at her petticoat. 'Master Peter Two-faced Fowler and Cousin Oh-so-shy Hester. *Well, well!*'

Chapter Eleven

'You knew!' Adorna scolded, sitting under a tree to have the tangles combed out of her hair. 'You knew it was him, so why could you not have told me?'

Bare to his waist, Sir Nicholas removed the comb from Maybelle's hand and signalled her to go. 'What good would it have done? Would it have made you any happier to know?' he said.

'That's not the point.'

'Then what is the point? He's an ambitious young rascal, but if he's what Hester wants, then where's the problem? She doesn't require anyone's permission, not even Uncle Samuel's. She can do as she likes.'

'She has no *experience* of men.'

'Well, she has now.' He grinned. 'What exactly *were* they doing?'

'Oh—men!' She snatched her hair away and held him off. 'Trust a man to miss the point entirely. He's taking advantage of her, can't you see?' She tried to evade him, but his arm across her shoulders threw her sideways into the grass, and she was caught beneath him with her damp hair like a veil of gauze over her face.

He held her hands away, enjoying her anger. 'While you, my fierce little filly, saw nothing amiss in taking advantage of Hester's inexperience, did you? Or of Fowler's so-called protection?'

'What do you mean? Let me up!'

'No. You'll stay here till we've had this out.'

'I shall not say a word, damn you.'

'Yes, you will. Now, what's all this righteous indignation about, eh? You're hopping mad because you tried to manipulate Hester and she decided to manipulate herself instead. Is that it? You tried to use Fowler to keep me at a distance and, when it didn't have the desired effect, he didn't stay around to mope for you as you expected him to do, but went dashing off after a more lucrative prize instead. So now you're mad at him, too, for being so quick off the mark. Did you really expect them to ask your permission, lass?'

'I'm not! I didn't!' she yelled. 'I don't care a damn what they do. They can do it on horseback for all I care, but why did they have to be so deceitful about it? Why did Hester make out she was interested in *you*? Why did Peter—pretend?'

'Why did either of them pretend?' he said, removing a strand of her hair to reveal an angry eye. 'Because they balked at telling you they didn't like your plan, I expect.'

'There *was* no plan!'

'Of course there was. D'ye think I don't know how you and Lady Marion tried to pair me off with Hester?

Or how you steered her in my direction and groomed her to try to make her more interesting? Then it began to get out of hand, didn't it?'

'That's most unfair! We wanted to help her to be more comfortable with our guests. All of them. She wasn't at ease in crowds.'

'Well, that's not changed, by the look of things. She couldn't wait to skip off alone, in spite of your help. And that's exactly what *you* wanted to do, isn't it?'

'On my own, sir, not with a lover. Not with anybody.'

'Which is what you've always done,' he continued, ignoring her interruption. 'Run away and hide when the going gets rough, when a man shows too much interest. Panic. Run home. Surround yourself with family and safe things so that you can avoid making any kind of commitment. Eh?'

'It's not like that,' she whispered, turning her head away, furious to be so misinterpreted. Yet how could she tell him that it was not simply a case of avoiding a commitment but evading men she didn't want to be with for more than an hour or two? Until now. To explain that to him, she would have to confess at least some of her feelings for him, and that was something she had no intention of doing. How could she, without first knowing for sure whether his pursuit of her was a temporary or a permanent one? She had watched his farewell to Lady Celia in the paradise at Richmond, and could share the woman's pain as if it had been her own.

'It's *not* like that,' she repeated, rounding on him.

'What d'ye think I've been doing these last few days if not making a commitment? You've had three whole days of my company, which is something no other man has ever had, and you were glad enough to take advantage of that, so it seemed. Yet now we have to wail about Hester's delicate feelings instead of mine. Well, go and *find* her!' She pushed at him in fury. 'Get off me! Go! She didn't look as if she was suffering too much when I saw her.' Angry tears stung her eyes as she struggled against him.

'So why do *you* think,' he said, holding her wrists, 'I came after you when I was needed at Kenilworth? Well, I'll tell you, woman. Because this is one dash for freedom you're not going to complete. You put yourself in my power and now you'll stay in it, not for three days, which for you must seem like a lifetime, but until you get the message that I'm in control. You've met your master, my beauty. Did I need to tell you that?'

'Leave me *alone*!'

'Not on your life! You've led me a merry dance since the beginning, and you've had Hester and Fowler and half the men at Court dancing to your tune, but no more, sweetheart. There's no one to run to out here and nowhere for you to hide, and we've got quite a way to go before we reach Richmond.'

She gave up the unequal struggle, his strength being far too great for her. 'I *hate* you!' she said, weeping. 'I could never expect you to understand.'

'Shh! Easy now. I understand far more than you think.'

His lips on hers suggested that he expected no reply, and certainly his kisses distanced her thoughts from Hester and Peter as nothing else could have done. Gradually, she softened and, while not returning his caresses, lay quietly while he brushed away her tears of vexation. He helped her to her feet and, while she watched the muscles of his chest ripple under the dusting of dark hair, he licked a handkerchief and wiped her face. 'Did you two actually get round to washing yourselves?' he said, sternly.

Suspecting that Adorna was not eager to meet Cousin Hester and the dastardly Peter at Wallingford, Sir Nicholas decided that this would be a good time to sleep under the stars. It was a balmy night, and they had enough food with them for at least two meals: bread, cheese, fruit and ale. Perkin's expedition into the town produced hot pies, roast chicken and flasks of wine, which they shared in a warm corner of a cattle-shelter where there was still enough hay for the horses.

With never enough house-room for servants, high or low, the men were not unused to such primitive accommodation and knew how to make themselves comfortable with only the barest essentials. The two women treated it as an adventure, though Adorna was noticeably subdued.

The distant bridge at Wallingford provided a focal point as she and Maybelle sat together on the river-bank, sharing the kind of silence that holds distant sounds only half-observed. Jumbled thoughts of the past and future combined in Adorna's mind with the doubts she hoped had faded, though they had not.

'He doesn't understand,' she whispered to Maybelle. 'What's a woman supposed to do when she doesn't want a man's company? Stand still and smile and let them believe she does?'

Maybelle threw a stick into the water and watched it swirl away. 'The problem is,' she said, 'that you've always had more than your fair share of men to seek your attention, so it's natural for you to have found places where they couldn't go. If you'd been Mistress Hester, you'd probably have been quite glad of their company. And I dare say she's accepted Master Fowler because he was the first man she was introduced to at Richmond. Do you remember?'

'Yes,' said Adorna. 'I do. I *do* remember. It was at the dinner party. They talked about—'

'Her father, Sir William.'

'That's right. So you think that's when it began?'

'Sure to be, but Mistress Hester's never had to find places to hide because, for one thing, she was hidden already and for another, no one went to look for her. With her new wealth it really doesn't matter whether she leaves the Queen's progress or not because she'll be seen to be like her father, an eccentric. He was, wasn't he?'

'He certainly was, likeable but quite strange. But why doesn't Sir Nicholas tell me what he has in mind for the future, Belle?'

'Because he's proud, I suppose. He may be waiting

for you, too.' She threw another stick into the water. 'Maybe it's up to you now.'

'And you, Belle? What about you and Perkin?'

'Oh…' she laughed, blushing a little '…we know where we are. He loves me and I love him, and that's all there is to it, really. We'll probably make babies together, I expect.'

'Babies?'

'Yes. You know, those little mewling things that come looking like screwed-up badly dyed leather. They're called babies, love.'

The description fulfilled its purpose in making Adorna smile but, all the same, it set her thinking about her mother's advice, which had come too late to be of much use, and the possible manufacture of one of those screwed-up leathery things.

As night descended, she lay in her lover's arms in a distant corner of the shelter on a thick bed of hay and cloaks and thought about that conversation and Maybelle's advice which, in the past, had not always been entirely appropriate.

'Have you thought,' she said ambiguously, 'what might happen if—?'

'Yes, sweetheart. Often,' he murmured.

She sighed and withdrew her hand from his chest, but he caught it and kept his hand over hers. 'I want it to look exactly like Lady Adorna Rayne,' he said. 'Unless it should turn out to be a boy, of course.'

She sat upright with a jolt to stare down at him in the gloom. 'How did you…?'

But again he pulled her back to him. 'Go to sleep,' he whispered. 'I told you I understand more than you think.' The next moment he was sound asleep, and her well-planned questioning had been disposed of in one quick riposte. Damn the man! Nevertheless, she fell asleep with a smile on her face for the third time in three nights.

During the night, however, she came half-awake to the unusual surroundings, the close hoots of owls, the breathing of the river, the warm bulk of the man she had come to love too quickly for comfort. Drowsily, she lifted herself over him, reminding herself of the taste of his chin, the contours of his cheeks, chin and brow. Her fingers burrowed seductively into his hair.

Without a word, he awoke and lent himself willingly to her investigations until, with an arm under her back, he reversed their positions in one quick flip that astounded her by its suddenness. She enveloped him with her legs and took him into her, hungrily and with a sudden urge that flared with a wild spontaneity like a forest fire. He responded like one who meets his mate in the still dark night and takes her, and satisfies her, and falls asleep again in her arms till dawn. Silently.

He was missing when she awoke and she lay for a moment or two, wondering if she had dreamed it, and what the day would hold for them. Maybelle came to her with a beaker of ale. 'He's exercising the bay,' she said. 'Come and see.'

In total concentration, the gleaming bay gelding and its rider executed manoeuvres similar to those they had performed at Kenilworth before the Queen, this time before an admiring audience of four. Sitting perfectly still in the saddle, Sir Nicholas guided the bay through its precise paces, moving sideways, crossing legs, pirouetting and dancing daintily, reminding Adorna of their partnership in quite a different setting. He dismounted and came to her, smiling. 'Your turn,' he said. 'Come on. A few basic moves to start with.' His eyes held another message that made her blush, but she did as she was told and discovered that under his guidance, she could manage many of the simpler movements. He corrected her; the horse obeyed. 'Well done,' he said, lifting her down. 'You learn quickly. We'll take that other palomino in hand when we get back home.'

She made no reply to that, for she had recently begun to take a perverse kind of pleasure from his authoritative manner, appreciating once again the sweetness of handing the reins to a capable and decisive man, following his direction and knowing that it was sure to be hers also.

They reached Pangbourne by evening and bathed amongst the swans in the River Pang, half-hidden by a bank of alders. The cygnets were curious, the parents protective and suspicious of the two humans who lingered in the warmest pools, quietly preening each other's plumage. Later, the two walked hand in hand through a field of poppies to join some late haymakers, sharing their ale like country lovers for the price of some help with the raking and the loading of carts. They stayed at an inn with the sign of a swan above the door, and made love with renewed passion well into the night.

By dawn, they were away again, heading eastwards at last.

Reading was a pleasant and bustling abbey town where they bought food but did not stay: there was, Sir Nicholas told her, a far prettier place than this a mile or two further on. He was right; Sonning-on-Thames had everything, including a village wedding which, by the time they arrived, had been in full swing all day and looked set to continue well into the night. Drawn into the festivities as anonymous guests of the happy couple, they ate, drank, and slept once more under the clear night sky along with many others who made their beds where they fell.

It was nearly noon when they crossed the bridge at Sonning and continued along the Oxfordshire side as far as Henley-on-Thames, crossing back again into Berkshire over the river. 'We could make it as far as Bisham,' Sir Nicholas said, after a stop to rest the horses, 'if you want to go on while it's still light.'

'Whatever you say,' Adorna replied, blowing down the open front of her bodice.

'May I help you with that?' he said.

'If you wish.'

He did, then looked at her intently. 'We've come a

long way, my lass, have we not? Is the lady tamed, then?'

'Will you still want to know in a year's time?'

'Probably not. I shall be able to answer it myself, by then.'

They cut across a loop of the river to arrive at Bisham Abbey by dusk, staying with Sir Edward and Lady Hoby. In return for tales of the Queen and her Court at Kenilworth, the Hobys showed the two lovers round their beautiful home, pointing out the huge bay window specially built for Her Majesty's visit some years earlier. Taking Adorna's apparent marriage in their stride, they asked no awkward questions but wished the couple good fortune and a large brood of children, which Sir Nicholas endorsed with a squeeze of her hand.

In the late evening, Adorna lured him into the private garden that had once been the monks' paradise, in some strange way connecting a mental image to a physical one that had something to do with his constancy. She could define it no more clearly than that, though she suspected by the way he smiled and indulged her that he knew what was passing through her mind.

From Bisham, they cut across to the little village of Cookham, where there was a smithy for the horses, and at Maidenhead they bridged the river again and came, in only a few more miles, within sight of the huge white towers of Windsor Castle like icebergs on the horizon.

They had come so far without needing to explain their new and unexpected espousal. The Hobys had accepted it without question and, so far, they had met no one who might do otherwise. But Windsor was a different matter, for here Sir Nicholas was known, as was the lovely daughter of Sir Thomas Pickering. According to Sir Nicholas, it was time for another decision.

'What kind of decision?' said Adorna, throwing crumbs of bread to a gaggle of ducks. They sat on the riverbank at Eton with the castle in the distance and, behind them, the open fields where Maybelle, Perkin and Lytton played a noisy and unruly game of football with an old pig's bladder they had found. The evening was not altogether peaceful.

'A decision, my lady,' Sir Nicholas said, lifting her left hand, 'concerning this.' He twisted the borrowed ring on her finger. 'This is all right as a temporary arrangement, but now I think it's about time we had something more convincing for nearer home, don't you? Unless you prefer to arrive at Richmond in two days' time as seemingly chaste as when you left?'

The breath tightened in her lungs and, still unsure of him, still half-expecting the worst to happen, she removed her hand from his, took the ring off and held it out to him. She did not know exactly what he meant, nor did she have the courage to ask him. 'There,' she said. 'Of course, you're right. I don't want my mother to see me wearing it after all that advice about the sanctity of marriage. You keep it. It may come in handy.'

He studied the distant expression on her face, folding her fingers over the ring. 'Adorna,' he said, 'what are you saying to me? What is it you think I'm saying to you?' His voice, full of concern, almost broke her heart.

'I don't know,' she said in a small voice, her words tripping up over a sudden need to weep. 'I don't know what you're saying, Nicholas, but if it's what...what I fear it might...be, then don't say any more. I cannot bear it.'

'Still so distrustful, after all this time?'

'I'm not distrustful, just...'

'Just unsettled? Unsure? I should have said it sooner, sweetheart.'

'Don't say it, please.'

'What, don't say that I love you? That I've loved you for weeks? Ached for you? Don't say that I want you to marry me? Is that what you don't want to hear, sweetheart? Come, my lass.' He pulled her into his arms and lowered her backwards on to the grass, his face close enough for her to feel his words. 'What did you think these last few days have been about, then? Did you really think I'd bed you all the way to Richmond then say thank you and goodbye and don't let your mother know? Is that what you thought?'

Tears had gathered in the corners of her eyes. 'I don't know...didn't know...what I was supposed to think,' she said, touching a scratch on his cheek. 'I hoped...I wanted you to say...but you didn't. How was I to know?'

'Ah!' He sighed. 'Would you believe that men can

be so careful that they sometimes get the timing wrong? Do you remember the first time I told you how lovely you are?'

'Yes.' She smiled, sniffing.

'And how you reacted to my poor timing?'

'Yes.'

'Because you'd heard it all before? And how many times have men told you they love you? Dozens?'

'Boys and old men,' she said. 'No one I could have loved in return.'

'So I thought you'd not want to hear how I felt about you for a while. I thought that if you wanted to know you'd ask me. Or perhaps tell me how you feel about me. And—'

'Shh!' She moved her finger to his lips. 'Then let me tell you how I feel. Let me tell you how I adore you. I've loved you from the beginning, Nicholas.'

'You mean it, sweetheart?'

'I mean it, truly. I thought it was hate. It's very confusing, isn't it?'

His kiss kept her mouth occupied for quite some time, during which she began to make some sense of their misunderstandings, the resulting confusion, and her own fears which had been left to grow for far too long.

'Very confusing,' he agreed 'And now?'

'I feared what you were doing to me,' she whispered against his cheek, 'and what you *could* do to me, if I let you. I've never loved before, you see, and it scared me, and I was madly jealous of all the others, even though I had no idea who they were.'

'So tell me again. I want to hear it at least twenty times a day.'

'I love you, Nicholas. Even when you were horrid to me, I loved you then, too.'

'Little snarling she-cat,' he grinned.

'I'm sorry.'

'Don't be. I loved it. I'd not want to marry a woman who couldn't stand up to me.'

'But what about Hester?'

'What about her? She was never in the running. She knew that.'

'I thought…' She bit her lip.

'I think you and she have a few things to discuss, don't you? There's more to Mistress Hester than meets the eye, obviously. She may not have been too sure about what she wants, but she certainly knows what she doesn't want. She has the Pickering trait, too.'

'What's that?'

'She's a fast learner.'

Their intimate laughter was brought to a sudden yelping conclusion by an inflated pig's bladder bouncing hard off the back of Nicholas's head, only to be retrieved by two lusty howling men who apparently lacked any respect, at that moment, for their master or his mistress.

Laughing, he helped her to stand. 'You've not replied to my proposal, I notice. Have you got used to the idea of being Lady Adorna Rayne, yet?'

She watched the three footballers chase away, Belle with her skirt pulled up between her legs. The idyll must be prolonged as it was, for two more days, at least. 'I think,' she said, 'I'll give you my answer at Richmond. Can you wait?'

'I can wait. And I think I know where I'll be when I wait.'

'Shh!' she said, smiling. 'Meanwhile, put this ring away and give it back to Master Burbage. It's fulfilled its purpose, but now I have to be myself or there'll be far more questions than I can answer.'

'Is your mother going to be shocked, d'ye think?'

'Slightly confused, more like, after all the protesting I've done.'

In the warm haven of his arms in a little inn at Eton, there was another matter to be attended to, though the answer was no more than a formality. 'Nicholas, would you really have told anyone about me taking Seton's part in the plays?'

He turned to her, stroking her hair and almost laughing. 'Think about it, sweetheart. Who would I tell? The earl? He'd be more than grateful to you, I should imagine, as Master Burbage and Seton were, as the rest of the company would have been, if they'd realised. They'd not want to be disbanded, would they? Your father would hardly shout about it, with his own family so closely involved, and any scandal involving the earl and his players would involve me, too, one way or another, as his servant. So I'd not want to put him in an embarrassing position either. Besides, I'm loyal. It makes no sense at all, my sweet, does it?'

'Yet you went along with the whole idea,' she said, trying to sound indignant.

'So I did.' He smiled. 'Who wouldn't? And we have Seton's nerves and wobbly voice to thank for it, and his most courageous sister. That took some doing, my love. I hope he appreciates what you did as much as I do.'

'I didn't really have much choice,' she said, knowing that he knew the truth of the matter as well as she did.

If they had not lingered in Windsor market, or played tennis at Hampton Court Palace, or met friends, or made a lengthy visit to one of Nicholas's brothers at Kingston-upon-Thames, they would certainly have reached Richmond sooner than they did. As it was, it was almost mid-afternoon when they wound their way up Paradise Road towards Sheen House, far more reconciled to each other than when they had set out. Their arrival was not far behind that of Sir Thomas Pickering and the Queen's Wardrobe, Leicester's Men, and the whole enormous slow-moving paraphernalia of baggage that beat them by less than an hour from a more direct route.

The courtyard was still teeming with men, horses and luggage, amongst which Sir Nicholas's small party made very little impression until the bright silvery toss of Adorna's hair caught the Master of Revels in mid-sentence. 'What…! What the *devil*?' he cried. 'Where have *you* come from?'

It took some time to explain. Seton joined in, as incredulous of his sister's sun-bronzed and unladylike appearance as of her obviously radiant happiness.

Lady Marion didn't care about the route they'd taken, which was all that interested the men, but about the daughter from whom she had had no news for well over a week. Close to tears, she hugged Adorna, leaving questions about her happiness to answer themselves. 'Hester arrived yesterday,' she said, wiping her tears. 'She's around somewhere.'

'Hester came back *here*?'

Her mother wobbled her head. 'Don't ask me,' she said, as confused as Adorna's prediction. 'I've no idea what's going on. I think your father is the only one so far who's come back the same as he went. Even Seton's got a new voice. Just listen to him.'

'Did Hester tell you what happened?'

Lady Marion rolled her eyes. 'You know what Hester's like. It'll be at least a month before we discover what she's been up to.'

In fact, it was nothing like a month, though it was not Hester, of course, who enlightened her cousin. But although Hester was unused to having to explain herself to others, there were certain things Adorna needed to know rather more urgently. The two hugged like sisters, too happy with the outcome of their own affairs to be affronted by the petty deceptions of the past.

Nevertheless, Hester was surprised by Adorna's appearance. 'Then you must have followed us…er, me,' she said, retrieving herself.

'Well, of course I followed you. You left rather abruptly and I was concerned. I thought you must have been upset by what you saw.'

'In your chamber? Oh, no. I went to tell you what I'd decided to do, but I didn't know Sir Nicholas was with you, so when I saw you were…er…busy, I left and went to find…er…to make arrangements. I wasn't upset at all.' She coiled her long brown hair into a rope, worn loose like a maiden, and taking at least five off her twenty-one years. Like Adorna, she was sunbrowned and sparkling with health and now, having discarded her stays, there was an elfin quality about her which had not shown itself before. 'Oh, dear,' she said, as the implications dawned upon her, 'did you think I was upset over Sir Nicholas? Yes, I can quite see that you would. It's all been a bit of a mix-up, hasn't it?'

'Hester,' Adorna said, tired of beating around the bush, 'I know that you travelled with Peter, and I don't mind. Really. I don't. Did you think I'd be annoyed about it?'

Hester stared. 'You *know*? I told Lady Marion I'd travelled with friends from the palace.'

'Of course. I told you, I followed you.'

'What, so close? You saw us?' The horrified expression grew.

It was time for some diplomacy. 'We caught sight of you in the distance—oh, I can't recall where it was—but Sir Nicholas had made enquiries before he left Kenilworth and he knew that you were in good company.'

'Oh, he's been so very kind.'

'Who, Peter?'

'Well, yes, but I meant Sir Nicholas. He promised

Uncle Samuel he'd keep an eye on me while I was here. Did you know that? I had it in one of my aunt's letters. I suppose I should have let him know where I was going, but when I saw that you and he had become friends at last, I realised I wouldn't have to pretend any more, so I forgot.'

'Pretend what, Hester?' said Adorna, noting the lack of regret.

'Well, pretend to be interested in him. You and Lady Marion were rather set on the idea, weren't you? And I felt obliged to make an effort. I thought I was doing quite well at one time when I saw that you were looking quite convinced, even though I knew it was a waste of time. Sir Nicholas has never seen me in *that* light, you know.'

So, it was as Sir Nicholas had said. Hester was so obliging. 'I see, so you and Peter found mutual comfort in each other.'

'Not exactly.' Hester smiled, suddenly coy. 'I think there was something between us at our first meeting, but at that time he was your friend, Adorna. He's *so* interesting though, isn't he? So dependable. It must have been Fate that sent me here to Richmond, don't you think?'

'And was it Fate that made you fall off your horse that day at the hunt?' Adorna could not resist the teasing laugh which Hester had the grace to echo.

'Oh, dear,' she said, twisting madly at the rope of hair. 'You realised that I was shamming, did you?'

No, Adorna had not, until now. 'So what was all that about?'

'Peter's idea. He thought that if I had a good reason to return home, your father would agree to let him escort me. But Sir Thomas didn't, so we just had to wait for another chance, and if we'd left it any longer Peter would have had to go on up to Staffordshire to check the security. I would have told you, Adorna, but I thought you'd be angry at me going with Peter. So we thought it best just to go and say nothing. Peter met me beyond the gate. It was so exciting. Neither of us could bear any more of that socialising, especially me. I thought it would have been fun, but it was such hard work. Our journey back was simply heavenly.'

'And the letters?'

'Oh, the letters. Well, it was the only way we could communicate, really, with so many people watching. Especially after I was confined to my room.'

'But what about Peter's position in the Queen's service? Surely he'll lose it?'

'Oh, that doesn't matter too much. We have all the money we need to live off without him having to earn anything. We'll probably travel to Italy soon.'

Well done, Peter, Adorna thought. Certainly this was a few steps up from Gentleman Controller of the Queen's Works. Yet it was only to be expected that, having had no reason to think about anyone except herself in twenty-one years, Hester would display a singular lack of interest in any doings except her own, and it was not long before Adorna realised that hers and Sir Nicholas's affairs were only relevant insofar as they affected Hester. Italy, she thought, would be about far enough.

It didn't seem to matter for, once the shock of having dozens of extra mouths to feed had passed, Lady Marion played hostess to the merriest crowd of people that either Adorna or Seton could remember. Young Adrian could not hear enough about his elder brother's performances before the Queen while congratulating him on the acquisition of a fine new baritone voice. Adrian, however, was ecstatic when Master Burbage, his hero, persuaded Sir Thomas to allow him to take over Seton's former role as principal female actor with the company. It was the only time any of them had seen Adrian speechless.

Seton would have wept, but found himself suddenly and inexplicably unable to. Instead, he clung to Adorna and shook with relief. 'Thank you, dear one,' he said for her ear alone. 'Thank you. I am the happiest man alive.'

This sentiment was contested later on after Sir Nicholas, in a rare moment of privacy, managed to corner Sir Thomas to ask him formally for the hand of his daughter in marriage, after which he no longer had to wonder which side of the family Adorna got her unpredictability from. Sir Thomas's exact reply was unrepeatable but, according to Sir Nicholas, contained the overtones of a command to the effect that he had bloody well taken the goods first and asked afterwards, so now he'd better be sharp and give a name to the bairn he'd no doubt spawned.

To Sir Nicholas's reminder that they had actually agreed at Kenilworth on a certain line of action—which dumbfounded yet another of the Pickering siblings—Sir Thomas replied that he had not believed it remotely likely that anyone would bed his daughter before her marriage, least of all Sir Nicholas to whom she seemed particularly ill disposed. He had, he said, agreed to him wooing her, not to getting her pregnant as fast as possible. Which was another good reason for the high good humour and air of complacency displayed by the Deputy Master of Horse as darkness fell over the garden at Sheen House.

People wandered quietly amongst the arbours and terraces or stood in shadowy chattering groups around the banqueting house as Sir Nicholas took Adorna's hand and caught the smile on her face. 'What?' he said.

'I'd not have believed I'd be won over either,' she said. 'Especially not by you.'

'Ah, then it's just as well I believe in myself, isn't it? Yet I'm not convinced that you didn't believe it. You kept it hidden, that's all.'

Unable to contradict him, for it was true, Adorna led him away from the garden, along the paved walkways, down steps and out beyond the house to Paradise Road where, in the wall along the grassy verge there was a door leading into the old friary paradise at the side of the Queen's palace garden. Past gnarled fruit trees and blowsy roses, straggling honeysuckle, golden-rod and fragrant lavender, she brought him to a stand where once he had waited for a woman while Adorna had watched, aching with envy and longing.

'Here,' she whispered. 'It was here, wasn't it?' She stood apart from him, hoping that he would know what she wanted. He did.

Stretching out his hands, he went to meet her and pulled her into his arms, enclosing her with strong hands whose warmth she could feel through the thin linen bodice. 'I knew it,' he whispered, kissing her eyelids. 'The paradise at Godstow nunnery, then at Kings Sutton, then at Bisham, and now here at Richmond. And this is where I tell you again that I want you to be my wife, the mother of my children, my companion, friend and lover. My adored Adorna. I want to keep you, protect you, give you my name. Will you be mine, sweetheart?'

For an answer, she quoted Beatrice's beautiful confession. '"Now I am persuaded to accept, to love, to be no more aloof, to say that what was mine shall now be yours, forsooth." Take my heart and my promise, beloved. I *am* yours; all of me. I think I always was since I first saw you just on this spot. I wanted you then so much. I willed you to come to me.'

His mouth roamed over her face as he spoke. 'And I would rather anyone had seen that farewell kiss but you. Saints, woman, I've never felt about another living soul as I do about you. Shall we have bairns, sweet lass, to give others the same sweet torment?'

'Bold, tenacious lads like their father?'

'Wilful Water Maidens like their mother. Tempestuous, passionate women that will test a man's resolve. We'll have a family of beauties, shall we, love?'

There were plenty of dark out-of-the-way corners amongst the old overgrown plots of the friary garden, places where they could lie on sun-warmed chamomile and clover to make urgent love as though time was running out on them instead of just beginning. Vaguely, they heard the chime of the clock over in the palace courtyard, the distant call of guests from Sir Thomas's garden and the faint laughter of lovers in the Queen's. But for them, the sweetest sounds were of their own soft moans of joy. Safe in his love and sure of his devotion, Adorna led him to paradise at last and herself to the mastership of the only man she had ever wanted, though it had taken her long enough to admit it.

They chuckled, remembering their first watery meeting. 'You were so unmannerly,' she said, sprinkling his chest with her hair. 'So high-handed. I think I hated you then.'

'You feared me. And you could hardly wait to hare off to your father's office, could you?'

'Where you barged in while I was trying on that ridiculous dress. Ogling me.'

His hand moved possessively over her naked breast. 'It was a rare sight. I saw far more than I could have hoped for. You didn't like my net, though. Did you?' He laughed softly, caressing her. 'How you fought me, eh?'

She turned her head into his neck. 'Shh! Don't remind me. It was shameful.'

'Not a bit of it! It was my triumph.' His hand stopped, and he lay over her, seeing the last glint of light in her eyes. 'And there was not a man in the hall who didn't envy me with Mistress Adorna Pickering in my arms. Netted. Well, I have you now, my beauty.'

'Here in paradise, for ever, love.' She smiled.

Adorna and Nicholas were married on August 5th, 1575, at Sheen House in Richmond in the presence of the Queen and the Earl of Leicester. Their first boy was born the following May in London, followed by two more boys and then a girl.

Author's Note

As the story states, Sir William Pickering was in fact a one-time contender for the Queen's hand. He was a brilliant eccentric who had a daughter named Hester to whom he left his entire fortune and his house in London. Nothing is known of this lady, or of her mother, but one lady about whom far more is known was the Countess of Essex, otherwise known as Lettice Knollys, to whose home in Staffordshire the progress moved from Kenilworth. The earl's long-standing love affair with the countess caused even more scandal when, shortly after her widowhood, they married in secret—an act of betrayal for which the Queen never forgave either of them.

Sir Christopher Hatton, Sir John Fortescue, Dr Dee, the Hobys and James Burbage are all real characters in history, and all the places mentioned in the story are real except Sheen House, which is imaginary. There was, however, a Sheen Manor, which the Queen gave to a former lady-in-waiting, the Swedish Marchioness of Northampton. Kings Sutton is now known as Sutton Courtney, and Kenilworth Castle is now a ruin. The Tudor Palace of Richmond covered about ten acres of land from what is now Old Palace Lane to Water Lane, but the only parts now remaining are the pink brick gateway into the Great Court and behind it, in Old Palace Yard, some original brickwork of the Tudor period which was once part of the Wardrobe. This was reconstructed in the early eighteenth century.

Queen Elizabeth I died in Richmond Palace in 1603, after which it declined in favour and was eventually demolished along with the remains of the old friary. We have seventeenth-century drawings of Antonis van Wyngaerde and Wenceslaus Hollar to show us what the buildings looked like.

However, the modern town of Richmond in Surrey retains names that remind us of its more serene past. Names such as Old Palace Lane, Water Lane, Friars Stile Road, Orchard Road, Manor Road, Vineyard Passage and, of course, Paradise Road, where, at Eton House, numbers 18 to 24, is situated the UK Head Office of the publisher of this book, Harlequin Mills & Boon, Ltd.

The excerpts from Seton's plays, read by Adorna and Sir Nicholas, are purely the invention of the author and are not taken, directly or indirectly, from anything written by anyone else, real or imaginary. Beatrice and Benedict may also have been Seton's own invention as borrowing, now known as plagiarism, was common and not illegal in Tudor England. And, since young William Shakespeare was open to all influences, this may have remained in his mind until he wrote *Much Ado About Nothing* in 1598/9. Similarly, Ovid's 'Titania' and the Germanic mythical 'Oberon', of the thirteenth-century romance *Huon of Bordeaux*, translated into English in 1534, were fair game for any author to use, as many did in later years. Shakespeare borrowed them both for *A Midsummer Night's Dream*.

*   *   *   *   *

A Most Unseemly Summer

JULIET LANDON

Chapter One

Lady Honoria Deventer shaded her eyes against the strengthening pale green rays that streamed into the best bedchamber at Sonning House. By her side, Lord Philip Deventer quietly opened the window, blowing a brittle winter cobweb into the garden below, where already a fuzz of new green covered the untidy plots.

Their joint attention was focussed on a tall and slender figure who stood motionless in the early sunshine, her dark mass of silky hair piled untidily on top of her head, her back curving into a neat waist without the support of whalebone stays. And though her face was turned from the house, her mother had guessed at its expression of sadness.

'What is wrong with her these days?' she whispered. 'So angry. So quiet.'

'She was not so quiet yesterday morning when she boxed the gardener's lad's ears, was she?' her husband replied.

'He was tipping birds' eggs out of their nests to feed the cat. He deserved it. But she was never so severe until recently, Philip. Perhaps I should find her a new tutor.'

'She'd be better off with a husband. A home. A few bairns.' The typically brusque response sent a shadow across his wife's face, which naturally he missed. His great hand wandered across her distended stomach, anticipating the gender of the new bulge, the first of a new strain of Deventers. Their combined families, eleven of his by his late wife and seven of hers by two previous husbands, would total nineteen by summer.

Lady Honoria nestled into him, covering his hand with her own. 'But she has a home here…' she turned her face up to him, suddenly unsure '…doesn't she? She's only nineteen, dearest, and she's always been good at managing a household. Until we moved here to Sonning,' she added as an afterthought. Lord Deventer's household had not appreciated her expertise.

'Well then, she can go down to Wheatley and manage *that*.'

'What d'ye mean?' Lady Honoria slowly turned within his arm, puzzled by his tone. 'To Wheatley Abbey? There's no one there, dear.'

'Yes, there is. Gascelin will be there now, after the winter break. He sent a message up last week. There'll be plenty of room for her in that big guesthouse, and she can make a start on the rooms in the

New House ready for our move. We could be away from here in the autumn, if they both get a move on.'

His new wife turned away, glancing at her daughter's lovely back with some scepticism. 'You cannot be serious, Philip. I know you and Felice haven't got to know each other too well yet, but I'll not have her packed off down to Hampshire on her own to work with that man. There'd be trouble.'

'Yes,' Lord Deventer replied, unhelpfully, 'but that man, as you call him, is the best surveyor and master builder this side of the Channel. Brilliant chap. And anyway, Hampshire's only the next county, love, not exactly the other side of the world. She can always come back if she finds the task too daunting.' He braced himself for his wife's predictable defence of her beloved and only daughter.

'Daunted? Felice? Never! But *he's* not the easiest man to work alongside, is he? You know what a perfectionist he is.'

Lord Deventer had chosen Sir Leon Gascelin for just that quality and was only too well aware that the last thing he would appreciate would be someone like young Lady Felice Marwelle getting under his feet. However, there were ways of overcoming that problem.

'Well,' he said, 'so is she, for that matter, and heaven knows the place is big enough for her to keep out of his way. He won't want much to do with a lass like her. He was after Levina again when I last heard.'

'Levina! Tch! Half the court is after Levina.' Hearing the amusement in his voice she quickly closed the window against his impending laughter. 'You'll send a message to prepare the best rooms for her? She'll be comfortable, Philip?'

'Of course she will, love,' he said, bending to kiss her downy neck. 'I'll send a man down today. She'll be in her element.'

'Today? So soon?'

'Yes, love. No time like the present, is there?'

If only the daughter had been so pliable.

The daughter, Lady Felice Marwelle, had surprised her stepfather by an unusual co-operation verging on enthusiasm over a means of escape that had occupied her mind almost incessantly in recent weeks. But her expectations of the comfort promised by her mother were dashed against the large stone gatehouse leading to Wheatley Abbey through which a large and untidy building site was framed.

The elegant but sour-faced steward held his ground, clinging to his staff with one hand and the wide spiked collar of a mastiff with the other. 'I received no orders from Sir Leon about a visit,' he said. Though his tone was courteous, his finality might have dismayed most of those present.

But the young lady astride the bay mare was remarkably steadfast, giving back stare for stare from large brown eyes rimmed with thick black lashes, beating down the watery pale ones that time had faded. 'That has no bearing whatever on the fact that I am here, now, with thirty members of Lord Deventer's household and a fair proportion of his possessions,' she replied, coolly. 'And in Sir Leon's absence you may take your orders from myself, Lady Felice Marwelle, Lord Deventer's stepdaughter. Is *that* good enough for you?'

'Lady,' the steward bowed stiffly, 'I beg your pardon, but the fact is that Sir Leon—'

'The fact is, steward, that we have been on the road for two days, at the end of which I was assured there would be lodging in the guesthouse available to us. Are rooms available or not?'

In truth, she was beginning to doubt whether the guesthouse would be the most suitable place to stay, after all, for although the fourteenth-century complex of buildings appeared to be more than adequate, they were far too close to the building site for comfort.

It was inevitable, of course, that any reconstruction work on this scale would cause some considerable mess, and although the abbey's original stones were being re-used, the sheer scale of the undertaking had turned the whole of the abbey precinct, once so well kept and peaceful, into a waste land. The large area between the gatehouse, guesthouse, abbey church and its old monastic buildings were stacked with stone and timber, scaffolding and hoists, with mounds of grit and sand, with the lean-to thatched sheds of the masons, carpenters, plasterers and tilers.

Most of the workers had finished for the day, but a group of grimy and wide-eyed young labourers hung round to see who would win the argument, Thomas Vyttery, steward, or this saucy young lass on the bay mare. They gawped at her and her two maids appreciatively until their attention was diverted by the steward's impressively muscular mastiff that suddenly noticed, through the legs of the lady's horse, two grey deerhounds almost as large as donkeys, standing passively but with bristling crests and lowered heads. Taking him by surprise, the mastiff wrenched itself out of the steward's grasp and fled for the safety of home with its tail between its legs, leaving the steward without his main prop.

'My lady, may I be permitted to suggest that, before you make a decision'—he was nothing if not formal—'you take a look at the inn in the village of Wheatley. You would have passed it on your way to the abbey. It's quite...'

Lady Felice was not listening. She was looking over to the right, beyond the church, towards a group of ancient stone-built dwellings that must once have been used by the monks for eating and sleeping before the terrible years of the Dissolution had driven them out. The message that Lord Deventer had received last week from his master builder and surveyor, Sir Leon Gascelin, had said that some of the rooms in the converted abbey would soon be ready for furnishing. Surely those must be the ones he meant.

'Those buildings over there. That must be Lord Deventer's New House, I take it?'

The steward did not need to look. 'The men are still working on that house, m'lady, and Sir Leon himself will be moving into the old Abbot's House within the next day or two.'

'Mr...?'

'Thomas Vyttery, m'lady.'

'Mr Vyttery, hand me the keys to the Abbot's House, if you please.'

The steward's voice quavered in alarm. 'By your leave, lady, I cannot do that. I shall be dismissed.'

'You will indeed, Mr Vyttery, if you refuse to obey me. I shall see that Lord Deventer replaces you with someone who knows more about hospitality than you do. Now, do as I say.' She held out a hand. 'No, don't try to remove any of the keys. I want the complete set—kitchens, stables, the lot. Thank you.'

In furiously silent remonstration, the impotent steward turned away without another word. Behind Felice, the cavalcade of waggons, carts, sumpter-horses, grooms and carters, cooks and kitchen-lads, household servants and officials lumbered into motion, creaking and swaying past the building site through ruts white with stone chippings and lime.

The fourteenth-century Abbot's House was on the

far side of the abbey buildings within the curve of
the river, far removed from the builders' clutter and
larger than Felice had imagined. There were signs
of extensive alterations and additions, enlarged windows and a stately carved porch with steps leading
up to an iron-bound door.

Sending the carts, waggons and pack-horses
round to the stableyard at the rear, Felice handed the
large bunch of keys to her house-steward, Mr Peale,
whose meteoric rise to the position had been ef-
fected especially for this venture. Still in his early
thirties, Henry Peale took his duties very seriously,
ushering his mistress up the steps into a series of
pine-panelled rooms with richly patterned ceilings
of white plaster that still held the pungent aroma of
newness. In the fading light, it was only possible for
them to estimate the rough dimensions, but the largest one on the first floor would do well enough for
Lady Felice's first night, and the rest of the household would bed down wherever they could.

It was testimony to the young lady's managerial
skills that a household, quickly assembled from her
stepfather's staff at Sonning in Berkshire, so soon
worked like a well-oiled machine to unload whatever was necessary for their immediate comfort and
leave the rest on the carts until they knew where to
put it. There was no question of assembling the
lady's bed, but when the candles and cressets were
lit at last, the well-swept rooms held a welcome that
had so far been denied them. So much for her step-

father's assurances of comfort, she muttered to Lydia, her eldest maid.

'We'll soon have it ship-shape,' Lydia said, drawing the unpinned sleeves over her mistress's wrists. 'But where's Sir Leon got to? Wasn't he supposed to have been expecting us?'

'Heaven knows. Obviously not where Lord Deventer thinks he is. More to the point, what's happened to the message he was sent?' She stepped out of her petticoat, beneath which she had worn a pair of soft leather breeches to protect her thighs from the chafing of the saddle. 'You and Elizabeth take the room next door, Lydie. I'll have the hounds in here with me.'

Perhaps it was these vexed questions that made her come instantly to life long before dawn and respond with a puzzled immediacy to her new surroundings. To investigate the moonlight flooding in broken ripples through the lattice, she crossed the room to the half-open window, watched by the two sprawling hounds. The scent of wood-ash hung in the air and in the silence she could hear her heart beating.

The moonlit landscape was held together by an assortment of textured greys that there had been no time for her to remember as trees or groups of sleeping water-fowl. A cloud slid beneath the moon reflected in the glassy river below and, as she watched, a series of counter-ripples slid across the water, chased by another, and then another. Across on the far side where the darkness was most dense, a disturbance broke the surface and, even before her eyes had registered it, she knew that it was a boat, that someone who rowed on the river had been caught by the moon. Then the boat disappeared, towing behind it a wide V of ripples.

Wide awake, she pulled on her leather breeches and her fine linen chemise, tucking it in and hurriedly buckling on the leather belt to hold them together. Then, without bothering to look for her boots, she commanded the hounds to stay and let herself silently out of the room. The wide staircase led down to the passageway where the front doors were locked and bolted. They were new and well oiled, allowing her to exit without attracting the attention of the sleeping servants. She was now almost directly below her own chamber window and only a few yards from the riverbank that dropped to a lower level, dotted with hawthorns and sleeping ducks.

She followed the river away from the Abbot's House in the direction of the boat, her bare feet making no sound on the grass. She kept low, putting the trees between herself and the river, passing the kitchens and the tumbledown wall of the kitchen garden and eventually finding herself on a grassy track that led to a wooden bridge and from there to the mill on the opposite side.

A small rowing boat was tied up below the bridge

and, as there was no other, she assumed it to be the one she had seen, suggesting that whoever had left it there was probably in the mill. The miller, perhaps, returning from a late night with friends?

The owls had ceased their hooting as she retraced her steps, the moonlit abbey now appearing from a different angle, the great tower of the church rising well above every rooftop. Rather than return by exactly the same route, she was drawn towards a gap in the old kitchen-garden wall that bordered the track, its stones paving a way into the place where monastic gardeners had once grown their vegetables. It was now impossible for her to make out any shape of plot or pathway, but she picked her way carefully towards the silhouetted gables of the Abbot's House, brushing the tops of the high weeds with her palms.

A slight sound behind her made her jump, and she turned, ready for flight, only her lightning reaction saving her from a hand that shot forward to grasp at her arm. She felt the fingers touch the linen of her sleeve, heard the breath of the one who would hold her, and then she swerved and fled, leaping and bounding like a hare without knowing which part of the wall ahead held the means of her escape.

She was tall, for a woman, but her pursuer's legs were longer than hers and she was forced to use every device to evade him, swerving and zig-zagging, ducking and doubling, hoping by these means to make him stumble. But it was she who stumbled on the rough ground that had not been cultivated for some twenty years or more, and that hesitation was enough for the man to catch her around the waist and swing her sideways, throwing her off-balance. She went crashing down into a bed of wild parsley and, before she had time to draw breath, his weight was over her, pressing her face-down into the weeds and forcing an involuntary yelp out of her lungs.

That was all she allowed herself, knowing that to reveal her identity might make her a greater prize than she already was. Let him think her a servant, a silly maid meeting her lover. It was not until he spoke that she realised how she must have appeared.

'Now, my lad, that was a merry little dance, eh? Let's introduce ourselves then, shall we? Then you can answer a few questions.' The voice that breathed softly into the back of her neck was nothing like a common labourer's, nor did he seem to be out of breath, but more like one who had enjoyed the chase, knowing he would win. He eased himself off her shoulders to kneel lightly astride her hips. 'Your name, lad?' he said.

Felice clenched her teeth, waiting for the persuasive blow to fall. This was something she had not reckoned on. Her face was deep in the shadow of long stalks and feathery leaves where the moonlight could not reach, her cheek pressed against the night-time coolness of the earth, which was to her advantage as soon as she felt his response to her silence.

'All right, lad, there are other ways.'

His hands were deft around her waist, searching her lower half for weapons and hesitating over the soft fabric of the chemise tucked into the belt. 'Hey! What's this, then?' he said more softly. Slowly, his hands moved upwards, spanning her back, his fingertips already well out of bounds. The next move would be too far.

Taking advantage of his shift in position, Felice twisted wildly, flailing backwards with one arm to hit hard at the side of his head with a crack that sent a wave of pain through her wrist. It took him by surprise, and although he was quick to recover his balance, it gave her the time she needed to roll beneath him and to push hard with one shoulder, using every ounce of force she could summon.

He swayed sideways but caught her again before she could free her legs from his weight, and then she fought madly, desperately, knowing that her boy's guise was not, after all, to be her safety. In panic, she tore at his shirt and sleeveless leather jerkin, missing his face but raking his neck and forearms and finally sinking her teeth into the base of his thumb as he grabbed at her wrists. She felt him flinch at that, giving her yet another chance to twist away, kicking and beating, desperate to be free of him.

She rolled, lashing out, but he rolled with her, over and over through the spring growth of chickweed and willow-herb and she was sure, without seeing his face, that he was actually enjoying her efforts, even while being hard pressed to contain them. At last she was stopped by an ancient half-buried wheelbarrow, and she lay, panting and exhausted, in an embrace so powerful that it hurt her ribs, immobilised by strong legs that encircled hers, her back against his chest and her wrists held fast beneath her chin by one of his hands.

She felt his chest shake in silent laughter while his free hand took her heavy plait and slipped the ribbon off the end, combing her thick hair loose with his fingers and letting fall a silken sheet of it across her face.

'There now, my beauty. Shall we stop pretending now. Eh? Fleet of foot and sharp of claw and tooth. That's hardly a lad's way now, is it? You're going to tell me who you are, then?'

Her resolve to remain silent wavered while her mind sought a quick answer to the question of his intentions; whether he would have as many qualms about violating a noblewoman as much as a village lass. Yet there was something about his persistent interrogation that suggested some other purpose behind his violent pursuit. Surely he would not have chased a lad with such ferocity if he'd had only rape in mind. But having discovered he held a woman, would he now change his purpose?

Panic, anger and dread screamed through her mind and left a sickly void at the pit of her stomach, for now his hand had come to rest upon the large silver buckle of her belt, loosening the thong in a leisurely mockery of her weakness.

'No,' she whispered, writhing. 'No...please!'

The hand stopped, but the voice was smiling. 'No? No, what? You're not going to tell me who I've captured? Are you a moon-spirit, perhaps?'

'No,' she whispered again. Having broken her silence, it seemed necessary now to insist. 'Let me go. Please.'

He spoke teasingly against her ear, his words touching her. 'Then I require some kind of proof that you're mortal, don't you agree? Do you have any suggestion of a harmless nature? Nothing too...irreparable?'

Holy saints! What was he talking about? Suggestions of a harmless nature? Nothing irreparable? Angered, obdurate, she remained silent, now becoming aware of the throbbing in her wrist. She tried twisting to bite at any part of him, but his hand tightened its grip as she writhed, his free hand gently easing the linen chemise from the safety of her breeches.

She stopped, again paralysed with foreboding.

'So, tell me who sent you here. Who are you working for?' His hand was still, waiting on the bare skin of her midriff, and when she again refused to answer, he shifted slightly, settling her sideways against him and wedging her head into his shoulder with one iron forearm.

Looking back on this episode, she was to wonder why she had not screamed, why she had suddenly been aware of her heart fluttering instead of beating, or why the dread had suddenly become tinged with a shade of illicit excitement. It was dark, she was to excuse herself later, and she had not been able to see when his mouth covered hers, and then all proper maidenly resistance was obscured by longings that had lain dormant over the long dark months of autumn and winter, waiting to be rekindled.

It was no excuse, of course, but it would have to serve in the absence of anything more persuasive. What was more, it was the certainty that she would never again encounter this stranger on any level that freed her mind and body to his direction. If she had believed, even for the space of one second, that they would ever meet again, she would have killed him rather than give what he took so expertly, what she gave without further protest.

She was not inexperienced, but this man was a master, claiming her mind, her total participation from start to finish. She was hardly aware when his hand moved upwards to capture her breasts and to explore them in minutest detail while his lips held hers in willing submission, suspending all resistance with cords of ecstasy. She moaned and pushed against him, feeling the brush of his hair on her eyelids, his warm hand caressing and fondling, her own hands now freed and hanging numbly out of harm's way, allowing him free access.

In the far distant reaches of her mind, a comparison stirred and settled again, dimly reminding her to take, while she had the chance. So she took, greedily and unsparing, surprising him by her need that, had he known it, had never before reached these dimensions. How could he have known what part he was playing in her desperation?

Responding immediately, he tipped her backwards on to the cool dark bed of greenery and lay on her, whispering to her like a voice of conscience that she must think...think. Unbelievably, he told her to think what she was doing.

It was a familiar word to her, one which she had not thought to hear again in this connection, and the senses that moments before had been submerged beneath a roaring storm of emotion now emerged, chilled and shaking, drawing her attention to the prickly coldness at her back and the pale shocked stare of the moon. Tears blinded her, shattering the white orb into a thousand pieces.

'Let me go,' she whispered yet again. 'Let me up now, I beg you.'

'Who are you? Tell me, for pity's sake, woman.'

She turned her head away, suddenly shamed by his limbs on hers, his hand slowly withdrawing, leaving her breast bleak and unloved. 'No, I'm nobody. Let me go.' The tears dripped off her chin.

His sigh betrayed disappointment and bewilderment, but there was to be no return to the former roles of captor and captive. He rolled away, lying motionless in the dark as Felice scrambled unsteadily to her feet and hobbled away with neither a word nor backward glance, wincing at the pains that now beset her like demons, clutching her chemise in both hands.

She could not know, nor did she turn to see whether he followed, nor did she know how she found her way out of that vast walled space and through the stone arch that had once been closed off by wooden gates. All she knew was that, suddenly, it was there, that the rough ground had changed to cobbles that hurt her feet unbearably, and that she used the pointed finials on the rooftop to show her where the Abbot's House was.

Predictably, Lydia scolded her mistress on all counts, especially for leaving the two deerhounds, Fen and Flint, behind. 'Whatever were you thinking of, love?' she whispered, anxious not to wake young Elizabeth. 'Why didn't you tell him who you were? He could have been somebody set to guard the site at nights. Here, hold your other foot up.'

Shivering, despite the woollen blanket, Felice obeyed but felt bound to defend herself. 'How could he be? All those who work here would know of our arrival. He'd know who I was, wouldn't he? But he didn't guess, and that shows he's a stranger to the place. Ouch! My wrist hurts, Lydie.'

'I'll send Elizabeth to find some comfrey as soon as it gets light. Now, that'll have to do till we can have some water sent up. Into bed, love.'

Bandaged and soothed and with a streak of dawn

already on the horizon, Felice gave in to the emotions that surged uncontrollably within her, awakened after their seven-month suppression. She had shared her heartache with no one, though faithful Lydia had been aware of her relationship with Father Timon, Lord Deventer's chaplain and Felice's tutor, and of the manner of his death. Now this stranger had forced her to confront the pain of an aching emptiness and to discover that it was, in fact, full to overflowing.

The revelation had both astounded her and filled her with guilt; what should have been kept sacred to Timon's memory had been squandered in a moment of sheer madness. Well, no one would know of that deplorable lapse, not even dear Lydia, and the man himself would now be many miles away.

But try as she would to replace that anonymous ruffian with the gentle Timon, the imprint of unknown hands on her, ruthlessly intimate, sent tremors of self-reproach through her aching body that were indistinguishable from bliss. The taste of his lips and their bruising intensity returned time and again to overcome all comparisons until, once again, she sobbed quietly into her pillow at the knowledge that *that* memory also would have to last for the rest of her life.

By first light, the servants were already astir under the direction of Mr Peale and Mr Dawson, the clerk of the kitchen from whom Lydia had obtained buckets of hot water. Elizabeth, a blonde-haired, scatter-brained maid of sixteen and the apple of Mr Dawson's discerning eye, had been sent off to find some comfrey for Felice's bruises while Felice herself, examining her upper arms and wrists, found exactly what she expected to find, rows of blue fingertip marks that were visible to Lydia from halfway across the room.

'Merciful heavens, love! I think you'll have to tell Sir Leon of this when he returns,' she said. 'It's something he ought to know about.'

'By the time Sir Leon Gascelin returns,' Felice replied, caustically, 'this lot will have disappeared.' She stirred the water in the wooden bucket with her feet, enjoying the comfort it gave to her cuts and scratches. 'And by the sound of him,' she went on, 'my well-being will probably be the last thing on his mind.'

'Lord Deventer said that of him? Surely not,' said Lydia, frowning.

'Not in so many words, but the implication was there, right enough. Keep out of his way. Don't interfere with his plans. And above all, remember that he's the high and mighty surveyor to whom we must all bow and scrape. Except that he's not available to bow and scrape to, so that gives us all time to practise, doesn't it? Pass me that comb, Lydie.' Thoughtfully, she untangled the long straight tresses, recalling how it had recently been undone by a man's fingers. 'I should wash it,' she mumbled.

A shout reached them from the courtyard below, then another, a deep angry voice that cracked across the general clatter of feet, hooves, buckets and boxes. Silence dropped like a stone.

Another piercing bark. 'Where, exactly?'

The reply was too quiet for them to hear, but Lydia mouthed the missing words, pointing a finger to the floor, her eyes wide with dismay.

'That doesn't sound like the steward,' whispered Felice.

Lydia crossed to the window but she was too late, and by the time she reached the door it had been flung open by a man who had to stoop to avoid hitting his head on the low medieval lintel. He straightened, immediately, his hand still on the latch, his advance suddenly halted by the sight of a stunningly beautiful woman sitting with her feet in a bucket, dressed in little except a sleeveless kirtle of fine linen, half-open down the front. It would have been impossible to say whose surprise was the greater, his or theirs.

'Get out!' Felice snapped, making no effort to dive for cover. If this was a colleague of the miserable steward, Thomas Vyttery, then his opinion of her was of no consequence. Yet this man had the most insolent manner.

He made no move to obey the command, but took in every detail of the untidy room as he bit back at her. 'This is my room! *You* get out!'

It took a while, albeit a short one, for his words

to register, for the only other person who could lay claim to the Abbot's House was Sir Leon Gascelin, and he was known to be away from home.

The man was tall and broad-chested, the embodiment of the power that she and Lydia had facetiously been applauding. His dark hair was a straight and glossy cap that jutted wilfully out over his forehead in spikes, close-cropped but unruly enough to catch on the white lace-edged collar of his opennecked shirt. Felice noticed the ambience of great physical strength and virility that surrounded him, even while motionless, and the way that Fen and Flint had gone to greet him with none of the natural hostility she would have preferred them to exhibit in the face of such rudeness.

He caressed the head of one of them with a strong well-shaped hand that showed a scattering of dark hairs along the back, while his straight brows drew together above narrowed eyes in what might have passed for either disapproval or puzzlement.

Felice's retort was equally adamant. 'This house belongs to Lord Deventer and I am here by his permission. As you see, I am making no plans to move out again. Now, if you require orders to bully my servants, I suggest you go and seek Sir Leon Gascelin, my lord's surveyor. That should occupy your time more fruitfully. You may go.' Leaning forward, she swished the water with her fingertips. 'Is this the last of the hot water, Lydie?'

Lydia's reply was drowned beneath the man's icy

words. 'I don't need to find him. I *am* Sir Leon
Gascelin.'

Slowly, Felice raised her head to look at him
through a curtain of hair, the hem of which dripped
with curving points of water. She had no idea of the
picture of loveliness she presented, yet on impulse
her hand reached out sideways for her linen chemise, the one she had worn yesterday, gathering it
to her in a loose bundle below her chin. Promptly,
Lydia came forward to drape a linen sheet around
her shoulders.

'Then I have the advantage of you, Sir Leon,'
Felice said over the loud drumming of her heart. 'I
was here first.'

'Then you can be the first to go, lady. I require
you to be out of here by mid-day. My steward tells
me that you call yourself Lady Felice Marwelle, but
Lord Deventer never mentioned anyone of that name
in my hearing. Do you have proof of your relationship to his lordship? Or are you perhaps his mistress
with the convenient sub-title of stepdaughter?' He
looked around him at the piles of clothes, pillows,
canvas bags and mattresses more typical of a squat-
ter's den than a lady's bedchamber. 'You'd not be
the first, you know.'

Outraged by his insolence, Felice shook with fury.
'My name, sir, is Lady Felice Marwelle, daughter of
the late Sir Paul Marwelle of Henley-on-Thames
who was the first husband of my mother, Lady Honoria Deventer. Lord Deventer is my mother's third

husband and therefore my second stepfather. I am not, and never will be, *any* man's mistress, nor am I in the habit of proving my identity to my stepfather's boorish acquaintances. His message would have made that unnecessary, but it appears that *that* went the same way as his recollection that he had a stepdaughter named Felice. He assured me that he sent a message three…four days ago for you to prepare rooms in the guest…' She could have bitten her tongue.

'So you decided on the Abbot's House instead. And there was *no* message, lady.'

'Then we share a mutual shock at the sight of each other, for which I am as sorry as you are, Sir Leon,' she said with biting sarcasm. She felt the unremitting examination of his eyes which she knew must have missed nothing by now: her swollen eyelids, her bruises, her soaking feet, all adding no doubt to his misinterpretation of her role. Defensively, she tried to justify herself whilst regretting the need to do so. 'I chose this dwelling, sir, because I am not used to living on a building-site, despite Lord Deventer's recommendations. Whether you received a message or not, I am here to prepare rooms in the New House next door ready for his lordship's occupation in the autumn. And I had strict instructions to keep well out of your way, which I could hardly do with any degree of success if our two households were thrown together, could I? Even a child could see that,' she said, looking out of the window towards the roof of the church. 'Now will you please remove yourself from my chamber, Sir Leon, and allow me to finish dressing? As you see, we are still in the middle of unpacking.'

Instead of leaving, Sir Leon closed the door behind him and came further into the room where the light from one of the large mullioned windows gave her the opportunity to see more of his extreme good looks, his abundant physical fitness. His long legs were well-muscled, encased in brown hose and knee-high leather riding boots; paned breeches of soft brown kid did nothing to disguise slim hips around which hung a sword-belt, and Felice assumed that he had stormed round here immediately on his return from some nearby accommodation, for otherwise it would have taken him longer to reach an out-of-the-way place like Wheatley.

'No,' he said, in answer to her request. 'I haven't finished yet, lady. You'll not dismiss me the way you dismissed my steward yesterday.'

Instantly, she rose to the bait. 'If your steward, Sir Leon, knows no better than to refuse both hospitality and welcome to travellers after a two-day journey, then it's time he was replaced. Clearly he's not up to the position.'

'If Thomas Vyttery is replaced at all, lady, it will be for handing you the keys to this house.'

'That was his only saving grace. The keys remain with me.'

'This is no place for women, not for a good few

months. We've barely started again after winter and there are dozens of men on the site,' he said, leaning against the window recess and glancing down into the courtyard below. It swarmed with men, but they were her servants, not his builders. 'And I have enough trouble getting them to keep their minds on the job without a bevy of women appearing round every corner.'

'Then put blinkers on them, sir!' she snapped. 'The direction of your men's interest is not my concern. I've been sent down here to fulfil a task and I intend to do it. Surely my presence cannot be the worst that's ever happened to you in your life. You appear to have survived, so far.'

'And you, Lady Felice Marwelle, have an extremely well-developed tongue for one so young. I begin to see why your stepfather was eager to remove you to the next county if you used it on him so freely, though he might have spared a thought for me while he was about it. He might have done even better to find you a husband with enough courage to tame you. I'd do it myself if I had the time.'

'Hah! You're sure it's only *time* you lack, Sir Leon? I seem to have heard that excuse more than once when skills are wanting. Now, if you'll excuse me, my feet are wrinkling like paper, and I *must* hone my tongue in private.'

It was not to be, however. Enter Mistress Elizabeth bearing a large armful of feathery green plants, her face flushed and prettily eager. Without taking stock of the situation in the chamber or sensing any of the tension, she headed directly for her mistress and dumped the green bundle on to her lap. 'My lady, look! Here's chervil for your bruises. There's a mass of it in the old kitchen garden. There, now!' She looked round, newly aware of the unenthusiastic audience and searching for approval.

Felice looked down at the offering. 'Chervil, Elizabeth?'

'Comfrey, Elizabeth,' said Lydia. 'You were told to gather comfrey.'

'Oh,' said Elizabeth, flatly.

'You have injuries, lady?' said Sir Leon. 'I didn't know that.' His deep voice adopted a conciliatory tone that made Felice look up sharply, her eyes suddenly wary.

'No, sir. Nothing to speak of. The journey yesterday, that's all.' In a last effort to persuade him to leave, she stood up, holding out the greenery to Lydia and taking a thoughtless step forward.

She went crashing down, tipping the bucket over and pitching herself face-first into a flood of tepid water, flinging the chervil into Sir Leon's path. He and Lydia leapt forward together, but he was there first with his hands beneath her bare armpits, heaving her upright between his straddled legs. Then, to everyone's astonishment, he lifted her up into his arms as if she weighed no more than a child and stood with her in the centre of the room as the two maids mopped at the flood around his feet.

Felice was rarely at a loss for words, but the shock of the fall, her wet and dishevelled state, and this arrogant man's unaccustomed closeness combined to make any coherent sound difficult, her sense of helplessness heightened by her sudden plunge from her high-horse to the floor.

His hands were under her knees and almost over one breast that pushed unashamedly proud and pink through the wet fabric; his face, only inches from hers, held an expression of concern bordering on consternation. He was watching her closely. Inspecting her. 'You hurt?' he said.

She peered at him through strands of wet hair, shaking her head and croaking one octave lower. 'Let me go, sir. Please.'

He hesitated, then looked around the room. 'Where?' he said.

'Anywhere.'

For a long moment—time waited upon them—their eyes locked in a confusion of emotions that ranged through disbelief, alarm and, on Felice's part, outright hostility. It was natural that she should have missed the admiration in his, for he did his best to conceal it, but she was close enough now to see his muscular neck where a long red scratch ran from beneath his chin and disappeared into the open neck of his shirt. His jaw was square and strong and his mouth, unsmiling but with lips parted as if about to speak, had a tiny red mark on the lower edge where perhaps his lover had bitten it in the height of passion. His breath reached her, sending a wave of familiar panic into her chest, and as her gaze wandered over his features on their own private search, he continued to watch her with a grey unwavering scrutiny, noting her bruised wrists before holding her eyes again.

Her gaze flinched and withdrew to the loosely hanging points of his doublet that should have tied it together; the aiglets that tipped each tie were spear-heads of pure gold. One of them was missing. She took refuge in the most inconsequential details while her breath stayed uncomfortably in her lungs, refusing to move and gripped by a terrible fear that seeped into every part of her, reviving a recent nightmare. She fought it, terrified of accepting its meaning.

His grip on her body tightened, pulling her closely in to him, then he strode over to the tumbled mattress where she had lain that night and placed her upon it, bending low enough for his forelock to brush against her eyelids. He stood upright, looking down at her and combing a hand through his hair that slithered back into the ridges like a tiled roof. Without another word, he picked up the grimy doeskin breeches she had worn in the garden, dropped them into her lap and strode past the sobbing Elizabeth and bustling Lydia and out of the room, without bothering to close the door. They heard his harsh shout to someone below them, and the two deerhounds stood with ears pricked, listening to the last phases of his departure.

Mistress Lydia was first to recover. 'For pity's sake, Elizabeth, stop snivelling and help me with this mess, will you? What's that you're fiddling with? Let me see.'

'I don't know. I found it under the chervil in the kitchen garden.' She held out her palm upon which lay a tiny golden spear-head with a hole through its shaft.

Lydia picked it up, turning it over in the light before handing it to her mistress. 'An aiglet,' she said. 'Somebody lost it. Now, lass...' she turned back to Elizabeth '...you get that wet mess off the floor and throw it out. Plants and men are rarely what they seem: that chervil is cow-parsley.'

Chapter Two

The unshakeable determination that Felice had shown to her early morning visitor regarding her occupation of the Abbot's House now collapsed like a pack of playing cards, and whereas she had earlier brushed aside Lydia's suggestion that they might as well return to Sonning, it now seemed imperative that the waggons were loaded without delay.

'We can't stay here, Lydie,' she said, still shaking. 'We just can't. Send a message down to find Mr Peale.'

Mistress Lydia Waterman had been with Felice long enough to become her close friend and ally and, at five years her senior, old enough to be her advisor, too. She was a red-haired beauty who had never yet given her heart to any man to hold for more than a week or two, and Felice loved her for her loyalty and almost brutal honesty.

'Think what you're doing, love,' said Lydia, businesslike. 'That's not the best way to handle it.'

Felice winced at the advice, given for the second time that day. 'I *have* thought. That was him!' she whispered, fiercely. 'This is his missing aiglet that Elizabeth found. He's a *fiend*, Lydie.'

Lydia lifted a dense pile of blue velvet up into her arms and held it above Felice's head. 'Arms up,' she said, lowering it. 'Losing an aiglet in the kitchen garden doesn't make him a fiend, love. And he didn't arrive here until now, so how could it have been him who chased you? Last night he'd have been miles away.'

'If he was near enough to get here so early he couldn't have been far away, Lydie. He must have been snooping while they believed he was away, looking for something…somebody. And I recognised the voice too, and the way he looked at me. I know that he knows. He wanted to humiliate me.'

'All men sound the same in the dark,' said Lydia, cynically. 'But he picked you up out of the water fast enough.'

'And he pretended to believe that I was Lord Deventer's mistress, too.'

'Perhaps he really believed it. His lordship's no saint, is he? It was an easy mistake to make, with him not recognising the name of Marwelle. Turn round, love, while I fasten you up.'

'I don't care. We're not staying. We can be away tomorrow.'

'No, we can't,' Lydia said with a mouthful of pins. 'Tomorrow's Sunday.'

Lydia's pragmatism could be shockingly unhelpful, yet not even she could be expected to share the torment that now shook Felice to the very core. The knowing stranger she had presumed would take her secret with him to the ends of the earth now proved to be the very person whose antagonism clearly matched her own, the one with whom she would not have shared the slightest confidence, let alone last night's disgraceful fiasco.

He would misconstrue it, naturally. What man would not? He would believe she was cheap, a silly lass who needed reminding to think before she allowed a man, a total stranger, to possess her, hence his whispered warning that should more typically have come from her rather than him. Oh, yes, he would revel in the misunderstanding: she would see it in his eyes at every meeting unless she packed her bags and left.

It was a misunderstanding she herself would have been hard-pressed to explain rationally, a private matter of the heart she had not discussed even with the worldly Lydia, for Father Timon had not been expected to know what it was frowned upon for priests to know, and his role of chaplain, confessor, tutor and friend had progressed further than was seemly for priests and maids of good breeding.

Timon Montefiore, aged twenty-eight, had taken up his duties in Lord Deventer's household soon after the latter's marriage to Lady Honoria Fyner, previously Marwelle, and perhaps it had been a mutual need for instant friendship that had been the catalyst for what followed.

Friendship developed into affection, and the affection deepened. As her mother's preoccupation with a new husband and a young step-family grew, Felice's previous role as deputy-mistress of their former home became redundant in Lord Deventer's austerely regimented household. Rudderless and overlooked by the flamboyant new stepfather, Felice had drifted more and more towards Timon, partly to remove herself from Lord Deventer's insensitivities and partly because Timon was always amiable and happy to see her. He had been exceptional in other ways; his teaching was leisurely and tender, arousing her only so far and no further, always with the promise of something more and with enough control for both of them. 'Think what you're doing,' was advice she heard regularly, though often enough accompanied by the lift of her hand towards his smiling lips and merry eyes.

She had discovered the inevitable anguish of love last summer when Timon had caught typhoid fever and her stepfather had had him quickly removed from his house to the hospice in Reading. Forbidden to visit him, Felice had been given no chance to say farewell and, during conversation at dinner a week later, she learned that he had died a few days before and was already buried. Lord Deventer was not sure where. Did it matter? he had said, bluntly. Until then, Felice had not known that love and pain were so closely intertwined.

Since that dreadful time last summer, no man's arms had held her, nor had any other man shared her thoughts until now. Her terrible silence had been explained by her mother as dislike of her new situation, exacerbated by talk of husbands, a remedy as painful as it was tactless to one who believed her heart to be irrevocably broken.

The usual agonies of guilt and punishment had been instilled into Felice from an early age and were now never far from her mind without the courteous priest to mitigate it. The replacement chaplain had been stern and astringent, not the kind to receive a desperate young woman's confidences, and she had been glad to accept any means of escape from a house of bitter-sweet memories upon which she had believed nothing would impose. But last night's experience had suggested otherwise in a far from tender manner, and her anger at her heart's betrayal was equal to her fury with the shiftless Fate who had plucked mockingly at the cords that bound her heart.

'Out of the frying-pan, into the fire' was a saying that occurred to her as she went about the first duties of the day, now demurely dressed in a blue velvet overskirt and bodice that set off the white under-sleeves embroidered with knotwork patterns. Black-work, they called it, except that this was blue and gold. Her hair was tidily coiled into a gold mesh caul at the nape of her neck almost as an act of defiance to the man who had warned her of his men's easily deflected attentions. At home, she would have worn a concealing black velvet French hood, yet she had never been overly concerned by prevailing fashions and saw no reason to conform now that there was no one to notice. That dreadful man had seen her at her worst; whatever he saw now would be an improvement.

The first floor was thronged with men carrying tables, stools, chests and cupboards and, in her chamber, several of the carpenters were erecting the great tester bed and hanging its curtains. The ground floor was the servants' domain, containing the great hall and steward's offices, but the top floor covered the length and breadth of the building, a massive room flooded with light from new oriel windows that reflected on to a magnificent plasterwork ceiling. Knowing that these additions were the result of the surveyor's vision, Felice tried hard to find fault with it, but came away with grudging admiration instead. It was no wonder he had been irked by her takeover.

She visited the kitchens across the courtyard next, but came close to being trampled underfoot by lads carrying boxes, baskets, pans and sacks; so, to give her feet some respite, she headed for an area at the back of the Abbot's House that gave access into the derelict square cloister. Here at last was peace where, in the enclosed warmth, the kitchen cat poured itself off a low wall at the sight of Flint and Fen and disappeared into the long grass.

Shelving her thoughts about how to make a dignified return home, she sat with her legs stretched out between the stone columns that topped the low wall, her eyes unconsciously planning a formal garden with perhaps a fountain in the centre. Not that it mattered; she did not intend to stay. She removed her shoes to inspect the soles of her feet in valuable privacy.

The deerhounds nosed about behind her, so their silence went unheeded until, sensing their absence, she turned to check on them. Their two heads could not have been closer beneath the hand of the tall intruder who stood silently in the shadows on the church side of the cloister, watching her.

Her heart lurched, pounding with a new rhythm, and she turned away, throwing her skirts over her bare ankles, pretending an unconcern she was far from feeling. She snapped her fingers, angrily and called, 'Flint! Fen! Come!'—by no means sure that they would obey but reluctant to turn to see.

The hounds returned to her side but they were not alone, nor had they obeyed her command but his, and she knew then that, like the steward deserted by his mastiff, she would never again be able to rely on them for protection. Angered by their inability to tell friend from foe, she snapped at them, 'Lie down!'

Sir Leon was laughing quietly at this calamity as he came to sit on the wall just beyond her feet and, as she began to swing them to the ground, he caught one ankle in a tight grip, making her flight impossible. 'No, lady,' he said. 'We have some unfinished business, do we not? A moment or two of your time, if you please.'

'Be brief, sir. And release my foot.'

She did not need to look at him to see that he had already started work, for he had discarded his doublet and now wore only the jerkin over his shirt, the sleeves of which were rolled up to expose well-muscled forearms. A deep V of bare chest showed in the opening, and his boots were powdered with stone-dust. Unhurried by her command, his hand slid away and spread across his knee. 'Well?' he said, tucking away the remnants of a smile.

She frowned at him, puzzled. 'Well, what, sir?'

'I'm allowing you to state your case before I state mine, Lady Felice Marwelle. And you need not be brief.'

'Nevertheless, I will be. You will be relieved to know that I intend to return to Sonning within the next few days.' She spoke to a row of purring pigeons on the angle of the wall behind him, disconcerted by his close attention, his attempted dominance even before words had been exchanged.

'Is that all?'

'Yes.'

'Then you've changed your mind about staying.'

'Yes,' she snapped. 'Don't ask me why. It's what you wanted, isn't it?'

'You changed your mind to please me?'

Her mouth tightened. 'No. It pleases *me*.'

'Then I'm sorry to disappoint you. I must reject your decision.'

'What?' She frowned, looking at him fully for the first time. 'You're in no position to reject it. I've already made it.' His eyes, she saw, were grey and still laughing.

'Then you can unmake it, my lady. You'll stay here and complete the task Lord Deventer set for you.'

Rather than continue a futile argument, Felice's response was to get up and leave him, but her body's slight message was deciphered even as it formed, and her ankle was caught again and held firmly.

'Ah, no!' he said. 'I'm aware of your aptitude for bringing discussions to an abrupt conclusion but really, you have to give them a chance to develop occasionally, don't you think so? Now, what d'ye think your stepfather will say when you tell him you haven't even seen the place yet?'

Riled by his insistence and by his continued hold on her ankle, she flared like a fuse. 'And what d'ye think he'll say, Sir Leon, when I tell him of the disgraceful way I've been received? Which I will!'

This did not have the effect she hoped for, no sign of contrition crossing his face. 'About mistaking you for one of his mistresses, you mean? That jest will keep him entertained for a month, my lady, as well you know. And if he'd intended to send a message to warn me of your arrival...'

'To *warn* you? Thank you!'

'...he would have done. Clearly he had no intention of doing so.'

'Why ever not, pray?'

'Because he knew damn well he'd have to look for another surveyor if he had. He knows my views about mixing work and women.'

Felice bent to clutch at her leg and yank it bodily out of his grasp, swinging her legs down on to the long grass. 'Then there will be three of us pleased, sir. There is nothing more to discuss, is there?'

'Correction. There'll be two of us pleased. You'll stay here with me.'

She sat, rigidly angry, with her hands clutching at the cool stone wall on each side of her. 'Sir Leon, I am usually quite good at understanding arguments, but when they are as obscure as yours I'm afraid I need some help. Explain to me, if you will. If you are so disturbed about having women near you, why have you suddenly decided that I must stay? I can only conclude that you must need to please Lord Deventer very much indeed to sacrifice your principles so easily. Do you need his approval so much, then?'

He allowed himself a smile before he replied, revealing white even teeth. 'Certainly I do. He pays me, you see, and the sooner this place is lived in, the sooner I can move on to others. I'm in demand, hereabouts.'

'Not by me!' she muttered under her breath. 'Barbarian!'

'Still sore?' He lowered his tone to match hers, catching the drift of her mind.

It was a mistake she regretted instantly, having no wish to discuss those terrible events, neither with him nor with anyone. Forgetting her shoes, she was quicker this time, managing to reach the centre of the overgrown quadrangle before her wrist was caught and she was brought to a halt. She shook off his grip and whirled to face him in a frenzy of rage.

'Don't touch me!' she snarled, her eyes blazing like coals. 'Don't *ever* lay a finger on me again, sir, or I swear I'll…I'll *kill* you! And don't think to dictate to me where and when I go. You are not my guardian.' She turned her back on him deliberately, but had no idea how to get out of the quadrangle without climbing shoeless over the low wall. Her heart thudded in an onslaught of anger. She hesitated, feeling the sharp tangle of weeds on her sore feet. There was an uncanny silence behind her.

'You'll need these to get out of here, my lady.' His voice came from where they had been sitting.

She knew he referred to her shoes but still she hesitated, wondering if it was worth risking more pain to her feet. The cloister walkways were littered with rubble.

'Come on,' he said, gently. 'We're going to have to talk if we're to work together.'

'We are *not* going to work together,' she snapped. 'I want nothing to do with this place. I'm going home.'

'You'll need your shoes, then.'

She turned and saw that he was sitting on the wall again with one leg on either side, holding up her shoes as bait. 'Throw them,' she said.

'Come and collect them.'

She looked away, then approached, eyeing his hands. She reached the wall just as he dropped them over on to the paved side, beyond her reach. 'Don't play games with me, Sir Leon. I'm not a child,' she snapped.

'Believe it or not, I had noticed that, but I'm determined you shall conclude this discussion in the proper manner, my lady, whether you like the idea or not. Now, please be seated. I am not at all disturbed by the idea of having women near me, as you see. Actually, it's something I'm learning to get the hang of.'

She knew he was being ridiculous. Any man who could move a woman so quickly and with such mastery was obviously no woman-hater. 'You have a long way to go,' she said, coldly. 'About twenty years should be enough.'

The smile returned. 'That's better. We're talking again. Now, my lady, I shall show you round the New House and we can discuss what's to be done in the best chambers on the upper floors. The lower one...'

'Sir Leon, you are under a misapprehension. I have already told you...'

'That you are not staying. Yes, I heard you, but I have decided that you are. If Deventer has entrusted you with the organisation of his household here at Wheatley, and to furnish his rooms, then he must think highly of your abilities. Surely you're not going to throw away the chance to enhance your credit with him and disappoint your mother, too? They would expect some kind of explanation from you. Do you have one available?'

'Yes, sir. As it happens, I do. I intend to tell them that you are impossible to work with and that our intense dislike of each other is mutual. Indeed, I cannot help feeling that my stepfather guessed how matters would stand before he sent me here, so I shall have no compunction about giving him chapter and verse.'

'Chapter *and* verse?'

'You are detestable!' she whispered, looking away.

'And you, as you have reminded me, are a woman, and therefore you will hardly be deceived by my very adequate reasons.'

'Not in the slightest. Nor would a child believe them.'

'Then how would it be if I were to inform your

parents of what happened last night?' he said, quietly.

She had not been looking until now, but the real intention behind his appalling question needed to be seen in his eyes. He could not be serious. But his expression told her differently. He was very serious.

'Oh, yes,' she whispered, her eyes narrowing against his steady gaze. 'Oh, yes, you would, wouldn't you? And if I told them you were talking nonsense?'

'Whose word would your stepfather take, d'ye think? Whose story would he *prefer* to believe, yours or mine? I could go into a fair amount of detail, if need be.'

She launched herself at him like a wildcat, her fingers curved like claws ready to rake at his cool grey eyes, his handsome insolent face, at anything to ruffle his intolerable superiority and to snatch back the memories he should never have been allowed to hold.

Her hands were caught and held well out of harm's way and, if she had hoped to knock him backwards against the stone column, she now found that it was she who was made to sit with one at her back while her arms were slowly and easily twisted behind her.

His arms encircled her, his face close to hers, and once again she was his captive and infuriated by his restraint. 'And don't let's bother about talk of killing me if I should lay a finger on you because I intend to, lady, one way or another. You threw me a care-less challenge earlier. Remember?'

Mutely, she glared at a point beyond his shoulder.

'Yes, well I've accepted it, so now we'll see how much skill is needed to tame you, shall we?'

She was provoked to scoff again. 'Oh, of course. That's what it's all about. First you pretend to be concerned with duty, yours and mine, and then you try threats. But after all that, it's a challenge, a silly challenge you men can never resist, can you? How pathetic! What a victory in the eyes of your peers when they hear how you took on a woman single-handed. How they'll applaud you. And how the women will sneer at your hard-won victory. Did you not know, Sir Leon, that a man can only make a woman do what she would have done anyway?' She had never believed it, but it added some small fuel to her argument.

'Ah, you think that, do you? Then go on believing it if you think it will help. It makes no difference, my beauty. Deventer sent you down here with more than his new house in mind, and somewhere inside that lovely head you have some conflicting messages of your own, haven't you, eh?'

Frantically, she struggled against him, not want-ing to hear his percipient remarks or suffer the un-bearable nearness of him again. Nor could she tol-erate his trespass into her capricious mind. 'Let me go!' she panted. 'Loose me! I want nothing to do with you.'

'You'll have a lot to do with me before we're through, so you can start by regarding me as your custodian, in spite of not wanting me. Deventer will approve of that, I know.'

'You insult me, sir. Since when has a custodian earned the right to abuse his charge as you have abused me?'

'Abuse, my lady? That was no abuse, and you know it. You'd stopped fighting me, remember.'

'I was exhausted,' she said, finding it increasingly difficult to think with his eyes roaming her face at such close quarters. 'You insulted me then as you do now. Let me go, Sir Leon. There will never be a time when I shall need a custodian, least of all a man like you. Go and find someone else to try your so-called skills on, and make sure it's dark so she sees you not.'

'Get used to the idea, my lady,' he said, releasing her. 'It will be with you for as long as it takes.' He picked up her shoes and held them by his side. 'Fight me as much as you like, but you'll discover who's master here, and I'll have you tamed by the end of summer.'

'A most unseemly summer, Sir Leon, if I intended to stay. But, you see, I don't. Now, give me my shoes.' She would have been surprised and perhaps a little disappointed if he had obeyed her, yet the temptation to nettle him was strong and her anger still so raw that she would have prolonged even this petty squabble just to win one small point. As it turned out, the victory was not entirely hers.

'Ask politely,' he said.

'I'll be damned if I will! Keep them!'

Her moment of recklessness was redeemed by voices that reached them through the open arch that had once been a doorway, the way she had entered. Lydia and Elizabeth were looking for her. 'My lady?' they called. 'Where are you?'

'Here,' she called back. 'Elizabeth, ask Sir Leon prettily for my shoes, there's a dear. He's been kind enough to carry them for me.' Without another glance at her self-appointed custodian, she held up one foot ready for its prize. '*Such* a gentleman,' she murmured, sweetly.

It was better than nothing. But she could not bring herself to elaborate on the scene to Lydia, who was not taken in by Sir Leon's stiff bow or by her mistress's attempt at nonchalance, her blazing eyes and pink cheeks.

'We're staying, then,' said Lydia, provocatively.

'Certainly not!' Felice told her, surreptitiously probing along her arms for more bruises. 'We're getting out of here at the first opportunity. Why?' She glanced at her maid's face. 'Don't tell me you'd like to stay.'

'Well…' Lydia half-smiled '…I've just discovered that he has a very good-looking valet called Adam.'

'Oh, Lydie! Don't complicate matters, there's a love.'

Another reason for Felice's reserve was that her discord with Sir Leon had now acquired a sizeable element of personal competition in which the prize was to be her pride, a commodity she was as determined to hold on to as he apparently was to possess. Removing herself from the field of contest would indicate that it was probably not worth the fight, leaving him to be the victor by default. And naturally, he would believe her to be afraid of him.

Perhaps even more serious was his threat to make Lord Deventer aware of their first encounter from which she had emerged the loser. While her stepfather would undoubtedly clap his surveyor on the back for taking advantage of such a golden opportunity, not to mention his night-time vigil, she herself would be severely censured for such conduct, irrespective of its initial purpose. The thought of Lord Deventer's coarse laughter brought waves of shame to her face enough to make any castigation pleasant by comparison. He would find her a husband, one who was more concerned about the size of her dowry than her reputation.

As for Sir Leon, any man who could use such an intimate and enigmatic incident as a threat was both unprincipled and despicable; he must know that that alone would be enough to keep her at Wheatley. Still, there was nothing to stop her making him regret his decision, though she expected that future encounters would be both rare and brief. Except to Lord Deventer, the man had absolutely nothing to recommend him.

The news that men had been seen traipsing through the kitchen garden had intrigued her until she discovered at suppertime that they had been repairing the gap in the wall by the side of the river path. And when she had asked by whose orders—it was, after all, in her domain—she had been told it was by Sir Leon's.

She might have let the matter rest at that; it would not do to display an inexplicable curiosity. But in the comforting darkness of her curtained bed, the soft images of the previous night took unnatural precedence over the day's conflicts and would not leave her in peace. It was as if, in the darkness, they were beyond regret. She had now seen the man with whom she had been entangled and, although hostile, it was not difficult for her to recall the way he had held, caressed and kissed her, nor to remember how her own body had flared out of control before the sudden quenching of prudence. In the dark, shame did not exist.

With only the moon to watch, she took Flint and Fen quietly downstairs out of the front door and round through the kitchen courtyard to the back of the house, the reverse of last night's frantic journey. At the entrance to the garden she stopped, confronted by the derelict place washed by moonlight where dear Timon's memory had been cruelly disturbed by one insane moment of bliss, the like of which she had never known with him. Was it because of his absence? Her longing? She thought not, but no one need know it. She need not admit it again, even to herself.

One of the deerhounds whined, then the other, both suddenly leaving her and bounding up the overgrown path into the darkness. Incensed by their preference for rabbits rather than her, she took a step forward, yelling into the silvery blackness, 'Flint! Fen! Come back here, damn you!'

They returned at the trot, ears flattened and tails flailing apologetically, but shattering her reminiscences and making her aware of their absurdity. 'Come!' she said, severely. 'Stupid hounds.'

This time, her return was unhurried and more thoughtful.

Had the next day been any other but Sunday, there would have been a good chance of avoiding the cause of her sleepless moments, but churchgoing was never an option unless one intended to attract the disapproval of the vicar and his churchwardens. Furthermore, as a close relative of the abbey's owner, Felice had a duty to attend.

She had had her hair braided and enclosed by a pearl-studded gold-mesh cap that appeared to be supported by a white lace collar. Over her elegant farthingale she wore a light woollen gown of rose-pink, a soft tone that complemented the honey of her flawless skin. As the early morning mist had not yet cleared, she wore a loose overgown of a deeper pink lined with grey squirrel, and she assumed Sir Leon's long examination of her to be approval of her outfit. But, as she had feared, she was given no choice of where to sit, the better benches being at the front and the church already well-filled. So his, 'Good morrow, my lady,' had to be acknowledged as if all were well between them.

Fortunately, there had been no time for more. The vicar, a lively and well-proportioned middle-aged man, was nothing like the sleepy village priest she had half-expected, and it was not until after the service when introductions were made that Felice discovered he was married to the lady who had been sitting beside her.

'Dame Celia Aycombe,' Sir Leon presented the lady, 'wife of the Reverend John Aycombe, vicar of Wheatley.'

Knowing of the new queen's objections to married clergy, Felice was surprised. Those who defied the royal displeasure usually kept themselves quietly busy in some isolated village which, she supposed, was what the Aycombes were doing. She had been equally surprised to see that Sir Leon's unwelcoming steward, Thomas Vyttery, had been assisting the vicar, and to discover that he also was married.

Dame Celia introduced the woman who had been sitting next to her and who had been craning forward in perpetual curiosity for most of the service. 'Dame

Audrey Vyttery,' she said to Felice, who saw a woman nearing her forties who must in her youth have been pretty when her eyes and mouth had still remembered how to smile. She was slight but over-dressed, and spangled with brooches and ribbons almost from neck to toe. Whereas the plumpish contented figure of Dame Celia held only a pair of leather gloves and a prayer book to complete her outfit, Dame Audrey fidgeted nervously with a pomander on a golden chain, an embroidered purse, a muff, a prayer book and a quite unnecessary feather fan. Acidly, she enquired whether Felice was to stay at Wheatley permanently and, if so, would she remain in the Abbot's House? She had understood Sir Leon to be moving in there.

Catching the direction of the enquiry, Felice put her mind at rest while speaking clearly enough for Sir Leon to hear. 'No, Dame Audrey. Certainly not. Indeed, I'm making plans to leave soon. This is merely a brief visit to check on progress for Lord Deventer.' Surprisingly, she thought she detected something like relief in the woman's eyes, but Dame Celia was vociferous in her reaction to the news.

Her pale eyes widened in surprise. 'Surely not, my lady. This will be May Week, when we have our holy days and games. You'll not return before we've given you a chance to see how we celebrate, will you?'

'Of course she'll not!' The answer came from halfway down the nave where the energetic vicar

approached them in a flurry of white. Billowing and
back-lit by the west door, he bore down upon them
like an angelic host. 'She'll not, will she, Sir Leon?
No one leaves Wheatley during the May Day revels,
least of all our patron's lovely daughter.'

Sir Leon, who appeared to find Felice's denial
more entertaining than serious, agreed somewhat
mechanically. 'Indeed not, vicar. I've already told
her she must stay.'

'Good…good.' The vicar beamed. 'That's settled,
then.'

'Then you approve of May Day revels, vicar?'
Felice said.

'Hah! It makes no difference whether I approve
or not, my lady. They'd still do it. I believe half the
fathers and mothers of Wheatley were conceived on
May Eve. Swim with the tide or drown, that's always been my motto, and it's stood me in good
stead, so far, as you can see. I keep an eye on things,
and so does my good lady here, and we baptise the
bairns who're born every new year. That's probably
why the church is so full. Now, have you seen the
new buildings yet, my lady? A work of art, you
know.'

'Not yet, sir.'

'Be glad to show you round myself, but the master builder must take precedence over a mere clerk
of works.' He grinned, glancing amiably at Sir Leon.

Sir Leon explained the vicar's mock-modesty.
'The Reverend Aycombe is also my clerk of works

for the building-site, my lady. Both he and Mr Vyttery hold two positions as priests and building officials.'

'Priests?' said Felice. 'Mr Vyttery is a priest?' She stared at Dame Audrey who simpered, icily.

'Oh, yes,' she said. 'May hasband was sacristan here at Wheatley Ebbey. Augustinian, you see. All the manks were priests.'

Felice nodded. If she was to be obliged to stay here, she had better learn something about the place. 'Of course. And you, vicar? You were at the abbey, too?'

'Abbot, my lady,' he beamed.

Not only married priests, but married monks. And Timon had told her more than once that it could never be done, that he was already courting danger by celebrating the Roman Catholic Mass in private which was why no one must know of his whereabouts. But, of course, he had been concerned for her safety: recusants were fined quite heavily these days.

It was later that morning as she passed through the courtyard behind the Abbot's House that Felice noticed something odd which she could not at first identify. The yard was always emptier on Sundays, yet the stables had to be cleaned out, even on the sabbath, and it was not until she remembered yesterday's bustle of men and furnishings that she realised what was missing. The carts. The waggons.

'William,' she called to the head groom. 'What have you done with the waggons?'

William came towards her, leading a burly bay stallion. 'Waggons, m'lady? Sent 'em back to Sonning yesterday.'

'What?'

Unruffled, the man rubbed the horse's nose affectionately. 'Gone back to Lord Deventer's. Sir Leon's orders. He said you'd not be needing 'em. He wants the stable space for his own 'osses. This one's his.' He pulled at the horse's forelock.

'Did he, indeed? And how in heaven's name shall I be able to return home without horses and waggons? Did you ask Sir Leon *that*?'

'Yes, m'lady,' William replied, not understanding her indignation. 'He said you'd be able to manage, one way or another, but there wasn't room for Lord Deventer's 'osses and his, too. He sent 'em all back, sumpter 'osses, too.'

'And the carters? He sent them back?'

'Only a few. He says the rest can stay and work here.'

'But carters don't do any other work, William. They cart.'

'Yes, m'lady. That's what they'll be doing for Sir Leon.'

'No, they will *not*!'

After quite a search of the New House and several missed turnings, she found the high-handed and mighty surveyor by crashing into him round a corner of one of the narrow pannelled passageways. He did not retreat, as she would have preferred him to do, but manoeuvred her backwards by her elbows until she sat with a thud upon a window-seat in the thickness of the wall.

'You certainly have a way with entrances and exits, my lady,' he said, smiling down at her. 'But I'm flattered by your haste to find me.'

'Don't be!' she said coldly, standing up again. 'Why have you removed my waggons and horses and appropriated my carters?'

He leaned an elbow on the top edge of the wavy-wood panelling and stuck his fingers into his thick hair, holding it off his forehead as if to see her better. 'Did you need them urgently?' he said, disarmingly.

'That is not the point. They were mine.'

'Yours, were they? Ah, and I thought they belonged to Deventer.'

'Don't mince words, Sir Leon. I needed them for my return to Sonning. You knew that.'

'Then you have a short memory, my lady, since we are not mincing words. I've already told you that you'll be staying here at Wheatley, and therefore the waggons and horses will be required by Deventer for his own use. Don't tell me you've forgotten our understanding already.'

'There is no *understanding*, Sir Leon. There never will be any understanding between us, not on any subject. And I want my waggons back. You have taken over my stables and my carters; do you intend to take over my kitchens next, by any chance?'

Languidly, he came to stand before her, easing her back again on to the window-seat, resting his hands on the panelling to prevent her escape. 'Not to mince words, my lady, I can take over the entire Abbot's House any time I choose, as I intended to do to clear the guesthouse for renovation. Would you prefer it if I did that sooner instead of later? We could pack in there quite cosily, eh?' He lowered his head to hers.

She gulped, her chest tightening at the new threat which she knew he was quite capable of carrying out, even at his own expense. 'No,' she whispered. 'But...'

'But what?'

'I...I did not agree to stay here. I *cannot* stay...in the...in the...'

'In the circumstances?'

She breathed out, slowly. 'Yes.'

'You are referring to our first meeting?'

She nodded, looking down at her lap and feeling an uncomfortable heat creeping up towards her ears.

'Which you find painful to recall?'

He was baiting her. 'Yes,' she flared, 'you know I do or you'd not insist on dragging it into every argument.'

His face came closer until he needed only to whisper. 'Then why, if it's so very painful, did you return to the garden last night, lady? To relive it, just a little? Eh?'

She looked into his eyes for a hint of laughter but there was none to be seen, only a grey and steady seriousness that gave nothing of either enjoyment or sympathy for her chagrin.

'Well?' he said.

'How do you know that?'

'I was there. I saw you.'

'The hounds...?'

'I sent them back to you.'

'I went to...to look at the wall. You had it repaired.'

'In the *dark*? Come now, lass, don't take me for a fool. You couldn't keep away, could you? You had to go to remind yourself or to chastise yourself. Which? Do you even *know* which?'

Goaded beyond caution, she broke the barrier of his arm and pushed past to stand well beyond his reach, panting with rage and humiliation. 'Yes, Sir Leon, I do know exactly why I returned, but never in a thousand years would you be able to understand. Of course,' she scoffed, 'you believe it was for your sake, naturally, being so full of yourself and all. But it was not, sir, I assure you. It was *not*. Did you believe you're the first man who's ever kissed me?'

She noticed the slight shake of his head before he answered. 'On the contrary, lady. I am quite convinced that I am not the one who lit the fire that rages inside you, and I also know that you are feeding it on some resentment that threatens to burn you up. Which is yet another reason why you'll be better down here at Wheatley doing what Deventer expects of you rather than moping about up in Sonning with little to do except think. Or are you so eager to continue wallowing in your problems unaided?'

'My problems, as you call them, are not your concern, Sir Leon, nor do I need anyone's aid either to wallow or work. And I'm stuck here with no transport, thanks to your interference, so what choice do I have now but to stay?'

'Less than you had before, which was what I intended.'

'You are insufferable, sir.'

'Nevertheless, you will suffer me, and I will tame you. Now you can go.'

'Thank you. I was going anyway.' She stalked away, fuming.

That prediction at least was true, though she missed the smile in his eyes that followed her first into a dark cupboard and then into a carpenter's bench and a pile of wood-shavings.

'Where the devil *am* I?' she turned and yelled at him, furiously.

His smile broke as he set off towards her.

'Come,' he said, laughing.

Chapter Three

Although the notion had taken root in Felice's mind that she might have to stay at Wheatley Abbey after all, Sir Leon's high-handed tactics hardly bore the hallmarks of subtle persuasion. Added to their disastrous introduction, it was this that made her almost wild with anger and humiliation to be so brazenly manipulated first by Lord Deventer and then by his surveyor. It was almost as if they saw it as some kind of game in which her wishes were totally irrelevant. As for his talk about taming her, well, that was ludicrous. Men's talk.

'Tamed, indeed!' she spat. 'You've bitten off more than you can comfortably chew, sir!' She threw a fistful of bread scraps to the gaggling ducks, scowling approvingly at their rowdiness.

Her companion on the afternoon stroll was Mistress Lydia Waterman, whose insight was heartwarming. 'Take no notice, love,' she called from further along the river's edge. 'You know what they're like. They have to be given a sense of purpose. We could do worse, though, than be stranded in a place like this, and at least you have plenty to do. Just look at it; it must have been swarming with monks twenty years ago.'

To one side of them the river cut a tight curve that enclosed the abbey on two sides before disappearing beyond the mill into woodland. Where the grass and meadowsweet had recovered from the builders' feet, creamy-white elder blossom drooped over ducks, geese and swans that jostled for food. They launched themselves into the water in dignified droves as Felice's two deerhounds pranced towards them.

Wheatley Abbey had been left in ruins for twenty years after the English monasteries were closed and their wealth taken by the present queen's father, Henry VIII. But the villagers had won permission to keep the church for their own use while the rest of the abbey buildings had been bought by Lord Deventer whose programme of rebuilding had already lasted two years. During that time, his talented thirty-year-old surveyor had restored and converted first the Abbot's House and then the New House, which had once been the monks' refectory, dormitory and cellarium. The enclosed cloister still awaited attention, and the guesthouse, which at present stood apart from the other buildings, was being used as Sir Leon's offices and some of the masons' accommodation. There was still plenty to be done, but work on the New House was almost complete: courtyards, kitchens, stables and smithy, storerooms and dairy had all been rebuilt from the monks' living quarters.

Even the church had had to adapt to the religious changes of the last twenty turbulent years. The young Queen Elizabeth was more reasonable than her forebears in her dealings with religion, but even she was not immune to pressure from her councillors to take a harder line with those who found the changes too difficult to accept, like Felice's mother, for instance. Lord Deventer himself cared little one way or the other but had taken on the young chaplain, Timon Montefiore, for the sake of his staunch Roman Catholic new wife who saw no harm in breaking the law every day of the week while relenting for an hour or two on Sundays, just to avoid being fined.

Felice and Lydia strolled along the river's edge in silence in the direction of the village and a wooden bridge under the dense white candles of a chestnut tree. A familiar figure came from the opposite side, joining them midway over the green swirling depths where a rowing boat was tied to one of the bridge supports. A clutch of small children fished with excited intensity, calling to Dame Celia as she crossed.

'They've been doing that for centuries,' she smiled. 'I did it myself when I was a wee child, though never on a Sunday.'

'You lived here as a child?' Felice said. 'I didn't realise.'

Slowly, they meandered along the opposite side of the river away from the thatched rooftops that appeared through the trees. Dame Celia pointed the way she had come. 'Down there,' she said, 'at the end of the village. You'd have passed Wheatley Manor the other day as you came through. My parents owned it, but now my brother and his family live there. John and I have the priest's house on the Wheatley estate.'

'So you went away to be educated, Dame Celia?' said Felice.

'With the nuns at Romsey until I was fifteen. It's only a few miles away. But it was closed down at the same time as Wheatley and everyone was turned out. I was fortunate in being able to come home, but the nuns and novices had a much harder time of it.'

They sat on a log that had recently been felled, its stump still oozing with sticky resin. Lydia sat on Dame Celia's other side. 'Then you didn't consider taking vows?' she said.

'Not I!' Dame Celia laughed. 'You see, John had been abbot of Wheatley only a year when the abbey closed. He was the youngest ever. And I had returned home to live when he took the post as chaplain to my parents, and as vicar at the church here. No one had better qualifications for those jobs than the former abbot. So that's how we came together.'

Felice's heart skipped a beat. Chaplain and employer's daughter. 'Did your parents approve?' she said.

Dame Celia's comfortable face crumpled in amusement. 'Certainly not, my lady. But John was given a goodly pension and he was very persuasive. But it was a very unsettled time, you know, with all the changes. At first, the former monks and nuns were allowed to marry; priests were even allowed to marry their former mistresses and concubines. Then the young King Edward decided they were not, and we swung from being Catholic to Protestant twice in the space of four reigns, m'lady, and it left everyone a bit troubled. Especially people like Dame Audrey and her Thomas.'

Felice recalled the steward's bejewelled wife, her sadly pretty face and her pseudo upper-class accents. 'Oh,' she said. 'Was Dame Audrey at Romsey Abbey, too?'

'She was a young novice when it all came to an end. Audrey Wintershulle, she was then, a very pretty girl.'

'But then she married the sacristan. Why was that so troublesome to her?'

'Well, you see, they were unfortunate because Thomas had been appointed only a few months before the date was set for the abbey's closure so he received only a small pension, barely enough to live on, so he took the job of chantry priest here at the church to say prayers for the dead. But then when the young King Edward came to the throne, all the chantry chapels were abolished and the money used for other purposes, schools and such-like. So poor Thomas was out of a job again. Then when the abbey was eventually sold off to Lord Deventer, Thomas was taken on as steward to oversee the property and maintain it. No one else could have done that better than Thomas; he knows the abbey like the back of his hand.'

'But what did he do for a living between times, Dame Celia? Surely he couldn't live off his pension alone?'

'John helped him out,' the dame said. 'He's been so good to them both.'

But on such a small pension, Felice wanted to ask, why did he take a wife? Especially one with such extravagant tastes. Surely the vicar's assistance didn't stretch as far as jewels and furs, did it? There was more she would like to have known about the strangely matched Vyttery couple, but she had no wish to pry. Instead, she turned her attention back to the vicar's wife who appeared to have suffered few financial problems, for all her simplicity of dress.

'And does your husband approve of all the alterations to the abbey?' She looked across the river to the New House of pale grey stone, solid and glittering with tiers of windows that only the very wealthy could afford in such quantity. It sat at an angle to the Abbot's House next door, dwarfing it by its sheer bulk and magnificence.

'Oh, John is very adaptable,' said Dame Celia. 'He's had to be with so many changes. But, yes, he admires Sir Leon's work. They've always got on well together.'

'They've known each other long?' Felice's question was casual, though she doubted whether it would deceive the motherly lady at her side.

'Only over the time they've been working together. Sir Leon's been responsible for several abbey conversions in the south. He'll never be short of work. Everyone thinks very highly of him.'

'Of him, or of his work? Isn't he somewhat difficult to work for?'

Dame Celia smiled and laid a gentle hand on Felice's pink sleeve. 'Men like him hate any interruption to their work, m'lady. They can only think of one thing at a time, not like we women. One has to humour them to keep the peace.'

Felice and Lydia laughed, having harboured the thought many times but not heard it said out loud by the wife of a former monk. 'Who does the little boat belong to, Dame Celia?' said Lydia. 'The one tied to the bridge back there.'

'It's the smith's. His cottage is next to the inn, very close to where the boat's tied up. He works the mill near the Abbot's House.'

'He works there?' Felice queried. 'I thought that's where the miller worked.'

'Yes,' Dame Celia smiled. 'Smith *is* the miller. That's not a cornmill, you see, but a water-powered forge used for the estate. It's easier for him to carry his heavy things in a boat from one bridge to the other.'

'Does he work at night?' said Lydia, brushing the mossy bits off her gown. 'We thought we heard the paddles going.'

'He works hard at his drinking,' the dame said, firmly. 'He doesn't have far to go for that. Have you seen inside the New House, yet?'

The idea of dispensing with Sir Leon as tour guide appealed to Felice almost as much as the idea that she could annoy him by her independence, and this was enough to hasten them across the bridge by the mill towards the great flight of stone steps that led to an impressive porch and an unlocked door.

The mansion that had seemed, only a few hours ago, to resemble a rabbit warren now spread from the front entrance in shining newness across pine floors, intricately plastered ceilings, panelled and painted walls, floor-to-ceiling windows and a marble chimney-piece that no one could have missed. It was while they stood in awe, taking in the grandeur of the carved staircase, that voices penetrated a heavy door behind them only seconds before it opened.

Felice tensed as she recognised one of them, and her quick turn to examine the coat-of-arms above the fireplace gave Dame Celia the chance to greet the men with far more geniality than Felice could have done.

'Sir Leon...John...and *Marcus*! Well, what are *you* doing here?'

Half-turning, Felice watched from a distance as her two disloyal deerhounds made a fuss of Sir Leon, and the newcomer named Marcus greeted Dame Celia with a familiar kiss to both cheeks. He was, she thought, probably a year or two younger than Sir Leon and of slighter build, but dashingly well set-off by an immaculate suit of honey-coloured velvet and satin, by white linen, lace, gold buttons and braids. His face was lean and good-humoured, almost handsome, his hair curled in a carelessly arranged fair mop that fell into heavy-lidded blue eyes. His manner exuded a gentle charm that contrasted immediately with Sir Leon's dark dynamism and animal grace.

His greeting to Dame Celia over, the man called Marcus made a beeline for Felice that forestalled any introduction, taking her by surprise with a bow and one hand placed over his heart. 'Ah, lady!' he sighed. 'If you would consent to marry me, here and now, we can use this good priest here, and yonder chapel, to unite our souls without delay. Now, tell me you consent or I shall go away and die.'

She was spared the need to find a suitably frivolous reply by Dame Celia's husband, the Reverend John Aycombe, who boomed cheerily, 'Argh! Take no notice of him, my lady. He'd embarrass the queen herself, he would. Get a grip on yourself, man. You can't go about scaring ladies like that.'

'He can, sir,' Sir Leon said, wearily. 'He does it all the time. Lady Felice, allow me to present to you a boyhood affliction...er, friend. Marcus Donne of Westminster. He'll be going home tomorrow.'

'He's wrong, my lady, as usual,' said Marcus Donne. 'I've no intention of going home for quite some time, I assure you. How could I go now?' He took her offered fingertips, kissing them with such protracted ardour that she was bound to pull herself free, laughing.

'Marcus Donne,' she said. 'A poet, of course.'

'Poet, playright and artist, my lady. And suitor to your hand.'

'Correction,' said Sir Leon, drily. 'He's a limner. Forget the rest.'

Mr Donne adopted an expression of exaggerated anguish. 'All right, I'm a limner and I came here expressly to paint your portrait, my lady. Will you sit for me, or will you break my heart with a refusal?'

'The latter,' Felice said, still laughing at his absurdity. 'Paint my maids instead. Here's Mistress Lydia, for you.'

The banter continued over Lydia's colourful beauty while Sir Leon came to stand by Felice's side. 'Well,' he said, 'having made a remarkably sedate entry, you may as well allow me to show you round.' He followed the direction of her eyes. 'He's only just arrived.'

'Delightful,' she murmured, purposely ignoring

his invitation. 'Such charming manners. What a welcome change.'

'Don't get carried away,' he replied. 'He puts on that performance for every woman, old or young, plain or pretty. He won't do for a husband.'

'That's not something that occupies my thoughts these days, Sir Leon. But thank you for the warning. It will make his flirtations all the more piquant.'

'Go ahead, but remember to take them with a hefty pinch of salt.'

'And you'll warn him about me, no doubt.'

'Naturally. I shall make him aware of our understanding.'

'Which I shall deny, sir.' She turned her scowl into a quick smile as the two Aycombes caught her eye.

'You'll deny it at your peril,' Sir Leon replied. Giving her no time to respond in the same vein, he turned to the others. 'Good. That's settled, then. A conducted tour to take stock of progress so far. This way, ladies and gentlemen, if you please.'

Inwardly seething at his continued provocation, Felice took Lydia's arm in a gesture intended to unite them against Marcus Donne's attempts at separation. It was while they were examining the beautifully carved pews in the small private chapel that Felice and Lydia, straying near the pulpit, noticed a battered leather chest upon the steps by the communion rail. They recognised it as one that had come from Sonning on one of the carts two days ago.

'It'll be the spare Latin bibles and altar plate that my mother wants out of the way,' Felice said.

Lydia agreed. 'And it'll not be needed here, either. I'll get someone to come and move it. It can go in the cellar for now.' But then the intention was put out of mind at the appearance of Adam Bystander, Sir Leon's tall good-looking valet who, having heard that Lydia was here, came to stake his claim before the notorious Mr Donne could do the same.

Lydia's interest in Adam was already established, being one of the reasons for Felice's decision to reconsider returning to Sonning. Lydia's ability to forget about men was the cause of much heartache; in fact, most men of her acquaintance would have agreed that her forgetting was too highly developed for her own good—certainly for theirs. It would be a pity, Lydia had said to Felice, to be rushed into a forgetting that would be premature, even by her standards.

The reason why the leather chest faded from Felice's memory was remarkably similar, for she now had to delude Marcus Donne into believing that she found him interesting, the Aycombes into believing that she was admiring every detail of the New House, Sir Leon into thinking that she was quite unmoved by his handsome presence and herself into believing that she was not watching him when, in fact, she was. It required all her concentration, especially as Adam Bystander had now weeded the willing Lydia away from her side.

However, the leather chest had also been noticed by the observant surveyor who, when his guests had been escorted away from the New House, returned for a closer examination. He found it to be unlocked, its stiffly studded lid at first unwilling, its contents unremarkable; bibles in the forbidden Latin, a linen altar-cloth spotted with iron mould, a priest's white surplice and a box of polished beechwood with a silver carrying handle.

He lifted it out on to a pew and sat down beside it, recognising it at once as a travelling box which priests had needed to celebrate mass before such rites were forbidden. The inside was lined with dark red leather, the contents still bright: a small silver chalice and plate, a crucifix, a candlestick, a rosary and a small leather-bound bible with a marker of old parchment still in place. The personal bible of a priest.

Angling himself towards the light, he opened the book to examine the fly-leaf and found the inscription in faded grey ink, the style bold and artistic. 'Timon Montefiore'. The bookmark was even more interesting, for instead of some biblical quotation or the owner's initials, it was intricately decorated with the letter *F*, with pierced hearts, arrows, teardrops, bolts of lightning, thorns and every conceivable symbol of passionate love that the owner could have contrived. What was more, it marked the beginning of the Song of Solomon made up of verses metaphorically comparing spiritual love to earthly love in an unmistakably erotic manner.

'Well, well,' Sir Leon breathed. For some moments, he held it while he explored the implications and then, on intuition, he turned to the back of the bible and found between the black end-papers a lock of silky dark brown hair tied with a fine gold thread. As if he had known it would be there, he stroked it with his thumb, feeling its softness. Then he replaced it and closed the book.

'So, that's what it's all about,' he whispered. 'And what happened to you, Father Timon? Did Lady Deventer discover your secret passion, perhaps? Dismissed, were you? No, of course not, or you'd have taken this with you, wouldn't you? Death, then? Was that it?'

Without any clear idea of what he intended to do with it, he replaced the contents and closed the lid of the leather chest, carrying the priest's sacrament box back to his room in the guesthouse.

Marcus Donne lay full-length upon his friend's bed, idly leafing through one of Sir Leon's notebooks of architectural drawings. He barely looked up as his friend entered and closed the door. 'Lovely,' he said. 'Amazingly lovely.'

Sir Leon placed the beechwood box on the floor beneath his table and then removed the book from Marcus's inquisitive fingers. 'Yes,' he said, 'I know she is. So why have you decided to come here now, of all times? Did your nose lead you to the scent of woman, or have you no work to do these days?'

Marcus swung his legs off the bed and stretched upwards with a smile. 'I told you. I'm between commissions.'

'You said that because John Aycombe was there. Now, what's the real reason? You're in hiding again, I take it.'

'Your man put my bags next door. Is that all right?'

'Yes. But tell me or I'll have them slung into the river.'

Marcus remained unperturbed by the threat. 'Well, I was in London, and a certain possessive husband took a dislike to me.' He grinned.

'Yes, husbands can get tediously possessive, I believe. So you were painting the lady's likeness, I suppose, and you couldn't concentrate. Is that it?'

'Well, she couldn't, either.' He and Sir Leon had known each other since they were boarded out at the London home of the late Queen Mary's Comptroller of the Household, during which both young men had made excellent connections. Being unlike each other in temperament, they had retained a brotherly friendship over the years and this was not the first time that Marcus had sought his friend's hospitality at Wheatley in order to lie low for a month or two. 'Oh,' he said, 'it'll all die down. And I can paint the glorious lady while I'm here, just to keep my hand in.'

'Just to keep your hand in what, exactly? Paint her, if she'll let you, but no more than that, my friend, or you'll be off back to London before your jealous husband has had time to forget your handi-work.'

'Whoo…oo! Steady, lad! What's all that about, eh? Has your lovely Levina stayed away too long, then?'

'She's *not* my Levina and mind your own busi-ness. Lady Felice Marwelle is in my guardianship while she's down here, so just remember that. De-venter sent her to sort out the New House and gar-dens and he's left no instructions for her to be dis-tracted by cuckolding limners and the like.'

'So you're her keeper, then. Is that it?'

'You'll not say as much to her, if you value your head, but that's the general way of things. She's my employer's daughter and I'm responsible for her.'

'Right,' said Marcus, rudely staring.

'And take that stupid grin off your face. Now lis-ten; you can keep your ears and eyes open while you're here. There's something going on at night. Thieving, I expect. That's the usual problem on building-sites. Rival builders stealing stuff. But so far I've not discovered anything missing.'

'So how d'ye know there's something going on?'

'A boat on the river at night. The only one here-abouts belongs to the chap who works the mill forge, but I've not been able to track him. I spent hours over the last two nights waiting to see if he comes through the kitchen garden or the other way round.'

'But no one came?'

'No.' His fingertips pressed gently against the deep toothmarks at the base of his thumb that still bled from time to time. 'Perhaps you could take a watch?'

'Sure. Anything else?'

Sir Leon glanced at the box under the table piled with books and ledgers, measuring instruments and letters. 'Yes,' he said, 'there is. What d'ye know about a priest called Montefiore?'

'Father Timon. Mmm...' Marcus's voice wavered, fruitily.

'You knew him?'

'No, but I met him. He was chaplain to the Paynefleetes.'

Sir Leon frowned, suddenly rivetted. 'The Paynefleetes here at Wheatley? Dame Celia's brother? I never knew that.'

'Well, that's not so surprising. The Paynefleetes of Wheatley Manor also have a house in London and they could have been there when you began work here. That's where I met him, but he left them soon afterwards.'

'You met him in London?'

'Yes. I painted the Paynefleetes' maid, Thomas Vyttery's daughter Frances. You didn't know that?'

'No, how do I know what you get up to in London? So Thomas's daughter was the Paynefleetes' maid, was she? He's never talked about her.'

'A dark-haired beauty, almost as lovely as—' He caught his friend's glare and retreated. 'Her mother, Dame Audrey, asked me to paint her daughter's portrait while she was with the Paynefleetes in London. So I did.'

'And what does this have to do with Timon Montefiore?'

Marcus spoke irritatingly slowly, as if to a child. 'Well, they were lovers. The maid and the chaplain.'

'Whew! F for Frances! How d'ye know?'

Marcus quirked an eyebrow at his friend's odd response. 'How do I *know*? For pity's sake, lad, I'm trained to *see*.'

'She died though, didn't she?'

'Yes, after young Montefiore had been packed off in a flurry of silence ostensibly because he was a Roman Catholic priest who was not supposed to be performing anywhere, let alone with a dissenting family like the Paynefleetes. Word gets round quickly in London, so I believe they packed him off to a Berkshire family where he's now probably busying himself with another patron's daughter, or maid, or whatever. The family managed to keep it all remarkably quiet, but I get to hear the gossip, you see. I didn't take to the man, particularly.'

The hairs on Sir Leon's arms bristled uncomfortably as he pictured the scene, against his will, of a young priest ingratiating himself into Deventer's family, charming the mother, seducing the daughter. Is that what had happened? F for Frances *and* for Felice, one or both? The sacrament box, unused and forgotten. A hasty departure. Her grief and anger. 'How old would he have been, this priest?' he said.

'Late twenties, perhaps. Soft-spoken. A quiet character. Intelligent, but not to be trusted, from what I gathered.'

'Thieving, you mean?'

'Dismissed for theft even before he reached the Paynefleetes, but that's only hearsay.'

'Then who on earth recommended him?'

'Leon, my friend, the priesthood closes ranks tighter than clams when one of them needs help. He wouldn't have any trouble finding another priest to recommend him.'

'So how does Dame Audrey find the money to pay for a portrait? I thought you were expensive.'

'I am, but I don't make a habit of asking my clients where they get their money from. I just collect it, with thanks.'

'Plus the gratuities. You're disgusting, Donne.' Sir Leon laughed.

'Delightfully so, and you're green with envy because building houses for wealthy old men doesn't give you the same opportunities. Or does it?'

'Come on down to the hall. You look as if you could do with the company of stout men, for a change.'

'How so?'

'Your brain's going soft, lad.'

Despite his conspicuously carefree manner, Sir Leon's curiosity was far from satisfied by the discovery of the wayward priest's inclinations or by his connection to two women who bore the same initial. Ironically, the apparent solution to the enigma of the Lady Felice's confusion had lasted only a short time before suffering more complications too difficult to unravel, though the priest's reputation indicated that he was capable of multiple offences.

And as if this was not enough, the sudden appearance of Marcus would do little to aid the self-imposed task of taming the beautiful sharp-tongued wildcat. She would use Marcus as a tool, and Marcus would play the part to the hilt, willingly skimming the bounds of the warning like a master. Well, let them do their worst; he had always been a match for Marcus, both intellectually and physically, and the lady herself would soon learn just how far she could go before he took her in hand again.

Sir Leon's guardianship of Lady Felice provided Marcus with a delicious temptation he had no intention of resisting. There had always been an element of rivalry in their good-tempered friendship, the latest and most serious manifestation of which was Sir Leon's erratic friendship with Lord Deventer's dazzling niece, Levina Deventer, which had previously irked Marcus more than he cared to admit. Any opportunity to pay his rival back in the same coin was something for which he had waited patiently, so it was no concern of his what Lord Deventer had instructed his surveyor to do; *he* would take the maid from under their noses. Clearly she had little liking for her new guardian; one had only to look at her to see how she resented his authority. Women were so transparent, bless them.

For Felice, Marcus Donne's arrival could not have been better timed. With the chivalrous and amusing limner, she could now show Sir Leon how little she cared for his presence or needed his ungenerous warning about the man's manners. He may have been the first limner she had ever met, but he was certainly not the first flirt. She knew exactly how to handle such men.

If only the same could be said of Sir Leon, who had put himself outside her experience from the start. With her horses and waggons gone, she had now no option but to comply with his decision concerning her immediate future, but she would make him regret his overbearing interference before the end of the week. That much was certain.

These resolutions were comforting for being easily acted upon; other hurts lay deeper and would have to wait for some more impressive retribution to salve them.

The opportunity for Marcus to acquaint himself more closely with his willing target came later on in the day as delicious aromas wafted across the courtyard from the kitchens of the Abbot's House.

The sun had lowered itself slowly until it rested upon the western edge of the cloister roof, flushing the derelict square with pink and accentuating the colour of Felice's gown. It was this vision that greeted Marcus Donne as he emerged from the shadows of the far side.

At first, Felice thought the sound of the door opening might be Sir Leon and she had been prepared to make a very dignified but obvious exit. But then the honey-coloured velvet caught her eye and she waited, half-pleased, half-disappointed. She watched as he looked around him as if to get his bearings and felt herself respond to his genuine pleasure at the sight of her, thinking that it would not be difficult to enjoy his company, for his charms were not all superficial.

The eager boyish smile was now replaced by that of a self-assured man who knew how to regulate his absurdities to suit his audience. With only the object of his interest to hear him, he could allow his flattery to fall more accurately, drop by precious drop. 'A Felice-itous meeting,' he said, approaching her through the untidy grass. 'A rose-washed Felice bathing in the sun's last rays. Now there's a picture waiting to be painted, my lady.'

'And I'm waiting for a summons to supper, Mr Donne,' she replied, prosaically. 'You're welcome to join us.'

'And I, my lady, am lost. But my host expects my presence at supper on my first day here and I dare not disappoint him.' He came to stand before her, smiling gravely. 'Pink is your colour. I shall paint you wearing that gown.' His eyes swept over her, lingering on the soft mounds of peachy skin where the stiff bodice supported from below, then returning to hold the unsureness in her eyes with a slow and lazy smile. 'Another evening, perhaps?'

She regretted her too-hasty invitation at once, and there was too much here to answer, so she answered none of it. 'This is the cloister, sir, where the monks studied and took their exercise, or so I believe. I shall make a garden here again as soon as I can organise my workers and draw up a plan. Whichever comes first.' She turned, leading the way to the sunny wall where she and Sir Leon had sat only yesterday. 'I'll have the walkway roofs repaired and this mess cleared...' she pointed with a pink shoe '...and then I'll have paths and plots and a fountain in the centre. Just there.' She nodded towards a heap of rubble, knowing that his eyes had not moved from her face and neck.

Marcus sat beside her on the wall and angled himself to lean against a pillar, resting one foot on the stonework between them. 'Go on,' he said, clasping his knee.

She knew the game but found it disconcerting, even so, to be expected to talk of mundane matters while a man drank his fill with his eyes and thought his own private thoughts. But with perhaps a little more effort she could do the same, for he was an artist and knew how to pose, how to show off his shapely legs, his prominently embroidered codpiece, and how to hold her attention with his own. Inevitably, his lack of response brought her monologue to a dwindling halt. 'You're not listening to me,' she chided him gently.

His eyes were sensuously invasive. 'I was... somewhere else,' he said, gesturing to prevent an impending withdrawal. 'No, don't go. It's a habit, I'm afraid, to watch rather than listen. But you must surely be used to having men look at you, my lady.' The voice was seductive, designed to entice confessions.

'I don't notice, sir,' she said, holding back a smile.

'Tch! Untruths already. What chance do we have of friendship then, would you say?' When she made no reply, he leaned forward to rest his chin upon his knee, refusing to release her from his intense scrutiny. 'You've not been here long, I understand, and I've only been here once before. Do you think we might explore the place together? My sense of direction is remarkably good, as a rule.'

For a second, it occurred to her that he might have been warned about her, but his expression was sincere and she saw no reason to refuse him as long as it fitted in with her duties. Better still, it would take her well out of Sir Leon's way. 'You're staying a while then, Mr Donne?'

'Long enough to paint your likeness, my lady.

That can take anything from three days to three months.' Now his eyes were merry, reminding Felice of another teasing smile and gentle laugh, of one who let her talk while he attended, unlike other men who believed only themselves to have anything worthwhile to say.

'Then I shall be glad to have your company, sir. With an escort, there'll be places I may visit that I'm not allowed to alone. Believe it or not, I'd like to see the work the men are doing on the building-site, especially the sculptors and wood-carvers, but I've been told not to go near them.'

The knee went down as Marcus Donne leaned even closer. 'What...you were warned off? Whatever for?'

Drawn into the charade, she shrugged her shoulders, wondering how far to go for his pity. 'Well, I can only suppose that Sir Leon's masons will suddenly go berserk at the sight of a woman,' she said, innocently, 'even though they're mostly old enough to be my father. He must employ some very unpredictable workmen, I fear.'

'But that's ridiculous! They're all respectable men. That cannot be the reason. Leon's never been vindictive, whatever else he may be.'

'Really?'

His fair brows drew together at that. 'I'm mistaken?'

'You know him better than I, but I can find no explanation other than vindictiveness for sending my horses, waggons and carters back to Sonning without my knowledge. I don't even have a horse of my own to ride, so I'll not be able to go far.'

Marcus made no attempt either to excuse or condemn his friend, realising that there must be more to this than mere pique. The lady had a fire held tightly under control, and her dislike of Leon could be useful as long as it was handled carefully. 'I brought several horses with me,' he said. 'At least two of them are suitable mounts for a lady. We'll use mine.'

'They're in the guesthouse stable?'

'Yes. Plenty of room over there now—most of his are out to grass.'

Felice looked beyond the arch where the end of the stableblock was just visible and where only that morning she had seen Sir Leon's bay stallion being quartered at the expense of hers. 'Then why not bring them over here so that I won't have to traipse over to Sir Leon's stable? My own saddle's still here.'

Their exchanged smiles enclosed an almost childlike conspiracy and Felice saw herself escaping at last from the despotic surveyor's reach.

The call for supper broke the mood as Mistress Lydia stepped through the archway in her search for Felice, then she halted as the door at the far end of the cloister opened to admit the young Elizabeth, followed closely by Sir Leon.

Elizabeth Pemberton had been hired only a year

ago mainly for her skills at needlework, which were indisputable. Sadly her skills in other directions were less remarkable for, no matter how repetitious her duties, she seemed unable to remember or anticipate what they were. She was sweet and gentle and well aware of the clerk of the kitchen's adoration, but his duties in that vital area were even less easy for her to accept, which was the prime cause of this latest drama. Both Felice and Lydia sometimes found the temptation to shake her almost irresistible, but this time it was unnecessary, for the lass was already well shaken.

Sir Leon led Elizabeth across the scruffy square plot where, in the pinkish fading light, Felice could see her tear-stained face and red nose and the way her arm rested trustingly along Sir Leon's.

His expression was anything but kindly as he voiced a command to Mistress Lydia without the slightest reference to her mistress. 'Mistress Waterman, be so good as to take this young lady indoors before I have another riot on my hands.'

Elizabeth, her bottom lip trembling, was passed over to Lydia who looked to Felice for approval, recognising the discourtesy to her mistress. But Felice intercepted the move, furious at being disregarded. Though reluctant to have words before servants, her first need was to know what had happened to cause Elizabeth's distress.

'One moment, if you please, Sir Leon. You seem to have overlooked the fact that I am responsible for

Mistress Pemberton and it is I who will decide where she goes. What happened? What is this riot you speak of?' She would have been grateful at this point to have had Marcus Donne at her elbow, but he remained discreetly on the wall, uninvolved, and she was left to face the surveyor's intimidating bulk on her own.

Sir Leon's eyes were like two dark slits of anger that bored accusingly into hers, but his voice was deceptively polite, 'Then if you are indeed responsible for her, my lady, may I suggest you take your obligations more seriously? Take her indoors, Mistress Waterman, if you please,' he snapped at Lydia.

Lydia prevaricated no longer, but took Elizabeth by the arm and led her away. As Felice turned to confront Sir Leon once more, she caught his glare at Marcus and the inclination of his head towards the door; a clear signal for him to leave.

Preparing for the storm, Felice toyed with the notion of imploring Marcus to stay but thought better of it, especially as the limner showed no inclination to dispute the command. The alternative was to follow her maids, but the prospect of venting her anger upon Sir Leon was too great to relinquish and she released it well before the cloister door had closed behind her new ally.

'I have never known such rudeness, such...'

'Spare me the tirade and yourself the energy my lady. If you've never known such rudeness, I've never known such irresponsibility. Have you no idea what your women are up to while you sit here lapping up compliments? Have you no control over them?'

'Yes, I have, Sir Leon, but I can hardly tie them both to my girdle-chain while I sit around lapping up compliments, as you so churlishly put it. Nor can I follow Mistress Elizabeth round like a shadow. If she gets into a predicament now and then, she can usually manage to get herself out of it. And tears follow as a matter of course, sir.'

Without warning, he took hold of her upper arm so tightly that she could feel his fingers through the padded sleeve, and marched her unceremoniously back to the low wall where she had been sitting with Marcus. 'So much for the sharp tongue, lady,' he growled, pressing her down on to the wall and sitting himself beside her. 'Now you can listen to mine, for a change.' He pointed to the distant door. 'Out there, your silly maid wandered alone into a crowd of apprentices and seemed to think it would be a good Sunday sport to play one rival gang off against the other. No matter that they've been warned about fighting, especially on the site, your lass actually egged them on and then wondered why *she* got roughed up at the same time. If those tears are part of an act, as you appear to believe, what does she do when she's truly scared, I wonder? If I'd not stopped them, she'd have been flat on her back by now in the mortar-maker's yard with a crowd of—'

'No!' Felice yelped, coming to her feet. 'You've said enough, sir! She's young. She doesn't think.'

'Those lads are young too, but they *do* think. Only of three things, I warrant you, but she'd better be told fast what they are or she'll be in more trouble again than she can handle. And if you'd been about your duty, my lady, instead of…'

'Instead of what, sir? Talking? Sitting? Sharing a pleasantry or two before I forget what a pleasantry sounds like? Is that a crime, suddenly? Should I lock her up in case one of your thick-headed apprentices gets one of his three thoughts in the wrong order?'

He stood, resting one foot on the wall and leaning towards her with an elbow on one knee, and though he had no intention of displaying in the way that Marcus Donne did, Felice was well able to see how his muscular thighs were more powerful, his chest deeper, his shoulders broader. 'Do what you like with her,' he said, 'only don't come running to me when she finds herself out of her depth again. I warned you of what might happen and now I've got fifteen lads to discipline tomorrow, thanks to your co-operation.'

'Then give your stupid apprentices more to think about, Sir Leon, and they'll have less time to fight over a young female. And don't give any more orders to my servants. Don't tell my guests when to leave. And don't blame me when your workers adopt your manners. I bid you good day, sir.' Giving him notice of her intention to leave had not been a part of her plan, but she was livid with anger and her plan had been turned on its head.

He caught her around the waist and swung her against the stone column, holding her resisting arms in a vice-like grip. 'I bid you good day also, my lady, but you've left one thing off your list, haven't you?' His body pressed hard against hers to make an off-beat duet of hearts between them.

'I forget nothing, sir, except your gracelessness,' she snarled.

There was nowhere for her head to go, and the impulse to watch as his mouth took hers gave her no chance to evade him as she knew she should have done. Besides, this was something her heart had begged for, desired and entreated, despite the strident callings of common sense and outrage, despite knowing that the kiss was derisive, meant to chasten, to mock her weakness and to demand her capitulation.

Whatever he had meant it to do, it did, as once again his mastery drove every thought from her mind except the dazing seduction of her lips. There was no need for her to respond in either direction, for he was taking without her permission, holding on to her wrists and thus giving her no reason to chastise herself for another uncontrollable participation. And had it not been for the closing of her eyes, she might have been able to pretend to be unmoved, but it was now too late for that.

He watched them open and slowly flicker into wakefulness. 'I believe you do forget, lady, that I will have the last word. And as long as you insist on forgetting, I shall insist on reminding you. Understand?'

She looked away, unable to meet the dominance in his grey eyes. 'No, Sir Leon, I do not understand any of this except that you are as careless of a woman's honour as the apprentices you are about to punish. Explain the difference to me...if you can.'

'The difference, my lady, is that your maid was in no position to appreciate those lads' attentions whereas the same cannot be said for you, can it? Or do you close your eyes and melt in any man's arms, eh?'

'You are despicable! Let me go!'

'The last word? Was that it?' he mocked, touching her lips with his to hold her silent. 'Good. That's better.'

But if she had thought to be released by her infuriated shove against his chest she was to find that it had the opposite effect, for her wrists were still held and her involuntary gasp was stifled by his mouth. He took his time, drawing her easily with him into a kiss that swamped her with wave upon wave of sensation until his hands released hers and found a way across her back and shoulders, bending her into him.

She clung, helplessly adrift, her gasp now surfacing to emerge as a cry that brought them both to their senses. His arms supported her and lowered her to the wall where she sat, hearing the swish of tall weeds against his legs as he strode away, neither of them knowing who had had the last word, after all.

Chapter Four

She had not thought he would take advantage of her again, not like that, and not after she had made abundantly clear her intense dislike of him. Unfortunately, telling herself repeatedly of her dislike did not have the effect upon her heart that she intended, for it remained entirely unconvinced and determined to recall how it felt to be held by him.

'Contemptible! Brute! Oaf!' she muttered, climbing into her great bed. 'It was meant to humiliate me, no more than that. Forget it. It means nothing either to him or to me.'

But she could not forget it and, at her lowest ebb in the blackest hours of the night, she again entertained the idea of escape on one of Mr Donne's horses. However, the practicalities of such a move were still being worked out as she fell asleep.

By morning, some of her original rebelliousness had recovered. With it came the hate and a soupçon of fear that Sir Leon was taking his role as custodian far too seriously.

Now she was determined more than ever to get on with her appointed task, to impress her stepfather by her amazing efficiency and resourcefulness, and to stay from under the feet of his surveyor, as she had been instructed to do. She dressed in her plainest brown bodice and skirt with sleeves to match over a white linen partlet that gathered round her neck in a neat frill. She requested Lydia to coil her hair into a net at the back of her head.

'Wouldn't you be better wearing your linen coif?' said Lydia, dutifully twisting the thick ropes of hair. 'After what happened yesterday?'

'No,' Felice replied, tersely. 'After what happened yesterday, it's that high and mighty surveyor who'd better watch out, not me.'

First she set about recruiting the services of three women to begin a clean-up of the servants' downstairs rooms at the New House. They were passing through the derelict cloister on their way to the building-site when she spied them through the archway, and in no time at all had re-directed them to collect brooms, buckets, mops and dusters from her own servants in the Abbot's House with orders to start in the scullery and work towards the big kitchen. She would come and inspect them in an hour.

The oldest of the three began a protest, saying that they were expected to carry lime for the plasterer who had not finished one of the ceilings but, having no choice but to obey, they quickly opted for the pleasanter task.

Felice went back to the stableyard where two young lads were carrying a heavy box between them by its rope handles. 'You two,' she called, 'leave that and come with me. I have a task for you.'

'Er...mistress...yer ladyship, we're not...'

'No excuses. Put that thing down and help. You can do that later.' Anyone in her yard was, after all, presumed to be one of her servants.

They lowered the box to the ground with a thud and followed Felice across the cobbles to where two more lads were sorting through a pile of rusty garden tools ready to clean them. 'Clean this lot up,' she told them, 'then take the best ones to the garden and start clearing. I'll get some more men to come and help as soon as I can find some.' The apprehensive looks exchanged by the two additions went entirely unnoticed.

She was prevented from returning to her indoor duties by the call of her own carpenter and his two lads. 'M'lady,' James said, pushing up his felt bonnet to scratch at his head, 'the carpenter on the site won't let us have any of his wood for the table and benches. He says to get our own.'

'I thought that's what we were doing, James. Surely it's all the same, isn't it?'

'Apparently not, m'lady. He says he has to account for every—'

Well able to imagine what the site carpenter had said, she cut off the explanation. 'Well, then, go and find a suitable tree, James. You have axes, don't you?'

'A tree, m'lady?' James frowned, pulling back his bonnet. 'Nay, you can't just fell a tree like that. You need a saw-pit to make planks, you know.'

'Then dig a saw-pit. It's only a table and benches you're making for the servants' hall, man, not for the high chamber. It can't be difficult.'

James blinked. 'No, m'lady. Right, we'll go and find a tree. C'mon, lads.' He tipped his head to the two staring lads and lurched off, muttering, in the direction of the nearest group of ash trees.

Crossing the servants' hall, Felice was suddenly confronted by a red-faced whiskered man wearing a leather apron over his doublet and a battered felt cap jammed down on to a mat of sawdust-coloured hair. His expression left her in no doubt of his displeasure.

Aggressively, Fen and Flint lowered their heads, rumbling a threat.

'Good day to you, carpenter,' Felice said, anticipating the man's reason for being here. He had probably come to explain about the wood.

'John Life, m'lady. Joiner for thirty years and more.' He snatched his hat off and then replaced it on a rim of hair. 'And I've come to fetch my lads and my box.'

To her surprise, Mr Life walked past her to the

outer door. 'Wait, Mr Life!' she called. 'Wait! What boys are you talking about?' But even as she spoke, the truth of the matter dawned on her. 'I stopped two lads in the stableyard...they had a box...I thought it was mine.'

With his hand on the latch, the joiner turned, addressing his remarks to the rushes on the floor rather than to the lady of the house. 'Them tools, *m'lady*, have been mine all my working life. Made each and every one of 'em myself, I did, when I were...'

'Mr Life...' Felice attempted to interrupt the flow.

'...an apprentice. And them two lads are mine, too. I'm paid to do a job for Sir Leon, *m'lady*, not to provide you...'

'Mr Life!' she yelled at him. 'They were coming out of my stable! Anyone who enters my stable without my permission will be put to my service and if you keep your damn box there in future I'll confiscate it, is that clear, as for your apprentices and tools I'll have them returned to you in due course, now you return the way you came sir.' Finally stopping to draw breath, she pointed to the opposite door.

He walked stiffly past her, still grumbling. 'I shall have to speak to Sir Leon about this...'

'You can speak to the devil himself, Mr Life, but don't ever speak to me in that tone again. Is that clear?'

Unperturbed, the clerk of the kitchen, who had

been waiting, seized the opportunity, list in hand. 'M'lady, would you?'

Felice sighed. 'Yes, Mr Dawson. Come, we'll sit over here. But first things first; let me get those lads and tools together again. Have the beehives started producing yet?'

There were still several areas of production not yet in full swing, one of which was the brewery, and it was while Felice was with her steward, Henry Peale, inspecting one of the outhouses for this purpose that a shadow filled the doorway. Until the thud in her breast had settled, she ignored it, knowing that a confrontation with Sir Leon was to be the inevitable outcome of John Life's dissent.

'Three hogsheads a month should be enough, m'lady,' Henry was saying as he turned to look at the intruder.

'A word with your mistress, Mr Peale, if you will.'

Henry bowed to them both, leaving Felice in midsentence to his departing back view. 'Sir Leon,' she said, coldly polite. 'I have already said that I am capable of giving orders to my own servants without your aid, I thank you.'

He leaned against the door frame, intentionally blocking the light and her escape, his rolled-up shirt sleeves exposing muscular wrists and forearms that sent a new wave of goose-bumps into her hair. His own looked as if he had combed it through with his fingers, making deep furrows from brow to crown. 'The question is, my lady, whether you are capable of *recognising* your own servants without my aid. It appears not.' His tone was bitingly sarcastic.

'I have had a similar discussion with Mr Life, sir, and I don't intend to repeat it to you. The joiner, his lads and tools have been reunited and I've told him to keep his tools out of my stable, that's all.'

'It was not only the joiner I had in mind. He's a miserable old fool who finds something to moan about every Monday morning, but he's the best this side of London and I won't have him upset or I shall lose him. You've already antagonised my steward, now it's the joiner, the carpenter and the plasterer. Did you have anyone else in mind for today? Some advance warning would be helpful.'

'I don't know what you're talking about, sir. Let me pass; I'm busy.' She knew it was probably the last thing he would do when he came further into the new brewhouse to stand before her, hands on hips, and she saw how the icy sarcasm only thinly veiled his anger.

'Is that so, my lady? Well, then, let me explain. Those women you commandeered to...'

'I did *not* commandeer them, I simply redirected...'

'...to clean the ground floor were to have been carrying lime for the plasterer who still has a ceiling to finish.'

'I thought...'

'Which I told you when I showed you the rooms yesterday. And what's more, the workmen on the ground floor are still fixing the shelvings and fittings and they don't need women sweeping round their feet while they're doing it.'

She blushed, biting her tongue on the reply.

'So if you must indulge your passion for cleaning everything in sight, would you mind starting at the top of the house with your own servants, not mine? I can't afford to lose my best plasterer at this point. And the next thing...'

'I don't want to hear about the next thing,' she croaked, trying to push past him.

But he side-stepped, barring her way with one hand against the wall. 'The next thing is that the carpenter does not have an unlimited supply of wood to be carted off for your pleasure. He has to account for every plank, every nail, every...'

'Oh, for pity's sake, spare me!' Felice said. 'I don't need the carpenter's damn wood, or his nails. There are plenty of trees hereabouts. We'll manage well enough, I thank you.'

'Don't think it,' he said, dropping his hand. 'No one fells a tree here without my permission.'

'Except me, Sir Leon. I have Lord Deventer's permission to obtain whatever I need to prepare the house for summer, and if you refuse to supply me with what I need I'll get them elsewhere. My own carpenter knows how to...'

'*What?*'

She walked past him to the door. '...to fell a tree.'

Roughly, her arm was held, and she was swung against the wall to face him again, this time in the full blaze of his anger. 'You did what? You gave orders? What orders...where?'

'I...I don't know. Wherever.' Her eyes skimmed the door at the sound of shouting. The door was pushed back with a sharp crack on to the wall. Her arm was released.

Henry Peale reappeared, flushed and breathless. 'Sir Leon! My lady! There's a fight...a brawl... they're trying to stop James and the lads from chopping the...'

He got no further, pushed aside as Sir Leon leapt through the doorway and across the courtyard, already running as he called, 'Where, man? Show me where they are.'

Picking up her skirts, Felice ran after them with Fen and Flint prancing alongside, yapping with excitement. Between the kitchen garden and the cemetery on the north side of the church, a line of ash trees had barely opened their leaves to make a delicate screen and it was here, much too close to the high wall and to the men who cleared the ground of rubble that the carpenter and his lads were in bloody conflict with each other. Both parties had axes and spades and both were using them to enforce their intentions, already resulting in cuts to foreheads, bleeding noses and lips, several broken teeth and tools. The fact that all six were Felice's own servants made the situation even more ludicrous: she would have preferred a display of amity amongst her own household, at least.

By the time she reached them they had been flung bodily aside by Sir Leon and Henry Peale, whose authority the men dared not challenge, and now they were scattered, dripping with blood and sweat.

Sir Leon was bawling at James as Felice approached. 'What in heaven's name d'ye think you're doing, man, felling a tree near a wall like that without ropes? What if it'd fallen into the garden, eh?'

'It would not, sir,' James said, holding a hand to his bleeding ear. 'We'd have had it falling the other way.'

'And how many trees have you felled in your time? Can't you see that you'd have taken the top of the wall off? Go, take your lads and stick their heads under the pump, then wait for my man to come and tend you. You'll need a stitch or two if you're to keep your ear.'

'There's no need for your help, sir,' Felice said. 'My ladies and I can do all that's necessary.' It was not the best choice of words.

'I'm sure you can, lady. It'll take you all afternoon to do what's necessary here, by the look of things. Thank God they're your men, not mine.'

She took the chastened men into the servants' hall, remonstrating all the way, yet knowing that it had been her own failure, her own over-eagerness, which had been at the root of the problem. So keen had she been to appear efficient that she had not stopped to consider every implication, and now it was her incompetence that had impressed Sir Leon most. And she *had* wanted to impress him, indirectly.

'I'm ashamed of you, James,' she said, unfairly.

'I could have done it with no damage. Now what are we going to do about the furniture?'

'Never mind that. What are we going to do about your ear?'

As things turned out, she and the maids had just begun to make bandages and to bathe wounds when Adam Bystander brought two servants with salves, a basket of moss to pack the cuts, styptic made of egg-whites and aloes bound with hair to stop the bleeding, and a jar of theriac, which Felice had always known as treacle. According to Adam, it was good for anything from burns to bronchitis.

With the mess washed away, the actual damage was much less than at first appeared, and even James's ear was stuck back together again with every prospect of success.

Adam Bystander was a good-looking young man of solid build, with crinkly hair the colour of hazelnuts and amused brown eyes that searched with a bold confidence whenever he listened or spoke. It was this quiet self-possession that Lydia found particularly attractive, even though they had spoken little when they had walked side by side yesterday. His fingers were skilful with the men's wounds and soon the tasks were complete, the debris of surgery cleared away.

Adam placed a hand over Lydia's wrist in full view of the others. 'Tonight?' he said, softly. 'You'll be there?'

Lydia blushed, glancing at her mistress. Felice nodded. 'Yes,' Lydia said. 'I dare say.'

Felice thanked the young men and sent them back, barely able to conceal her wretchedness at the way her good intentions had fallen, one after the other, like a row of ninepins. Still smarting from Sir Leon's latest tongue-lashing, she went back to the brewery where she could cool off, alone. Her own workers would keep the affair to themselves and eventually dismiss it entirely; they would never lay any blame at her door. But that was small comfort when one person in particular whose good opinion she had hoped to gain now held her in the utmost contempt.

It was Marcus Donne who came to the rescue, news of the latest affray having travelled fast across the ruins of Wheatley. Marcus was always avid for news. He appeared as Felice emerged from the new brewhouse and walked by her side into the vast kitchen garden where clearance had resumed after the fracas. There would be no escape from his en-quiries, she knew that. Bracing herself, she tried to make light of it but he was trained to notice every detail: he was also determined to make what capital he could out of his lovely companion's problems.

'You're upset, dear lady,' he purred. 'I can see it in your eyes. Don't allow him to affect you so. You did your best. No one could have done more. How were you to know what his plans were?' And so on.

'I could have asked, I suppose.'

'He'd not have told you. Anyone can see he's in no mood to co-operate. I suppose he was still angry about the apprentices.'

'He told you what happened...yesterday?'

'By the time I reached the guesthouse it was everywhere. Was he very severe? I know he can be.'

'He was angry. He had every right to be.'

'You're too fair, my lady. But then, he's your guardian and I suppose you feel an obligation to be loyal to him.'

'He's *what*? My guardian? God's truth, whatever next!' She stopped in her tracks and stared at the fair-haired man with the disarming blue eyes. 'Where did you get that notion, for pity's sake?'

'From him, my lady. Why, have I said something to upset you?'

'No, Mr Donne, nothing at all, but I'd like you to know that, whatever Sir Leon tells you about any relationship, guardianship, custody or understanding, it has absolutely no foundation in fact. Lord Deventer has not appointed him to any position except that of surveyor. He is not my keeper and I am not his responsibility. I owe him no obedience or favours of any kind except to keep out of his way. There, now, does that explain things, or have I missed something out?'

'Whew!' Marcus Donne stroked his chin, making a mental note of the exact blue of the whites of her eyes, and of the slightly swollen lids. Last night's, he judged, being expert at such things. 'Yes, indeed it does, my lady. In which case you will perhaps be free to accept an invitation to accompany me to the May Eve bonfire tonight. We're both strangers here so we may as well stick together. Yes?'

'Yes,' she said, with rather more force than was necessary.

'Good. Then I shall collect you at dusk. Now, will you show me the new bit of wall? Ah, there it is with a door to the river path. How convenient. The men will soon have this place tidied up.'

Felice stared at the patch where flattened stems looked as if someone had rolled on them, and her hand automatically closed over the silk pouch hanging from her waist. Inside it nestled a tiny gold object in the shape of a spear-head. 'Yes,' she said. 'I'm sure they will. The sooner the better.'

It did not usually take Felice so long to be dressed, nor would she have made quite so much effort for Marcus Donne if there had not also been another's interest to hold. Naturally, she would not admit it, but her heart knew why she was taking so much care and why her mind was already racing ahead to find a chink in the surveyor's implacable exterior that would allow the point of a dagger to penetrate. She smiled at her reflection in the silvered mirror, recalling how Sir Leon's apparent weakness was to have his orders contravened.

In the last light of day, the bedchamber of the Abbot's House came alive with softly glowing reflections on its patterned ceiling, tapestried walls and multi-paned windows that shone like jewels. Some had coloured glass at the top that cast pools of colour on to the rush-strewn floor, catching the toes of her soft red leather shoes with patches of amber and blue. There was now no sign of the previous mess: her flute and sheet-music lay tidily upon the chest, her writing table and prie-dieu stood to one side, her bed now hung with pretty but faded curtains and an oddly ill-matched but favourite coverlet. It was her own room, private and cherished.

She smoothed her hands down her bodice and tiny waist, turning sideways for a reflected view of the green-blue shot taffeta. 'Thank you, Lydie and Elizabeth,' she said to the two admiring maids. 'Now go and get ready, quickly.' She dabbed rosewater on to her wrists and neck, well satisfied.

The two deerhounds rose to their feet as the maids disappeared into the adjoining bedchamber that had once been the abbot's small chapel. Their heads were lowered, watching the door to the stairway with pricked ears, their whip-like tails beginning a slow swing that gained speed as the door opened.

'Mr D—' Felice began her greeting before her smile faded. The tall powerful figure of Sir Leon took her so much by surprise that he had time to close the door before her heart could regain its natural rhythm. The large chamber appeared to shrink. She turned away to hide the sudden flush of confusion. 'My entrances and exits may be somewhat dramatic, Sir Leon, but at least they give you some warning, which is more than can be said for yours. Do you never knock?'

He chuckled. 'No, not on my own doors, my lady. Do you?' He looked around the chamber with approval, this time. 'You've made some progress in here since my last visit. Pity the same can't be said of everything else, but I believe you're beginning to see who's in charge here, so we'll soon be working well together.' His patronising tone raised her hackles immediately, as he had known it would, but he gave her no time to defend herself. 'First thing tomorrow—'

'Sir Leon, if you will excuse me, I'm preparing to go to the bonfire. It had occurred to me that you might have come to apologise, but I'm obviously being far too optimistic. May we discuss business some other time, do you think? Tomorrow morning, first thing?'

'Apology?' His laugh was deep and rich. And genuine. 'Ah, no, lady. Not after I saved so many of your men's lives. But certainly we can talk in the morning, if you prefer. My men will be waiting at cock-crow, but I shall instruct them to knock first, of course.' With that mysterious announcement he turned towards the door. 'Have a pleasant evening.'

'Er...wait! Please.'

His hand paused upon the latch. 'Yes?'

He held her eyes and, even from that distance, Felice understood that here was something significant thinly disguised as the ordinary discourse of colleagues. Yet nothing about this man had been ordinary, so far, especially not his exceptional charisma which was all the more potent for being totally natural, as unlike Marcus's posturing as it was possible to be. Or Timon's quiet charm, for that matter. 'Mr Donne will be calling for me,' she said, for want of something better to say.

'Yes, I know.'

'Well, yes, of course you would. I expect he told you that we spoke this afternoon.'

Sir Leon removed his hand from the latch and strolled across to the deep window-seat where he sat, filling it with his frame. With his back to the fading light, his dark head was surrounded by a pink glow that caught his chiselled features like a crag at sunset. He rested his hands on his thighs, his feet wide apart. 'He told me. Yes. Which is why I'm here. But it can wait. I didn't want to take your servants completely by surprise, that's all.' His tone was deceptively agreeable.

Completely at a loss, Felice shook her head. 'Please make yourself clear, Sir Leon. Is this some new chastisement you've devised because of what happened today?'

'Lady...' he sounded hurt, '...you malign me. Of course not. You're already aware of my plans to move out of the guesthouse. You knew that before you moved in here. Now I cannot begin any rebuilding over there until it's cleared, and the New House must be kept clear for your preparations, which leaves this place as the only shelter for me and my men. I came to tell you that my men will be here with my furnishings at dawn ready to bring them in. I hope it doesn't rain. There'll be room enough in here for me and my equipment, and our limner friend will not be staying long, whatever he chooses to believe. Plenty of room upstairs.' He looked around him as if to decide where to place his belongings, measuring the bed with deliberate interest.

'No!' said Felice, in a choked voice.

He looked at her in mild surprise, without comment.

'No,' she said again. 'This is preposterous, Sir Leon, and you know it.' She sat heavily upon a low stool with her skirt billowing around her, outwardly calm but trembling with fear beneath the embroidered bodice. Thankfully, no one could collapse inside a whalebone corset. 'You cannot do this. You agreed.'

'Ah...agreements. Easy to forget, eh?'

'Not *so* easy, sir, since it was made at our first meeting.'

'The day before yesterday. And you remember that because it was in your favour, no doubt; yet the one we made later in the day seems to have escaped your memory presumably because you didn't like the sound of it. Understandable, but bad practice. Perhaps we should have put it into writing.' He leaned back on to the window-panes and folded his arms across his wide chest, his eyes never once leaving her face.

Agreement? Felice struggled to understand what he meant, then her blood slowed in her veins and she felt a prickling along the nape of her neck as she remembered her vehement denial only that afternoon to the over-sympathetic Marcus. It came back to her, detail by detail, as if in a dream, knowing that it had erupted in a moment of fury.

'I shall tell him of our understanding,' he had said.

'And I shall deny it.'

'Deny it at your peril.'

And she had denied it. 'No, Sir Leon, I did not forget. I denied it as I told you I would because I cannot accept it. You must have known that.'

'Cannot, or will not?'

'Both.'

'Then the only way for me to enforce it, my lady, is to show that it exists. Two unrelated people of the opposite sex living closely under one roof are expected to have an understanding of some sort, are they not? And by the time I've spent a night or two in this room, that understanding will be more or less impossible to shake off, however hard you deny it. It should give the village women something to talk about.'

She thought of Marcus's horses, soon to be in her stable.

'No,' he said, reading her thoughts. 'You'll not get far.'

Fuming, and reeling from the cleverness of his scheme, she glared at his darkening silhouette as if he were the devil himself. 'I hate you,' she whispered. 'I *hate* you!'

For an answer, he swung his gaze slowly from her face to the wide curtained bed and back again. 'Easily remedied,' he whispered back.

'What is it you want from me, sir? Be truthful for once, if you please.'

'I think you know, lady. First, I'll have an acknowledgement of our relationship, a public one, and then I'll have the obedience that goes with it. And then I'll consider delaying my move into these rooms for the time being. That's not too much to demand, I think.'

'*You* may not think so, but I cannot for the life of me understand why, when you hold my honour in such contempt, you wish to publicise a relationship which must be as abhorrent to you as it is to me. Surely you could allow me to get on with my appointed task without wrapping it up in this ridiculous garb? My stepfather failed in his duty to my mother when he sent me here unannounced, but I cannot believe he'd have wanted my freedom curtailed so severely, my means of transport taken away, my every move watched and criticised, my servants ordered, my person manhandled by an unscrupulous stranger. It's intolerable!' She stood and turned aside, her voice trembling with fatigue and anger. 'Now you want everyone to believe you're… I'm…we're…'

'Lovers?' he said from across the room. 'No, but that's not quite as abhorrent as you seem to think it is, nor is the impression I've gained from our brief encounters, whatever you intended.'

'Don't shame me any further, sir, I beg you. Say no more on that.'

'Why? Because you can't explain it? Because it brings back memories still raw, does it?'

'Stop!' she yelled. '*Stop* it!' Tears welled into her eyes as a sea of confusion surged into her breast. 'You'd be the *last* person to understand.'

'Wrong. I might even understand before you do. However, one thing at a time. When word gets round that you're down here, as it will, there'll be few who believe Deventer had nothing in mind but a straightforward working relationship, even if he did.'

'Ah, I see! You have a reputation to uphold. Yes, I can see how that would matter to you,' she said, scornfully through her angry tears. 'Well, don't keep it bright at my expense, sir. I can forge my own relationships without my stepfather's help. Or yours.'

'Steady, lass. You're running ahead of yourself again. We're talking about a guardianship, remember, at the moment.'

'Do guardians make love to their wards then, these days?'

'It certainly wouldn't be the first time it's happened. But it will stop tongues clacking for a while, that's the main advantage.'

'This…this guardianship, Sir Leon. It would not involve further…intimacies? Do I have your assurance on that?'

He came slowly to his feet and approached her like a cat until he was close enough to read her face in the gloom. 'I do not think, my lady, that you are in a position to bargain, are you? Shall we get the first stage over with first, then we'll see about the rest?'

'Blackmail, Sir Leon. How many stages are there? Where do they lead? And what do I get out of it, exactly? I don't relish the idea of acquiring a colourful reputation like the men and women at court. Mine was white when I came down here to Wheatley and I'd like it to be the same kind of white when this fiasco comes to an end.'

'White, was it, lady?' he whispered. 'You're sure of that, are you?'

She swung her head away, mortified by his inference. 'I was speaking of my reputation, sir, nothing else. I do not want my name linked with yours merely for your convenience. Indeed, I don't want it linked with yours for any reason.'

'Then that must be one of the disadvantages of being a woman,' he said, pitilessly. 'Now, do we continue this discussion in front of Donne, or have we reached some kind of conclusion?'

'Guardianship, is it? Is that a notch up from custodian, or a notch down? Do remind me,' she said, scathingly.

'That's what Deventer would have had in mind, I believe. It will do to begin with.'

'Hypocrite!' she spat. 'As if you care a damn what Lord Deventer has in mind.'

'That's the wildcat. Now we begin to understand one another. You'll tell Donne this evening what the situation is, without the drama, if you please. Say your anger made you forget; anything you like, but make it clear. Now, come here.'

She remained rooted to the spot, glaring at the darkening windows.

'Come here, Felice.'

Trembling inside, she went to him, dreading what was to come and fearful that her inevitable response would mock at all she had been asserting. 'No,' she whispered. 'Please don't.'

His hand reached out and slipped round to the back of her neck, drawing her lips towards his. 'So it's not me you want, then? Someone still nagging you, is he? Then change your mind, lady, before I change it for you.' He released her with only the tenderest brush of his lips across hers like the touch of a moth's wing, leaving her to wonder not only what he meant by that but whether his strange demand would really be as uncomfortable as she was making it out to be.

Chapter Five

The discovery that Marcus Donne had not, after all, revealed the details of their afternoon's conversation to Sir Leon came as something of a relief to Felice, who had hoped for Marcus's confidence, at least. Nevertheless, she was extremely angry that her outburst that afternoon had somehow landed her deeper than ever into Sir Leon's power.

'Then how did he know?' she said, keeping her voice low so as not to be overheard along the busy pathway to the village. Torch-boys carried flaming brands before them, sending plumes of smoke over their heads and dancing shadows across the moving figures. 'If you didn't tell him what I'd said, how on earth could he have known?'

'Dear lady,' Marcus said, clamping her hand between his sleeve and doublet, 'if I spilled private conversations so easily I'd never be employed again, believe me. I am nothing if not discreet. I can only assume that when I'd told him how upset you were, his intuition told him that you may also have said something rash. Anyway, there's no harm done, is there? He scolded you yet again and made you promise to put the matter straight, which you have done, so nothing's changed, has it? He'd already told me that he was responsible for you as soon as I arrived. Yours was a natural reaction, my lady; think no more about it,' he said, not believing for one moment that she would take his advice any more than he himself would. This would not be a difficult conquest, with the lady already halfway there.

What nonsense, Felice thought. Everything's changed. If details of this guardianship are not all over Wheatley by now, they will be by the end of this night, for although Sir Leon's threat had been based on speculation, she would now have to accept his authority in everything or suffer the consequences. Lord Deventer's direct intervention in this matter was not something she could count on. Most disturbing of all was Sir Leon's refusal to promise no further intimacies and his cryptic message about changing her mind. It didn't need changing. She did want him, but not while her loyalty still belonged elsewhere and not while Sir Leon's only intention was to gain her obedience and to win her stepfather's approval. For her, it was a heartbreaking situation to be in; for him it would no doubt continue to be highly entertaining.

Until that evening, Felice had not realised how

many people were employed at the abbey as builders, craftsmen, labourers and servants, kitchen and stablemen. Behind and before her they streamed into the village over the little bridge, past the thatched cottages and towards the village green where a mountain of wood, mostly from the building-site, was ready to be lit. May Eve was the beginning of summer and the start of festivities that not even the church was able to prevent.

It was only when she joined the group that included the Reverend John Aycombe and Dame Celia, Thomas and Audrey Vyttery and the complete Paynefleete family that Felice realised she and Marcus had been closely followed by Sir Leon Gascelin. She prayed he'd not overheard them.

On all sides of the wide green, cottages huddled together in the darkness; against the paler western sky rose the stone bulk of Wheatley Manor, where Dame Celia's brother and his family lived. These were the Paynefleetes, whose generations of wealth and nobility gave them extraordinary advantages in every sphere, property in several southern counties and, not least, the distinction of lighting the May Eve fires.

It was a crowded and merry occasion with laughter and shrieks of excitement as the flames licked and roared, sending sparks into the black sky and lighting rosy faces. Last year's chestnuts were thrown into the red-hot ashes to roast; there were gingerbreads to eat and dripping slices of roasted ox from the manor kitchens, hunks of new bread, honey-coated apples on sticks and barrels of perry, cider and ale.

Lydia stood with the protective Adam, who successfully warded off attempts to draw her into the chain-dance until she herself pulled him along. Elizabeth followed on with Mr Dawson of the kitchen and a clutch of other hopefuls, and Felice silently prayed that the lass would not take too much of the potent cider to which Marcus had taken a liking.

She had managed to evade any direct contact with Sir Leon, but he seemed never to be far away until the rowdiness intensified and even the vicar appeared to approve of the horseplay. Then, when her eyes searched for him for reassurance, he and the Vytterys had gone, and Marcus's impatient hand around her waist was anything but protective.

'C'mon,' he insisted. 'It's the dain-chance. Everybody's got to do the dain-chance on May-hic! Hey there! Wait for us! C'mon, Feleesh. Put your cider down.'

Hastily, Felice relinquished her drink to Dame Celia, who laughed her approval of Marcus's enthusiasm while the two were drawn into a thirty-strong chain of bodies and dragged along a sinuously snaking path around the fire, through groups of people, along the dark track and round to the fire again. Old and young, lively and infirm, all those in the chaindance wreathed about, broke and reformed, gathered newcomers and whopped untuneful snatches of song to the sound of pipes and drums. The din was deafening.

In the dark, the chain of hands broke with a sudden tug, and Marcus fell heavily backwards, cannoning into Felice and knocking her into the man behind whose sweaty hand caught at her shoulder as she fell, pulling at her sleeve. Instantly, the pile-up of bodies collapsed into helpless cider-inflamed laughter, tangling arms and legs and, for the most part, rendering them unwilling and unable to recover. Two men were lying on her skirts, preventing her escape, while another was taking the opportunity to kiss her neck with wet and smelly lips and an unconcern for her identity that caused her to lash out in all directions. Which body was Marcus she had no idea, for the darkness was intense.

She yelled, screaming to be free of groping hands, and then there were grunts and yelps and spaces beyond her, a pair of arms encircling her, pulling her upwards. 'No...no!' she yelled. 'Get off! Get away!'

'Hush, lass. It's me. Come this way...come on. I've got you.'

She stepped on bodies and over them, supported by strong hands and an arm about her waist, unable to see but recognising the voice. His voice. 'My shoe!' she called out. 'I've lost a shoe!'

'No matter. Leave it. Are you hurt?'

'Er...no, I don't think so. Oh, no!'

'What?'

'My hair. My net has come undone and my sleeve's ripped off.'

They stood apart from the screeching mêlée but close to each other, Felice taking an unexpected comfort from the rock-firm stability of Sir Leon's embrace, and making no protest as he redeemed the silver mesh from the tangle of her hair and shook the rest of it out over her shoulders.

'There. Now take your other shoe off. You'll walk more easily. D'ye want me to carry you?'

'No.' She shook her head. 'Thank you, I can manage now.' She pushed herself away, but he enveloped her in his long cloak and kept an arm about her waist, holding her firmly to his side.

'Come,' he said, walking her towards the pink glow in the distance. 'There must be some advantages in having a guardian. Hold on to me.'

Obediently, she slipped her shoulder beneath his and walked barefoot over the cool grass towards the fire, thankful that the occasion itself provided an excuse for such familiarities. Half-expecting him to release her from his protection, she halted at the edge of the crowd and dropped her arm from his waist. 'I think…er…I should find Lydia,' she said.

'Adam's with her. She'll be safe with him.'

'Yes, but…'

'And Mistress Pemberton is over there, see. And you're staying with me.' As if to reinforce his words, he drew her on through the crowds towards those she had left, greeting them with laughs and accepting a juicy slice of beef with which he fed her.

She stood with her back to his chest, enclosed with him in the same woollen cloak and with one of his arms across her like a barrier. As her hair found its way into her mouth, he swept it aside with his thumb.

'What happened?' said Dame Celia. 'Trampled underfoot?'

With her mouth full, Felice nodded, blissfully unconcerned by the unkempt sight she now presented. The fire was warm on her face and feet and the cider had begun to release the cares of the day, taking them away beyond recall, and as she turned her face upwards to watch a shower of sparks, she felt his chin on her forehead and knew an intense longing she had never experienced before with any other man.

'What happened to Marcus?' Dame Celia asked, merrily.

Felice felt Sir Leon smile into her hair. 'With Betty,' he laughed.

'Who's Betty?' she said.

Dame Celia's face was a picture of shocked amusement, her rolling eyes almost providing the answer. 'The village…er…'

Sir Leon's arm tightened. 'Betty is a very accommodating lady,' he said. 'Marcus will be all right with Betty until about noon tomorrow.'

'Does she know him, then?'

'She certainly will by noon tomorrow, my lady. Now, will you open your mouth for a piece of this sticky apple? You can ask Marcus himself for more details when he recovers.'

The noise and dancing continued as they took their leave of their hosts and headed away from the fire's glowing warmth, still clinging like lovers and calling goodnight to the groups and couples and shadowy forms. And despite the soreness of her feet, Felice was scarcely aware of the rough ground on that dark and silent walk back to the abbey. Almost silent.

'My head feels funny,' she whispered.

'I should have warned you. It's the cider. Take it slowly.'

'There's something I was supposed to be saying to you. Something angry.'

'That goes without saying. It'll keep till tomorrow. And I know what it is, anyway.'

'How do you?'

'I just do. Wait!' he whispered. 'Stop! What's that?' They had reached the part of the path that ran parallel to the river across the front of the New House. A new moon caught a patch of shining water where V-shaped ripples dragged along behind a shadow that made a soft plash-plash in the quiet air. An owl hooted, and the moving shadow answered it.

'Do rowing boats hoot?' Felice whispered.

'They seem to at Wheatley,' he replied. 'Keep still. Let it pass.'

They waited until it had disappeared up-river towards the mill, then continued their slow amble towards the Abbot's House. When he passed her porch and continued along the river path towards the mill, she made no objection to the detour.

In sight of the mill's dark outline they waited, flattening themselves against the high wall of the kitchen garden as the boat returned on the river's flow, one oar steering expertly away from the bank. Then it was gone. Footsteps approached softly out of the darkness and, without any warning, Felice was pushed hard against the wall by the engulfing warmth of Sir Leon and held immobile as a shadowy figure passed them.

Her nose was against his neck and the faint but intoxicating aroma of his maleness overcame her senses, heightening the longing she had felt earlier and clouding all but the desire to be kissed, to submit, to accept and give without reserve. But the moments passed as he listened, twisting his head away to watch.

He took her arm in one hand and opened the new garden door with the other. 'Come this way,' he whispered, urgently. 'I want to see where he's going. If he's returning to the abbey buildings we can head him off quicker this way, and if he's going to the village we can watch from the kitchens.'

Baffled, uninterested and disappointed, she

slipped with him through the door where there had recently been a mere gap in the wall. Vaguely, she recalled how she had walked the same route in bare feet, a brief moment of bliss and a sudden parting. Then, she had been glad to get away from him: now, she would have given anything to stay, to begin again and make a better conclusion.

Forgetting her bare feet, Sir Leon hurried her along the dark path that the workers had begun to restore. The cloak slipped and trailed over one shoulder, dragging her torn sleeve further down and jabbing her flesh with the pins that attached it to the bodice. Removable sleeves could be a boon, but not when one was being hauled through a midnight garden.

Exasperated by his haste and especially by the redirection of his interest, she pulled her hand out of his to clutch at the spiteful pins at the top of her sleeve, yanking it away in anger. 'You go on,' she said. 'I'll catch you up.'

'Stay where you are. I'll come back for you.'

He dived away into the blackness towards the garden entrance, leaving her to wrestle with her bulky skirts, heavy cloak and drooping sleeve. Then, seething with indignation and frustration, she hitched it all up into her arms and stalked after him, ignoring his command to wait.

'Wait on yourself, Sir Leon,' she muttered, heatedly. 'And then wait some more. We'll see who can wait longest.' Purposely avoiding his route, she ran round to the back door of the Abbot's House and let herself into the pantry, up to the servants' hall on the first floor and up again to her bedchamber without being noticed. There, fumbling and tangling with an array of laces, hooks, pins and ties, her head swirling madly, she fell onto the bed. She was asleep before she touched the pillow, and this was how Elizabeth and Lydia found her only ten minutes later. It was another half-hour before Adam Bystander knocked on the door to ask Lydia if her mistress was in there, by any chance.

'Well, of course she is,' she replied, pertly. 'Where else would she be?'

As the pagan festival of May Day could not be allowed to exist in its own right, it was given a cloak of respectability by the feast days of Saints Peter and James, who drew a much-reduced congregation the morning after the bonfire. Admittedly, it was early, many of the worshippers holding their heads for reasons other than prayer, but Dames Celia and Audrey were predictably staid.

'You all right, my lady? You look rather pale,' said Dame Celia to Felice at the end of the service.

'Headache,' said Felice, thinking that the strong communion wine could not have helped matters. The sun pouring in through the large eastern window hurt her eyes, and she turned away with a frown.

The events of last night had drifted through the

service in a concoction of memories, both irksome and pleasant, those concerning Sir Leon being particularly difficult to untangle. She recalled a sense of temporary compromise that had developed into an expectation on her part which, she now realised, was probably more to do with the cider than anything else. And after her earlier request for no more intimacies, she supposed it was only natural for him to grant a lady's request. All the same, she found it hard to suppress her indignation that he had so easily been able to overcome any urges he might have felt in favour of a cursed boat on the river. At least she now understood why he had been in the garden that night, thinking that she had been involved in these mysterious activities. She also remembered what she had meant to say to him about yesterday's conversation with Marcus, but that would now have to wait, for he had not taken his place by her side in church, and she assumed he must still be asleep.

She was wrong; he was waiting at the back of the church, though if she had expected him to say something she was to be disappointed; his bland greeting was general rather than particular. The man was so unpredictable.

He wore the new style of knee-length breeches known as Venetians, brown with vertical panes of silver-grey to match his doublet. He swept off his feathered velvet cap and bowed, smiling, apparently unaffected by the cider. Marcus was nowhere to be seen.

The light at the western door was even more intense. Unable to remove her frown at the pains in her head and feet, Felice's first words to Sir Leon came out with a sourness she had not intended. 'Good day to you, sir. It looks as if both you and the vicar will have to make do with anyone you can find today, doesn't it?'

'Oh,' he replied, 'there'll be no work done on the site today. Most of the young ones are still out there in the woods and the older ones find it hard to hold their ale, these days. Dame Audrey,' he remarked to the steward's hovering wife, 'you're looking particularly grand today. Will you be at the festivities later on?'

Dame Audrey had not spared any available space on her bright green silk bodice on which to hang a brooch or jewelled pin, and even her girdle-chain was weighted with clinking objects as she moved: scissors, a tiny watch, spectacle-case and a golden locket no larger than the palm of a lady's hand.

Her reply was predictable, in view of her early departure from last night's bonfire. 'No, Sir Leon. May hasband and aye have always trade to observe the calendar according to Her Majethy's decree, you know. Aye think our vicar should show his disapproval of these goings-on bay benning them. Heaven only knows what these silly lesses will hev on their hends in nane manths' tame.'

The silly lasses to whom she referred were at that moment filtering out of the woodland that surrounded the village and abbey, arm in arm with the lads and carrying boughs of May blossom with which to decorate the May Queen's bower. There would be maypole dancing, music and laughter, of which the Vytterys apparently disapproved.

Felice could find no suitable response to that, nor did she care to scan Sir Leon's face for signs of amusement, but there was no need, his eyes having caught a more interesting topic.

'Heaven knows, indeed, Dame Audrey. Is that a locket hanging from your girdle? A portrait?' He bent to look at it more closely, then at her. 'May I?'

For a moment, Dame Audrey hesitated, as if about to refuse, then she relented and hauled it up by its chain and lowered it carefully into Sir Leon's waiting hand. 'You may open it, if you wish,' she said.

The tiny domed lid sprang back to reveal a portrait of a young woman, her face no larger than Sir Leon's thumb-nail. She was dark and very lovely, her hair covered by a close-fitting black cap, her oval face enclosed in a small frilled collar, her eyes dark brown and red-rimmed as if she was prone to weeping.

Felice peered, equally enchanted. The young lady's hair was as dark as her own but Dame Audrey was fair-haired and blue-eyed, her husband grey-haired, his eyes pale. So who was the young lady? 'A relative, Dame Audrey?' she said. 'She's very good-looking.'

'My daughter Frances, my lady,' the dame said,

quietly, taking the locket out of Sir Leon's hands and closing the lid. She held it lovingly like a new-hatched chick.

Completely taken by surprise, Felice realised that she should perhaps have waited longer for information instead of pressing for it, but her next question slipped out in the same uncontrolled fashion. 'Does she live hereabouts, dame?'

Dame Celia stepped in to save her friend. 'We lost her, my lady, just over a year ago. This is Mr Donne's portrait of her. We still miss her so.'

Felice's head thudded. On impulse, she took Dame Audrey's hands between her own and held them tenderly. 'I'm so sorry, dear lady. Truly I am. I would never have…oh, dear…that was clumsy of me. Do please forgive me.' She took a pretty lace handkerchief from her sleeve-band and handed it to Dame Audrey, and the situation was overtaken by the boisterous arrival of the Reverend Aycombe who appeared not to notice that group's momentary unease.

Felice, however, was troubled by the incident, particularly as she felt she could have been warned in advance about the Vytterys' personal tragedy, which did much to explain their obvious unhappiness. If only she had known.

There was no denying that the quality of the painting was excellent, perfect in every detail and as lifelike as if the young Frances Vyttery had been sitting there inside the golden filigree case. Upon the bright blue background, Felice had noticed the date, *Anno Domini* 1559, painted in a delicate scrolling hand, and she wondered again how Dame Audrey was able to afford such a valuable object, or whether Marcus Donne had presented it to her as a gift. And how well had he known his subject? A miniature portrait was a personal object usually commissioned by a husband, wife or lover.

Partly to escape the May Day rituals, Felice slipped away to the kitchen garden to discover what had once grown there and to make a rough plan for the men to use the next day. Lydia was the first to understand: her mistress's feet were still sore, she still had a sick headache, and she didn't want the effort of making herself affable to Sir Leon. Or to Marcus, for that matter.

'Here, love,' Lydia said with genuine sympathy. 'Take your pad of paper with you, and your charcoal. Make your plan on that, and don't bother about young Elizabeth; we'll keep an eye on her. Here, take an apple with you.'

Felice was sitting in the shade of a drooping ash tree when Sir Leon found her, her head leaning back against the flaking whitewashed wall, the pad of paper discarded by her side.

He took her noisily discouraging sigh in good part. 'I know, I know,' he said, reassuringly. 'You wanted to be alone, you've got a sore head and, most of all, you wanted to avoid me. And now your plans won't work.' He came to sit on the old bench beside her.

'How d'ye know they won't?' she said, without moving.

He picked up the pad of paper and looked at the mess of lines, scribbles and rubbings-out, turned it round several times and smiled. 'Well, I suppose it depends on what you have in mind,' he said, turning it again.

Lethargically, she took it from him. 'It makes sense to me,' she said, looking at her plan and then at the acreage before them. 'That's the northern side.' She tapped the top edge of the paper.

Delicately, he gave the paper a quarter turn. 'Yes?' he said.

'Go away. I know what I'm doing. And why could you not have told me about the Vytterys' daughter? You must have known.'

'There didn't seem to be an appropriate time to suddenly start talking of the Vytterys' daughter. Not even then. It's the first time I've seen the portrait; perhaps she wears it because Marcus is here.'

'You've not seen it before?'

'Never.'

'But you knew she'd died,' she accused. 'What happened?'

'I've no idea. Thomas has never mentioned it and I've not asked. I didn't even know Marcus had painted her until he told me on Sunday. Now, lady, am I absolved?'

'No. How did you know the details of my conversation with Mr Donne?'

'I didn't know.'

She opened her eyes and turned to stare at him in disbelief. 'Then how did you know I'd denied anything?'

'Denied our understanding? I guessed you would at the first opportunity. And I was right, wasn't I?'

'What if you'd been wrong?'

'You'd soon have let me know. It was worth a chance. I got what I wanted.'

'It was dishonest, sir.'

'No. All's fair in love and war, they say.'

'Thank you for the warning. So you won't object if I do the same.'

'Try it, by all means, my lady. I shall soon let you know if I do.'

'I'm sure you will, sir, but I doubt I shall know the difference, your objections coming so thick and fast.'

'Whew! Sharp! Now, would you like me to help you to plan the gardens? I could draw you a rough diagram and you can tell me how you want it set out.'

'No, thank you. You've disapproved of everything I've done, so far. It would be a complete waste of time to tell you how I want anything.'

His chest gave a deep chuckle like a rumble of thunder. 'Oh, dear. That cider has a lot to answer for, doesn't it? I didn't want you tamed *that* fast, lass, not when I was beginning to enjoy myself. Here,' he said, taking the paper from her, 'let me make a start and then you can heartily disapprove of everything I do, just to get even. Yes?'

She could not resist a smile as she watched him stroll away with the pad and charcoal, drawing without looking. 'And if you see a red shoe anywhere,' she called, 'it's mine,' and closed her eyes again.

'You lost them both? Serves you right for walking off.'

Two encounters so close together without a fight began to look like the beginnings of a truce, at last. Even more so when, for the next two hours, they plotted the kitchen garden in something approaching harmony, if one discounted the occasional disagreement about the points of the compass.

'Look,' he said in exasperation. 'Over there you can see the apse of the church. Which way does the apse always point?'

'East.'

He took her shoulders and faced her in the same direction. 'East,' he said. 'Now, point to the north.'

She stuck out her right arm but he pushed it down and pulled up the other, holding her wrist out. 'North. So *that* is the south-facing wall where the apricots and medlars will grow. Right?'

'But you just said....'

'No, the other side of it faces north. This side faces south.'

'Did you find my shoe?'

'Look over there.'

She discovered it perched on the handle of the old broken-down wheelbarrow that she had bumped into during their first confrontation but, as he had suspected, she would not go to collect it. Finally he retrieved it himself, making her blush angrily at his unashamedly teasing laughter.

Sir Leon had not asked why she had left him last night without an explanation, so she assumed it did not matter to him, nor would she raise the subject of the mysterious man and his boat in case he asked her for reasons she would have found uncomfortable to provide. Even so, she would like to have known why he had decided to spend the afternoon with her instead of at the May Day games.

From the kitchen garden they went to the cloister for more planning, by which time Felice was bound to assume that he enjoyed her company almost as much as she enjoyed his, in spite of the air of controlled antagonism that held the delicious promise of a fight. If he was intent on taming her, there was no reason why she should make it easy for him.

By comparison, the company of Marcus Donne that same evening held none of the same undercurrents. He was unfailingly charming and amusing. He told her as much as he could remember about the accommodating Betty and, with almost no persuasion, went on to talk about people he had met and painted. He remembered very little about his time with her at the bonfire last night but begged her to forgive his lapse; the cider was liquid gunpowder, he said.

He hoped her guardian had not been too tedious.

'Tolerable,' she said. 'Have you known him long, Mr Donne?'

'Since we were lads. He's a mite older than me, but we've always been friends. We meet when we're both in London.'

'Sir Leon has a house in London?'

'Yes, on the Strand, but his other house is in Winchester. He does most of his entertaining in London, though.'

'Entertaining who?'

With some difficulty, Marcus contained the smile that threatened the seriousness of her barely concealed interest. Leon had berated him for his less-than-chivalrous conduct last night, particularly for failing to care for Lady Felice as he should have done. Added to this, the buxom Betty had made demands upon him that no country-bred lass ought to know about. His pocket had suffered, too.

'Who?' he said, guilelessly. 'Oh, Leon's always been popular in court circles. He's well sought after, especially by the ladies.'

'Ah, of course.'

Marcus had no intention of letting the subject rest there. 'He's been linked with so many of the court beauties: Lady Arabella Yarwood, the Countess of

Minster's twin daughters, Marie St. George, Levina Deventer, Dorothea...'

'Who? Levina? My stepfather's niece? He knows *her*?'

'Why, yes. Of course, I almost forgot. You're related, are you not?'

'Only by marriage, thank heaven, and then only distantly. So Sir Leon and Levina have been friends, have they?'

'Still are, my lady. That affair's been on and off the boil for the last three years. They're mad about each other, but her money's tied up till her father dies. Pity, really. They make a fine pair.'

'But Sir Leon cannot be short of money, surely. And he'd not allow that to stand in his way, would he?'

'Hah!' Marcus barked with genuine regret, but appreciating the sudden pain in her eyes. 'Houses and servants cost money to keep up, dear lady, as you well know. There's not a man alive who can afford to ignore the wealth that comes with his chosen one, or the lack of it. She'll need considerable funds to keep her happy. Court beauties come expensive, my lady, and none more so than the lovely Levina. That one demands the best of everything.'

Heavy ice-crystals formed around Felice's heart, chilling the blood in her veins. Lord Deventer's notorious niece was the one he would have liked Felice to emulate more closely. She was about four years older than Felice, handsome rather than beautiful, overflowing with vitality, extravagance and style, demanding and holding the attention of everyone within her circle. The two of them had met only last year at the height of Felice's grief over Father Timon, and her dislike of the dashing niece was then transparently mutual.

Felice was no prude, but news of Levina's persistent scandals which Lord Deventer found so diverting sounded to her more desperate than amusing, and the thought of Sir Leon being the favourite of her many lovers made Felice feel sick with disgust that he could show such little discrimination in his choice of women when he could have had the best.

'What is it, my lady?' Marcus asked, tenderly. 'You are unwell?'

'No,' she whispered. 'I saw the portrait you painted for Dame Audrey today. It's beautiful. She's very proud of it.'

'Thank you. She should be; it's one of my best.'

'Did you know that Frances Vyttery had died?'

'Oh, I heard. Summer sickness, I suppose.'

'Yes, I suppose so. It must have cost Dame Audrey a great deal of money, Mr Donne. The portrait, I mean.'

'I would paint your likeness for nothing, my lady.'

'Well, thank you, but doesn't one need a loved one to give it to?'

'I have an idea. We will share it. I shall allow

you to keep it for six months and then I have it for the next six. Then it would belong to both of us.'

At last she smiled, liking the sound of his offer, but that night she wept bitter tears at the relentless inconstancy of her mind and the uncontrollable jealousy that twisted her innards. Now, it seemed that she must accept her heart's involvement with a different existence in which her love for Timon bore no part. She had been used to calling it love, but the overwhelming emotion that now held her in its terrible grasp was something she could never have imagined. It was a sickness; a madness. Men died of it, she'd heard, and women, too. She could well believe it. It would have been more bearable if she had thought that his heart was similarly obsessed, but she knew that it could not be, and the notion that she might have to suffer this pain for the rest of her life was the blackest thought of all.

Being a stranger to the real thing, Felice could hardly be expected to know the other side-effects of love—like anger, for instance, anger that she had not discovered more about the object of her desire before falling beneath his spell. It was unfair. Illogical. She was sure she would not have succumbed to this dreadful affliction if she had known he could love someone like Levina Deventer.

Just as disturbing was Marcus Donne's cynical implication that it was only Levina's lack of a substantial inheritance that was keeping Sir Leon from marriage with her. After three years, what other reason could there be? Levina was the fourth child of Lord Deventer's youngest brother and had therefore never been in the running for anything more than a modest allowance and the promise of a limited dowry. Her extravagances in London were largely financed by friends, lovers and sundry indulgent relatives, including her uncle, none of whom could be relied on to subscribe to a marriage-fund to line the purse of a prospective husband. Her father, with other offspring to finance, would never be as wealthy as his eldest brother whereas the Lady Felice Marwelle, as the eldest daughter of the late Sir Paul, was potentially wealthier by far than Levina could ever hope to be, for all her show.

As dark hour after hour crawled by, these implications grew out of all proportion, finally convincing Felice that Sir Leon Gascelin's real reason for taking her in hand was most likely to ingratiate himself into Lord Deventer's favour, to obtain his permission to marry her and then to avail himself of her considerable marriage-portion which would allow him to set the abominable Levina up as his mistress in his London home. He would be able to squander it to his heart's content while she, Felice, would be kept contentedly manicuring the gardens here at Wheatley near her mother and their growing family. Her mother would naturally be happy with the latter arrangement, and Lord Deventer with all of it.

If love could turn to hate in an instant, the discovery of this ghastly plan would have turned the tables completely and for all time. Unfortunately, one of the other side-effects was that the two were often inexplicably entwined, and Felice found that she was unable to untangle them, being so new to love.

Having sown the seeds, Marcus Donne sat back to watch with interest as the situation developed over the next few days, assuming that Felice's increased interest in him was due to his escalating interest in her. Confident that his plan was working well, he saw nothing particularly significant in the tension that always surrounded the meetings between the lady and her guardian, not even when the sound of their voices could be heard above the hammering and sawing.

He heard Felice's fierce reprimand as he rounded the corner of the great staircase in the New House. 'You're impossible!' she yelled. 'And anyway, it's my mother I'm trying to please, sir. If her tastes happen to disagree with yours, that's unfortunate, but she's the one who'll be living here.'

'I don't care who's going to live here,' Sir Leon was heard to reply, 'you'll not cover those walls with painted cloths. It's tapestries or nothing. You may have an old-fashioned mother, but I have a reputation.'

It sounded to Marcus as if the lady was walking away, but then a door slammed and the argument continued. 'If you must bawl at me, do it when we don't have an audience of workmen. I've not brought enough tapestries with me from Sonning for all these walls. If you'd built them to fit the hangings, as other builders do—'

'Other builders can do what they like. And if you'd spend more time preparing some lists instead of posing for our limner friend, you'd know more about what was needed up here.'

Marcus heard a rattle of paper and saw a flash of white. 'What d'ye think this is? Whilst you've been fiddling about out there, I've been in here since early morning making lists as long as my arm. And what good will that do when I've no way of getting to the merchants? Shall I *walk* to Winchester?'

'Give them to me. I'll see they get there.'

'Not on your life, sir. You'd change everything on them. And what I do with Mr Donne is not your concern.'

'It's very much my concern, my lady. Don't get too friendly,' Sir Leon snapped.

'Why ever not?'

Marcus strained to catch the reply but the door nearest him was the next to close, and all their words were cut off.

'Because,' Sir Leon said, speaking more quietly, 'our friend's interest tends to gravitate from a lady's face with alarming speed. Don't say I've not warned you.'

Contemptuously, Felice turned to go. 'Then you two have more in common than I thought, sir. I bid you good day. I must not keep him waiting any longer. Thank you for another warning, but I find his attentions more appealing than yours.'

His stride reached her before she reached the door. 'His attentions? What are you saying? Has he touched you?' His eyes were suddenly like cold steel, demanding the truth of the matter.

But Felice was determined to press the point, even if it hurt her most. 'Yes,' she said, refusing to lower her eyes modestly. 'Yes, he has. He took my chin and moved my head into the correct position. He has such gentle hands, Sir Leon.'

He placed a hand on the wall to prevent her escape. 'Is that so, lady? Well, then, allow me to remind you yet again that if ever his hands stray into your guardian's territory, he'll be on the road to London faster than you can blink. Do I make myself clear?'

'No, sir. You are being your usual obscure self, I fear. A guardian may not claim any part of his ward as his *territory*, especially without her permission.'

'I can easily prove you wrong on that point also. Do you wish for a demonstration? I can oblige,' he said, lowering his head to hers.

'Your concern for my safety is touching, Sir Leon, but it sits rather at odds with your offer. Am I to believe that you want for yourself what you would deny your friend?'

'Believe what you wish, but as soon as your mind has decided to accept what your body is telling you, we can have a more serious discussion on the matter. Until then, lady, stop playing games and get on with what you're supposed to be doing, for all our sakes. Is that any clearer?'

'But for one small point. By "games" I suppose you mean having my likeness painted?'

'Now who's being obscure?' He opened the door to let her pass.

It was not the outcome to the argument she had wanted, having left her with no score to speak of·in her favour. And having felt at one point as if she might win, she was now left with a far-from-winning smile to greet Mr Donne on the stairway.

'Yes,' she answered his call, rather too loudly. 'I'm coming down. There's little more I can do up here until I get more co-operation.'

It was made no easier for her to accept Sir Leon's warnings by knowing that they were to some extent justified, if a little exaggerated. While finding it impossible not to like Mr Donne, and not to be impressed by his painting ability, she was well aware that his interest was not confined to her face alone.

If anything, his attitude towards her was intensifying from the friendly to the lover-like, and Felice's jibe about his gentle hands was not entirely a device to rouse her guardian's anger. The painter's hand had strayed only yesterday to the nape of her neck where a tendril of hair had been caught by her starched collar, and she knew that the caress that followed was not part of the rescue. It had interested rather than aroused her, for though Marcus Donne's fair good looks had a certain attraction, his manner was too similar to Timon's to be comfortable, which she now understood to be a diluted version of the real thing.

Nevertheless, despite Sir Leon's obvious concern, Felice was quite sure she could manage the situation and emerge unscathed with a portrait, for what she had purposely failed to tell Sir Leon was that Mistress Lydia had been with them at every sitting, so far. Marcus had made use of the excellent light in the large chamber above Felice's, the windows on both sides giving superb views of the conventual buildings on one side and the river and woodland on the other.

After a two-hour session, Marcus took advantage of Lydia's departure down the stairs to approach Felice as she looked through the window to the courtyard below. He slipped an arm about her waist and held her, gently, speaking just below her ear. 'Perhaps you could find a task for Mistress Lydia to do at our next sitting, do you think? There are one or two areas I'd like to examine in more detail. In private.'

The temptation to defy Sir Leon, even for the wrong reasons, was strong, but so was the memory of his hands on her, his potent kisses. Voices from the stairway interrupted them and, taking Marcus's hand, she peeled it away and slid it to one side, giving him no answer.

Dame Celia Aycombe, the vicar's homely wife, appeared in the doorway, her face glowing with the exertion of two flights of stairs. 'My dears,' she said, 'how are things progressing?'

'Coming along nicely,' said Marcus. 'Another day or two, perhaps.'

Chapter Six

With Dame Celia, Felice found some respite from Sir Leon's seemingly constant differences of opinion on everything ranging from the decoration on the walls to the size of the candlesticks. But as they walked together through the spacious rooms of the New House, the dame's sympathy was not quite of the same order as Marcus Donne's.

'He does have such very good taste though, my dear,' Dame Celia said. 'He knows all the latest trends; indeed, I believe his *is* the latest trend.'

'Tapestries on walls are nothing new, Dame Celia. That's what he's insisting on in the best bed-chamber.'

'Jan van der Straet's are,' she said. 'Sir Leon was one of the first to use his designs here in England before he was snapped up by the Medici in Florence. There's no one here who can compete with the Flemings, you know. I'd follow Sir Leon's advice every time.'

Felice's resistance to the surveyor's ideas had not been based on any sense of her own superiority but on her mother's strong preferences that had collected the showiest items from the homes of three husbands and crammed them all together. To Lady Deventer, if you had it, you showed it, discrimination being an excuse for not having it. This placed Felice in some difficulty since she could easily predict how her mother would react to Sir Leon's restrained elegance.

They entered the best bedchamber through a nest of smaller rooms with cupboards as big as closets. Even without furnishings, everything was proportionate and pleasing to the eye.

Dame Celia had not missed the ups and downs of Felice's relationships. 'I'm glad you and Marcus are such good friends. When will the portrait be finished? Are you pleased so far?'

Felice swept a hand across a sawdust-covered window-seat and sat sideways to the view beyond. 'I hope it will be as attractive as Dame Audrey's,' she said. 'Was Frances an only child?'

'The only one,' Dame Celia said, opening a door on the far side of the room. 'Where does this lead?'

'Nowhere. It's a maid's room, I think. What did she die of?'

'Your mother will be needing a new nursery nearby. Does she breast-feed or use a wet-nurse? What did she die of?' she repeated, closing the door.

'Childbirth, my dear. They lost the baby, too. Very sad business.'

Felice knew how common such deaths were but this was something she had not expected to hear. 'But...she wasn't married, was she?'

'Frances? No, dear, she wasn't. That makes it even sadder.'

'What happened, Dame Celia?'

The lady was preoccupied with the pattern of gilded knot-work on the ceiling. 'Lovely...lovely,' she whispered. 'Well, she was sent off to have her child in Winchester with one of Audrey's friends who lives at the Sisterne House—you know, the home for sisters who'd been at the nunneries in the area. Of course she'd have been allowed back to live with my brother's family here in Wheatley if she'd lived—not as a lady's maid, but they'd have found some kind of work for her, if only so that she could leave the child with her parents. Such a silly girl, getting herself caught like that.'

The sun sparkled on the river, sending shimmering diamonds across its surface, and Felice wondered for a fleeting moment what she was doing there in that strangely echoing room, hearing about the tragic death of an unknown woman whom this kindly woman was calling silly. 'Who was the father?' she asked. 'Do you know?'

Dame Celia's short laugh held no humour. 'Oh, it could have been one of several men, I believe. She never lacked for admirers in London, and my brother and his wife entertained almost constantly. It was hushed up in case my brother was held responsible for the girl's safety, but if a lass is determined to court danger, she will, no matter what her employers do to prevent it. I feel sorry for the Vytterys. They'd have loved a grandchild.'

'And did they hold your brother responsible, dame?'

'No, I don't think so. They've been very philosophical about it, though I doubt not that they're still grieved.'

'She was a lovely woman.'

'Yes, a lot like you in some respects, dark-eyed and the same independent spirit. Everyone loved her.' She wandered off into the next room, calling back to Felice, 'Now this could be the nursery, my lady. Come and see what you think.'

'Marcus Donne!' Felice said emphatically to Lydia at supper that evening. 'There can't be any doubt about it.'

Lydia disagreed. 'I don't know how you can be so sure when Dame Celia believes it could have been one of several. Besides, he wouldn't...'

'He would, Lydie! And he painted her portrait in London and that means he had plenty of time to get to know her. Look how fast he tried to impose himself on me. Nobody's safe with him, even Sir Leon told me that. I saw the weeping in her eyes on that portrait.'

'I still think you're being too hasty. He's a flirt, and maybe he goes a bit too far when he thinks he can get away with it, but he'd not last long as an artist if he sired a brat every time he paints a woman's portrait.'

'That's as may be, but I believe Sir Leon knows more about Marcus's reasons for being here instead of in London. Keeping out of someone's way, I suspect. Well, I'm not going to sit for him again, Lydie. A man who can carry on as if nothing had happened in those circumstances is an unprincipled wretch, and I want nothing more to do with him or his portrait.'

For the next few days, Felice made herself unavailable to the fervent, if puzzled, Mr Donne until he came to realise that something other than the pressure of work was causing a hiatus. Careful to make no particular mention of the problem to Sir Leon in case it should be misconstrued, it was none the less only a matter of time before the observant surveyor noticed what was happening. Or rather, what was not happening.

'Four days?' he said to the limner. 'Of course she's available. She's been keeping out of my way too, but at least I know why. Which is more than you seem to, my friend. What happened at the last sitting?'

'I painted. She sat,' Marcus snapped. 'What else can I tell you?'

'You were alone?'

Marcus sighed. 'No. Mistress Waterman's always been there.'

'Oh, really? She didn't tell me that.'

'No. She doesn't tell you much, does she? You should try listening.'

So it was with that in mind that he sought Felice out in one of the small downstairs offices in the New House where she and Mr Peale, the house steward, sat before a pile of lists, ledgers and accounts.

'Ah...' Felice looked up from her list '...here's Sir Leon come to tell us that we cannot have this room because he wants it. Good day to you, sir. We were just moving out. Come, Henry.'

Still smarting from Marcus's rebuke, Sir Leon bit back his retort and spoke to the steward first. 'Henry, the men have just brought up the eel traps from the dam. If Mr Dawson wants a basket or two, get him to send his lads over to my kitchen and say I sent them. But be quick.'

'Yes, sir. Indeed I will. Thank you. Please excuse me, my lady.'

'Certainly, Henry. And where may I send one of your men, Sir Leon?'

'Felice,' he said, closing the door.

'Oh, dear, now what have I done?'

'It's not that which brings me here.'

'All right, what haven't I done? I can't wait to hear.' She gathered her papers as she spoke, convinced that she was being moved on.

'No, don't go. I shall be using the offices on the other side. Stay here, if you wish.'

'I probably won't, but thank you. Now, my sins of omission. What are they this time?'

He leaned against the door and folded his arms, conscious of her bristling hostility and not knowing how to dispel it. She was wild, like a fearful creature, mistrustful, vulnerable and full of resentments. And too beautiful for words. 'No sins,' he said. 'I wondered what Marcus has been up to, that's all.'

Her eyes searched his for some meaning. 'How should I know? He lives in the guesthouse with you, doesn't he?'

'You've not been sitting for him for four days. He believes you're avoiding him.'

'Then you should be well satisfied. It was you who repeatedly told me not to get too friendly. You've been careful not to offer me a sensible alternative but, as you see, I'm taking your advice until something mutually acceptable appears.'

'Felice,' he said, again.

'Yes?'

She was not making it easy. Why should she? 'Felice, has Marcus been misbehaving?'

'With me? No. Is that all?'

'Not with you, then with whom?'

She looked away. 'Ask him. It's none of my business.'

'With Lydia? Elizabeth?'

'Oh, for heaven's sake! Of course not. Don't let's

go through all the possibilities, *please*. The dairy-maid and the laundrymaid haven't complained, either.'

'There's something wrong and I need to know what it is.'

'Why?' she flared. 'You've spent plenty of time telling me how not to do this and that, who not to make a friend of, who not to think of, who I should forget. Now you think there's something amiss when I stop doing what you've been telling me not to do in the first place. Make lists, you said...' she waved an arm at the pile of papers '...I'm making them. Look...look! Are they wrong, too?' By now her voice had become raw with anger, and tears had begun to flood her eyes. 'Tell me,' she croaked. 'Put me in my place again. I can take it.'

He wanted to take her in his arms, but knew that she would fight him off. 'No, it's nothing to do with any of that. You've done well. But if there's something happened between you and Marcus...'

'All right!' she spat. 'If it will make you go away any faster I'll tell you why I'm not sitting for him. It's because he's an unscrupulous lecher who carries on seducing women even after the mother of his child has died in childbirth. A man who can do that is too ungodly even for my company. There now, does that satisfy your needs?'

Sir Leon's arms slowly unfolded. 'What?' he said, frowning. '*Marcus*? Nay, you cannot mean...

Marcus?' He swept a hand round his jaw, holding it together. 'How do you know all this?'

'I *know* it!'

'Yes, but how? You can't make that kind of accusation without evidence. Proof. Do you have proof?'

'Well, of course I do, sir. You've seen his portrait of the Vytterys' daughter that he painted in London at the Paynefleetes. Well, it was after that that she was sent off to Winchester to have a child, and it was there she died last year while he went on painting and trying it on with every available female. You said it yourself, plain or pretty, it makes no difference. He's responsible for two deaths, Sir Leon, and he has the gall to behave as if nothing has happened. It's indecent. What more proof do you need than that?'

'But Felice, none of that is proof. It's not even evidence, it's more like supposition. Because a woman has her portrait painted a few months before she has a child, you can't pin the blame on the painter, just like that. Think of all…'

'How do you know it was only a few months? Did he tell you that?'

'Well, no, but I know when he was at the Paynefleetes' London home and I happen to know when the Vytterys' daughter died because Dame Celia told us, didn't she? I admit that the dates are close, but that doesn't mean he must be responsible. He's not the only man in London to know the Paynefleetes' household.'

'You're protecting him. After all you've said to warn me, and now suddenly when your warnings take shape you'll not believe it. I might have known.'

'Felice, will you stop to think. Think!' he said, firmly but gently, instantly reminding her of that same instruction delivered under such different circumstances.

She covered her face, unable to look at him or be seen.

'I'm sorry. Listen a while. Are you listening?'

She nodded into her hands.

'Do you really think that Marcus would have the effrontery, and the insensitivity, to return to Wheatley if he'd been guilty of what you say? Do you really think the Vytterys and the Aycombes would remain his friends if they believed that he could have been the one involved with Frances Vyttery? And the Paynefleetes: do you think they'd allow him anywhere near if he'd betrayed their trust in that way? Of course they'd not. Marcus may be a womaniser, but he's not stupid enough to put his profession in jeopardy to *that* extent. You've no doubt deduced that he's here to lie low for a while, but not for anything like the Frances Vyttery tragedy. That's not Marcus's way of doing things.'

Felice sat on her stool and stared woodenly out of the window where men had begun to clear the cloister of debris and weeds. 'I'd better apologise to him,' she whispered.

'Have you accused him, then?'

'No, not personally.'

'Then there's nothing to apologise for, is there? Leave it to me.'

'No…no! You cannot tell him.' She turned to him in alarm. 'You must not.'

'I won't. I'll say you've been busy trying to please me. Isn't that what you were doing these last four days?'

'No, sir. He knows I'm not stupid enough to attempt the impossible.'

'Has it been as bad as that, lass?'

She declined to answer that. 'So, if it was not Marcus, who was it?'

He trod the ground carefully, picking his way through the facts he knew and those he was not able to reveal, aware that she sat like a hawk ready to pounce on any mistake. 'Well, that's not something that need concern us, is it? I don't know how much the Vytterys and the Paynefleetes know, but I believe it's best if we put it to the back of our minds. She was obviously a foolish woman, wasn't she?'

Despite all his care, his painstaking route led him straight into the trap, and now she reacted to his heedless censure with all the instincts of a she-wolf with her litter. Her eyes blazed angrily. 'Oh, yes, indeed, sir, she was, wasn't she? But I believe she might have been as confused as I am about who to trust and who not to. It's an affliction we foolish women are prone to, didn't you know that? We're sent here and there to do this and that, and we're forced to obey and accept anyone who sets himself up as a protector without knowing whether they're wolves in sheep's clothing or sheep disguised as wolves. It's all very confusing. And then, to cap it all, we have bairns and die. Now that's *really* foolish!'

She turned her back on him, attempting to hide her pain as well as her fury. But he had seen both. He had been told to listen, and now he heard a mixture of anguish and confusion, insecurity and bitterness, and a personal experience that she had so far done all she could to hide. And while he suspected what form this had taken, there was still no way of telling how deeply she had been involved, whether the priest's real passion had been for the mother of his child or for the lovely young woman who came after. Perhaps he would never know.

He broke the heavy uncomfortable silence of the little room as gently as he was able. 'No, not foolish, my lady. Forgive me. It was the wrong word to use. Men can be so clumsy with words. She paid a heavy price. Too heavy. But men become confused every bit as readily as women, remember, when they read women's signals they're not meant to see. That's what I warned you about with Marcus; the more experienced the man the more signals he picks up, and then the woman had better not send any she prefers to keep to herself.'

'Sometimes she cannot help it, sir,' she said, in a small voice.

'As you say, sometimes she cannot help it.'

'And then what's she supposed to do? What else can she do but pretend that these private longings don't exist?'

'Why so? Would it not be better for her to talk about them?'

'No, sir, I think not. She would have to be very sure of her confidante before she could trust him to share her thoughts. Men in particular are so clumsy, as you've just pointed out.' She kept her back to him, her fingers toying abstractedly with the ivory needlecase at the end of her girdle-chain, impressing her fingertips with its sharply carved roses.

Sir Leon could see that she was shaking. 'Felice,' he said.

'Please...leave me. Go, sir.'

'I'll speak to Marcus.'

'Yes, thank you,' she whispered.

It was some time before she stopped shaking and before the words between them had settled, still tangled with double meanings that both of them had recognised and understood. But not until now had she known that he could be lost for words.

As the brilliance of the sun slanted through the windows, Felice stood motionless in the upper room of the Abbot's House contemplating the tiny half-finished portrait of herself on Marcus's miniature easel. It fitted into the lid of his travelling paintbox and had been covered over by a fine silk cloth to keep any dust off its surface, as was also the array of paints and brushes, oyster-shell palettes and packets of dried pigments. The limner even wore silk shirts so that no fibres escaped on to the ultra-smooth vellum surface of the painting. His hair was always newly washed, his nails immaculate.

The portrait already showed a miniature Felice, a steady gaze into the distance and the fine outline of the three-quarter view that limners favoured, the shadowless and peach-toned skin. But Felice could not see the likeness to the Vytterys' daughter that Dame Celia had mentioned, perhaps for politeness' sake, except in the dark hair and eyes. Yet in how many other ways had they been alike?

'Like it?' A voice spoke from the doorway.

'Marcus! Oh, I didn't hear you come up. Er...yes, it's looking good. It'll soon be finished now, I suppose?'

He strolled forward and replaced its silken shroud. 'Not for a while, I fear. Another time, perhaps.' His long delicate fingers roamed deftly over his tools, collecting them and placing them one by one in the box. 'I must pack them, my lady.' He smiled at her, gravely.

'Marcus, stop! What d'ye mean? You're not going, are you?'

He stopped, still holding a squirrel-hair brush. He took her chin in one hand to hold her face still, dragging the brush's sensuous furriness around her oval face from ear to ear and smiling at her startled blink. 'Going? Yes, my lady, I must go. Say you'll miss me. Say you'll die of a broken heart.' He touched her lips with the tip of the brush. 'Say it, even if you don't mean it.' His smile was of pure blue-eyed mischief.

'I shall miss you, Marcus. Truly. I cannot promise the broken heart, nor do I understand why you're going. Has Sir Leon told you you must?'

'Not exactly.' Marcus's squirrel brush was now following the line of each fine dark eyebrow. 'Keep still.'

'Then what?'

'Let's say it was a mutual decision. We both think it best if I were not here. He believes I may be a distraction, I think. No, don't open your mouth, I'm painting it.'

Impatiently, she held the brush aside. 'Marcus, that's ridiculous. I need someone to distract me from these endless lists. You can have a bed up here if he wants you out of the guesthouse.'

'He's about to move out of there himself tomorrow into some of the ground-floor rooms at the back of the New House but, no. That's not the real reason I'm going. I must get another commission, you see. I cannot afford to be without work for too long.'

'Yes, I see. But I wish you were not leaving me here.'

He touched the tip of her nose impertinently. 'Then come with me, lady.'

'To London?'

'Why not? My horses are in your stables. Let's use them.'

It would not do, nor did she believe him to be too serious about the idea. She could not live with Marcus, nor did she have contacts in London, but the idea was too good to dismiss without some further thought. 'Must it be London?' she said.

He shrugged. 'Personally, I'd rather not, but it's where I live and where I know the work to be.'

'Then why not go to Sonning instead and paint my mother?'

'Sonning? Isn't that in wildest Berkshire, somewhere?'

She went to take his arm, threading hers through a crust of pale grey-embroidered satin and surprising him by her sudden affection. 'Wildest? Hardly. It's near Reading, and that's nearer to London than Wheatley is.'

Catching the drift of her mind, he looked down at her in amusement. 'I see. And the road to Sonning passes through Winchester. Is that it?'

'And I need to reach Winchester with my lists.'

'And you need an escort.'

'I need an escort and a horse or two, sir.'

'How convenient. And where do you stay in Winchester?'

'With my mother's friend, Lady Mary West. We stayed there overnight on our way down here: she'll be pleased to see me again so soon.'

'And what about permission to leave Wheatley, my lady? Am I correct in thinking that you intend to forgo that?'

'You are correct. All I need is for a certain person to be too occupied by a house-move to notice what I'm doing. It shouldn't be difficult.'

'And what of your mother? Will Lady Deventer want to have her portrait painted?'

'She will if I send her a letter for you to carry. At the same time you'll be able to tell Lord Deventer how things progress here at the abbey and what a fine job I'm making of things.'

'And how well you get on with your guardian?'

'Er...no, Marcus. It's best if you say nothing of that. It's not his concern, but you may tell him I'll be ordering goods for the New House in his name from merchants in Winchester. He'd better know of that.'

'Right. So I'll go and make myself agreeable to your lady mother. Is she as lovely as her daughter, by any chance?'

'She's very pretty. She's also seven months' pregnant.'

Not for a moment did Felice think that her mother's pregnancy would make any difference to

Marcus's interest in her as a sitter, not with a hefty fee to be had. After all, he had painted the Vytterys' daughter in the same, though probably less advanced condition, though Sir Leon had been right to suggest that they should now put that subject out of mind, especially since she had mistaken Marcus so unjustly.

However, this was not the only subject she must try to forget during the day-long ride to Winchester over rough tracks bordered with white hawthorn and alive with cheeky hedge-sparrows. Spontaneous plans, Marcus had told her, were often the best, this one being perfectly timed to remove herself from the one who nowadays dominated her thoughts. It also gave her the chance to be truly independent of him.

She must, she told herself, get to the merchants to order more beds and linen, mattresses and pillows, more tableware and silver, kitchenware and food supplies. The lists were extensive, yet the prospect of all this in the days ahead could barely compensate for the ache in her breast and the knowledge that any annoyance she had inflicted upon Sir Leon by her escape was nothing to the gnawing emptiness she had inflicted upon herself. It did little good to compare it with that which she had felt over Timon, for now she had to contend with the whereabouts of Sir Leon's affections as well as her own.

She had no doubt that he would wait until her

return, berate her soundly, then carry on from where they'd left off, but this diversion would help to show that, if Marcus was a distraction, that was exactly what she needed.

They had left Elizabeth behind because, Felice had told the weeping girl, Mr Donne had only enough spare horses for herself, for Lydia to ride pillion behind Mr Peale whose help she must have, and for a packhorse. Even this had taken some re-arranging, their so-called furtive escape eventually becoming so difficult to conceal that it was a wonder the whole of Wheatley had not heard what was go-ing on, even through the clamour of cock-crow and church-bells.

But the drizzling rain that followed them towards Winchester soon cleared, drying their cloaks with a gusting wind and scattering them with a confetti of white petals. It was late afternoon when they passed through the great West Gate into the High Street still seething with traders and last-minute buyers, porters and journeymen, tinkers, pedlars, beggars and drunks who reeled tipsily out of noisy inns.

'Keep going,' Felice called to Marcus's men who led the way. 'On past the cathedral and then turn right.' South, she said to herself, if the apse is still in the same place. 'It's called Colebrook Street, Marcus.'

Here in the eastern corner it was quieter, leafed with pale new trees and lined with houses enclosing the area that had once been Saint Mary's Abbey.

Just beyond the little church of Saint Peter stood a large timbered house within a spacious corner plot made by the high city wall, the home of one of Winchester's best-known citizens, Lady Mary West.

The outward ambience of serenity was deceptive, for the Winchester widow was larger than life in every respect, booming her welcome to the unexpected guests as if she had known of their imminent arrival. She sailed down the wide panelled passageway to meet them from the garden that bathed brilliantly in the evening sun, the sides of her wide bell-farthingale knocking against everything, sending a silver tray crashing to the floor and her pet spaniel yelping for cover. 'Hah! Back already, m'dear?' she called merrily. 'Brought a beau with you this time? Well, if it's my approval you're after you'd better bring him out here where I can see him. What's his name?'

This unnerving habit of talking about those in her presence had been known to alienate people, especially men. But Felice succumbed to the mighty embrace of the padded figure whose magnificence would have made even the queen's ladies blink, and told her who and what Marcus was. As she had expected, Lady West took to his extravagant chivalry like a duck to water, linking her arm through his and noisily accepting his flattery without a single contradiction. Felice's worries fell away; it was as if she had come home.

For all Lady West's bluff heartiness, she was perceptive and exceptionally wise, kindly, and alarmingly undaunted by men; her reputation as a Roman Catholic recusant was well known to the citizens of Winchester, many of whom sheltered beneath her authority. She had regularly been fined for non-attendance at the parish church, but not even the threat of gaol would make her change her mode of worship to this new-fangled Church of England. She had survived the changes of the last twenty years, and now the Winchester authorities were beginning to admit defeat.

She had been a friend of Felice's mother for many years; she knew Lord Deventer and, although she was aware that his surveyor was a neighbour of hers, she had never met the elusive man. However, it took her very little time to read between the lines of Felice's apparent disenchantment and Marcus Donne's somewhat premature departure from Wheatley. As the mother of a large grown-up family, she was still close enough to their doubts and disputes to understand love's cheating ways.

As she waved farewell to Marcus early next morning, she was sure that Felice would not have seen the last of him, having about him a keenness that in Felice was only skin-deep. He was pleasant, but nowhere near strong enough for this young lady who was of her father's mould rather than her mother's.

'There now,' she said to Felice as soon as Marcus's cavalcade was out of sight. 'No more men for a while. How does that suit you?'

'Well enough, I thank you,' said Felice with some feeling, but smiling to sugar the impulsive reply. 'I like him, though.'

'Who wouldn't, my dear? I imagine your mother will, too. Now, shall we take a look at your lists and decide where to begin? I know all the best merchants in Winchester. And perhaps it's time to take a look through your wardrobe, while you're here, and bring it up to date. My tailor is very good; how about a trip to him, for a start?'

Felice and Lydia eyed each other's dresses critically, not for the first time. Lady Honoria Deventer's energies of late had not been directed towards her daughter's appearance, nor had Felice shown much interest in the styles she knew to be changing, little by little, the paddings and slashings, stiffenings and quiltings, the furs, puffs and braids. A farthingale was something she had never found to be practical enough for her purposes, and the one she had taken with her to Wheatley had been impossible to transport on the packhorse to Winchester during her escape. Now she was being offered a chance to remedy all that, and it was no coincidence that an image of the glamourous Levina Deventer passed before her mind as she said, 'I think it's about time too, my lady. I cannot tell you when I last had a new gown, and poor Lydie's been wearing my cast-offs for these two years or more.'

Lady West's high-class tailor, William Symonds, had a shop below his house in The Pentice, just off the High Street where, as a former mayor, he lived amongst Winchester's wealthiest citizens. One look at the well-stocked shelves told Felice that she was not going to finish her business here without paying heavily for it, yet, once amongst the bolts of velvet, taffeta, tiffany and silk damask, she succumbed to the excitement of having the exotic fabrics draped over her. All around the shop were rows of farthingales and ready-made corsets, half-made bodices and drawings of sleeve-details, kirtles, embroidered chemises and partlets, rolls of gold braid and fine linen for collars, lace, feathers and patterned bands. She stopped thinking about the cost, nor did she balk for long at Lady West's inducement to be more daring.

'With your looks and colouring, you can get away with anything,' Lady West said loudly from the other side of the colourful shop. 'Here's some lustie-gallant,' she called. 'And what about this incarnate?'

'Not red,' Felice said, wincing at the ruby brilliance. 'I've never been comfortable in red.'

'Nonsense, love. Tell her, Mistress Lydia, if you please. Red suits her.'

Persuaded, Felice chose an orange-red called Catherine pear, a bluish-white known as milk-and-water, and a colourful silk called medley which they told her was the height of fashion, though she would have preferred willow. Naturally, it took them all morning, though the servants carried back to Cole-brook Street only the farthingale and two exquisitely made corsets, enough fine lawn for several cool smocks for summer and, from the hosier, three pairs of real silk stockings.

'Shoes this afternoon,' said Lady West, energetically.

The change of environment, the indulgence of pleasing oneself and the stimulating company of her hostess, not to mention that sudden relaxation of tensions, was an intoxicating mixture that Felice could not recall ever having tasted before. Still laughing at some silliness of Lydia's, she tripped happily down the wide staircase of Cool Brook House, resting on the lower landing where the balustrade balanced a massive pineapple on its angle. Lady West's voice mingled with a man's, flowing across the panelled hallway from the garden and causing Felice to hesitate rather than intrude upon their conversation.

Her heart somersaulted inside her new whalebone corset, her hand stiffening upon the smooth wood as the tone of the man's voice reached her softly through Lady West's loud chatter, and she knew then that all her hopes and fears had converged like tributaries into one fast-flowing river. He had come to find her.

It was immediately obvious that he had not come from Wheatley that day; his deep gold and sage-green doublet and matching trunk-hose that showed no sign of dust was set off by spotless white at the neck and wrists. He greeted her with a courtly bow, sweeping off his green velvet hat around which curled a peacock feather and, having replaced it, treated her to a lazy smile that took in every detail of her unwelcoming expression. 'My lady,' he said.

'Sir Leon. You are here on business?'

'Part business, part pleasure,' he said. 'We could have travelled together if you'd told me of your intentions.'

Lady West looked at Felice in surprise, but said nothing.

'Yes, sir. I realise that. Do you stay long?'

'Long enough to help you with the purchases and to escort you back to Wheatley.'

'I may be here some time, sir. Perhaps you'd better…'

'Good. These things are best not rushed. Lady West tells me you've not fixed a date for your return.'

'I've made no decisions of any kind except what new gowns to wear. On that I was given some encouragement; quite an unusual experience for me these days. That alone tempts me to outstay my welcome.'

Lady West was not slow to sense the hostile undercurrents on Felice's part. 'Impossible,' she said. 'Your welcome extends indefinitely, my dear. For ever, if you wish. My home is yours. Now, please excuse me if I leave you for a moment or two; I shall return presently.' She touched Felice's arm in passing.

Sir Leon bowed and waited for Felice to speak. When she did not, he held out a hand, hoping for hers. 'Come now,' he said, softly. 'Our parting was not on such bad terms, was it? Did you think I'd be angry?'

'At taking matters into my own hands? Certainly it had crossed my mind, since it takes only that much to anger you.'

'Well, then,' he said, smiling at her waspishness, 'now that we're both here, shall we begin anew, since we left our disagreements at Wheatley?'

'But we didn't, did we, Sir Leon? I brought my lists with me and I intend to order everything on them. Mr Donne went on to Sonning.'

'Yes, I know.'

'Elizabeth told you, I suppose,' she said, with resignation.

'She had no choice. I asked her.'

'Of course. So you followed, just to make sure I didn't go with Marcus.'

'I was scarce a half-hour behind you, lass,' he said, quietly. 'I knew exactly where you were going and I followed because you are my responsibility. I want no changes of mind while you're in Winchester. I take it that Lady West hasn't been made aware of our relationship?'

Alarm flared in her eyes, giving an edge to her tone. 'No, naturally I've told her nothing of that. If it makes no sense to me, I can hardly expect Lady West to understand it.'

'I think you misjudge the lady's abilities, Felice. She'll understand if I tell her. And why should she be kept in the dark when all Wheatley and your parents know?'

'My *what*? You've been in contact with them?'

'Well, of course I have. I'm in contact with Deventer constantly for one reason or another.' He drew her towards a wooden bench, the back of which rested against a high yew hedge that sheltered them from the house. 'Come, sit awhile. It's what friends do, you know.' He felt the resistance in her hand and smiled at her vacillation.

Finally, she sat, eyeing him warily. 'So they know of this clever arrangement, and they agree with you, of course.'

'Of course.'

'And Lord Deventer must be wondering why he hadn't thought of the idea himself. It never ceases to amaze me, Sir Leon, how men can know so much more about what women need than the women themselves. I don't suppose you could give me some warning of the next stage in your plans, sir, or would that be asking for the moon, d'ye think?'

'Probably. But perhaps when you begin to trust me, when you begin to take me into your confidence, then I'll start to tell you of my plans for you.'

'I already know of your plans for me, sir,' she retorted. 'I would have had to be alarmingly stupid not to have seen through them by now. It was the timing of them to which I referred.'

'Yes, that was also what I referred to. Perhaps we could work on that together, eh?' His fingers lifted a dark tendril of hair from her neck and replaced it on top of her head, scorching her with his touch and drying her next words before they could emerge. He waited, patiently. 'Well?'

'I came here for two reasons, Sir Leon,' she whispered, eventually. 'One was to continue the task my stepfather set for me, and...'

'And?'

'And the other...' She looked sideways at his hands and found herself unable to speak with any real conviction.

'Was to evade me. Yes, I knew that, too. I shall help you with one but not the other. We did it once before, remember? We can do it again.'

He referred to the planning of the garden, she knew, but things had changed since then. The painted face of Levina Deventer laughed silently over his shoulder and disappeared. 'I doubt it, sir,' she whispered, 'as long as others come between us.'

'Then tell him to go,' he said.

Chapter Seven

Lady West mopped a dribble of onion sauce from her mouth and laid her linen damask napkin upon the white tablecloth. 'It's been done before, my dear,' she said, philosophically, reaching for the lamb pie. She took the edge of the crust in her fingers and made a cut to each side, lifting the wedge on to her trencher. 'A young lady tries to escape her guardian's custody. Well, so what's new? The only thing that *does* surprise me is that he came after you so fast. Few guardians of my experience have taken their responsibilities as seriously as that.'

To be truthful, it was not only that which had surprised her, though it would have been unhelpful to say so. Astonishment would have been closer to describing how she felt when the man portrayed as the overbearing, interfering, arrogant and thoroughly unpleasant surveyor turned out to be a courteous, charming, and extremely handsome man of some considerable style, all of which spoke volumes to explain Felice's hostility. Hardly surprising was her convenient memory-lapse concerning the roles of guardianship and ward, which she obviously resented as much as he intended to enforce.

'Not too surprising, if you think about it, my lady,' Felice replied, dipping a piece of her manchet-bread into the sauce and watching it soak upwards. 'He's doing his best to please my stepfather, of course. He'll find my inheritance more than useful when he comes to make an offer for my hand. *That's* what it's all about.' She eyed the bowl of saffron-yellow frumenty but decided against it. 'The insulting part is that I'm not supposed to be able to see through it.'

'Felice, my dear...' Lady West looked hard at the piece of lamb on its way to her mouth '...you cannot seriously believe it.' She popped it in and chewed happily while she explained, defying table manners in her enthusiasm. 'I'd not met Sir Leon until today, but I've seen his house, I know his men, and I know what he's worth. I know,' she said, licking her fingers, 'what *everybody*'s worth in Winchester. He's a man of substance known to the council as a subsidy-man, one of the top ten taxpayers. And I don't for a moment believe that he needs to find himself a wealthy wife or he'd have found one by now.' She waved a little finger to a waiting servant. 'Help the ladies to the salad,' she said. 'Lettuce and cucumbers picked today. And apart from that,' she went on, picking out a leaf of red cabbage as the bowl passed in front of her, 'it's hardly likely that Deventer will have discussed any details of your inheritance with Gascelin, even though he is your guardian.'

'I doubt my stepfather knows the details himself.'

'There you are, then. It's not the money, my dear. You can take it from me.'

Fitting so neatly into Felice's theory, it was hard to let go of the idea so, as if to help her, Lady West took her two guests in her carriage on a tour of the town during which the coachman had orders to go via the Staple Garden and Northgate. Being an extravagant lady in every respect, Lady West's claim to know everyone's worth was bound to be exaggerated, but Felice and Lydia soon found out that this was not so as snippets of information about owners, occupations, families, religion, misdemeanours and aspirations, wealth and social standing came leaking out, much of them keeping them in stitches of laughter.

'Diverted all his sewage into next-door's cellar,' she went on, waving to an acquaintance. 'They couldn't make out where the smell was coming from for three months. Now he's the town clerk, so it obviously didn't hamper *his* movements.'

Up in the north-west corner of the city wall, most of the ground was taken up by gardens and orchards where once the wool-merchants had held their wool market, known as the staple. There were few houses here, but the largest one stood alone within tree-lined walls, allowing them only a glimpse through wrought-iron gates at the pink brickwork and silvered pepperpot domes capping hexagonal towers, and acres of shining glass that caught the sun.

South-facing, no doubt, Felice thought.

The coach slowed to a walking pace. 'Built only a few years ago on the site of four houses,' Lady West told them. 'He owns several shops in the town, including the best goldsmith.'

'And a tapestry merchant, by any chance?'

'Yes. Jonn Skinner, last year's mayor. How did you know that?'

'I daresay he'll be well represented at Wheatley Abbey,' Felice replied, with a sigh. But by the time they had returned home via the great Norman castle, the Kingsgate, the boys' college and the bishop's palace, Felice was utterly convinced that no other house in Winchester compared for sheer beauty and size to the one owned and built by Sir Leon Gascelin.

Well satisfied with the impressions she had been able to change with such relative ease, Lady West began to understand something of her lovely young guest's animosity towards her stepfather's surveyor. Having set his own highly individual ideas so firmly around a new project, he would have had to be a saint not to be exasperated by a nineteen-year-old maid's insistence on her mother's preferences. Honoria's conception of good taste had not improved during three marriages and a large brood of children. Heaven only knew how much of it her daughter had absorbed.

Accordingly, Lady West's private predictions materialised when Sir Leon paid an unfashionably early visit to Cool Brook House the next morning as she was speaking to her chaplain after mass in her tiny chapel. The man hurried off at Sir Leon's appearance, anxious not to be identified.

'A difficult life,' she whispered, loudly. 'They have to be so courageous, these days, never being sure of their friends. Come on, Sir Leon. I've had wine and wafers sent into the garden. The wasps are already showing an interest.'

'You were expecting guests, my lady?'

She raised her eyebrows and darted a look at him, sideways. 'You, Sir Leon. Just yourself. I may be old, but I know a thing or two.'

He smiled and held out his arm for support down the stone steps. 'I'm sure you do, my lady. That's partly why I've come, to find you alone.'

'Ask away,' she said, allowing herself to be seated in a basket chair. She handed him a tall Venetian glass of elderflower cordial that glistened like honey between his fingers. 'You'll want to know more about Lady Felice, I expect; this guardianship was a rather hurried business, I take it.'

'An emergency device,' he said. 'She'd have

abandoned the task if I'd not thought of something drastic. Deventer approves.'

Lady West nodded. 'And she doesn't.'

Sir Leon seated himself opposite her, facing the early sun. His legs were shapely and well muscled, clad tightly in dark green hose as far as his thighs, his glinting grey eyes well aware of his hostess's admiring scrutiny. He waited for her to continue.

'Well, you've come for some information, though I may not give it, for all that.'

The grey eyes laughed back at her warning. 'I'd not expect you to betray any confidences, my lady, but I'd like to know something about Lord Deventer's chaplain.'

'Then why don't you ask him yourself?'

'Because he'd want to know of my interest, and I prefer him not to.'

'You're not one of the queen's spies, are you?'

He knew she was not too serious: this woman knew everyone's persuasions without asking. 'Did you know the Deventer's chaplain before the present one?' he said.

'Before Bart Sedburgh? Yes, Father Timon. He came from the Paynefleetes of Wheatley. You'll know them, of course.'

'Yes, I know them well enough. Have you any idea who recommended him to Lady Honoria when he left Wheatley?'

'Yes. I did.'

'You?'

'Why so surprised? Roman Catholics have to stick together in these precarious times, sir. We have to help each other. Hakon Paynefleete knows I have contacts of the same faith, and when he asked me if could find a position for Father Timon, I put him in touch with Honoria. She wanted someone suitable to tutor hers and Deventer's combined broods. They have a clutch of young lads, you know.'

'I see. Did Hakon Paynefleete give any reason why Father Timon was leaving him?'

'Said he'd been told that if he didn't get rid of the chaplain he'd be clapped in gaol. Paynefleete, that is, not the chaplain. *He*'d be hanged, most like. You know what it's like in London where the Paynefleetes have a house. If you ask me, it was a bit foolish taking him with them; I'd not last long if I lived there; I'm fortunate to be tolerated here.'

'So Hakon told you *he* was in danger?'

'Correct. But the chaplain wasn't with Deventer long before he died, you know. Did you know that?'

'I had heard. Sad business. He was well liked, I believe.'

Sir Leon was staggered by Hakon Paynefleete's deceit. In spite of the chaplain's dishonourable conduct with their maid, the Vytterys' daughter, he was nevertheless allowed to move on to another family. 'Lady West,' he said, 'does Lady Felice know that it was you who recommended Father Timon to her mother?'

'I doubt it. It was not her concern, after all, and

we all have to be so careful about giving information on the whereabouts of priests. Why, has she spoken of him?'

'No, not a word. Nor would I like her to know that we've been speaking of him, my lady. As you say, it's not her concern.' Anticipating her next question, he went on, quickly. 'I'd like to assist Lady Felice with her purchases for the abbey while I'm here. Would you allow me to call, to take her into town...shopping? I have one or two workshops I'd like her to see.'

'On foot?'

His smile was audible. 'I have horses for her and Mistress Waterman. She and my valet have taken a fancy to each other, you see. May I bring them round?'

'If they're as comely as yourself, sir, Felice and Lydia will not be able to resist them, will they? But don't head directly for John Skinner's tapestry workshop, I beg you. That would be exceedingly undiplomatic.'

If Sir Leon had expected to find the same compliance in this ward as in her hostess, he was to be disappointed. She protested, in private to begin with, at some feeling of betrayal. 'My lady' she said, 'I've come all this way expressly to shop *without* him. I'll not go through all those arguments again, and one cannot dispute before merchants, can one? He'll get his own way, no matter what I've decided, and I may as well not have any say at all.'

'I think you'll find, my dear, that away from Wheatley Sir Leon will be quite prepared to accept your choices on most things.' Lady West had good reason to believe this, having advised him to begin with the household goods with which his tastes counted for little. 'Begin at the linen-hall on Ceap Street and don't let them charge you more than three shillings for tablecloths, ten for quilts and four for a pair of sheets.'

'I had hoped to go with you, my lady,' said Felice.

'You shall, my dear, you shall. For the important purchases, we'll go together. Plenty of time.'

'This is quite ridiculous,' she snapped to Lydia later on. 'It's bad enough having him here in Winchester without having to be watched over when I'm buying. Can't we give him the slip, Lydie?'

She said something very similar to Sir Leon himself as he came into the large terraced garden wearing high riding-boots and looking very sure of himself. 'No, sir,' she said, watching two butterflies chase each other around the spikes of lavender. 'I'm sorry, but today I've made other arrangements.' She had no wish to sound petulant, but this was getting uncomfortably close to the manoeuvring tactics she had striven so hard to avoid, his impeccable courtesy here at Cool Brook House melting no ice with her.

It might have impressed Lady West, but she herself knew the cutting edge of his tongue, and his inflexibility.

'Oh, dear,' Sir Leon said, 'Mistress Waterman was so looking...'

'Oh, don't give me *that*!' she snarled, suddenly angry. 'Yes, I know Lydia wanted to ride with your Mr Bystander, but we are talking of more important issues than that, Sir Leon, we are talking of making me do something I am determined not to do. Now, I suggest that, to settle the argument, *you* take the lists and shop on your own. That way at least one of us will be pleased. Here you are.' She held them out, catching Lydia's eye as she did so. 'What's funny?' she said, crossly.

'Come,' said Lydia, laying a gentle hand on her arm. 'Just come and look at this.'

'Oh, no! If it's a carriage, forget it.'

'It's not. Come on.'

Reluctantly, she was led by the hand through the door in the garden wall and into the cobbled stable-yard where grooms talked, holding horses. They spread out as the group approached, bringing one horse forward to meet Felice, a pure white mare with a long mane and tail like unspun silk, dark eyes and muzzle, ears pricked delicately towards her. Its legs were fine, tail held high, coat shining like satin.

'Oh,' Felice said. 'Oh, you...you *beautiful* thing.' She halted, looking with reproach at Sir Leon's amusement. 'This is most unfair,' she whispered. '*Most* unfair!'

'No. As I said, all's fair in love and war. Sheer bribery,' he whispered back. 'Think you can ride her?'

The saddle was new pale Spanish leather embossed with a scrolling pattern, the stirrups of chased silver, the bridle studded and patchworked with coloured leathers and silver; the effect was exquisitely delicate.

Neither of them had seen Sir Leon ride before on his powerful dark bay stallion whose eyes rolled continually towards the two mares, Lydia's being a pretty light chestnut with a blonde mane and tail. With Adam, they made an impressive quartet but, with three servants bringing up the rear, they turned every head on the streets of Winchester.

As Sir Leon had said, it was sheer bribery, but it worked, and the next days were unbelievably different from the contentious times at Wheatley when good relations had been a mere oasis in a desert of conflicts from which Felice had not been able to find an escape except by the easiest route of giving in.

After the linen-hall they had visited the carpenter on Middle Brook Street to look at designs for bulbous-legged tables, chairs with wider-than-usual seats for ladies' skirts, massive court cupboards and tester beds with richly carved surfaces, wide enough for a small family.

'When my own carpenter is allowed access to

some good wood,' Felice said archly to Sir Leon as he lifted her up into the saddle yet again, 'I'll be able to set him to making some pallets and joined stools. At the moment, he's using whatever he can scrounge.'

Sir Leon arranged her skirts over her legs, hardly rising to the bait. 'At the moment, my lady,' he said, 'your carpenter has already made extra pallets and joined stools and is now using my best oak to make a set of shutters for your bedchamber windows.' He held her eyes, boldly.

'Oh,' she said. 'You gave orders to my carpenter?'

'Certainly I did. We both felt it was the safer course.'

Only a few days ago, she would have made a fuss, on principle, but now she was content to let it pass, there being no point to make.

'Where next, my lady? The mercer, is it?'

'No, silverware, if you please.'

'Jewry Street,' he said to Adam. 'Isaac Goldsmith's shop, then home.'

Felice was tempted to argue, almost to test him. 'No, not home. To the apothecary, I think, and then the brewer.'

'They'll be putting up their shutters in another ten minutes,' Sir Leon said, swinging himself up into the saddle. 'How long d'ye need with the goldsmith, five minutes?'

'An hour, at least.'

'Well, then, which is it to be?'

There was something quite delicious in losing an argument one didn't need to win anyway, a far cry from the unseemly Wheatley squabbles.

She had thanked him for the beautiful white mare, warmly and sincerely, though each night she wondered what lay behind this amazing change from severity to kindliness. She called the mare Pavane because her movements were graceful, like the dance, and she was allowed to stable both mares in Lady West's stables which, they said, was another mark of his new trust in her.

Sir Leon's new easy manner was the cause of some sleepy discussion at night when the two women lay side by side, tired after the day's exertions followed by a sociable evening.

'I'd no idea he had a singing voice,' Felice whispered. 'It's rather good.'

'Beautiful,' Lydia said. 'It almost made me cry when he sang about summer turning to cold December. He was looking at you, you know.'

'Yes, and thinking about someone else, no doubt. But he plays the lute well, too. I loved his duet with Adam. Do you think he's intentionally showing us his other side, Lydie, or is it just coincidence? He wants us to go and see his house tomorrow; Lady West's dying to have a look inside.'

'So am I, love. Tomorrow's Sunday. No shopping.'

'Early church; the little one across the road.'

'She doesn't attend the cathedral?'

'Once a month to avoid being fined and to see who she can see.'

They rolled over, back to warm back, and fell into the silent darkness. A muffled question found its way out, before sleep. 'Hasn't he kissed you since we came?'

'No. Not once.'

'Not even tried?'

'No.'

'Are you relieved?'

'Relieved. Puzzled. I don't know, Lydie. Perhaps this is just his new friendly phase. At least I can deal with this. I think.'

In the dark, Lydia did not see her mistress's eyes fill with tears, but she felt the sudden spasm, and laid a gentle hand upon her thigh until it ceased.

In the little church of St Peter Colebrook, which had formerly belonged to the nunnery of St Mary, the changes from Roman Catholic to Protestant were less obvious than in most other Winchester churches. The altar was still where it had always been, the statues and crucifixes, officially banned by the queen, were here tolerated by the town council because of Lady West's formidable influence, her large donations being responsible for the upkeep of the church and the priest's stipend.

The congregation still had a sprinkling of former

nuns from both St Mary's and from Romsey Abbey, most of them living either at St John's Hospital near the Eastgate or at the Sisterne House in the southern suburbs outside the city wall.

Lady West introduced Felice to some of them, noisily as usual, promising to find Sister Winifred and Mistress Godden, both of whom had been at Romsey and would be sure to know Dame Celia and Dame Audrey of Wheatley. Sister Winifred was not hard to find after the service, not daring to ignore Lady West's bellow outside the western door. The elderly black-clad sister turned with an expression of patient exasperation and waited for Lady West's magnificent black amplitude to bear down upon her like a gigantic magpie.

'Most of them are deaf,' Lady West yelled at Felice. 'You have to shout at them, poor things. Winifred, dear, where've you been?'

Good-natured or not, the question came as an extra discomfort to Sister Winifred. The former Romsey nun, unlike the two Wheatley dames, preferred to retain her habit, her name, and her nun-like demeanour, keeping her eyes downcast until the proper introduction had been made. Then she looked up, showing Felice the world-weariness and disillusionment in the drooping eyelids and mouth that she had seen in Dame Audrey's once-pretty face.

Contrary to Lady West's announcement, Sister Winifred was not deaf and so, while the noisy benevolent magpie was discussing the finer points of the sermon with the priest, Felice, Lydia and the former nun strolled towards the little wicket gate that enclosed the cemetery.

'Lady West believes you may remember two ladies I've recently met who now live at Wheatley. Former nuns of Romsey like yourself, I believe.'

'I was Mistress of the Novices there until it closed,' said Sister Winifred in a small disciplined voice. 'You must be referring to Celia Paynefleete and Audrey Wintershulle, I suppose, though Celia was never a novice.' There was no joy in her admission, and Felice saw instantly that there had been neither friendship nor close connection between them. She was, after all, a good ten years their senior, and there would be little by way of gossip to be had from this dame's tight-lipped mouth. 'Good families, both of them, but that doesn't count for much nowadays, does it?' she said.

In the context of her reduced circumstances at the hospital for poor but well-bred ladies, Sister Winifred's dour remark was understandable, but Felice suspected another meaning. 'The Paynefleetes are Dame Celia's brother and sister-in-law,' she said, 'but the name of Wintershulle is not a familiar one. Are they a local family?'

'Well, for all they helped their daughter, they may as well have lived on the moon. Families usually stick together in times of trouble, but not the Wintershulles. They didn't want to know.'

Felice's arms crawled with prickling hairs. She

had been mistaken, the tight-lipped mouth was not so much reluctant as bursting from want of a hearing. Discretion told Felice not to encourage her, but the words slipped out so easily. 'Know what, sister?'

Sister Winifred gripped the wicket gate with swollen knuckles, also fighting with the habit of discipline but, as she pushed the gate open, the inner defences were breached, breaking through into an outburst that carried more weight than mere gossip. 'They didn't want her back when Romsey closed down,' she said. 'Celia was all right. She hadn't taken her vows and she'd kept her nose clean. Not like young Audrey; she should never have been allowed to train as a novice. It was against my advice, though I blame those young priests at Wheatley. It's always as much the man's fault, isn't it?'

Felice glanced at Lydia, seeing a mirror there of her own horror. 'Yes,' she whispered, mechanically. 'They get away lightly, sister.'

Three abreast, they trod the pathway through long mounds, gravestones and bundles of flowers, not far distant from the chatter of church-goers. *Go on, woman. Go on.*

'That was the trouble,' Sister Winifred said, bitterly. 'The nunneries always needed priests to take our services, to instruct our novices, see to our accounts, hear confessions, administer…ah, heaven only knows what they administered. For most of them it didn't much matter; they knew their days were numbered and many of them were too young, anyway. *Far* too young. It was not good for those young lasses.'

'There was trouble?' said Lydia.

'Tch! Trouble!' Sister Winifred shook her head, hardly looking up. 'By the time we closed down in the spring of thirty-nine, the young Wintershulle lass was three or four months gone with child and not a soul wanted to know about it. Not even the father.'

'The Wheatley sacristan? Thomas Vyttery?'

'Aye. They had the devil's own job to get him to admit it and marry the lass. Celia's father took her in till they were married. He even gave them a cottage to live in and Father Thomas a job in the church.'

'Chantry priest, I believe.'

'Aye, but chantries were closed down soon after—you'll not remember that—so his job went, too. Life seemed to go sour on them, while young Celia and her family had it easy by comparison. Like mother, like daughter.' She sighed, shaking her head. 'I've said enough, my lady, she being a friend of yours, and all.'

'Well...er, not exactly. Wait, please.' Felice touched Sister Winifred's arm, pleading for her to stay, to tell her the rest which she half-knew already. 'Like daughter, you said? That would be Frances, would it?'

Lady West's voice called lustily from the church end of the path, putting an end to further enquiries, though Felice felt that Sister Winifred would have answered, given the chance.

'I'm not the one to be telling you this,' the sister said. 'It's Ellen Godden you ought to be talking to. She and that Wintershulle lass were friends. She's usually here at church on Sunday mornings, but not today.'

'Where does she live, sister?'

'The Sisterne House. Quite a few Romsey women there. I bid you good day, my lady. My way lies yonder.' She left them so hurriedly that it was obvious she regretted what she'd said and wished to avoid Lady West's inevitable questioning.

'Well, dears. What have you been chattering about, eh? Come, you can tell me as we walk, but hurry, it's starting to rain.'

In their hurry, the conversation mercifully turned to the general instead of the particular yet, in the shelter of Cool Brook House, Lydia could see her mistress's determination to investigate further.

'Don't,' she said. 'Let it lie, love. It's nothing to do with us, is it?'

'Not directly, no. But I must know, Lydie.'

'Why? Why must you?'

'You know why. Because whoever was responsible got off scot-free, didn't he? And I want to know who it was could do that to a maid and walk away smiling. She was pregnant, Lydie. She was my age. It broke her mother's heart. You saw Dame

Audrey, wretched and bitter. They've all clammed up to protect her, but they're protecting the monster who did it, too.'

'I'll come with you.'

'No. Stay here, Lydie. I'll only be half an hour or so. Lady West's having a nap, so I'll be back before she wakes.'

'It's raining. You'll get soaked. Do let me come.'

Felice was adamant about her need to meet Ellen Godden and to go alone. It was Sunday afternoon, she reminded her maid, and few people would be about, especially on a damp day. She dressed in loose comfortable clothes, sensible shoes, dark hooded cloak and a purse of coins to pay the porter of the Sisterne House, once known as the Sustren Spital, the small hospital for former nuns. Her white mare would be an obvious target for thieves and, anyway, it was not far on foot, she said, giving Lydia a last hug and slipping out through the garden door.

The pathway led on to a track through a field bordered by dripping may-blossom and now slippery with wet grass, the fine rain whipping uncomfortably across her, wrapping her skirt around her legs. The town wall was locked at Kingsgate, but the small postern door was opened for her, allowing her access into the southern suburbs where well-built houses were surrounded by plots and orchards. The deeply rutted track was already filling with brown water and the grey sky was low over the town, cutting out the light and obscuring the great tower of the cathedral behind her. But the Sisterne House was further than she thought, and soon she was obliged to stop and look back at the now straggling cottages, sure she must have passed it.

A young lad passed furtively by, carrying two dead rabbits and calling his lurchers to heel, making Felice wish that she had not left Flint and Fen behind at Wheatley. At her enquiry, he pointed away from the town into the distant field where a cluster of whitewashed thatched cottages huddled together in a sweeping cloud of rain.

'Over there,' he said, looking her up and down. 'You in trouble then, lady?'

She was tempted to box his ears, but gave him a groat from her purse instead and thanked him. By the time she reached the muddy courtyard and ramshackle stables the rain had soaked through to her shoulders and legs, numbing her hands and face. The porter at the lodge was unwelcoming but came alive at the sight of a half-crown which Felice had the wit to hold on to until she had his full cooperation. 'This is to let me in *and* out,' she said. 'Understand? I am Lady Felice Marwelle, staying at Lady West's residence.'

It had the desired effect; he led her towards a dark passageway and a series of battered wooden doors, one of which had studs and bars across it.

'Mistress Godden,' the porter said, pointing. 'She'll be able to help you, my lady.'

Felice frowned. 'It's not...' but stopped at the man's pale stare, realising how it must seem to him. This was, after all, where Audrey Vyttery's daughter had come to have her child.

Mistress Godden answered the door herself, but cautiously, as if to resent any disturbance, her eyes already sympathetic. 'Yes?' she whispered.

'Lady Felice Marwelle. An acquaintance of Dame Audrey Vyttery. May I speak with you, briefly?'

Instantly, the woman held the door against her visitor, her eyes widening in alarm. 'Nay, look...m'lady, I'm simply a goodwife. I had nothing to do with...'

'No, wait, Mistress Godden! I've not been *sent* by her. In fact, she knows nothing of my visit. I have no axe to grind, I assure you. Please, may we not speak? I'll not take much of your time.'

'I've got a lass here. Well, she'll be a while yet, and you're soaked. Come on in.' She opened the door just wide enough for Felice to squeeze through, shooting heavy bolts into position with a cracking sound. 'You in trouble yourself, then?' she said, searching Felice's trim figure.

Mistress Ellen Godden was probably of Dame Audrey's age, and her years at the nunnery in Romsey were now, like hers, only a distant memory. Apart from being clothed entirely in black, except for a grubby brown-stained apron, there was nothing to reveal her former vocation, not even her manner, which was confident and openly curious. Wisps of grey hair lay across her forehead, and these she continually pushed away, showing nails caked with grime. Quickly, she untied her apron and threw it into a corner.

The room was small and would have been ill lit even without the day's heavy cloud, and it took a moment or two for Felice to see that one wall was a woollen curtain where the end of a pallet and a pair of bare feet could be seen. A groan came from behind the curtain.

Mistress Godden turned towards the sound. 'Pant!' she called, motioning Felice to sit. She gave a wry smile. 'First one,' she said. 'Always takes longest.'

Felice took a stool, horrified by the squalid place where spiders' webs hung like lace across the steamed-up window, and a table was piled high with grey towels, linen bundles and soiled clothes, bowls and a pair of rusting shears, a wooden bucket and a large tabby cat eating the remains of a mouse.

'No,' she said, holding back a sudden urge to be sick. 'No, I'm not in any trouble, mistress. Sister Winifred told me where I might find you.'

'Then it must be urgent, m'lady, for you to come on a day like this. And if it's information you want about Audrey's lass, I can't help you. I'm not supposed to be doing this, you know. It's a man's job, according to them, that is. They'll have me for a witch if word gets round.'

'From what I've heard already, mistress, it doesn't

appear to be much of a secret, but I can understand your need for caution. Perhaps a small contribution will make things easier?' She brought her purse forward and delved, showing the midwife two gold coins.

'What is it you wish to know, lady? About Audrey's lass, is it?'

'If you please.'

'Tch!' Mistress Godden turned irritably towards the curtain again. 'Pant!' she called. 'Go on, keep panting. You've got hours to go yet, lass! Well,' she said to Felice, 'I suppose if she'd wanted to go on living, she would have. But she didn't see? The babe was dead inside her. Had a terrible time getting it out, and she didn't help much.'

Felice had begun to shiver. 'Wasn't her mother here to help?'

'Heavens, no. I managed alone, as I always do.'

'I knew that Frances Vyttery died, mistress, but what I need to know is the identity of the father. Can you help me there?'

The woman looked away, clearly uncomfortable with the turn of the interrogation. 'Ah…now…look. I'm just involved with the mother and child, not the father. If they wanted *him* to be known, they'd not be coming to me, would they? None of my business, that end of things, m'lady. Why not ask Dame Audrey herself, eh?' She stood up, disturbing another cat as she did so. It sniffed at the apron on the floor and began to lick it.

The gorge rose in Felice's throat, tempting her to give up and go. The two gold crowns pressed into her hand, and she delved for yet another one, holding them out to Mistress Godden. 'Please,' she whispered. 'I believe you can tell me. Am I correct?'

The midwife studied them and sighed. 'You'll not be revenged,' she said, indulgently. 'Whatever your reason for wanting to know, you'll never be glad for knowing. They'll never change, m'lady. No amount of knowing will ever make a difference to them and they'll never pay for it like women do. Ask her,' she said, tipping her head towards the curtain.

'All the same, I need to know. Was it her employer, Hakon Paynefleete? Is that why no one will say anything?' She believed she had hit the mark when Mistress Godden sat down again rather quickly, making both cats look up in alarm, but the woman shook her head, searching Felice's eyes for an alternative way round the truth.

'Nay,' she said. 'She and her mother both got caught in the same net, didn't they? Audrey with her priest and Frances with hers.'

'What? Her *priest*?'

'Aye. Paynefleetes had a young chaplain at that time. They got rid of him, quietly, of course. No fuss. Sent him packing, but it was too late, even for herbs. Frances was well gone. I reckon he should have married her but they wouldn't have that, the Paynefleetes. They weren't supposed to be having a chaplain, let alone a married one, and by the time the young lass came here she'd tried several times to get rid of it. I reckon that's why she was in such a state.'

Shivering and nauseous, and heartily wishing she had taken Lydia's advice, she stood up to go, holding the coins towards the woman.

'That's a lot of money,' the woman said, suddenly reticent.

'Yes, it is. Who was this cowardly chaplain? Where did he go?'

'Ah, as to that, m'lady, I can only tell you half. He had an Italian sounding name. Monte-something?'

Felice swayed and clutched at the filthy cluttered court-cupboard. 'Montefiore?' she whispered.

'That's it!' the midwife's face lit up in recognition. 'Father Timon, the lass called him. Been lovers for the best part of a year, from what I could gather.' She held out a hand and took the coins. 'You know him, then? My, but you've gone white as a sheet, m'lady. Here, sit down and—'

'Unbolt the door! Let me out of here!'

But the howl from behind the curtain rose to a scream and Felice had just enough time to wrestle with the bolts, wrench the door open and slam it shut again before lurching blindly down the darkened passageway and out into the pouring rain. Gasping with shock and seeing nothing she recognised, she blundered across a yard and through a flock of preening geese, splashing through deep puddles and into marshy ground that ripped off her shoes, one after the other, throwing her like an unshod horse on to her hands and knees.

Time and again she fell, sobbing dry rasping moans, whipped by the rain and lashed by a new unrelenting wind. A clap of thunder cracked above her, and she ran through sheets of lightning that showed her only mile upon mile of water-meadow and, far off in the distance, a solid square tower that some reasoning told her must be the cathedral. The point that the cathedral was not situated within water-meadows entirely escaped her.

Headlong she stumbled, blind and uncaring, towards a wooden thatched building that in the semi-darkness she took to be a house. Then, almost screaming with frustration, she found that it had only one door. She lifted the wooden bar that held it shut, pushed at the heavy panels and fell face-downwards on to a dry floor scattered with clover-hay and there, as the storm in her heart matched the one outside, she gave in to torrents of blackest despair.

Less concerned by Sir Leon's obvious anger than for her mistress's safety, Lydia squared up to him with commendable courage. 'She wouldn't *let* me go with her, sir. I pleaded, but she insisted on going alone.'

'Two hours, you say?'

'More than that, sir. It was just after the mid-day

meal, and she said it was not far, but I fear she must be soaked, if not lost.'

Sir Leon was very wet, his hair stuck down like black leather, his face as grim as anything Lydia had seen at Wheatley. With his valet, he had arrived at Cool Brook House to escort Felice to his home, only to find that he was too late to prevent her from doing what he had prayed she would not do. It had been the main reason for his vigilance, and now he had only himself to blame. 'Little fool,' he muttered. 'Come, Adam. I know where this place is. We'll find her, mistress.'

Lady West collided with them at the door. 'Ah, Sir Leon. What a pleasant...oh! You're not staying?' she called after them.

The Sisterne House was no place for men, so it was hardly surprising when their imperious demands met with a disappointing response. Mistress Godden was in the middle of a difficult 'illness' and could not be disturbed, not even by money, which said something for her commitment. Sir Leon and Adam rode on, picking their way through deep mud and belting rain to the roar of thunder, their way lit by blue-white flashes that made the horses dance in alarm. It was during one such illumination that Adam spotted Felice's shoes.

'Right. That's it!' said Sir Leon. 'She's gone ahead. You go back, Adam, and tell Lady West I've found her. Tell them she's safe.'

'But, sir…' Adam yelled above the din.

'Tell them, Adam. There's only one place she can shelter round here and that's either at St Cross or in one of the barns. I'll soon find out. Go!'

The wooden bar of the door was still swinging loosely in the wind as he pushed and led the big bay stallion inside, almost tripping over a woman's wet cloak covered with hay. The air was warm and sweet-smelling, and even in the darkness Sir Leon had no difficulty unsaddling the horse and leading him over to a pile of loose hay.

'There you are, my lad,' he said, softly. 'Try some of that while I have a look round. And don't let anybody in. Or out.'

Chapter Eight

Through swollen eyelids, Felice saw the door open and, from her hiding place at the back of an empty byre, knew that it was a man and horse who, like herself, probably sought shelter from the rain. She had piled hay into a dense mound and, in the safety of the darkness, had stripped off most of her wet outer clothing and laid it over the wooden partitions to dry. Now, she began to wish she had not.

Silently, she wormed herself even further down into the prickling warmth, willing herself to be invisible as flashes of lightning lit up the intricate network of rafters above her. The man waited, watching, and then began a leisurely removal of his wet clothes and boots, laying them as she had done over the nearest partition. By this time his identity was clear and her outrage was doubled. Her teeth chattered with fury at his intrusion.

The thunder drowned out all other sounds, but she knew his search had begun as he moved from stall to stall, stopping as he came across her wet clothes, waiting again for the next terrifying flash to show him her whereabouts. Suddenly, the tension was too much. Like a hare, she leapt aside and over the partition into the next stall, then the next, crashing into the black shadowy form of his horse and away to the other side of the great barn where empty sacks were piled high like a wall. She snatched one and threw it in his direction, not waiting to see him catch it but dodging his closeness in a mad, irrational, frenzied panic, fleeing his outstretched hand and feeling his warm laugh on her back.

Her chemise was still damp, hampering her legs, so she pulled it between them and ran blindly across the stone floor, feeling the hay thicken underfoot and hold her like heavy water. She fell, rolled away, and was stopped by the bulk of him landing on top of her, pushing her deep down and giving her no leverage. As in a recurring dream, she knew that something similar had happened before, that she had fought and escaped, and that she and her attacker were unknown to each other. Yet this time, knowing seemed to make no difference, for she refused to acknowledge him, plead with him, or remind him of that time when neither of them had claimed a victory. This time, her anger was greater than her fear, and the damage she had every intention of inflicting upon him would be little to the damage her pride had suffered within the last hour.

Unable to budge him, she used tooth and claw

savagely and without a shred of mercy, biting hard into his arm and raking his bare chest with her nails, kneeing him when he rolled away in surprise and hearing with satisfaction the grunt of pain. But he was tough, and quick, and she was not allowed to get away as she had believed she might in the face of such unmitigated aggression.

Again, he threw her backwards and found her wrists, holding them in a cruel grip above her head that left her no means of retaliation. As if she had been in water, she felt herself drowning, awash with hair, hay and the restricting weight of his body. Mercifully, she felt him rise and drag her upwards, lift her out of the suffocating deepness into his arms, holding her close against his body, still powerless to move but free of the stifling, seething bog of hay. She sat across him, unable to do more than pant, gasping at the air in raucous mouthfuls, already aware that her intentions were now even more confused against the enclosing safety of his arms.

'No...no!' she sobbed. 'Not you.'

'Shh!' he whispered, rocking her. 'This is no time for talking.'

'Let me go!'

'No. Not this time.' As if wading through foam, he carried her easily to where the stallion stood quietly munching in one of the stalls, and there she was deposited, in front of the horse's nose, on the hay. He spoke to the stallion, not to her. 'Keep her there, lad.' He patted his neck and disappeared, leaving

Felice to wait with only the horse's massive head before her, lit by the occasional flash of lightning. The dull roar of rain came to her like the sound of a waterfall, and the crack of thunder muffled his return.

She felt his wet hair against her cheek and forehead as he carried her to the byre where she had first hid and where he had now spread a layer of empty sacks over the hay to make a smooth deep-filled bed. Enclosed by partitions on three sides and by the floor of the hay-loft above, the new imposition of his caring and the closeness of his body emphasised her own change of direction.

'This is not what I...' she began, defensively.

'I know. You want to fight me...hurt me... anybody. But I believe I have a better idea.'

'You always believe you have a better idea,' she snarled.

He smiled, laying her down. 'Yes, but just this once you might agree with me. I think it's quite possible.' He lay half across her, resting upon his elbows and lifting the strands of damp hair away from her face, unsticking them from her neck.

'What are you doing?' she whispered.

'Starting where we left off last time.'

'You told me to *think*,' she protested. 'You said...'

'That was then, and you did well to think in the circumstances. But now he's out of the way, and you need think no more.'

She writhed, pushing at him in anger. 'Just like that! Stop thinking! You believe it's that easy, don't you? What do *you* know...or care?' Out of control, her fists beat at him but were caught again and held away, and although she did her best to evade him, his mouth silenced her angry protests and showed her how easy it was to stop thinking.

'I do know, and I do care,' he said, releasing her wrists, 'and we'll talk about it later.' He would have liked to have asked her if she was still a virgin, not knowing how far the priest had progressed with his instruction, but he knew she would resent such an enquiry and anyway, he would soon discover the answer for himself. But she was full of bitterness and hate, needing to take out her aggression on him, for want of a better adversary, and a fight was not going to be the pleasantest initiation for a virgin into the delights of love-making. It would require all his skills as a lover to turn her understandable antagonism into rapture.

He did not start where they had left off in the garden that night; he began at the beginning with sweet searching kisses that caught her attention and held it completely. And slowly, for they had all the time in the world, his kisses deepened and moved away from her lips downwards, covering her throat, and when he thought she might revert to angry words again, he found that her eyes were closed with tears filling the corners and falling into her hair.

Without comment, he eased her damp chemise

over her head, folded it up and placed it beneath her hips, freeing her beautiful firm breasts to his mouth and hands and, still with the spectre of the deceiving priest between them, made her gasp at his softly biting caresses. Her arms came up at last and held his head, taking part in the rite, enfolding him, fondling his ears and damp hair, searching the wide expanse of his shoulders.

She caught at his hand as it slid over her stomach to begin its quest towards the secretive quivering place and, although her legs parted of their own accord, the grip on his hand told him all he needed to know about her body's ownership. She had given it to no one; of that he was sure.

He rested his hand, letting it lie beneath hers. 'It's all right,' he said. 'I know. I'm the first, and I shall be the only one. You're mine, woman. You've been mine from the beginning, and you'll be mine to the end.'

'The guardianship...?'

'Was to hold you. This is to hold you even faster.'

Almost imperceptibly, his hand was allowed to continue on its way, exploring, persuasive and then insistent on an entry that was followed immediately by the gentle assault of his body, reaching even further into her, making her cry out in an excitement that instantly craved for more.

Expertly, he dipped and stroked, heightening the exquisite tension and stretching it almost to breaking point as she abandoned herself utterly to his mastery, moaning with the yielding pleasure of it.

The thunder rolled away and the rain continued to lash the deep thatch above them, sending the wind to whine and moan around the corners to harmonise with the cries of the enraptured woman within, and time lengthened as the light faded completely. He had not known her need was so great, nor had she recognised it for what it was, an emptiness to be filled, a hunger to be satisfied. So when the time came that she believed her needs had been met, a wave of feverish excitement surged through her body, taking her completely by surprise and making her swing away sideways to escape its force.

But Sir Leon had anticipated its arrival after his lengthy preparation, and he brought her back under him, twisting his hand into her long hair to keep her there. Relentlessly, but with supreme control, he guided her through the climax and heard her cries of ecstasy, felt her heave beneath him and then the fierce clasp of her fingers on his arms gradually relax. Understanding her bewilderment, he pulled her tenderly into his arms to lay in a close embrace and they stayed there, without speaking. They heard someone enter and leave again almost immediately, and they knew that the worst of the storm had passed.

Aware of a slight tremor in her body, he pulled her even closer and swept his hand down her back, pulling her hair away from the new tears. 'Do you want to tell me?' he whispered.

'I cannot,' she said. 'It hurts.' There was a silence, then came her remembrance that his questions were no longer ambiguous concerning her previous relationship but now quite specific. 'You knew?' she gulped.

'A fair idea,' he replied. 'Conjecture, mostly.'

'About the Sisterne House, too?'

'That was a guess. It would not have been St Cross Hospital; that's for men. And Mistress Godden has something of a reputation. I take it you found out what you wanted to know. Is that why it hurts?'

'Yes.'

'Your first love?'

She nodded.

'And now?' His arm tightened again as he kissed her forehead. 'Will he go, d'ye think? Will he leave us alone?'

It was an impossible question to answer at that moment, her wounds being so fresh and the new experience of his loving being so persuasively close. She could have promised to forget, but the events of the afternoon were etched clearly in her mind, though jumbled and far too poignant, and a promise would be meaningless after that. Just as terrible was the confluence of this most recent commitment and her concern about the placing of his heart, for now she was reminded that men's hearts were not necessarily where their loving was. It was what she had wanted, but did she know any more about *him* than she had about Father Timon? A woman's shriek pierced her thoughts.

'Eventually,' she said. 'Being a man, I'm sure he will.'

The bitterness was not lost upon him. He swung himself over her, leaning upon one elbow to look at her in the dimness, every soft word now clear in the hay-scented stillness. 'Is that what you think, my lady? That I'll leave you, after this?' His fingers slipped into her hair.

Again she felt the incredible surging of desire where each part of his body touched hers, and the black fears about his attachment to Levina Deventer were whisked away into the depths like bats into a cave. Without answering him, she held his beautiful head between her hands and drew it close to her mouth. 'Love me again,' she breathed into him. 'Show me.'

'I *will* show you,' he said. 'I have that much in my favour.'

Thomas Vyttery, Sir Leon's perpetually unsmiling steward, stood in his employer's office in the upper storey of the guesthouse, waiting for some response to his request. Unconsciously, the hand by his side clenched and unclenched, its fingers seeking each other's reassurance. His other hand held a sheet of papers that hovered over Sir Leon's desk as if about to be dropped in some impatience. Or despair.

The Reverend John Aycombe, seated on the stool at the desk, tidied a pile of notes with exaggerated slowness and lay them carefully to one side. Then he tipped his black cap forward on to his forehead, scratched at the base of his hairline and righted it, tying the strings beneath his chin.

'We've had our orders, Thomas,' he said with maddening calmness. 'That's all there is to it, I'm afraid. You'll have to take it up with Sir Leon when he returns.' His immobility suggested that he knew this answer was not going to satisfy the former sacristan of Wheatley Abbey.

Thomas's paper stopped hovering and landed with a smack on the desk, though the effect on the former abbot was minimal.

'And you know as well as I,' Thomas Vyttery said, testily, 'that that's *not* all there is to it. It's bad enough having that…that *woman* down here messing up our plans…'

'Your plans, Thomas. *Your* plans.'

'…without this to make matters worse. You told me you'd dissuade him from moving the sacristy to the north-west end and from digging up the chapter-house floor, and now I see they've been given the go-ahead. They're about to start on it. Today. Look!' His bony finger jabbed at the pile of papers. 'And I'm expected to feed them while they do it.'

Almost tenderly, John Aycombe, Master of

Works, pushed the guilty papers out of Thomas's reach. 'I said I'd try, Thomas, and I did. But Lady Felice wants to start work on the garden that will cover the old cloister and the foundations of the chapter-house, and Sir Leon's decided that we need the sacristy space for our expanding congregation.'

'*You* decided that, Father Abbot. You decided that yourself, didn't you?'

John Aycombe sighed and looked away. They had rarely seen eye to eye though they'd known each other as novices, professed monks, priests, and as contenders for the abbacy, then as abbot and sacristan, though he himself had scraped in by a whisker with the casting vote of the Bishop of Salisbury. Since when he and Thomas and half the inmates had shared a bone of contention, their promises of loyalty made in the knowledge that the last abbot would be handsomely pensioned off, whereas the rest of them would not. John had done what he could to sweeten the pill by appointing Father Thomas as sacristan. Except that Father Thomas had expected to be appointed prior, no less. John had not wanted Thomas Vyttery to be prior any more than he'd wanted him to be sacristan, and now he often wondered which of the offices, if any, would have satisfied him.

'No, Thomas,' he protested mildly. 'Of course I didn't. But if the congregation is swelling year by year, it stands to reason that we have to make more space available for them. You saw what a squash it was on Sunday, and soon we'll have the whole of Lord Deventer's household with us, so what better time to do it than while we have the builders here, on site? Anyway, all churches nowadays have vestries at the other end of the church.'

Such irrelevancies were like a red rag to a bull.

'Have you forgot?' Thomas poked at John Aycombe's shoulder to bring him down to earth. 'Look at me, John Aycombe! Have you forgot who's buried in the chapter-house? Have you forgot how I get a living, the living you promised me would outlast me and Audrey? Well, *have* you?'

John Aycombe's bottom lip was sucked in and released. Of course he'd not forgotten. How could he? But Thomas should have let go of these old affairs by now and got on with the present: there were others who had suffered as much, if not more, one way and another.

'No, I've not forgotten who's buried there, Thomas, any more than I've forgotten your relationship with him. That kind of thing was very much disapproved of, you know, and maybe the time has come for you to let him rest in peace.' Too late he realised the absurdity of the chastisement when the grave was about to be well pounded by the feet of builders and more rubble before Lady Felice's garden was constructed over it, in which state not even Thomas would be able to visit it as he had done in supposed secret these last twenty years and more. As abbot, he should not have allowed the friendship to continue, but the end was in sight by then, and what did it matter? 'And as for the living you speak of,' he went on rapidly before Thomas could pick him up, 'you and Audrey have done very well out of it, man. You can hardly complain that the deal was ungenerous, not after all this time. I suggest that you remove what you can before the men begin and leave the rest where it is. As I said, there's nothing I can do until Sir Leon's return.'

Thomas Vyttery's usual pallor had changed to an unhealthy green, his hands now clenched into tight fists. He took a noisy rasping breath. 'Take it *now*?' he almost screeched. 'In broad daylight just as they're about to start knocking the wall out? Have you taken leave of your senses? How can I do that, John Aycombe? Tell me. And while you're about it, think back to the time when you needed *my* help, if you will. You've always had the best of the bargain, haven't you? Always landed on your feet, in spite of—'

'That's enough, Thomas!' John Aycombe rose to his feet, as sure of his authority as he'd always been, even as Wheatley's youngest abbot. He would not listen to his catalogue of accusations. He had tried to put matters right; no man could have done more, and Thomas Vyttery had done a good deal better than the rest of them for a decent living.

His shoe caught the corner of a beechwood box that stood on the floor beneath Sir Leon's desk. 'Listen, Thomas,' he said. 'I have a lot of catching up to do. Some of the men got drunk over May Eve and now I find that one's been thieving and gone missing. We'll talk about this later, eh? Do what you can for the time being. Nay, cheer up, man. All good things have to come to an end some time, don't they? You must have known that, so it's no great surprise. I'll catch up with you later.'

He smiled behind the closing door. What a fuss about nothing. Yet he stood for a few moments as his smile faded, wondering what other good things would come to an end, and had he made as much effort to forget things as he was advising Thomas Vyttery to do? The bottom lip ventured inwards again.

From the stool, he bent forward and lifted the beechwood box on to the desk, recognising it immediately as a Catholic priest's portable mass set. Why had he not noticed this before? And what was it doing here in Sir Leon's room? Carefully, he lifted the lid, exposing the red leather lining, the silver chalice and plate, the rosary, crucifix and candlestick, the small box of wafers. A small well-thumbed bible held a bookmark of parchment.

Fumbling, and in sudden haste, he opened the book and found the owner's signature, Timon Montefiore, then the symbols that required no explanation and the initial *F*. Now his chest tightened painfully as he glanced at the verses, knowing them by heart, and from there to the end-page where the lock of hair still lay in a soft curl. His hands shook and tears trickled down his face, falling on to his chest like glass beads.

'The sins of the fathers,' he whispered. 'The sins of the fathers.'

After a long time, he gathered himself together, replaced the items in the box and closed the lid. He would leave it until dark, and then he would collect it when the men had finished work on the site. It would not be difficult to explain its absence to Sir Leon: thieves were an ever-present menace.

Shaking with anger, Thomas Vyttery marched down the nave of the church and entered the sacristy, closing the door with a slam and at once shutting out the chatter and clatter of workmen who already gathered like vultures. He looked around him at the shelves where the daily vestments of the clergy were folded in neat piles, candles laid in order of size, boxes and casks, bibles, prayer-books and chests of tools for repairing and cleaning the organ, the clock and the two remaining bells. Years ago, these same shelves had gleamed with polished plate; vestments had lit the small room with their glowing colours, purple, red and green, sparkling with gold thread and jewels. Now all was black and white, plain and functional.

All good things come to an end, indeed. Trust John Aycombe to think of that glib comment when everything he touched turned to gold. A knock on the door made him turn in fury. 'I told you to…'

The intruder did not hesitate politely, but stepped inside and closed the door behind him—a thick-set man wearing a filthy leather apron over his tunic, tied round the middle with twine, his grimy shirt-sleeves rolled up to his biceps. His head was enclosed in a flap-eared cap that framed his ruddy face like a pig in a bonnet.

Thomas turned back to his study of the cope-chest. 'What do *you* want?' he said.

'You'll be wanting some help with that lot then, eh?' said the smith. 'So, considering that I'm the only one around here that you can trust, here I am. How's that for Christian charity, Father Thomas?'

'I've told you not to call me that, Smith. It's not appropriate. And why have you come here in the daytime, for pity's sake? What d'ye think that lot out there will make of it?' He tipped his head towards the door. 'Well, since you're here you might as well stay and help. It's in both our interests.'

'Ah, well. That's what we have to discuss, isn't it, Mr Vyttery? Just like you'll have to discuss with the gardeners how to avoid trampling all over that friend of yours outside where the chapter-house used to be. Now that's going to be a tricky one, isn't it, Mr Vyttery?'

Thomas stared at the smith, whose brawny arms were now folded implacably across his leather apron in as uncompromising a pose as one could devise. Thomas would not ask what the objectionable man meant, for it was plain that his extra help would require extra money. 'Forget it!' he snapped. 'I'll manage alone.'

'Ah, but you see, Mr Vyttery, it's not quite as simple as that, is it? I can't forget, can I? As you said, it's now in both our interests, and I don't think you're in a position to refuse my offer of help right now.' His face crumpled into a bland smile at the blatant animosity in the steward's eyes. 'You see, I might just have a word with Sir Leon, when he returns. Or I might even have a word with the gardener and tell him he needn't be too careful when…ah! No, you don't, old man. You'll have to put a bit o' weight on before you can tackle Ben Smith.'

Thomas's thin patience had broken. Without his usual caution, his assault upon the smith had reached only chest-height before his wrist was caught and held away in a painful sideways twist. 'Toad!' he yelped. 'Don't you *dare* speak of that to *anyone*, do you hear? No one!'

His wrist was released in a push that unbalanced him further. 'No one? Well then, you'd better co-operate, Mr Vyttery, or that superior you were so friendly with might get a little disturbed, and so might Sir Leon and Lord Deventer. Now you'd not like that, would you? Don't forget, old man, that I was digging these graves as a lad when you were Father Thomas, and I've seen what you and he used to get up to.'

'Money,' said Thomas, panting and holding his

arm. 'I suppose you think your help's worth more now than it was at the beginning? You've changed your tune, Smith. You were glad at one time to accept whatever I could spare.'

'Ah, but things have hotted up, you see, with that flighty young filly having plans for this and that. Got Sir Leon round her little finger already. Things've changed, Mr Vyttery. I'll need twice as much now, sir.'

'For one damned boat trip a week? God in heaven, man!'

Smith was at Thomas's throat like a bull-mastiff, holding his black tunic in one great fist beneath Thomas's tangled white beard. 'Yes, Mr Bloody Vyttery! And just *you* try taking a boat up-river in the pitch dark and see how far you get. If I'd got caught you'd have denied anything to do with it, wouldn't you?' He shook the fistful of fabric. 'Eh? I'd have been on my own, yes? Yet I only have to tell Sir Leon where to look, don't I, and that would put you back to square one. Now, let's talk about a real reward.' On the penultimate word, he threw Thomas backward on to the cope-chest like a rag doll.

Righting himself, Thomas wiped away a trickle of blood from his bitten lip, his fright and anger allowing him barely enough breath to speak. 'Lock the door,' he wheezed. 'I don't want that lot in here.

Now, if you'll just pass me that tool chest up there…?'

The smith obeyed, willingly.

The incident of Felice's visit to the Sisterne House brought her nearer to a quarrel with her maid than she had ever been before. It was not only that Lydia was expected to know where her mistress was, but that Felice had gone knowing that the outcome would not be to her liking, that she had refused Lydia's company and therefore her comfort and, worst of all, she had then taken an irrevocable step that defied any attempts at reason.

'Reason has nothing to do with it,' Felice said, defiantly. 'I couldn't have held him off, even if I'd wanted to.'

'And you didn't want to. Well, obviously what you saw in Mistress Godden's room didn't shock you enough to stop you having a go yourself, did it? Let's just hope nothing comes of it, that's all.'

'Oh, Lydie, don't spoil it for me. It was the only good thing that came out of the whole afternoon. He knew it was what I needed.'

'What *he* needed,' Lydia muttered, tying the cord at the end of Felice's plait with a vicious tug. 'It remains to be seen what his intentions are.'

There was nothing to be said to that, for it was a subject Felice had not broached, fearing the same lack of devotion Timon had demonstrated, and although he had said that she would be his to the end, he had not been too precise about the time span or her role within it.

'We were to have seen his house today,' Lydia said, shaking Felice's skirt with a loud crack. 'Adam came back like a drowned rat, and I was left not knowing how much to tell Lady West.'

'I'm sorry, Lydie. I should have shared it with you. I'm still confused.' Her voice tailed off into a whisper, heralding another weeping.

'Nay...love!'' Lydia relented, taking her mistress into her arms. 'Don't weep any more. We're back to Wheatley on Tuesday and we'll soon see how things turn out after that, eh? And you've seen more of him than you expected to, haven't you, one way or another?'

The tears turned to laughter at Lydia's forthright views, especially when she admitted to a slight case of sour grapes at the non-appearance of a convenient hay-filled barn and a thunderstorm.

But the following day, their last in Winchester, brought with it not only more torrential rain but an exhausted messenger from Wheatley who almost fell from his horse on to the cobbled courtyard of Sir Leon Gascelin's stables.

It was late afternoon, and Sir Leon had just returned from Cool Brook House. 'Will! What on earth do you do here, lad? Why...what is it?'

'Bad news, sir,' Will gasped, clutching at his lathered horse for support. 'Fire, sir. Last night at the guesthouse. Whole place went up.'

'Merciful saints, no! Fire? Anyone hurt?'

Will shook his head, searching for a way to begin. Suddenly, his face crumpled. 'Mr Aycombe, sir. Nobody can find him. They think…oh, God!'

'John Aycombe, *lost*? In the guesthouse at night?'

'Aye, sir. Mr Vyttery's fair demented, he is. Place is still smouldering. Most of the men were in the village, so they couldn't stop it spreading. Sparks flew across, sir, and caught the stable thatches and then the stables went up, and…'

'The horses? Any horses inside?'

'No, sir. They'd all been moved across to the Abbot's House stables, like you said. But some of the mason's lodges went up. It's a mess, sir. I came as fast as I could.' His face was still grimy and wet with sweat.

'We'll be away at first light in the morning. Take Will inside, you lads, and tend him.' He turned to his steward. 'Samuel, get a message to Cool Brook House, will you? Tell the ladies we must be away fast at dawn.' He shook his head in disbelief. 'John Aycombe. I can scarce take it in. But what was he doing there, for pity's sake? Most of my stuff was being moved out as I left.'

The first light on the following day revealed dark lakes of water in the lowest fields, the roadways more like rivers, the tracks deep with mud. Some of the wooden bridges had collapsed in the floodwaters and the fords were treacherous, but the group of riders had gone on ahead, leaving the packhorses and extra waggons to make their own pace, and although they cursed the appalling conditions, Felice and Lydia were determined not to lag behind.

Their leave-taking from Cool Brook House was genuinely affectionate, the ebullient Lady West being completely unruffled by her guest's short lapse of common sense which, she said kindly, was by no means a unique affliction. Furthermore, her observations concerning a certain relationship had proved to be as close to the truth as one could get, whatever differences the two had once had now being apparently resolved. She was glad to have been instrumental in their new accord, at which rather pompous announcement she and Lydia had winked at each other, knowingly.

Squalling rain dogged them on their uncomfortable journey, stinging their faces, soaking their legs and chilling their hands into numbness. Waggonteams approaching from the opposite direction were not inclined to deviate, the riders being forced to make detours and new routes wherever the ground was easiest. But there was a certain joy in the discomfort, none the less, whenever Sir Leon's grey eyes caught hers, reminding her that she was now his more than ever she had been Timon's.

The damp clothes chafed on her new Spanish leather saddle, but predictably her comment was misinterpreted. 'Sore?' he said, his eyes twinkling mischievously. 'We should be able to find a cure for that, m'lady.'

It was late in the day when they reached Wheatley and the wooded approach to the abbey where the rain had done just as much damage as it had to the rest of Hampshire. The wooden bridge beneath the chestnuts was now awash, and the horses had to be led, resisting and nervous, across the slippery planks towards a building-site blackened, wrecked, steaming and chaotic. Soaking men still wrestled with masonry, their faces resolute and unemotional, fire being a common enough hazard to every householder these days.

Grooms came running to lead the horses and to be first with the news. 'Haven't found the vicar yet, sir. They're still looking,' said one.

Another had more recent news. 'Smith's missing too, sir.'

'What?' said Sir Leon, dismounting. 'Ben Smith? What the devil was *he* doing in the guesthouse? What's been going on while I've been away?'

'No, sir. Not in the guesthouse. Drowned, they think. Boat's missing, too.'

'Since when?'

'His woman hasn't seen him since last night, but the river's too swollen for a search. We'll have to wait a day or two for it to go down, sir.'

'Where's Thomas?' Sir Leon snapped.

'At home, sir. He wanted to help search, but it's too dangerous for an old man like him, and he was taking too many risks. Too upset to know what he was doing, they said.'

'And Dame Celia?'

'With her brother at the manor, sir. All your things were moved into the offices at the back of the New House…well, most of them, anyway. I think there was your table and a few odd bits still to go, but nothing important. Shall you and Mr Bystander be sleeping over there now, sir?' The lad glanced up at the rain-soaked ladies and their mud-spattered mounts.

'Mr Bystander and me'll not be sleeping at all until we've made a few arrangements, lad. Go and make some space in the stables and tell the head groom to come and see me. We shall have Lord Deventer down here in a day or two, if he responds to my message.'

'Yes, sir.' The lad took another appreciative glance at the two new horses, determined to be the one to care for them and wondering at the same time what the gifts betokened, considering her ladyship's hasty departure with Sir Leon's artist friend a week ago.

Chapter Nine

That evening left no time for reflections on relationships or understandings or even on the future, the needs of the men on the site taking paramount importance over everything else. The servants and workers were both numerous and capable, but relieved to have their surveyor once more in charge, more than filling the gap left by the missing clerk of works, John Aycombe. Felice had time only for a quick change into dry clothes and an even quicker bite to eat before she was over in the kitchens of the New House to see what was needed to produce enough food for them all, the kitchens at the guest-house having been demolished. The place had been due for reconstruction, but not as drastically as this. No one seemed to know how it had happened.

As well as having dozens of exhausted men to feed and accommodate in every nook and cranny, there were wounds to dress, burned hands, black eyes, cuts and bruises and a broken collar-bone, mountains of wet clothes to dry and clean ones to regenerate from every available source. Most of the guesthouse's last inmates had been slow to move out and had therefore lost many of their possessions, but goodnaturedly settled into the outhouses and stable-lofts, granaries, storerooms and even in the newly built kennels awaiting Lord Deventer's hounds.

The kitchens of the Abbot's House worked over-time that night, preparing food that the guesthouse could not. Kitchen lads carried sacks, boxes and bas-kets over to the new kitchens that were being put into service for the first time. Animal carcasses had to be re-hung, extra bread to be made.

At one point, Sir Leon found Felice coming away from the great larder where the meat waited to be cooked, the ubiquitous list in one hand. 'You should not be in here, lass,' he said to her, softly, steering her away into the passageway. 'This is no place for a lady. Besides, it's time you'd finished.'

'Yes, I know,' she said, wearily. 'This is the last check. Where've you been?'

'Searching the ruins. We found him.' He brushed a grimy hand across his forehead and leaned against the whitewashed wall where a blazing torch lit his tired face.

'You found him...oh!' Felice's hand went to her mouth. 'Badly burned?'

'No, not at all. He'd fallen into one of the emptied cavities beneath the stone stairs where we'd been keeping some stoneware bottles. It's one of the few

places the fire didn't reach because there's nothing
to burn. There was rubble and collapsed beams all
around him, but it looks rather as if he'd got lost in
the smoke and hit his head on the lintel as he fell.
He's got a massive bruise on his forehead, but I'm
beginning to wonder if he didn't simply have a sei-
zure and collapse. He'd been complaining of chest
pains for some time.'

'Oh, poor man! But why was he there at that time
of night? Was he working late?'

'That's how it looks, sweetheart. I can think of
no other reason.'

'Finish now,' she pleaded. 'You can do no more
tonight.'

He looked at her without smiling, passing a hand
quickly over her breasts. 'Can I not, woman? Then
you don't know me so well.' He pulled her to him,
crushing her inside one arm and kissing her hungrily, almost desperately. 'Go to bed,' he said. 'I'll
come to you as soon as I can.'

Resuming their vigilance of their mistress, the two
hounds followed her lazily back to the Abbot's
House and to the familiar bedchamber where Lydia
and Elizabeth waited and repaired men's torn and
singed clothing. The rain had stopped at last, but the
night air was full of woodsmoke and the stench of
burnt bedding and, in her own room, the many windows were steamed with warm damp garments that
hung before the blazing fire. But her bed was
warmed, and sleep came instantly.

* * *

Several hours later, she propped herself up against the pillows to watch Leon undress before the glowing fire. He stretched, gracefully, like a beautiful night creature whose skin bulged tautly over muscles, whose chest was deep, his limbs lithe and strong. And as he gradually became aware of her attention, he turned and stood to watch her, full-face and unashamed, showing himself for the first time. He came to her and sat on the bed, slowly peeling away the covers that she held up to her chin.

She was well used to nakedness and to her maids' reactions to it, but the scrutiny of such a man made her aware of every tingling surface even more than in the darkness; being able to see where his eyes examined as well as his hands seemed to double the thrill of each impending caress.

His fingers drew her long plait to one side, indicating where his next interest would fall but not the breathtaking excitement of it and, as she watched his eyes, the sensation of his fingertips plotting the ripe fullness of each breast, drawing slowly towards the hardening peaks, tipped her head back as if by a magic thread. Her eyes closed as she reached out for him and smoothed her hands over his magnificent shoulders, allowing herself to be taken into his mouth, melting her body for his delight.

She moaned, half-drowning in desire, and was swung round sideways across the bed, craving for the nakedness of him along her length. She heard his soft laugh. 'So soon set aflame, my wildcat, as

I knew you could be. I could keep your burning all night, couldn't I? Eh? Shall I tame you now?'

'Brute! I hate you!' she whispered. It was all she could say to sting him and to manage her fear of his unconcealed arrogance. Lydia's warning floated aimlessly through her mind, mildly chastising her for knowing his body before she knew his mind, but she gave it no foothold. Still suffering quietly from the blow to her pride, she knew that this was the only way to salve it, to put Timon in the shade and make him totally redundant. Yet using one lover as an antidote for another was a dangerous drug, especially when she now knew that she had herself been used as a remedy for another.

The time for teasing passed, and his loving took her into realms she could never have dreamed of where she truly believed that, at times, he was as moved by her performance as she was by his. She had no means of knowing whether his hunger was always great enough to take him on in a seemingly endless union that changed in pace but never flagged, or whether she was an exception for him. But in all other things, he had never seemed like the kind of man who would use superlatives so freely, just for the sake of kindness; on the contrary, she had discovered to her cost that his praises were usually so stinting as to be almost non-existent. Now, however, it was as if he was the one who would burn all night.

'Sleep, brute,' she whispered at last.

'Tired, sweetheart? Have I tired you out?' He reached across her for the ale cup and held it to her lips, cradling her head.

'I'm still new to it, despite what you seem to believe.'

He finished what was left in the beaker and replaced it, lying on top of her, lightly. 'And exactly what do I seem to believe?'

'Well, that I've had some experience, for a start.'

'Which you have.' He kissed her nose. 'But let me tell you something, woman. Your newness, as you call it, feels more like a natural aptitude to me. You have a freshness, it's true, a delicious wonderment that takes the art of making love to a different level, but you also have a fire that feeds a man's passion as quickly as he burns it. I knew it when I held you in the garden that night. I've known it ever since. It's there in the daytime and it flares almost out of control here in the night, and that's priceless, my beauty. You know how to take a man's soul, but you also know how to give. You're an amazingly gifted virgin, my sweet.' He smiled, touching her lips with his. 'New, experienced; demanding, giving; sweet and fierce. A rare mixture and I intend to keep it. I'd not have you tamed too far. Have I been too brutal with you?'

'Very,' she said, enjoying the chance to disturb him. 'Is it any wonder I tried to leave? I believe you're impossible to please.'

'Difficult, but not impossible.' He rolled off her

and held her close to his side. 'But I don't throw praise about indiscriminately, otherwise it becomes worthless. When I give it, I mean it.' He yawned.

'You're making me sound like a permanent fixture, Sir Leon.' She caught his yawn and snuggled closer to him. 'Is that what you intend? Do I become one of your mistresses, the one kept at Wheatley, or is there some other role for me? Perhaps you should tell me before Lord Deventer himself asks me about it. He is coming down here, didn't you say?'

But it was too late. The rhythmic sound of his breathing told her that these were questions that should have been asked earlier.

With so many questions of her own left unasked, the prospect of having to supply Lord Deventer with some answers was not something to which Felice looked forward. It was far easier to prepare for his physical comforts than to face an inquisition regarding her new and deepening relationship with his surveyor which, so far, had been the cause of nothing but confusion. Fortunately the chance to put these problems to one side came early the next day when the waggons from Winchester arrived piled high with the purchases for the New House, and as this was the moment for which she had been waiting, she felt obliged to be in at least four places at once as the pieces were carried, assembled and manhandled. Then at last the best bedchamber, several of the guest chambers, the great hall, withdrawing room and parlour began to shrink with the addition of beds, chests, tables and stools, hangings and all the paraphernalia of living. There were the inevitable hitches, misunderstandings and arguments, but Sir Leon's previously critical manner was noticeably tempered by a need to set the place to rights as soon as possible.

To Felice's question about when they should expect Lord Deventer, Sir Leon was bound to admit, 'I really don't know. He's sent no word ahead, but I've no doubt he'll be anxious to see the damage. Is his room ready now?'

'Yes, everything. Beds made up and fires lit.'

'Kitchens?'

'Yes, ovens and spits working, larders stocked.'

'You've worked miracles. And I've got a load of trout from the Paynefleetes' fishpond, so with two kitchens working and all the supplies from Winchester, we should be able to manage. Have you heard anything from Dame Audrey?'

'Yes. I went to call on her.'

She and Lydia had called early upon both Dame Audrey and Dame Celia, the newly widowed vicar's wife. At her brother's house, the widow was in the comforting arms of her family, shocked but calm. She had known of her husband's chest pains but could not think what he was doing at the guesthouse when she had believed him to be at the church.

The brief visit to Thomas Vyttery's small but well-appointed house was not half so reassuring.

Dame Audrey had hurriedly bundled away the embroidery she had been working on a sizeable frame which she was strangely anxious Felice should not see, and all questions to Mr Vyttery had been fielded by her as if she was afraid he would say something of interest. Which Felice didn't think was very likely. It had been a tense but revealing visit.

There had been one moment, as Dame Audrey was showing them out, when Felice detected a softening in the anxious woman's attitude as if she would like to have confided in her, but it passed with the usual acid smile and an evasion of eye contact, and any thought that Felice had had about speaking of their daughter's tragic death was abandoned. Waste of time, Lydia had said on their way back.

It was a time for abandoned discussions, apparently. The one Felice had been preparing to ask Sir Leon about how much of their new relationship to reveal to her stepfather was cut short by a cry from the outer door. A servant, breathless and damp, could hardly wait to reach his master. 'The boat, sir! They've found the boat!' he yelled.

'How many times have you been told not to yell across the hall, lad?' Sir Leon frowned. 'Whose boat? Smith's? But no body?'

The man's excited voice dropped obediently. 'No body yet, sir, just the boat. It was on the bottom, weighted down with...'

'Shh! Not here, lad.' Sir Leon led the way outside into the heavy overcast greyness of the late afternoon where a crowd of men carried a dark boat across from the river towards the ruined guesthouse. 'On the bottom, you say?'

'Yes, sir. Come and look. Two heavy sacks smashed straight through the hull. That's what filled it with water and took it down just below the mill bridge.'

The two sacks had already been cut open by inquisitive fingers, their contents marvelled at and hurriedly replaced. Gold plate, jewel-studded chalices, censors, chains and rings, beakers of silver, salt-cellars as big as buckets, clasps, buckles and bowls, priceless gems from the monastic church that were supposed by now to have been in the London coffers of the Royal Treasury.

'Riddle solved,' he told Felice later. 'The boat-man was Smith stealing treasure from the church vaults that somebody had taken good care to hide from the king's receivers when the abbey closed twenty years ago.'

'But someone was helping him,' she said. 'The man who passed us on the river-path on the night of the bonfire.'

He took her elbow and turned her to face him in the darkly panelled entrance to the Abbot's House, enfolding her waist with his arms. 'I'm rather surprised, my lady, that you can remember anything of what happened that evening. Personally I'm more inclined to remember what didn't happen because a certain person took it into her head to stalk off in a huff.'

'Did she so, sir? I wonder why. Perhaps it was because she felt herself to be playing second fiddle to a shadow. If so, who could blame her?'

'Second fiddle, lady? Is that what needled her, then?'

She could have told him, before his mouth stopped her, that any woman so unsure of a man would be unnerved by his slightest lack of attention, especially when every other condition was tailor-made to suit his purpose. But as his embrace bent her into the strong curve of his body, the searchingly tender warmth of his kisses banished those lingering doubts, reminding her only of the hunger she had felt then, of the decision to give herself without reserve, if he had asked it. Fiercely, avidly, and trembling with a sudden surge of love for him, she slid a hand around his bare neck and into his hair that felt damp and warm, seeking even more sensations to add to her store whilst being aware that this was not to be hers for long. Like Timon, he would go. Like Timon, he had never been hers from the start.

'Tonight,' he whispered. 'I'll come to you tonight. Wait for me, this time. No more playing second fiddle to shadows, eh?'

Even without Lord Deventer's imminent arrival, there would still have been much to do to restore order to the chaos that followed the fire, for now her carefully laid plans for the rooms, particularly those on the ground floor, had had to be revised, and the New House, which had once appeared vast and spacious, had suddenly become cramped with men and their belongings. She had worked tirelessly all day, but was still finding shortcomings which Lord Deventer would surely mention, if she did not. Reluctantly, she had to admit that, but for him, she would probably not have been so fastidious. Then she allowed herself to be lulled into a sense of false security by the lateness of the hour and, instead of going to change out of her housewifely grimy clothes, she loosed her hair and took a last stroll into the orchard to check that the beehives had been closed for the night.

It was here, beneath the low leafy boughs of the apple and damson trees, that she was found by young Elizabeth who, overcome by her excitement, quite forgot to tell her why she was being sought. 'Suppertime, I think,' said the scatty girl, giggling. 'Oh, no…wait, it's not that, is it? Oh, yes,' she giggled again, reminded by someone's warm knuckle recently caressing her cheek, 'My lord says he's hungry and to hurry.'

'My *lord*?' said Felice. 'Are you telling me… oh…good grief!'

With loose hair flying and a new tear in her gown from the old wicket gate, Felice sped out of the orchard, across the stable yard and round the front of the Abbot's House where she was instantly caught up in the tail-end of Lord Deventer's retinue of men, packhorses, waggons and, rising above it all, the leather-covered roof of a coach.

'My mother?' she said to Elizabeth. 'You didn't say my mother was here. Now what on earth possessed him to bring her all this way?' The words dried on her lips as the carriage moved away, leaving its occupant to walk with Sir Leon arm-in-arm up the front steps of the New House. Even from this distance, Felice noticed the woman's swaying voluptuousness inside the long pointed bodice and extravagantly wide farthingale that almost swamped Sir Leon's legs with shimmering folds of silk.

'What a ridiculous gown for travelling in,' Felice snapped.

'I thought it was rather...' Elizabeth began but, seeing her mistress's face, thought better of it. 'Who is she?'

'Lord Deventer's niece,' came the terse reply. 'Levina.'

'What a pretty name.' Fortunately for Elizabeth, her eyes were too fully occupied with the woman's glamorous and totally impractical costume to notice Felice's murderous look.

It was not something Felice had feared because she had never for one moment expected it. Not here, of all places. He would have disappeared to London, eventually. That woman would have reappeared at Sonning, but not here at Wheatley, to claim her property so soon.

In a haze of anger and jealousy, she heard her name being called and, turning to search the crowd, came face to face with Marcus Donne who, in spite of being usually so observant, failed to recognise any of the signs that a woman would know as uncompromising dislike of a rival.

'My lady,' he called, holding out two hands to take hers. 'You could not do without me, could you? Tell me you need me, or I'll die.' His laughing face begged for some witty reply and forced her to relent.

'Marcus Donne,' she said, smiling. 'There is no one in the world I would rather see at this time. Truly. But why have you come? Not merely to see the damage, I hope?'

The truth, had he been able to part with it, was that after only three days of Levina's visit to her uncle's house at Sonning, he was not willing to be left behind while she chased off to Wheatley to see Leon at the first opportunity. If she and Leon saw fit to resume their inconstant friendship, then he would resume his with the ward. Not to *see* the damage, but to do some.

'To see you, my lady,' he said, making her blush with his bold eyes that made no secret study of her loosened hair and dishevelled appearance. 'You should have sat for me like that. 'Twould have been my best ever.'

'I must go in, Marcus. Loose my hands, if you please. Will you come with me? It should be interesting finding rooms for everybody.'

It proved to be more impossible than interesting, it having escaped Lord Deventer's comprehension that a disaster and an unready house was hardly the place to bring an extended retinue of guests and their servants, especially a guest as elaborate as his niece.

Her strident voice had already reached the high-notes of demand by the time Felice and Marcus entered the great hall, her silver-grey spangled silk gown almost eclipsing Lord Deventer's orange-red legs and puffed breeches. 'Lord, how cold it is in here! Bring my bags, man! And find a chamber for me at the front of the house overlooking the lake.'

'It's a river, Levina,' Sir Leon told her. 'And we've put Lord Deventer at the front of the house, I believe.'

'Then change it, Leon dear. He won't mind, will you, dearest uncle?'

Dearest uncle spied Felice, and though he held her glance with little obvious approval, he preferred to reply to his niece before greeting his stepdaughter. 'Of course I don't mind. Give her what she needs...ah, here's the one we need to show us to our rooms. Do we have hot water, Felice?'

If that was to be her only greeting, Felice was willing to accept it, but Sir Leon was not. 'My lady,' he said, drawing her forward, 'will you act as hostess to our guests? You ladies know each other, I believe?'

Regardless of protocol, it was Levina's extra four years that motivated her to assume an instant superiority over a titled lady. 'Yes, we met once, didn't we, though I cannot remember much about you.' Her open stare was conspicuously cold. 'Have we caught you in the middle of your toilette?' she asked with undisguised sarcasm, glancing sideways at her uncle for approval of the jibe.

'Good day to you, Mistress Deventer.' Felice inclined her head and then, turning to her uncle, curtsied dutifully with a natural grace that put her distant relative's sneers to shame. 'You are welcome, my lord. And, yes, we have hot water and fires ready for you upstairs.' As she spoke, she reached up to gather her long dark hair into her hands, twist it quickly and hold the heavy coil up onto the crown of her head from where silken wisps drifted downwards into the curve of her long neck.

She heard Marcus suck in his breath behind her and felt the stares of everyone nearby, including her stepfather, but it was to Levina she spoke again. 'There now. Toilette completed. I'll get my maid to find you a chamber, mistress, while I show my stepfather to his.' Keeping her hair up with one hand, she brushed past the hugely puffed shoulder of her ill-mannered guest, called her two deerhounds to heel and led the way up the wide staircase to the accompaniment of silent admiration.

It was an ordeal she could never have repeated. Even so, it had an effect upon her stepfather she could not have foreseen, softening his abrupt manner and, she suspected, causing him to see her in a somewhat different light.

'Change rooms by all means, if you wish, my lord,' she said, dropping her hair. 'As you know, some are large, some not so large, but this is the one you and my mother will eventually occupy. Do you have a message from her to me?'

'Ahem! Er…yes, indeed.' He spoke too loudly, still astounded by the stranger he thought he knew. 'Yes, she's well. Sends her…er…love. Right, this'll do nicely, I thank thee. Looks better now with a few bits of…oh, where's *that* bed come from?'

'Winchester, my lord. It cost you twenty pounds. Curtains and bed linen and extra…'

'Yes, right! It'll do well enough. Do we get any supper?'

His boorishness never ceased to make her wonder. 'Supper has been waiting this last half-hour, my lord. We shall have it served as soon as you are ready for it.' She glanced at his state of unreadiness and judged it might take another two minutes, by his standards. He would once have been handsome, she thought, in a heavily flamboyant way, but was now even more coarsened by an over-indulgence of every appetite, from what she knew of him. His hair was thick and almost white, making him appear taller than his impressive six feet, his eyes heavy-lidded and wrinkled and cleverly concealed from view. With a large family to tend, it was obvious why her mother found him attractive.

'Good,' he said. 'And where's young Donne going to lay his head?'

Having given the matter no thought, she opened
the doors that led off the great bedchamber, showing
Lord Deventer's servants where they could sleep
and keep their master's belongings, noting with
some relief how her two hounds kept close to her
heels and refused any offers of friendship. The matter of Marcus Donne's head would easily be resolved, one way or another.

Recovering her equanimity was no new thing for
Mistress Deventer and soon her voice was heard carrying across the first floor. Failing the room at the
front, she would have one near Sir Leon's. Obligingly, Felice replied, 'Certainly, mistress, if that's
what you prefer. He's downstairs near all the men.
The rooms are minute, but you'll have constant
company, and you'll be able to check each of them
in at night and out again at dawn. This way,' she
called, merrily, knowing that the yapping woman
would not be following.

She had brought an army of servants, three maids
(one for her hair alone) and enough baggage for a
year. Felice's main concern was where to accommodate them all, even in such a large house, for until
the extra beds came from Sonning there would be
less than enough. For a moment or two, she and
Lydia watched the hysterics, unable to decide
whether it was put on for their benefit or whether
the woman was truly overwrought. They were fas-

cinated by her costly furs and jewels, her neck ruffs, shoes, paddings and wirings.

'Probably collapse when all that's removed,' whispered Lydia rudely, closing the door on the scene. 'Did you see the bum-roll? Fancy having to wear that thing tied round her waist like a monstrous sausage.'

They had been fascinated also by Mistress Deventer's striking attractiveness and her obvious skill with cosmetics that reddened her cheeks and lips and accentuated her arched brows with an unnatural black that looked odd, they thought, with her fair hair. In what they presumed was the latest fashion, Levina's blonde tresses were drawn back off her face and rolled over a heart-shaped pad, its point on her forehead, the rest of it covered by a jewelled cap which included several waving feathers. But it was the dress itself that had made them stare, being a bell-shaped contraption of Lady West's dimensions and sumptuous combination of bright reds and golds enriched with embroidery, braids, jewels and frills at neck and wrist, balloons of padding on each shoulder and a tightness as far as the elbow.

'Just as well Sir Leon designed wide doors,' Lydia muttered, following her mistress down the stairs. 'She'd never get into the Abbot's House.'

'It seems to keep the men on their toes,' Felice remarked drily, thinking of Sir Leon's undisguised pleasure at her appearance, 'but he'll not find me competing on those terms. Popinjay!' she growled.

Lydia smiled. She had seen the men's looks at Felice's artlessness just now and, in her experience, the competition was already won.

After that disconcerting introduction, it was not to be expected that the two Deventers would even notice what was being presented at supper or the impeccable service at the table by newly liveried servants, the new linen napery, the silver plate and matching spoons and knives, all unpacked that day. The new kitchen yielded a feast which the superb Levina picked at distastefully and her ravenous uncle wolfed down without even tasting: trout and pike with oranges in their mouths, loins of beef, mutton and veal, capons and conies, new-baked bread, young lettuces and radishes, apple fritters, clotted cream and six different sauces.

'I'd have liked a marchpane,' Levina said, loudly, as the last dishes were removed. 'Her Majesty's confectioners…'

Sir Leon interrupted the comparison. 'We had a major disaster here only a day ago,' he said, 'and this is the first meal from our new kitchen. Lady Felice and I returned from Winchester only twenty-four hours ago, mistress.'

Far from being grateful for this intervention, Felice was on the defensive from the start. 'I don't need you to make excuses for me,' she said, attempting to outpace her guardian along the cloister walkway at the back of the New House. Having done her duty, she was attempting a quick exit to her own abode when Sir Leon caught up with her.

'It was not an excuse,' he said, catching her arm. 'And look where you're going or you'll fall over those slabs of stone. Listen to me!'

'I don't want to listen to you.'

He held her back against the wall, making a cage of his arms. 'Listen! I was not making excuses. It was an amazing meal, considering how—'

'There! There you are! *Considering!* It was an amazing meal by anybody's standards, including hers. Perhaps you think she could do better.'

'What is it, lass? I can see you don't much care for each other, but you've only met her once before. She's harmless enough. Plenty of show, I grant, but that's only a cover. Don't take it all so seriously, sweetheart.'

'That you and she have been lovers for years? Is *that* something I'm not supposed to take too seriously? That she wants a room near yours? That, too? That she's spent all evening ogling you, her uncle and Marcus in turns? Truly, I don't know whether that's serious or ridiculous. What say you?'

He sighed. 'What I say is this, if you'll hear me. She and I had a brief affair two years ago, and since then I've seen very little of her except in public. Deventer has always believed I should make an offer for her, and I suppose that's why he took the chance to bring her down here with him.' He would have continued, but Felice was in no mood to hear the rest.

'Well, then, don't waste another moment here with me, Sir Leon. You've explained to me already how you have to please my stepfather. He pays you, you reminded me once. And I have some old wounds to lick, remember? Now, let me pass. I'm tired.' She pushed against his arm, freeing herself and leaping away into the darkness towards the arch where, on the stable block, a torch burned and waved crazily in the gusting wind.

Having previously schooled herself to say nothing of that to him, to refuse any kind of competition with the outrageous Levina and, most of all, to refrain from any mention of her own recent wounds, she stood for some time in the darkness shaking with vexation at her own stupidity and lack of control. If anything could be guaranteed to send him into Levina's company more quickly, it was her revelation of jealousy. And after that, how could she expect that he would come to her that night, as he had said he would?

His excuse, if one could call it that, was that Lord Deventer had wanted to talk with him and had kept him up until the early hours of the morning. It was perfectly reasonable, Lydia told her, but Felice was not open to reason and preferred to torture herself with other explanations. Coolly polite, she had thanked him for coming to tell her, making it impossible for him to share an intimate caress in front of the servants who had brought her breakfast up from the kitchen, a bowl of porridge and a beaker of weak ale.

Her next visitor of the morning was Marcus, who sat beside her on the chest and scooped a fingerful of her porridge into his mouth, his stillness suiting her mood.

'Sleep well?' she asked, moving her bowl towards him.

'No,' he whispered. 'Four men snoring in the same room, all in different keys and not one of them could keep time.'

Felice's guffaw was most unladylike. 'Oh, dear, Marcus,' she said, licking splutters of porridge off her hands, 'I'm sorry. I was so busy with the other two that you were left to fend for yourself. Do forgive me. I'll find a better place for you, I promise.'

'Last time I was here, you offered me the big chamber up there...' he pointed to the plaster ceiling '...where I was painting your portrait. Is that offer still open?'

On the face of it, there was no reason why it should not be, yet there had been developments since then which he clearly knew nothing of and which were in a state of flux that she could not predict one way or the other. But it was not so very unusual for people to sleep wherever there was a space, and she had already offered it to him once. Why not again?

'Of course,' she said. 'I can't think why I didn't offer it to you yesterday. I'd rather you used it than anyone else.'

'Thank you, m'lady.' He kissed her cheek and took another fingerful of her breakfast. 'I'll move my things across later on. My lad can stay too, I take it?'

'Does he snore out of key?' she said in mock severity.

'Soundless. I'd not employ him otherwise, believe me. And while I'm here I could finish off your portrait. I expect Leon and the amazing Levina will want time to themselves, so why don't we do the same? Would you like that? Lady Honoria was pleased with hers, I believe.'

'Yes, so you said. I'm glad. He still admires her, then?'

'Who, Leon? Well, if his attentions last night were anything to go by I'd say they'll be resuming negotiations almost immediately.' He laughed at his witticism. 'But let them get on with it. She's a determined lady, that one. Hey, have you finished with this already?'

Felice nodded, feeling her stomach revolt at the thoughts.

'Then you don't mind if I finish it up for you?'

After he'd gone to collect his belongings, she sat for a long time pondering over what Marcus had implied, not only regarding the resumption of the old love affair but also that neither he nor the other guests had been made aware of the new relationship between herself and Sir Leon, neither by hint, gesture or declaration. What was she to read into this but that he intended to keep it secret, that it was not intended to last? Like Timon.

Chapter Ten

At any other time, Felice would have seen it as essential that Sir Leon should spend most of his time with his employer, on the site, and in discussion with the master craftsmen who were not being paid to stand around idly. Whatever time was left over, he would be expected to pay some attention to his guests. But being unsure of herself as well as him, in fact being unsure of everything, Felice felt unable to see things without a strong bias, consequently overplaying her hand and making matters worse at the same time. Every look, word or smile in Levina's direction was noted; every advance in her own direction was received as coolly as before their visit to Winchester, and Sir Leon was given no opportunity to put matters to rights. His anger at Marcus's new lodging added yet more fuel to her resentment.

'What the hell d'ye think you're doing, woman,' he snapped at her later that day, 'inviting him to sleep up there? Give him half a wink and he'll be down those stairs and into your bed. Is that what you want?'

'What does it matter to you, sir, who I have in my bed? I don't care a damn who you have in yours.'

'What's that supposed to mean?'

'Think about it, Sir Leon. Your room is as close to Mistress Deventer's as mine is to Mr Donne's, so presumably you have only to give *her* half a wink and she'll be—'

'Felice...stop it! This is ridiculous. Come *back* here!'

Her efforts to escape were this time halted by Lord Deventer, who had lagged behind his surveyor to speak to the master plasterer. With a mixture of curiosity and amusement, he caught Sir Leon's words and the defiant expression on his stepdaughter's beautiful but angry face.

'Now then, lad.' He laughed. 'You told me it was working out quite well, this new guardianship. Is this a good day for it, or a bad one? Perhaps it's not suiting you as well as I believed, young lady.'

'I don't know what you were led to believe, my lord, but I was never asked for my approval of the arrangement, nor have I ever accepted it.' Boldly, she gave back stare for stare, ignoring the warning in Sir Leon's eyes. 'Sir Leon seems to believe he can order my life, but he's mistaken. I'm perfectly able to choose a guardian of my own whose interests are less complex than his.'

'Complex?' Lord Deventer bellowed. 'Doesn't sound all that complex to me. Well, never mind that now; we've more important things to settle, like clearing this mess up before her ladyship comes down. Ye've still plenty to do in the New House, lass. It's coming together, but it'll take a while yet.'

'Thank you, my lord,' Felice said with acid sweetness. 'Your praise is as unstinting as ever, like your appreciation.' She marched off calling sharply to Fen and Flint whose loyalties were, as usual, divided.

'Unstinting?' Lord Deventer said. 'Is that good? Never did understand the lass's high-falutin' words.'

'I'm not sure that I do either, sir,' said Sir Leon, watching her go.

Levina Deventer did not appear on either of the two following days until after a light dinner in her room at midday, after which she had no difficulty in commanding Sir Leon's and Lord Deventer's attentions without even setting foot out of the New House into the messy realms of workmen. To this predictable pattern of behaviour Felice could only ascribe one thing, giving herself every reason, or so she thought, to make her appearance there at mealtimes and then to disappear on her own business.

Sir Leon had not thought fit to visit the Abbot's House on any pretext at night, and on the one daytime occasion had found her sitting for the limner in his large sunlit room upstairs. He had not stayed long, and Felice had had to strain every muscle to avoid running after him to beg him to take her in his arms.

Suppertime was a formal meal taken together in the large hall for convenience, where all the workers gathered and where the glorious Levina could entertain the whole company simply by her airs and graces. Her loudly caustic remarks, usually at someone's expense, and her dazzling clothes were like the moon to a swarm of moths beside which Felice's quieter hues could not compete. Good manners and graciousness being the duty of every hostess, she began to wonder if perhaps the roles were being reversed when Mistress Deventer issued orders to the servers to remove some of the dishes and bring in others, to tell the musicians to play more softly so that she could hear herself speak. Felice would have stayed on, as etiquette demanded, but this time she doubted whether anyone, except perhaps Marcus, would notice her absence. The atrocious Levina's domination of the scene was getting out of hand.

She slipped away into the kitchen passage and out through the back door into the cloister, stumbling over slabs in the wrong direction and eventually coming to the door leading into the church. Dim lights burned here and there as she closed the door quietly and made her way towards them, fighting the pain in her breast. She stopped to listen, not sure whether what she heard was the wind or voices, but a fine line of light appeared under the heavily studded door on her right, the door to the sacristy and, knowing no reason why anyone should be there at that time of night, turned the iron ring to lift the latch. Silently, the door opened, the flickering light of a single candle illuminating the pale and horrified faces of Thomas Vyttery and his wife Dame Audrey.

Their combined stares compelled her to take in the scene and comment on it, to put them out of their misery. The small room had recently been cleared of its contents, ready for demolition, but the one remaining item was the cope-chest, far too large to remove until the wall was knocked down. Shaped like a quarter-circle, it stood massively on several small feet, its iron-bound lid being used as a table for its previous contents, a mountain of embroidered and jewelled vestments worn by the old abbots of Wheatley Abbey, their colours glowing richly, winking with jewels and gold thread, priceless on the continent where Roman Catholicism was allowed.

The steady glare of Thomas Vyttery's animosity was more potent this time than it had been at their first meeting when even his mastiff had deserted him, but now the candlelight showed up something she had not seen before, a terrible sadness in the pale watery stare. Beads of perspiration stood out on his brow and his hands listlessly tidied papers that had been set out before them. 'Come inside, my lady,' he said, tiredly. 'You followed us, I suppose?'

'You supposed wrongly, Mr Vyttery. There is no reason why I should follow you, but now I'm here you may find it more convenient to tell me what you're doing with vestments that should by now be in the king's treasury. I'm bound to reach the wrong conclusions otherwise. Is there a stool for me, Dame Audrey?'

The steward's wife had avoided Felice's eyes, so far, but now blinked in surprise at the request. 'Yes, of course.' She placed the stool at Felice's feet, sliding away a pile of velvet and silk stoles and a jewelled mitre thick with gold thread, as if to keep it out of her reach.

But Felice could not resist touching it. 'The gold alone must be worth hundreds of pounds,' she said. 'There must be a good reason why you've chosen to—'

'There was no *choice*, my lady,' the steward almost spat through his beard. 'There *was* no choice!' His hands shook over the papers and Dame Audrey looked away, acutely embarrassed by her husband's sudden outburst.

'Please, Thomas!' she whispered. 'Don't!'

He turned to her, snarling. 'I have to, woman! Can you not see that she knows? I expect she knew it all before she came. She looked as if she did.'

'Know what, Mr Vyttery? I wish you would tell me so that I can understand. You're a man of God, so you can hardly have been breaking the law with a light heart all these years, I'm sure. Nor your wife.'

'My *wife*!' The words came out with a venom that stopped Felice's breath and made her glance at the poor woman who stood opposite.

Dame Audrey had turned white, her eyes round with horror. 'Don't say any more, Thomas, I beg you,' she said, forgetting her previous mincing accents.

'Well, you tell her, then,' Thomas snapped. 'She's come here to find out, so she may as well have the whole story. Tell her, woman, and be damned to the lot of 'em. He's gone now, so it's hardly going to damage his reputation, is it?'

'I don't know how to start,' Dame Audrey whispered.

'Start at the beginning. Go on, tell her every sordid detail. Let's see if she'll understand as much as she thinks she will.'

'Was it blackmail? Tell me, Dame Audrey,' said Felice.

The poor lady shook her head, her face transparent against the creamy-white linen of her coif. 'You knew I'd been a novice at Romsey Abbey, my lady?'

'Yes, Dame Celia told me that.'

'See?' Thomas muttered.

'And you knew that…'

'Oh, for pity's sake!' Thomas's interruption startled them both as he turned to face them. 'From the beginning, Audrey, not halfway: the beginning is with Abbot John Aycombe, isn't it?'

'Perhaps you should tell me, Mr Vyttery,' said Felice, laying her fingertips upon his sleeve.

He looked down at them and began quietly to talk. 'When the old abbot died, m'lady, John Aycombe and myself were the next choice, but he was the old abbot's favourite. Always genial, John was, and mightily ambitious. John was elected by a whisker, though by that time we all knew that the end was in sight for the abbeys. We also knew that whoever was abbot at the time would be sent off with a good pension and enough perquisites to keep him comfortable, once he was out in the world, and that the rest of us would have to fend for ourselves any way we could.

'John made me sacristan, but he could have done much more, m'lady. He chose not to. But then he suddenly needed my help.'

'Thomas…no!'

'We're telling her everything,' he said to his wife. 'Clever John Aycombe, Abbot of Wheatley, got a young novice from Romsey Abbey in the family way. A bright, vivacious sixteen-year-old called Audrey Wintershulle. No, it was not *me*, my lady,' he said, taking in Felice's shocked expression, 'it was John Aycombe who fathered a child on Audrey. I don't blame her. I never have done. I blame him. He knew full well what he was doing and he knew how to wriggle out of it, too.'

'Merciful heavens!' Felice said. 'Why did he not accept responsibility?'

'Because,' Thomas continued, 'by that time he'd made his plans for the inevitable retirement, even though he was only young. Audrey's parents refused to take her back once they discovered she was pregnant so she had no dowry and no home, and that was no good for John Aycombe because by that time he'd set his sights on Celia Paynefleete, who was fifteen at the time, a pupil with the nuns at Romsey. Well-connected, wealthy, friends of the former abbot and a much better catch than a Wintershulle.'

'Oh, my dear,' Felice said. 'I'm so very sorry. I'd no idea it was like that. What happened to you?'

'Celia's family took me in,' Dame Audrey said, looking down at her hands, 'but John never told Celia that he was the father of my child, and to this day she still doesn't know. He wanted nothing to do with me,' she said. 'I had nothing to offer him.'

'A child?'

'He didn't want that. It would have done his reputation no good.'

Thomas Vyttery continued the story. 'Well, whether for good or evil, Sir Paul Paynefleete, Celia's father, discovered John's misconduct at Romsey, and although Celia persuaded her father to let her marry John, he withheld his permission until a father had been found for the child Audrey was expecting. He didn't want any scandal rubbing off on to his family, you see. So John had to find somebody to marry his...'

'Thomas!'

'Yes, well. Anyway, he came to me with the proposal. Me, of all people. He didn't mind *my* reputation being tarnished.'

'But you agreed, out of charity,' Felice suggested.

'Out of greed. And necessity. Because I didn't know how I was going to live otherwise. He got me the job of chantry-priest here at the church, which paid very little, but he'd got himself the position as Paynefleete's chaplain *and* vicar, a wealthy patron, a future wife and dowry, and a pension from the crown. Not bad, eh? He offered me, if I would help him out, the treasure from the church and the abbey that we'd hidden from the king's receivers. Oh, we let them have some of the stuff, enough to keep them quiet, but we were a very wealthy abbey and only I knew what we had down there—' he pointed to the floor '—in the vault and in that great cope-chest. He told me I could have access to all of it if I'd marry Audrey and foster their child as my own. And I agreed.

'Celia's father let us have our cottage rent-free, and Audrey had Frances there. And John Aycombe never once recognised her as his, even though he baptised her.'

Dame Audrey dabbed at her eyes, recalling the pain. 'You're shocked, my lady. Men can do this kind of thing, you see. Even the best of them.'

'*Best* of them?' snarled Thomas. 'John Aycombe's best was all show. You should know that better than anyone.'

'I think Dame Audrey meant it in a social context, sir,' Felice said gently. 'He always struck me as being totally upright. But I thought nuns were not allowed to marry for many years after the abbeys were closed.'

'There was a lot of confusion,' said Dame Audrey. 'I was only a novice, so no one could argue that I'd gone beyond the first stage of acceptance. And at that time I cared little about what happened to me, so I accepted the arrangements in return for a roof over my head. What choice did I have? But Thomas has had the worst of it by far. He made a home for me and my child. He's suffered torments over the years over this...' she indicated the piles of costly fabrics '...though he was not depriving anyone except the king's treasury. He was a young man with all of life ahead of him, yet he took me in my condition with never a word of reproach. Neither Celia nor her brother know the truth of it; they believe John Aycombe to have been a saint, and so does everyone else. But I've seen what he's done to my Thomas.'

From the corner of her eye, Felice saw that Thomas was looking intently at his wife with an unusual kindliness, placing a gnarled hand tenderly over hers. 'She looked a lot like you, our Frances, m'lady,' he said. 'Dark-haired, slender. A lovely lass, she was.'

Until that moment, Felice had been congratulating herself on her composure but, at this, her self-possession began to disintegrate.

Thomas Vyttery, introspective and bitter, did not notice. 'I expect you've pieced together what happened there,' he said. 'It was John Aycombe who recommended a certain young chaplain to the Paynefleetes who then betrayed our daughter just as *he*'d betrayed Audrey all those years before. And by that means, my lady, we lost our finest treasure.' When no reply came from Felice, he turned to look and saw the tears streaming down her face. 'Nay, lass, Don't be upset. Too late for weeping now. It's done, and John Aycombe's gone.'

'The fire?' Felice whispered.

'Nothing to do with me,' Thomas said. 'I'd not have wished that on any man, not even him. Now we have to clear out of here because they're about to knock this place down and we have to get this lot away somehow.'

'How do you usually do it, Mr Vyttery?'

'Oh, you may as well know. There's a vault under here full of church treasure still. Ben Smith used to take sackfuls of it along an underground passageway to a cellar in the Abbot's House, and from there down the river to my cottage.'

'I see. And that's going to be difficult now he's… er, gone.'

'Impossible. I can't carry it, nor can Audrey. We were just checking through to see what we ought not to leave behind, but that's academic now, I suppose. You'll be telling Sir Leon and Lord Deventer, of course.'

'No, Mr Vyttery, I shall be telling no one.' Felice stood, wiping her tears with the back of her hand. 'It's no business of mine what you do with it; the secret is as safe with me as it has been with you, and that applies to what you told me about your lovely Frances. I know how you must grieve.'

'No one can know that, m'lady. By now we might have had not only a daughter but a grandchild, too, but for that man.'

And by now, I might also have been where she is.
The terrible thought reeled through her mind as she passed once more into the cool cloister and into the waiting arms of Marcus Donne who held her, racked with sobbing and unable to tell him what the matter was.

'You've been to the church…yes…I know. I waited for you. Did it not help? There…don't cry. Come, I'll take you home. Lean on me, Felice.'

She could not tell him that her fears were as much for what might yet happen as for what had already happened, that she had been a fool, that she loved a man who could never be hers.

His comfort was brotherly and gentle, his arms by no means threatening and his curiosity we trolled. He assumed, as anyone would, that fairs of the past weeks were catching up with her, and what woman wouldn't be overwrought with Leon throwing his weight around, and now her stepfather? Quietly, he rocked her as they sat before a low fire while Mistress Lydia wondered whether she was being cynical in seeing this as the next step in the limner's cautious seduction.

Sleep came near dawn but did not stay, and Felice roused Lydia and Elizabeth to dress her and to begin their duties earlier than usual. In the New House, most of the men had drifted out on to the site, and so her hopes of catching sight of Sir Leon came to nothing as she greeted the servants, checked lists with Mr Peale and Mr Dawson, and showed her presence.

Upstairs, all was quiet except for the squeak of a new floorboard and a muffled sneeze from Lord Deventer's chamber but then, as Felice entered the small darkened closet where clean linen was kept, she heard an unmistakable sound coming from the opposite door that led into Levina's chamber. She froze, straining her ears to be sure, asking herself what the woman could have eaten to cause such a violent reaction. It came again, followed by a moan, then a voice and more retching. Morning sickness. Was it her, Levina, or one of her maids?

She tapped on the door merely as a formality and, as a gap appeared, held it with one hand. come in!' she said decisively, moving for-

ward. No one looked up as she entered, lcast of all
the heaving woman who knelt at a stool with her
head in a basin, her blonde hair tied in a damp bundle that straggled down and stuck to her cheeks.
Two young maids stood helplessly by, their expressions blankly unsympathetic. The room was in a
state of chaos.

'Clear this room up,' Felice snapped at them,
whipping them into action with her eyes. 'And open
that window.' Quickly, she bent to Levina and eased
her shoulders back, away from the stinking basin.
'Come, mistress. That's probably enough now, isn't
it? Come...into bed.'

Directing the maids to remove the bowl and clean
it, she half-carried the fainting woman to the bed
and tucked her up warmly, tidied her hair and wiped
her white perspiring face. Then she shooed the
maids into the anteroom and chastised them
soundly, sending one for a warm posset from the
kitchen and the other for a brick from the oven to
warm her mistress's feet. 'Two minutes!' she said,
sharply. 'Or you lose your jobs.'

Looking at Levina's pallor, Felice could now understand the need for the heavy cosmetics, the late
appearance each day, the loss of appetite. She sat
down on the bed as the patient's eyes opened, this
time showing wariness rather than animosity but
reading Felice's concern and responding to it with a
wan smile. 'Serves me right,' she whispered.

'Pregnant?'

'Yes. I've missed three of my courses. I'll not be able to hide it much longer.'

'Then why come all this way? The journey's so rough.'

'How innocent you are. That's one way of getting rid of it. And anyway, I had to see Leon.'

Felice held her breath, not wanting to hear but unable to stop herself from asking the dreaded question. 'He's the baby's father?'

The pale lips compressed, and Levina turned her head away. 'No, he's not,' she whispered. 'It would have been easier if he had been, but I can't make the dates fit when they obviously don't. We haven't been lovers for years. Friends, but not lovers. I don't even know who the father is.'

'So you wanted to ask Sir Leon's advice, is that it?'

Levina turned to look fully at Felice, showing her a ghost of the showy, noisy, ill-mannered harridan who had done her best to turn Felice's life upside-down over the last few days, demanding and criticising, trading on her own longer friendship with Sir Leon and on Lord Deventer's lusty approval. And even now she was willing to continue taking. 'No,' she said. 'I don't need anyone's advice. It's a husband I need. Leon will help me out.'

Staring, accepting the implications at a snail's pace, Felice shook her head in an attempt to clear it. 'You mean, you're going to ask Sir Leon...?'

'To marry me. Yes. He will. We've always helped

each other out, one way or another. I haven't mentioned it to him yet. Uncle Philip's been with him
most of the time. In fact, it was Uncle Philip who
suggested the idea.'

'My stepfather knows, then?'

'Oh, yes. He always warned me that this could
happen but…well, you know how it is. Wise after
the event, eh?' Her smile was watery but far from
self-pitying, and apparently she expected Felice to
understand not only how easy it was to become
pregnant but how easy to find a solution to the problem. Her cold-blooded audacity was almost unbe-
lievable.

'Wouldn't you rather find out who the father is?'

Levina shook her head. 'Needle in a haystack,'
she said. 'Besides, I'd rather not marry any of them.
Leon will be far more reliable as a husband.'

'You love him, then?'

'Hah! Love? What's that got to do with anything?
No, Felice, of course I don't, nor does he love me.
Never has. Men don't take a woman to bed for love,
at least not in my experience. But if a woman gets
caught, it's up to her to do something about it. No
hole-in-a-corner midwife for me. I want a house and
servants to look after me and a wealthy husband to
keep me in clothes and carriages. Leon has an eye
for such things, doesn't he?'

With a cold numbness creeping up her arms, Felice did her best to smile in agreement, suddenly
desperate not to allow this callous creature to know

of her heartache. 'He certainly does, mistress. I'd stay there a while, if I were you, and try the warm posset. It'll make you feel stronger.'

Dazed and sickened, she clutched at the heavily ornamented balustrade and took each step slowly downwards, plagued by the memory of that dark fetid room in Winchester where a young woman lay groaning and afraid. Would that be the fate of Levina if her plans did not materialise? Could a woman stand by and allow that to happen, knowing how the Vytters' daughter had expected care and found criminal irresponsibility that her parents could never have suspected? This woman's plight was here and now; her own was not yet established: there would be no question of sacrifice when Leon had never been truly hers, nor she his. And even if it were true that he had no love for Levina, his undeniable friendship for her would be enough to help her through this crisis.

Once again, Lydia was horrified, outraged and adamant that Felice should not give in to this heartless manipulation, having had good evidence from Adam Bystander that his master was behaving like a man in love. 'You cannot let her do it!' she pleaded, following Felice into the newly set-up brewery. 'Pregnant or not, she's a bitch and you've got to fight her over this. Tell him you love him, or he'll believe you don't, and then this…this *harpy* will get her clutches into him for good.'

Aimlessly moving bowls from here to there, Fe-

... only the appalling dilemma of a woman who, denied help when she most needed it, could easily forfeit her life.

'Rubbish!' Lydia said, taking an earthenware jug from Felice and replacing it on the stone shelf. 'She'll not come to any harm. You don't suppose Sir Leon's the only string to her bow, do you? She may not know who the father is, but she'll have a damn good idea, believe me. You think she needs Sir Leon more than you do, don't you?'

'Yes.'

'Well, you're wrong! She's aiming for him because Lord Deventer put her up to it because he's always wanted the match. You said so yourself only yesterday. You're being mawkishly sentimental, love, and it's time *you* showed your talons, too. Oh, what *is* it, Elizabeth?'

Mistress Elizabeth Pemberton, in and out of love like a butterfly, had some news of a most inappropriate nature. 'The waggons have arrived from Winchester,' she said, eyeing Felice's tears.

'They arrived two days ago,' Lydia snapped.

'No, these have the gowns from the man on the Pentice. Shall I unpack them, my lady?'

'No,' Felice croaked. 'Leave them in their boxes.'

Lydia's unvoiced command contradicted this, and it was fortunate that Elizabeth, for all her failings, had learned to lip-read.

It was also fortunate that Lydia stayed close to her mistress for the next few hours in the expecta-

tion that something might happen to propel Felice
into action. It did, but not in the direction Lydia had
hoped, even though she had managed to steer her
towards the small room that Sir Leon called his office with a view to pushing her inside and closing
the door.

Voices reached them from the passageway causing Lydia to frown, crossly. 'Tch! He's got someone
with him.'

Quickly, Felice turned away. 'Let's make it another time,' she hissed.

Lydia restrained her. 'Shh! Listen. Someone's
weeping.'

'It's her!' Anger and curiosity combined to make
her investigate, and unwillingly she moved forward
until she could see into the room where Sir Leon
stood by his table piled with papers, an account-
book still open. Levina stood close to him with her
forehead on his shoulder, comforted by his arms, his
head bent to one side as if to catch her sobbing
words. He said something to her and she nodded,
and Felice could watch no more.

'Now do you believe me?' she growled to Lydia.

'No,' said Lydia. 'I'll not believe it, even now.'

But for Felice, it was the evidence she needed that
she had no place in Sir Leon's future, evidence she
would not have had the humiliation of witnessing,
she told Lydia, if she'd followed her own advice

instead of hers. Lydia was unrepentant. If her mistress lost Sir Leon, she would lose her Adam, and that would be a new and unacceptable experience for Mistress Lydia. Something had to be done.

On the top floor of the Abbot's House, Marcus Donne laid down his fine squirrel-hair paintbrush with a sigh and looked reproachfully at his lovely subject as yet another tear dripped off the point of her chin. As no explanation followed, he took a stool across to her and sat so that he could take her hands in his. 'What is it?' he whispered. 'This is the second time in two days. There's a problem, isn't there?'

'I'm sorry,' she said. 'Shall we try again later?'

'When your eyes are red with weeping? No, dear lady. I think it's better if you tell me about it, then I can see what's to be done.'

'Nothing's to be done, Marcus.'

'Ah,' he smiled. 'Don't you believe it. If it's Leon, leave him to me. Has he been severe again? I thought you two were…hush, love. Don't distress yourself. What's he been up to?'

Felice blew her nose, noisily. 'No…nothing, really. It was all a terrible mistake. Nothing. I'm being silly.'

'No,' Marcus said, slowly. 'No, there's something here I don't quite understand. Tell me to mind my own business, but has he…did he become *more* than friendly while you were in Winchester? Has he taken you to bed?'

Felice was silent, twisting her handkerchief in her fingers.

'He has, hasn't he? The swine. And now on your return there's my lovely Levina to bring him to heel, and all the while he's telling me to keep off his pitch and sending me packing when I refuse.' His voice throbbed with anger. 'I should give him a good thrashing for this. My God, I should!'

She laid a hand on his arm. 'Don't interfere, Marcus. I know you mean well and I'm touched, but he and Levina are—did you say *your* lovely Levina? You're in love with her, Marcus?'

'Oh lord, always have been. I've never bothered her. Nothing to offer on the scale that *she* needs things. I doubt she even knows. But look, if you and Leon have been lovers, you must be getting a bit worried. Did he talk of marriage to you? Has he told your stepfather?'

'No,' she said. 'He'll marry Levina. I'm sure of it.'

'And leave you to fend for yourself? Not without a word from me, he won't!' He stood up, pulling her up with him and surprising her with his uncharacteristic anger. 'Listen to me, Felice. He's not going to get away with this. This time he's overstepped the mark. It's no surprise that he's taken up with Levina again, but if he doesn't agree to marry you, I will. With or without his permission. He can't tie a woman hand and foot like this. No, it's no good protesting. I've made my mind up.'

'You cannot do it, dear Marcus. I must find my own solution to the problem.'

His voice dropped as he kissed her knuckles. 'You just have, Felice. It's me.'

'I cannot allow you to do this,' she called after him as he left her. 'I couldn't ask you to…'

'You're not asking me to,' he called back from the stairway. 'I'm asking you.'

Sir Leon was standing in the middle of the blackened ruins with a flapping plan in his hands when Marcus found him talking with two of his masons. All around them, men were clearing rubble, sawing up charred beams and clambering along the walls while, in the distance, Lord Deventer stood talking to a black-gowned gentleman and his clerk.

One of the masons took the plan and rolled it up. 'Right, sir,' he said, looking at Marcus. 'We'll get on, then. Good day to you, Mr Donne.'

'The coroner,' Sir Leon said in answer to Marcus's enquiring glance. 'And you'll be getting dust all over you in this place, lad. Come away.' He was dressed in working-clothes—leather boots, knee-length breeches and open-necked white shirt—that set off his dark handsomeness and large frame in a way that Marcus was well able to appreciate, as a painter.

But Marcus was in no mood to be impressed. 'Yes,' he said, tersely. 'A word in private is what I have in mind, Leon, if you please. Unless you want this crowd to hear what I've to say.'

'Why, what is it? Something wrong?' Sir Leon stepped over a pile of masonry and out through the courtyard piled with salvaged materials, and on towards the river. 'Now, is this private enough for you? And if you've come to tell me about Levina being…'

'I've come to talk about Lady Felice, Leon, if you can get Levina out of your head for a moment or two. Perhaps it's time you gave some thought to her instead.'

'Wait a minute, my friend! What the hell are you talking about? For one thing, Levina's not *in* my head and, for another, what d'ye think I've been doing since all this happened, sitting on my backside? I've been out here in every daylight hour, working on plans half the bloody night, talking to Deventer about his ideas, siting new lodges that were burnt down, ordering replacement materials, with all my clerk of works' duties to cover and much of my steward's as well. Lady Felice has had her hands so full she's hardly given me the time of day, and I've no time to find out any more than that. So what's eating at you, for pity's sake?'

'I'll tell you what's eating me, you thick-headed arrogant churl.' Marcus grabbed at Sir Leon's arm and yanked him round to face him. Then, with amazing velocity, he smashed a fist into his friend's face, catching him on the jaw and knocking him backwards a couple of paces, taking him completely unawares. 'That's what's eating me, my friend,' he said, keeping his distance. 'That's for telling me to keep off your property while *you* put her in the same danger you pretend to be so concerned about. And now when the lass doesn't know whether she's coming or going, you leave her to stew while you prance about with *another* woman you've picked up and dropped at random for the past three years. It's time you heeded your own warnings, my lad, because this can't go on. You have responsibilities, or had you forgotten?'

Sir Leon looked at the blood on his fingertips and touched his lip again. 'Marcus, you're not making any sense. I haven't left Felice to stew, as you seem to believe. She won't have anything to do with me, and I've been too busy with Deventer and all this lot.' He waved an arm towards the site where already men were gazing in astonishment at the man who had just managed to get one under the surveyor's guard. 'And anyway, what's this danger she's supposed to be in? She's mine, and she knows she is.'

'She knows nothing of the kind, you great oaf!' Marcus yelled, infuriated by his friend's defence. '*I*'m going to marry her, if you won't!'

'Really. And you've told her so, have you?'

'Yes, I have.'

'Then you can untell her.'

'I'll be damned if I will! You can't marry them both, or did you think you could?'

'Both? You believe I'm going to marry Levina…oh, God, Marcus! Get a hold of yourself, lad! Of course I'm not. We've not been…'

But whatever they had not been was unexplained before Marcus took another swing at his friend in a blind fury of jealousy. This time the blow was knocked brutally aside and Marcus was hustled backwards against a tree-trunk, struggling to keep his balance. 'Why not?' he yelled.

'Why not? Ask her yourself. You seem to be developing a skill in counselling,' Sir Leon yelled back. 'She might begin to see you as husband-material at last, which is more than anyone else can, but you can forget your chivalry towards Lady Felice, my friend. I've told you, she's *mine*! And if she's having doubts about that, that's none of your concern, limner. Your profession allows you to gain women's confidences; mine doesn't. My love-life has to wait until my patron has shifted himself from under my bloody feet!'

'Love? What do you know about love, builder?'

'More than you, paint-dabbler, but I don't splash it around so much.'

'Well then, perhaps I can show you how to make a splash.' Marcus lunged towards his friend who now stood with his back to the river on the debris-strewn banks that had only recently been covered with water. He was caught and knocked sideways

by a huge fist, making him stumble and hcsitate before tackling Sir Leon again. But though he faced
the abbey, he was oblivious to Lord Deventer's approach or to the coroner's expression of astonishment. Madly, he rushed forward with both fists flying, but his adversary was prepared, lifting him high
off the ground in a bear-hug, tossing him above his
head as if he were a child and hurling him into the
river to the applause of a crowd of men from the
distant courtyard.

'Cool off!' Sir Leon yelled.

Lord Deventer's voice held no hint of censure.
'Well, Gascelin? So your patron gets under your
bloody feet, does he?'

But although the bend in the river was not deep
at that point, the current was swift and Sir Leon had
no wish to prolong his friend's humiliation before
an audience. However, before he could wade in, several of the men ran forward to rescue Marcus, eager
for any diversion, and soon there was a thrashing
group of them, pulling and shouting.

'Get him out,' called Lord Deventer. 'Time's
money!'

'Yes, my lord,' one of them called back. 'But
there's another body here.'

'Well, pull it out, then.'

With Marcus doing his share, fair hair darkly
plastered on to his forehead, they dragged a bloated
body, face downwards, up on to the bank. Still tangled around one wrist was a bulging sack, the cord

of which had cut deeply into his skin. Undoubtedly it was what had held him under the water since the night of the fire.

'Ben Smith,' said one man, rolling the body over.

'So it is,' said Sir Leon. 'Come, Marcus. Give me your hand.'

'I came here to give you a hiding, lad,' Marcus said, coughing, 'not to do your dirty work for you. And you're going to lose that lovely lass if you don't look to it. She's in love with you, you know.'

'And how would you know that, limner?'

Marcus peeled off his soaking doublet and threw it down on to the ground with a loud smack. 'Well, what d'ye think *I*'ve been doing for the last few days while I've been painting her? Looking at your damned ceiling? Before Winchester and after Winchester. Think I can't tell the difference in a woman's eyes by now, my fine friend? See to it, before it's too late.'

'I intend to. Go and get some clothes on before *you* catch a chill.'

Lord Deventer moved in as Marcus squelched away. 'Now, Gascelin, if you have a moment I'd like you to…hey! Where are you off to?'

'Business, sir!' Sir Leon called, striding after Marcus. 'Urgent business.'

In Felice's bedchamber, the vibrant new clothes from Winchester that spread like a peacock's tail across the bed had lost the appeal they'd had a week or so ago when Lady West's views had been accepted. Nevertheless, both Lydia and Elizabeth agreed that red suited her peach complexion and dark hair, quelling all Felice's arguments that it made her feel uncomfortable. 'It's not my colour,' she grumbled, as they hooked and pinned her into it. 'It makes me look like an over-ripe strawberry.'

'Stand still,' said Lydia with a row of pins between her lips. 'If the men like Levina's bright showy clothes, they'll like yours, too. If you can't beat 'em, then join 'em, love. And if they like her powder and painted lips, presumably they'll like yours even better.'

'No, Lydie! I'm not…'

'Only a dab, love, to brighten your pale cheeks. Just a quick dab.'

The quick dab became a classic case of too many cooks spoiling the broth, and yet such was the state of Felice's insecurity that she felt unable to rely on her own judgement alone, admitting to herself that, as none of her hopes and plans had worked too well so far, there was little harm in trying someone else's. So she submitted to the frills and festoons, the brooches and rings, the tightly-braided hair over padding with the silly hat on top, the collapsible farthingale made of willow-hoops that she had not worn since Winchester. She stood, scowling, while they painted her eyebrows more thickly, reddened her cheeks and lips, powdered her skin and made her almost unrecognisable while assuring her that, if it did nothing else, it would at least draw some of the attention away from that scheming callous hussy Levina.

Feeling that she may as well have held a mask before her face as have one painted on her, she took up her duties in the hall of the New House as the servers were preparing the tables for the mid-day meal where, disconcerted by the apparition before them, several of the lads crashed into each other, dropping their dishes and contents. Flint and Fen dashed in to gobble up the mess, refusing to take any notice of the strange woman who called them off and growling at one lad who dared to lay a hand on their collars.

The appearance of Thomas Vyttery did nothing to help matters, for his cowardly mastiff, unable to escape the scene, was instantly seen as a rival for the new food supply on the floor, and the fight that ensued was weighted against him from the start. Felice was in despair, hampered by the contraptions under her clothes and everything that dangled from them.

A man's deep voice cracked across the pandemonium. 'Flint! Fen! Come here!'

Without another look at the terrified mastiff, the two deerhounds slunk away and padded, heads and tails down, to Sir Leon's side where they flattened themselves on to the floor like two grey rugs.

'What's going on, Thomas?' Sir Leon said. 'And

who's…my *God*! What on earth?' He stared at Felice, aghast, his face a picture of dismay.

She knew, as soon as she saw it, that she had done the wrong thing, that she should not have given in to this absurdity, that far from finding her attractive, he found it all repulsive. There was nothing to say to him, not even in her own defence, while he stood there, taking in every detail. She whirled on one high heel and made a frantic dash for the door behind Mr Vyttery, not knowing where it led.

He dodged to one side, blinking in astonishment and remonstrating with the large powerful figure who followed with giant strides. 'Nay, sir. Leave her be! Ye can see she's upset. Leave her!'

'Get out of my way, Thomas!'

The passageway was a narrow one leading to a flight of stone stairs down which a liveried servant came, his arms piled high with white folded linen tablecloths larger than bed sheets. There was no way past him. Felice turned to confront her angry guardian, trapped between the two of them.

'Leave me alone!' she snarled at him. 'No…!' She tried to ward him off with her hands but he caught them without any attempt to persuasion or reason, holding her easily as he whipped the top cloth off the startled servant's pile, shook it out and wrapped it round her like a shroud before she could free herself from his grasp.

Imprisoned in this white cocoon, she fought and twisted as she was bent forward over his knee and, held in that position, her skirts were lifted, her great bell-shaped farthingale untied from her waist and dropped to the floor like a pool, her skirts replaced.

'That's a start,' she heard him say. 'Now for the rest.'

'No...no!' she wailed. 'How dare you do this? How *dare* you?'

He was not inclined to answer, but lifted her up into his arms instead and, ignoring the speechless man on the stairs, stepped over the white fabric puddle and marched with his writhing bundle across the hall. The same people were there who had seen them leave moments before, this time with mouths open in amazement at the spectacle of their mistress being carted off like a side of bacon by a grim-faced Sir Leon.

He stopped alongside Lydia who had been, to her credit, prepared to follow them. 'Mistress Lydia,' he said. 'Take this daft thing off her head, if you please, and collect that tent from the passageway before someone camps out in it.'

Lydia complied, and then had no choice but to see her mistress swung round and carried off, still protesting, to Sir Leon's room that overlooked the cloister. And while the drama was ended for those in the hall, for Felice it was only just beginning, all the more dramatic because he was too furious to speak and she too furious to keep silent.

Still constrained by the winding-sheet, she was laid on the bed and held there while he began a thorough removal of the crude cosmetics that could do nothing to make her lovelier, only the opposite. Taking a handful of the cloth, he soaped her face, ignoring her protests and her tears and then, as her own features were restored, dried her more tenderly. Next, he unbraided her hair, turning her face-downwards to reach the back and teasing out each coil until it was loose and covering the pillow.

By this time, Felice's tears had run dry, though her anger had not, and now the full force of it was vented into his pillow in a rage of helplessness and unmitigated jealousy. And although she felt nothing but relief to be free of her disguise, the motivation for it could not be removed so easily. The harridan Levina was a she-wolf, did he not know that? Was he blind? Too besotted to care?

'I'll give you all the answers you need when I've got you out of this,' he said. 'And who in heaven's name told you to wear this colour? Do you not know that red's no colour for you?'

'Of course I do!' she yelped into the pillow. 'But if that loud-mouthed hoyden can wear it, so can I.'

'Ah, so that's it! Well, you're wrong. You can't.' Preventing her from turning over by a hand on her hips, he deftly unhooked her bodice and then, with his dagger, cut through the laces of her whalebone stays, removing all her casings like a shrimp from its shell. It was an easy matter after that to peel off the under-layers, one by one, until she was nakedly resisting any further peelings by holding on to his

wrist behind her back in the belief that she was re-
straining him, not herself.

'No more,' she said, through a sheet of hair.
'Leave my silk stockings on.'

'Then let go of my wrist.'

She felt his hand explore the prettily tied garter
ribbons and then continue on its own search of her
thighs and buttocks, felt his tender kisses follow the
path of his hand, moving upwards over hips, waist
and shoulders. 'No,' she whispered. 'I don't want
you. Marcus has offered to marry me. You go and
marry Levina. You deserve each other.'

His sigh turned into a soft laugh as he lifted the
mass of hair off her neck and allowed his mouth to
roam warmly over her skin. She could see his face
from the corner of her eye. 'You've got it all sewn
up, haven't you, you two? Eh? Well, my fierce
beauty, you can undo all your plans because mine
were made as soon as I saw you, weeks ago.' His
lips nibbled at her beautiful shoulders. 'And they've
not changed since then.'

'Oh, I knew exactly what your plans were from
the start, Sir Leon. Whether I'm a wife to please my
stepfather or a mistress to suit you, I'm supposed to
share my life with that monster upstairs who doesn't
even know the father of her own child. Well, if
you…'

'Will you shut up for a moment, woman?'

With a deft flip of her hips, he turned her on to
her back and drew the hair away from her face. His

kiss did more than silence her words, it reached down into her heart and gentled it, soothing its pain. 'Now,' he whispered, 'shall we leave her out of it, my lady, and speak of something more interesting? Of the first time we met, in the Abbot's House?'

'I hated you then and I hate you now,' she said, caressing the side of his finger with her teeth.

His lips twitched. 'Yes, but there was more to it than that, wasn't there? You hated the idea of being disturbed out of your unhappiness, and you hated me because I represented your stepfather. You were determined not to accept my control. And now, you believe my heart is elsewhere when it's always been yours, from that very first moment.'

She had not heard him speak of hearts and emotions before, only her adeptness at loving, which was not the same. Yet now he was saying it with such tender conviction she could hardly believe what she was hearing. 'But you couldn't have…you were so rude…so unpleasant.'

'We'd already met, remember? Look here.' He delved inside the lining of his waistband and drew out a long shining blue ribbon, now very creased, and dangled it before her.

'That's mine!'

'Yours, woman. Pulled off the end of a thick plait of silken hair one night in a moonlit garden, the same hair that you piled up on top of your head to show them all what a real woman looks like, just a few days ago. My heart nearly burst with love and pride, sweetheart, and when you're my wife, you'll wear your hair like this for me, as it is now. No paint. No more attempts to look like those wenches at court. Nothing can improve on this, my love.' His hand swept over her body, setting it alight.

'Your wife?' she whispered. 'No rivals?'

'Still unconvinced? There never have been any rivals, sweetheart. That woman thrives on mischief; I found that out soon enough. We've remained friends over the years, and I'm bound to remain polite to my patron's relatives...'

'You were not polite to me!'

'...but she knew damn well I'd not go so far as to marry her just to find a name for her brat.'

'She asked you, then?'

'Oh, yes, she tried it on. She has all the audacity of the devil, but I'm not stupid enough for that, and she knows it.'

'What about the tears?'

'You saw?'

'Some of it.'

'The tears were because I said no. Deventer had already told me of the problem, and I'd told him I couldn't help. But I've been so frantically busy since they came, love, that I've hardly had time to sleep, what with the loss of John and all. I'm sorry. I should have made you listen to me, but you seemed not to want me. *Did* you want me?'

'Wanted you. Ached for you. Forgive me, I was

desperate. I was sure you loved her. Marcus told me you did.'

'Another little trouble-maker we could do without. I think we should make him marry Levina.'

'He's in love with her.'

'I know. The trouble is, he can't afford her.'

'Then speak to Lord Deventer. Perhaps he'll help.' She began to untie the cords of his shirt. 'What's he going to say about you and me?'

'He'll not be too surprised, sweetheart. He admitted he'd brought Levina down here in the hope that I'd help her out of her predicament, but I don't owe him any favours of that kind. Not in my personal life; he has no influence there. As for you, my fierce ward, he already guessed how things are between us when he saw you that first evening with your hair down, not caring a damn for any of them. He tried to change my mind, of course, but he knows that if he refuses his consent, he'll lose both of us. He's got the picture, my love.' His hands caressed as they had done at that first meeting, intimately. 'And my mind's been made up since I caught you in the garden, my sweet. I knew you must be a beauty, but I'd no idea just how beautiful until I saw you that morning with your feet in a bucket of water. And then I had you in my arms, wet and angry. I could scarcely believe my good fortune...'

'And I was afraid of you.'

'...I wanted to eat you.'

'And I loved you, I think.'

'Love me now, Felice. Be my wife. I want no one but you.'

'I do love you. I will. But what was all that talk of taming? Not *that* much of a challenge, surely?'

'To anger you. I love your wildness, your wilfullness. I adore you, woman.'

The voluminous white tablecloth wrapped their limbs, and a wrinkled hair-ribbon slid between its folds like a reflection of blue sky on the sea, and it was as if the sudden release of all misunderstandings and doubts gave their loving a new direction, a never-ending gentleness in which time had no part. All inhibitions dissolved as Felice gave herself up to him in a total surrender that brought both laughter and tears and wave upon wave of joy into her heart, now repaired, restored and intact again. Suddenly she was living, flying, and whole.

The notion that Marcus and Levina should solve each other's problems found favour with everyone, even Lord Deventer who would have done anything to ensure his niece's future happiness. Relieved to see Felice's glowing contentment, Marcus fussed around Levina like a dog with two tails, caring not one whit that Lord Deventer and Sir Leon had insisted that she tell him the exact truth of her condition. It made no difference to Marcus; he would take her in any condition, though the lady's uncle had made the path remarkably smooth with a generous annual allowance.

Supper that evening was an informal meal at which Felice was allowed to dress in the new pale-blue watery silk that Sir Leon said was exactly right for a wanton moon-spirit. And even though the grave coroner and his clerk were their guests, Sir Leon would have her hair only loosely knotted with a crumpled blue ribbon.

The coroner wanted to know how the fire had started, but no one was sure except that one of the injured was a man who had only recently been dismissed for drunkenness. He should not have been there at all, and so far had not confessed to anything. As for what John Aycombe had been doing in the guesthouse so late, no one knew the answer to that, either.

'You say he had a beechwood box with him?' the coroner said to Sir Leon. 'Have I seen it yet?' He knew he had not.

'It's one that belongs to me, sir,' Sir Leon said. 'Nothing much in it.'

'Then what did he want with it?'

'He was probably taking it across to my new office. I can't think of any other reason. Can you, Thomas?'

'No, sir. John would have had his reasons, I don't doubt. He always did.' Deep in the pocket of his black gown, Thomas's hand closed around a fold of linen that Sir Leon had given him only that morning after their private conversation. It was soft and yielding and gave no indication of its contents, a curling lock of dark brown hair tied with a fine gold thread. There had not, apparently, been anything for Thomas to tell him that he'd not already discovered for himself.

The cloister was deep in shadow, lit faintly by a distant torch that flickered in the stableyard beyond and by a moon that had only just risen above the church roof. Already the walkways had been cleared, and the square that had once been rubble-filled was stacked out with strings and trenches ready for new beds to be laid and, at the end near the sacristy, a rectangular grave-slab had appeared which Felice had not seen before.

Hand in hand, the two lovers approached. 'Who was it?' she said.

'The sub-prior. We'll not disturb him. He was a friend of Thomas's, I believe.'

'Then we must dig carefully round him and plant rosebushes. Would he like that, d'ye think? And rosemary, for remembrance?'

'Yes, my love, he'd like that.' He took her in his arms and saw the moon reflected in her eyes. 'Do you remember sitting here? How we fought?' His kiss reminded her, sending shocks of pleasure through her that once she had tried guiltily to deny.

'I remember another fight, sir,' she said, 'when you lost something, too.' Against the pale moon, Felice held a golden pointed thing shaped like a tiny spear-head. 'This?' she whispered.

'My missing aiglet! Where did you find it? You've had it all this time, next to your heart?'

'Most of the time,' she teased. 'This has been a *most* unseemly summer, has it not, sir?'

But if she thought she would be allowed to have the last word, just for once, she was reminded otherwise. 'Unforgettable,' he whispered, his lips teasing hers, 'not unseemly. Unless you wish to argue the point?'

* * * * *

Discover more romance at

www.millsandboon.co.uk

- ❤ WIN great prizes in our exclusive competitions
- ❤ BUY new titles before they hit the shops
- ❤ BROWSE new books and REVIEW your favourites
- ❤ SAVE on new books with the Mills & Boon® Bookclub™
- ❤ DISCOVER new authors

PLUS, to chat about your favourite reads, get the latest news and find special offers:

- Find us on facebook.com/millsandboon
- Follow us on twitter.com/millsandboonuk
- ❤ Sign up to our newsletter at millsandboon.co.uk

The World of Mills & Boon®

There's a Mills & Boon® series that's perfect for you. We publish ten series and, with new titles every month, you never have to wait long for your favourite to come along.

By Request
Relive the romance with the best of the best
12 stories every month

Cherish™
Experience the ultimate rush of falling in love
12 new stories every month

Desire™
Passionate and dramatic love stories
6 new stories every month

nocturne™
An exhilarating underworld of dark desires
Up to 3 new stories every mor